Italian
BACHELORS

RUTHLESS
PROPOSITIONS

ITALIAN BACHELORS
COLLECTION

July 2017   August 2017   September 2017

October 2017   November 2017   December 2017

Italian
BACHELORS

FIONA HARPER
CATHY WILLIAMS
LEANNE BANKS

MILLS & BOON

Published in Great Britain 2017
By Mills & Boon, an imprint of HarperCollins*Publishers*
1 London Bridge Street, London, SE1 9GF

ITALIAN BACHELORS: RUTHLESS PROPOSITIONS © 2017
Harlequin Books S.A.

Taming Her Italian Boss © 2014 Fiona Harper
The Uncompromising Italian © 2014 Cathy Williams
Secrets of the Playboy's Bride © 2010 Leanne Banks

ISBN: 978-0-263-93132-7

09-0817

Our policy is to use papers that are natural, renewable and recyclable products and made from wood grown in sustainable forests.
The logging and manufacturing processes conform to the legal environmental regulations of the country of origin.

Printed and bound in Spain
by CPI, Barcelona

TAMING HER ITALIAN BOSS

FIONA HARPER

As a child, **Fiona Harper** was constantly teased for either having her nose in a book or living in a dream world. Things haven't changed much since then, but at least in writing she's found a use for her runaway imagination. After studying dance at university, Fiona worked as a dancer, teacher and choreographer, before trading in that career for video-editing and production. When she became a mother she cut back on her working hours to spend time with her children, and when her littlest one started school she found a few spare moments to rediscover an old but not forgotten love – writing.

Fiona lives in London, but her other favourite places to be are the Highlands of Scotland and the Kent countryside on a summer's afternoon. She loves cooking good food and anything cinnamon-flavoured. Of course, she still can't keep away from a good book or a good movie – especially romances – but only if she's stocked up with tissues, because she knows she will need them by the end, be it happy or sad. Her favourite things in the world are her wonderful husband, who has learned to decipher her incoherent ramblings, and her two daughters.

CHAPTER ONE

'YOU WANT ME to give you a job?'

The woman staring across the desk at Ruby didn't look convinced. The London traffic rumbled outside the first-floor office as the woman looked her up and down. Her gaze swept down over Ruby's patchwork corduroy jacket, miniskirt with brightly coloured leggings peeking out from underneath, and ended at the canvas shoes that were *almost* the right shade of purple to match the streaks in her short hair.

Ruby nodded. 'Yes.'

'Humph,' the woman said.

Ruby couldn't help noticing her flawlessly cut black suit and equally flawlessly cut hair. She'd bet that the famous Thalia Benson of the Benson Agency hadn't come about her latest style after she'd got fed up with the long stringy bits dangling in her breakfast cereal and convinced her flatmate to take scissors to it.

'And Layla Babbington recommended you try here?'

Ruby nodded again. Layla had been one of her best friends at boarding school. When she'd heard that Ruby was looking for a job—and one that preferably took her out of the country ASAP—she'd suggested the top-class nannying agency. 'Don't let old Benson fool you for a moment,' she'd told Ruby. 'Thalia's a pussycat underneath, and she likes someone with a bit of gumption. The two of you will get along famously.'

Now that she was sitting on the far side of Thalia Benson's desk, under scrutiny as if she were a rogue germ on a high-chair tray, Ruby wasn't so sure.

'Such a pity she had to go and marry that baronet she was working for,' Benson muttered. 'Lost one of my best girls *and* a plum contract.'

She looked up quickly at Ruby, as if she'd realised she'd said that out loud. Ruby looked back at her, expression open and calm. She didn't care what the nanny provider to the rich and famous thought about her clients. She just wanted a job that got her out of London. Fast.

'So...' Ms Benson said in one long drawn-out syllable while she shuffled a few papers on her desk. 'What qualifications do you have?'

'For nannying?' Ruby asked, resisting the urge to fidget.

Benson didn't answer, but her eyebrows lifted in a what-do-you-think? kind of gesture.

Ruby took a deep breath. 'Well...I've always been very good with kids, and I'm practical and creative and hard-working—'

The other woman cut her off by holding up a hand. She was looking wearier by the second. 'I mean professional qualifications. Diploma in Childcare and Education, BTEC...Montessori training?'

Ruby let the rest of that big breath out. She'd been preparing to keep talking for as long as possible, and she'd only used up a third of her lung capacity before Benson had interrupted her. Not a good start. She took another, smaller breath, giving herself a chance to compose a different reply.

'Not exactly.'

No one had said it was going to be a *great* reply.

Thalia Benson gave her a frosty look. 'Either one has

qualifications or one hasn't. It tends to be a black-or-white kind of thing.'

Ruby swallowed. 'I know I haven't got any *traditional* childcare qualifications, but I was hoping I could enlist with your new travelling nanny service. Short-term placements. What I lack in letters after my name I make up for in organisation, flexibility and common sense.'

Benson's ears pricked up at the mention of common sense. She obviously liked those words. Ruby decided to press home her main advantage. 'And I've travelled all over the world since I was a small child. There aren't many places I haven't been to. I also speak four languages—French, Spanish, Italian and a bit of Malagasy.'

Ms Benson tipped her head slightly. 'You've spent time in Madagascar?' The look of disbelief on her face suggested she thought Ruby had gone a bit too far in padding out her CV.

'My parents and I lived there for three years when I was a child.'

Benson's eyes narrowed. *'Inona voavoa?'* she suddenly said, surprising Ruby.

The reply came back automatically. How was she? *'Tsara be.'*

Benson's eyes widened, and for the first time since Ruby had walked through the office door and sat down she looked interested. She picked up the blank form sitting in front of her and started writing. 'Ruby Long, wasn't it?'

'Lange,' Ruby replied. 'With an *e*.'

Benson looked up. 'Like Patrick Lange?'

Ruby nodded. 'Exactly like that.' She didn't normally like mentioning her connection to the globetrotting TV presenter whose nature documentaries were the jewel in the crown of British television, but she could see more than a glimmer of interest in Thalia Benson's eyes, and she really, *really* wanted to be out of the country when good old Dad got back from The Cook Islands in two days' time. 'He's my father,' she added.

The other woman stopped messing around with the form, put it squarely down on the desk and folded her hands on top of it. 'Well, Ms Lange, I don't usually hire nannies without qualifications, not even for short-term positions, but maybe there's something you could do round the office over the summer. Our intern has just disappeared off to go backpacking.'

Ruby blinked. Once again, someone had heard the name 'Lange' and the real person opposite them had become invisible. Once again, mentioning her father had opened a door only for it to be slammed shut again. When would she ever learn?

'That's very generous, Ms Benson, but I wasn't really looking for a clerical position.'

Thalia nodded, but Ruby knew she hadn't taken her seriously at all. From the smile on the other woman's face, she could tell Thalia was wondering how much cachet it would bring her business if she could wheel Ruby out at the annual garden party to impress her clientele, maybe even get national treasure Patrick Lange to show up.

That wasn't Ruby's style at all. She'd been offered plenty of jobs where she could cash in on her father's status by doing something vastly overpaid for not a lot of effort, and she'd turned every one of them down. All she wanted was for someone to see *her* potential for once, to need her for herself, not just what her family connections could bring. Surely that wasn't too much to ask. Unfortunately, Ruby suspected Ms Thalia Benson wasn't that rare individual. She rose from her side of the desk, opened the office door and indicated Ruby should return to the waiting area. 'Why don't you take a seat outside, and I'll see what I can do?'

Ruby smiled back and nodded, rising from her chair. She'd give Thalia Benson fifteen minutes, and if she hadn't come up with something solid by then, she was out of here. Life was too short to hang around when something wasn't working. Onwards and upwards, that was her motto.

Everything in the waiting area was shades of stone and heather and aubergine. The furniture screamed under-stated—and overpriced—elegance. The only clue that the Benson Agency had anything to do with children was a pot of crayons and some drawing paper on the low coffee table between two sectional sofas. When Thalia's office door closed, Ruby shrugged then sat down. She'd always loved drawing. She picked up a bright red crayon and started doo-dling on a blank sheet. Maybe she'd go for fire engine–red streaks in her hair next time they needed touching up....

She spent the next five minutes doing a pretty passable cartoon of Thalia Benson while she waited. In the pic-ture, Thalia dripped sophistication and charm, but she was dressed up like the Child Catcher from the famous movie, locking a scared boy in a cage.

As the minutes ticked by Ruby became more and more sure this was a waste of her time. The only thing she needed to decide before she left was whether to fold the drawing up and discreetly stick it in her pocket, or if she should prop it on the console table against the far wall so it was the first thing prospective clients saw when they walked in the door.

She was holding the paper in her hands, dithering about whether to crease it in half or smooth it out flat, when the door crashed open and a tall and rather determined-looking man strode in. Ruby only noticed the small, dark-haired girl he had in tow when he was halfway to Thalia Benson's of-fice. The child was wailing loudly, her eyes squeezed shut and her mouth wide open, and the only reason she didn't bump into any of the furniture was because she was being propelled along at speed in her father's wake, protected by his bulk.

The receptionist bobbed around him, trying to tell him

he needed to make an appointment, but he didn't alter his trajectory in the slightest. Ruby put her cartoon down on the table and watched with interest.

'I need to see the person in charge and I need to see them now,' he told the receptionist, entirely unmoved by her expression of complete horror or her rapid arm gestures.

Ruby bit back a smile. She might just stick around to see how this played out.

'If you'll just give me a second, Mr...er...I'll see whether Ms Benson is available.'

The man finally gave the receptionist about 5 per cent of his attention. He glanced at her, and as he did so the little girl stopped crying for a second and looked in Ruby's direction. She started up again almost immediately, but it was half-hearted this time, more for show than from distress.

'Mr Martin,' he announced, looking down at the receptionist. He stepped forward again. Ruby wasn't sure how it happened—whether he let go of the girl's hand or whether she did that tricksy, slippery-palm thing that all toddlers seemed to know—but suddenly father and child were disconnected.

The receptionist beat Mr Tall and Determined to Thalia's door, knocking on it a mere split second before he reached for the handle, and she just about saved face as she blurted out his name. He marched into the room and slammed the door behind him.

Once he was inside, the little girl sniffed and fell silent. She and Ruby regarded each other for a moment, then Ruby smiled and offered her a bright yellow crayon.

Max looked at the woman behind the desk. She was staring at him and her mouth was hanging open. Just a little. 'I need one of your travelling nannies as soon as possible.'

The woman—Benson, was it?—closed her jaw silently and with one quick, almost unnoticeable appraising glance she took in his handmade suit and Italian shoes and decided to play nice. Most people did.

'Of course, Mr Martin.' She smiled at him. 'I just need to get a few details from you and then I'll go through my staff list. We should be able to start interviewing soon.' She looked down at a big diary on her desk and started flipping through it. 'How about Thursday?' she asked, looking back up at him.

Max stared back at her. He thought he'd been pretty clear. What part of 'as soon as possible' did she not understand? 'I need someone today.'

'Today?' she croaked. Her gaze flew to the clock on the wall.

Max knew what it said—three-thirty.

The day had started off fairly normally, but then his sister had shown up at his office just before ten and, as things often did when the women in his family were concerned, it had got steadily more chaotic since then.

'Preferably within the next half hour,' he added. 'I have to be at the airport by five.'

'B-but how old is the child? How long do you need someone for? What kind of expertise do you require?'

He ignored her questions and pulled a folded computer printout from his suit pocket. There was no point wasting time on details if she wasn't going to be able to help him. 'I came to you because your website says you provide a speedy and efficient service—travelling nannies for every occasion. I need to know whether that's true.'

She drew herself up ramrod straight in her chair and looked him in the eye. 'Listen, Mr Martin, I don't know what sort of establishment you think I run here, but—'

He held up a hand, cutting her off. He knew he was steamrollering over all the pleasantries, but that couldn't be helped. 'The best nanny agency in London, I'd heard.

Which is why I came to you in an emergency. Have you got someone? If not, I won't waste any more of your time.'

She pursed her lips, but her expression softened. He hadn't been flattering her—not really his style—but a few timely truths hadn't hurt his case. 'I can help.' She sighed and Max relaxed just a little. She'd much rather have told him it was impossible, he guessed, but the kind of fee she was measuring him up for with her beady little eyes was hard to say no to. 'At the very least, let me know the sex and age of the charge,' she added.

Max shrugged. 'Girl,' he said. 'Older than one and younger than school age. Other than that I'm not quite sure. Why don't you take a look and see what you think?'

The woman's eyes almost popped out of her head. 'She's here?'

Max nodded. Where the hell else did the woman think she'd be?

'And you left her outside? Alone?'

He frowned. He hadn't thought about that for one second. Which was exactly why he needed to hire someone who would. Anyway, he hadn't left Sofia completely alone. There had been the flappy woman...

Ms Benson sprang from the desk, threw the door open and rushed into the waiting area beyond her office. There, colouring in with the tip of her tongue caught at one side of her mouth, was Sofia. Max suddenly noticed something: the noise had stopped. That horrible wailing, like an air-raid siren. It had driven him to distraction all day.

'Here...try purple for the flower,' a young woman, kneeling next to Sofia, was saying. Sofia, instead of acting like a child possessed with the spirit of a banshee, just calmly accepted the crayon from the woman and carried on scribbling. After a few moments, both woman and child stopped what they were doing and lifted their heads to look at the two adults towering over them. The identical expression of mild curiosity they both wore was rather disconcerting.

Max turned to the agency owner. 'I want her,' he said, nodding at the kneeling woman who, he was just starting to notice, had odd-coloured bits in her hair.

Benson gave out a nervous laugh. 'I'm afraid she doesn't work here.'

Max raised his eyebrows.

'Not yet,' she added quickly. 'But I'm sure you'd be better off with one of our other nannies who—'

He turned away and looked at the strange pixie-like woman and the little girl again. For the first time in what seemed like weeks, although it had probably only been hours, Sofia was quiet and calm and acting like the normal child he vaguely remembered. 'No. I want *her.*'

Something deep down in his gut told him this woman had what he needed. To be honest, he really didn't care what it was. It was twenty-five to four and he had to get going. 'What do you say?' he asked the her directly.

The woman finished colouring in a pink rose on the sheet of paper she and Sofia were sharing before she answered. She flicked a glance at the agency owner. 'She's right. I don't even work here.'

'I don't care about that,' he told her. 'You have all the skills I want. It's you I need.'

She blinked and looked at him hard, as if she was trying to work out whether he was serious or not. Normally people didn't have to think about that.

'What if the job isn't what *I* need?' she asked. 'I don't think I should accept without hearing the terms.'

Max checked his watch again. 'Fine, fine,' he said wearily. 'Have it your way. We'll interview in the car. But hurry up! We've got a plane to catch.' And then he marched from the offices of the Benson Agency leaving its proprietor standing open-mouthed behind him.

CHAPTER TWO

IT TOOK RUBY all of two seconds to drop the crayon she was holding, scoop up the child next to her and run after him into the bright sunshine of a May afternoon. God did indeed move in mysterious ways!

And so did Mr...whatever his name was.

Those long legs had carried him down the stairs to street level very fast. When she burst from the agency's understated door onto one of the back roads behind Oxford Street, she had to look in both directions before she spotted him heading towards a sleek black car parked on a double yellow.

She was about to run after him when she had a what's-wrong-with-this-picture? moment. Hang on. Why was she holding his child while he waltzed off with barely a backward glance? It was as if, in his rush to conquer the next obstacle, he'd totally forgotten his daughter even existed. She looked down at the little girl, who was quite happy hitched onto her hip, watching a big red double-decker bus rumbling past the end of the road. She might not realise just how insensitive her father was being at the moment, just how much it hurt when one understood how extraneous they were to a parent's life, but one day she'd be old enough to notice. Ruby clamped her lips together and marched towards the car. No child deserved that.

She walked up to him, peeled the child off her hip and

handed her over. 'Here,' she said breezily. 'I think you forgot this.'

The look of utter bewilderment on his face would have been funny if she hadn't been so angry. He took the girl from Ruby and held her out at arm's length so her legs dangled above the chewing-gum-splattered pavement. Now it was free of toddler, Ruby put her hand on her hip and raised her eyebrows.

He was saved from answering by the most horrendous howling. It took her a few moments to realise it was the child making the sound. The ear-splitting noise bounced off the tall buildings and echoed round the narrow street.

'Take it back!' he said. 'You're the only one who can make it stop!'

Ruby took her hands off her hips and folded her arms. '*It* has a name, I should think.'

He offered the screaming bundle of arms and legs over, but Ruby stepped back. He patted the little girl's back, trying to soothe her, but it just made her cry all the harder. The look of sheer panic on his face was actually quite endearing, she decided, especially as it went some way to softening that 'ruler of the universe' thing he had going on. He was just as out of his depth as she was, wasn't he?

His eyes pleaded with her. 'Sofia. Her name is Sofia.'

Ruby gave him a sweet smile and unfolded her arms to accept the little girl. She still didn't know whether following this through was a good idea, but the only other option was working for her dad. He'd flipped when he'd found out she'd given in her notice at the vintage fashion shop in Covent Garden.

Considering that her father didn't pay an awful lot of interest the rest of the time, Ruby had been shocked he'd noticed, let alone cared. He was usually always too busy off saving the planet to worry about what his only child got up to, but this had lit his fuse for some reason.

According to him, Ruby needed a job. Ruby needed to grow up. Ruby needed to stop flitting around and settle to something.

He'd laid down a very clear ultimatum before he'd left for the South Pacific—get a proper job by the time he returned, or he'd create a position for her in his production company. Once there, she'd never escape. She'd never get promoted. She'd be doomed to being *What's her name? You know, Patrick Lange's daughter...*for ever.

Sofia grabbed for Ruby as her father handed her back over, clinging to her like the baby lemurs Ruby had got used to seeing in the Madagascan bush. A rush of protective warmth flooded up from her feet and landed in her chest.

She looked up at the man towering above her. 'And, before I get in that car, we might as well continue with the information gathering. I'd offer to shake your hand but, as you can see—' she nodded to Sofia, who'd burrowed her head in the crook of her neck '—it's in use at the moment. I'm Ruby Lange. With an *e*.'

He looked at her blankly, recognising neither her name nor the need for a response. 'And you are?' she prompted.

He blinked and seemed to recover himself. 'Max Martin.'

Ruby shifted Sofia to a more comfortable position on her hip. 'Pleased to meet you, Mr Martin.' She looked inside the dark interior of the limo. 'Now, are we going to start this interview or what?'

Max sat frowning in the back of the limo. He wasn't quite sure what had just happened. One minute he'd been fully in charge of the situation, and the next he'd been ushered into his own car by a woman who looked as if she'd had a fight with a jumble sale—and lost.

She turned to face him, her eyes large and enquiring as

she looked at him over the top of Sofia's car seat, which was
strapped between them. 'Fire away,' she said, then waited.

He looked back at her.

'I thought this was supposed to be an interview.'

She was right. He had agreed to that, but the truth of the
matter was that, unless she declared herself to be a drug-
addicted mass murderer, the job was hers. He didn't have
time to find anyone else.

He studied his new employee carefully. The women he
interacted with on a daily basis definitely didn't dress like
this. It was all colour and jarring patterns. Somehow it
made her look very young. And, right there, he had his
first question.

'How old are you?'

She blinked but held his gaze. 'Twenty-four.'

Old enough, then. If he'd had to guess, he'd have put her
at a couple of years younger. Didn't matter, though. If she
could do the job, she could do the job, and the fact that the
small bundle of arms and legs strapped into the car seat
was finally silent was all the evidence he needed.

He checked his watch. He really didn't have time to chit-
chat, so if she wanted to answer questions, he'd dispense
with the pleasantries and get on with the pertinent ones.
'How far away do you live?'

For the first time since he'd set eyes on her, she looked
surprised.

'Can we get there in under half an hour?'

She frowned. 'Pimlico. So, yes… But why—?'

'Can you pack a bag in under ten minutes?'

She raised her eyebrows.

'In my experience, most women can't,' he said. 'I don't
actually understand why, though.' It seemed a simple
enough task, after all. 'I believe it may have something to
do with shoes.'

'My parents dragged me round the globe—twice—in

my formative years,' she replied crisply. 'I can pack a bag in under five if I have to.'

Max smiled. And not just the distant but polite variety he rolled out at business meetings. This was the real deal. The nanny stopped looking quite so confrontational and her eyes widened. Max leaned forward and instructed the driver to head for Pimlico.

He felt a tapping on his shoulder, a neatly trimmed fingernail made its presence known through the fabric of his suit sleeve. He sat back in his seat and found her looking at him. 'I haven't agreed to take the job yet.'

She wasn't one to beat about the bush, was she? But, then again, neither was he.

'Will you?'

She folded her arms. 'I need to ask *you* a few questions first.'

For some reason Max found himself smiling again. It felt odd, he realised. Not stiff or forced, just unfamiliar. As if he'd forgotten how and had suddenly remembered. But he hadn't had a lot to smile about this year, had he?

'Fire away,' he said.

Was that a flicker of a smile he saw behind those eyes? If it was, it was swiftly contradicted by a stubborn lift of her chin. 'Well, Mr Martin, you seem to have skipped over some of the details.'

'Such as?'

'Such as: how long will you be requiring my services?'

Oh, those kinds of details. 'A week, hopefully. Possibly two.'

She made a funny little you-win-some-you-lose-some kind of expression.

A nasty cold feeling shot through him. She wasn't going to back out already, was she? 'Too long?'

She shook her head. 'I'd have been happy for it to be longer, but it'll do.'

They looked at each other for a couple of seconds. Her eyes narrowed slightly as she delivered her next question. 'So why do you need a nanny for your daughter in such a hurry? I think I'd like to know why the previous one left.'

Max sat bolt upright in his seat. 'My daughter? Sofia's not my daughter!'

The nanny—or *almost* nanny, he reminded himself—gave him a wry look. 'See? This is what I'm talking about... *details.*'

Max ignored the comment. He was great with details. But nowadays he paid other people to concentrate on the trivial nit-picky things so he could do the important stuff. It worked—most of the time—because he had assistants and deputies to spring into action whenever he required them to, but when it came to his personal life he had no such army of willing helpers. Probably because he didn't have much of a personal life. It irritated him that this mismatched young woman had highlighted a failing he hadn't realised he had. Still, he could manage details, sketchy or otherwise, if he tried.

'Sofia is my niece.'

'Oh...'

Max usually found the vagaries of the female mind something of a mystery. He was always managing to put his foot in it with the women in his life—when he had time for any—but he found this one unusually easy to read. The expression that accompanied her breathy sigh of realisation clearly said, *Well, that explains a lot.*

'Let's just say that I had not planned to be child-minding today.'

She pressed her lips together, as if to stop herself from laughing. 'You mean you were left holding the baby.... Literally.'

He nodded. 'My sister is an...actress.'

At least, she'd been trying to be the last five years.

'Oh! Has she been in anything I've heard of?'

Max let out a sigh. 'Probably not. But she got a call from her agent this morning about an audition for a "smallish part in a biggish film". Something with…' what was the name? '…Jared Fisher in it.'

The nanny's eyes widened. 'Wow! He's really h—' She shut her mouth abruptly and nibbled her top lip with her teeth. 'What I meant to say was, what a fabulous opportunity for her.'

'Apparently so. She got the job, but they wanted her in L.A. right away. The actress who was supposed to be playing the part came down with appendicitis and it was now or never.'

Secretly he wondered if it would have been better if his little sister had sloped despondently into his office later that afternoon, collected her daughter and had gone home. She'd always had a bit of a bohemian lifestyle, and they'd lost touch while she'd travelled the world, working her way from one restaurant to another as she waited for her 'big break'. But then Sofia had come along and she'd settled down in London. He really didn't know if this was a good idea.

Maybe things might have been different if they'd grown up in the same house after their parents had split, but, while he'd benefited from the steadying influence of their English father, Gia had stayed with their mother, a woman who had turned fickle and inconsistent into an art form.

They had grown apart as teenagers, living in different countries, with totally different goals, values and personalities, but he was trying to make up for it now they were more a part of each other's lives.

Gia always accused him of butting his nose in where it wasn't wanted and trying to run her life for her, but she always said it with a smile and she was annoyingly difficult to argue with. Perhaps that was why, when she'd turned up at his office that morning with Sofia and had begged him to help her, her eyes full of hope and longing, he hadn't been able to say no.

'And what about you?' he asked. 'Why do you need a job in such a hurry?'

She rolled her eyes. 'It was either this, or my father was threatening to make me work for him.'

'You don't want to work for the family firm?'

She pulled a face. 'I'd rather jump off the top of The Shard! Wouldn't you?'

Max stiffened. 'I now head up the business my father built from nothing.'

An unexpected stab of pain hit him in his ribcage, and then came the roll of dark emotion that always followed. Life had been much simpler when he'd been able to bury it all so deep it had been as if it hadn't existed. 'There's something to be said for family loyalty,' he added gruffly. 'For loyalty full stop, actually.'

She looked a little uncomfortable, but waltzed her way out of the awkward moment with a quip. 'Well, I'm quite prepared to be loyal to your family. Just as long as you don't ask me to get entangled with mine. Parents are fine and all that, but I'd rather keep them at a safe distance.'

Max couldn't help but think of his mother, and he decided not to quiz Ruby any further on her motives. It wasn't going to alter whether he hired her or not for a couple of weeks. If this had been for a more permanent fixture in his life, it might have been a different matter.

'So, why do you need a travelling nanny?' Her face lit up. 'Are we going to Hollywood?'

She sounded just like Gia. Max resisted the urge to close his eyes and wish this were all a bad dream, that he'd wake up in bed, his nice, ordered life back.

'I'm taking Sofia to stay with her grandmother,' he said. It was the only possible solution. All he had to do now was convince his mother of that. 'I can't possibly babysit a toddler for the next fortnight, even if I knew how to. I have three weeks to turn around an important work situation and I can't take any time off.'

The shock of realising he'd have to cope with Sofia on his own while Gia was away had been bad enough, but then his biggest client had phoned, slinging a spanner in the works. Now he couldn't afford even an hour off work, let alone a fortnight. He needed time to think. Space. Peace and quiet. And Sofia brought none of those things with her in her tiny, howling package.

Hopefully he'd get Sofia installed at his mother's, then he'd be able to fly back and be at his desk first thing Monday, only half a day lost. It had been Gia's idea, and, while he didn't relish having to take time out to deliver Sofia, at least his sister's moment of destiny had come on a Friday morning. He'd stay overnight to make sure they all settled in and leave the nanny with his mother. He'd thought of everything.

The girl gave him a sideways look. 'So work is important to you? More than family?' She didn't look impressed.

Max gave her one of his patented you-don't-know-what-you're-talking-about looks. *Of course* family was important! That was why he had to seal this deal. He was determined to carry on and finish what he and his father had started together, to ensure that his dad's dream was fulfilled.

'I'm a thirty-something bachelor with a riverside apartment that has split-level floors with no railings, stairs with no banisters and no outside space except a balcony with a hundred-foot drop to the Thames. Do *you* think it would be the responsible thing to allow a child to live there?'

He could see her wrestling with herself, but finally she shook her head.

'Taking her to her grandmother's is the most sensible and practical thing to do—for everybody.'

He looked up. They'd crossed the river now and could only be minutes from her home. If she said no he'd just drop her off and they'd never see each other again. And he'd have to wrestle a screaming Sofia all the way to her grandmother's on his own.

'So, Miss Lange with an *e*, will you take the job?'

She inhaled and held the breath for a few seconds before glancing up at her building, then she let the air out again. 'I have one last question.'

'Which is?'

The corners of her mouth curled up, as if she couldn't quite believe he hadn't mentioned this himself. 'You really are a big-picture kind of guy, aren't you?'

Yes, he was. 'How did you know?'

'There's another detail you've forgotten, a rather important one. If I'm going to be your travelling nanny, I kind of need to know where we'll be travelling to.'

Ah, yes. Another good point. He cleared his throat. 'Italy,' he said. 'We're going to Venice.'

Ruby's hand shot out, her long slender fingers stretched towards him. 'Done.' He half expected her to spit in her palm, but she just looked steadily at him.

He encased her smaller hand in his own, feeling the warmth of her palm, the softness of her skin. Something tiny but powerful tingled all the way up his arm. He shook her hand. 'It's a deal,' he said, his voice rumbling in his own ears. 'You're hired.'

But as he pulled his hand away he started to wonder if he knew exactly what he'd got himself into.

CHAPTER THREE

RUBY SHOULD HAVE realised when the limo driver gingerly put her hastily packed canvas rucksack into the boot that this journey was going to be different. She was used to travelling, used to crowded terminals in international airports teeming with the whole spectrum of human life. She was used to queuing just to buy a bottle of water and browsing the endless shops filled with travel gadgets in order to fill the time. She was used to playing 'hunt the chair' in the departure hall, and dozing on it with her jacket for a pillow when she found one.

She was not used to hushed and elegant lounges in small city airports, free food, drink and entertainment. Even though her father could easily afford to fly business class everywhere, he refused to, preferring what he called 'real' travel. If he wasn't squished into Economy or standing at a three-mile queue at Immigration it wasn't a real trip. Of course, the public loved him for it. Privately, Ruby had always wondered why dust and the ubiquitous Jeep with dodgy suspension were more 'authentic' than air-conditioned coaches these days, but she wasn't daft enough to argue with him. He was disappointed in her enough already.

She sighed. It had been better when Mum had been alive. Even though she'd done exactly the same job, travelled along with him and presented the programmes alongside him, she'd always been good at hugs and sending postcards and presents to boarding school to let Ruby know that just because she was out of sight, it didn't mean she was out of mind. Her father was no good at that stuff. And after she'd died he'd channelled his grief into his work, meaning he lost himself in it more than he ever had done before.

Ruby found herself a spot on the edge of a designer sofa in the lounge and reached for the bowl of macadamia nuts on the table in front of her, only scooping two or three out with her fingers and popping them quickly into her mouth, then she returned to doodling on a paper napkin with a pen she'd pulled out of her bag.

It was supposed to have been easier once the journey got under way. She'd thought that at least the 'travelling' part of being a travelling nanny would be inside her comfort zone. *Wrong again, Ruby.* And she didn't even have anything work-related to do to keep her mind off her awkwardness, because Sofia, obviously exhausted by the sheer graft of tantruming half the day, was stretched out on the plush sofa with her thumb in her mouth, fast asleep and completely unaware of her surroundings.

Her new boss didn't make it any easier. He'd hardly made eye contact with her since they'd left her flat, let alone talked to her. He was a right barrel of laughs.

She filled the short time they had by quickly sketching him as he remained, granite-like and motionless, hunched over his laptop; the only parts of him moving were his eyes and his fingers. She used only a few lines to get the back of his head and his jaw right, leaving the strokes bare and uncompromising, then settled down to reproducing the wrinkles on the arms of his jacket, the soft shock of dark thick hair that was trimmed to perfection at his nape.

Thankfully, once the flight was called and they had to head to the gate and board the plane, Ruby started to feel a little more normal. Jollying a freshly woken toddler along kept her occupied. It wasn't that difficult. Sofia was a sweet child, even if the quiet curiosity hid a will of steel, like her uncle's. Poor child must have been scared and upset when she'd seen her mother disappear out of Max's office without her. It was no wonder she'd screamed the place down.

As the plane began its descent to Marco Polo airport Ruby began to feel the familiar quiver of excitement she always got at arriving somewhere new. She'd always wanted to visit Venice, had even begged her father to go when she'd been younger, but he hadn't been interested. It was a man-made construction, built on stilts in the middle of a lagoon, and the city itself had few open green spaces, let alone rare wildlife—unless you had an unusual passion for pigeons. Ruby didn't care about that. She liked cities. And this one—*La Serenissima*, as it used to be known—was supposed to be the jewel of them all.

It was a disappointment, then, to discover that they weren't going to be arriving in Venice by boat, as many visitors did. Instead Max had ordered a car to take them along the main road towards the city of Mestre, which then turned onto the seemingly endless bridge that stretched from the land to the city across the lagoon.

Sofia began to whine. Although she'd had that brief nap at the airport, the poor little girl looked ready to drop. Ruby did her best to calm her down, and it helped, but what the child really needed was someone she knew. She might have taken to her new nanny, but Ruby was still a stranger. As was her uncle, Ruby guessed. The sooner she was reunited with her grandmother, the better.

The car pulled to a halt and Ruby looked up. Her face fell. Usually, she liked catching the first glimpse of a new place, seeing it as a far-off dot on the horizon, and getting more and more excited as it got closer and closer. This evening, she'd been so busy distracting Sofia back from the verge of another tantrum, she'd missed all of that. They'd arrived at a large square full of buses. They were in Venice at last, and yet this didn't look magical at all. The Piaz-zala Roma looked very much like any other busy transport hub in any busy city.

People were everywhere. They spilled off the large orange buses that seemed to arrive and leave every few minutes, dragging luggage behind them as they set off on foot, maps in hands; or they queued wearily and waited for the buses to empty so they could clamber inside and head back to the mainland.

The driver started unloading the bags. Ruby took her rucksack from the boot before this one had a chance to be snooty about it, then reached inside and unclipped Sofia from her car seat. The little girl grizzled softly as she clung round Ruby's neck. They walked a short distance to a wait-ing motor launch on the side of a nearby canal. But Ruby was too busy trying to work out if the sticky substance Sofia had just wiped onto her neck was tears or snot to really pay attention. The boat driver nodded a greeting to Max, and then started up the engine.

For the next few minutes they took a dizzying route through the narrow canals—the equivalent of back streets, she supposed—and she could hardly see more than white-washed or brick walls, oddly placed ornate windows high up in them, or the odd washing line strung with underwear, waving like unconventional bunting above their heads. But then they emerged onto the Grand Canal and Ruby was glad she was sitting down, with Sofia's weight anchoring her to her seat in the back of the boat, because she surely would have thumped down onto her backside if she'd been standing up.

She'd never seen so many beautiful buildings in one place. All were ornately decorated with arches and win-dows and balconies. Some were crested with intricate cren-ellations that reminded her of royal icing fit for a wedding cake. Others were the most beautiful colours, the old stone worn and warmed by both the salt of the lagoon water that lapped at their bases and the soft sun dangling effortlessly in a misty sky.

She was still sitting there with her mouth open when the boat puttered to a stop outside a grand-looking palazzo. Instantly, two uniformed men dashed out of an ornate wooden door and onto the small, private landing stage, complete with the red-and-white-striped poles, and collected their bags and helped them from the boat. One tried to relieve Ruby of Sofia, but the little girl wouldn't have it. She clung so hard to Ruby's neck that Ruby almost choked. She had to make do with letting one of the men steady her as she clambered, a little off balance, onto the small stone jetty.

Ruby looked up. The building was very elegant. Traditional Venetian style, its tall windows topped with almost church-like stonework. Surely nobody real could live anywhere quite so beautiful?

Max must have decided she was dawdling, because he huffed something and turned.

She shook her head slightly. 'Your mother lives *here*?'

He thought she was being slow again. She could tell by the way he was looking at her, a weary sense of disbelief on his features. 'Of course my mother doesn't live here. It's a hotel.'

Maybe it was because she was tired and Sofia felt like a lead weight, or maybe it was because this had probably been the strangest day of her life so far, but she bristled. 'You said we were taking Sofia to see your mother. You didn't say anything about a hotel.'

'Didn't I?'

'No, you didn't,' she said darkly, and then muttered under her breath, '*Details*, Mr Martin.'

He waited until they had walked through the lobby and were whooshing upwards in a shiny mirrored lift before he spoke again. 'This is the Lagoon Palace Hotel. Sofia is tired.' He nodded in her direction, where the child was still clamped onto Ruby's shoulder like an oversized limpet. It was the first time he'd even given a hint he'd remembered his niece existed since she'd taken over. And, consequently, the fact he'd even noticed Sofia was exhausted took Ruby by surprise. 'It'll be a lot less fuss if we settle in here this evening and go and see my mother in the morning.'

Ruby opened her mouth to ask why, then shut it again. A flicker of a look had passed across his features, tensing his jaw and setting his shoulders. She was only too well acquainted with that look. Some people rushed into their parents' arms after a separation, but other people? Well, sometimes they needed a chance to mentally prepare themselves.

She just hadn't expected Max Martin, who seemed to have life buttoned up and marching to his tune, to be one of her fellow throng.

The inside of the Lagoon Palace was a surprise. Ruby had expected it to be full of ornate furniture, antiques and brocade, but the style was a mix of classic and contemporary. The original features of the building were intact, such as the tall marble fireplaces, the plasterwork and painted ceilings, but the decor was modern, with furnishings in bold, bright colours and rich textures.

The suite Max had booked had a main living area overlooking the Grand Canal and a bedroom on either side. A low, modern sofa in cherry-red velvet faced the windows and two matching armchairs sat at right angles. The end tables were a funky organic shape and the walls were the same colour as the furnishings. Other than that it was all dark wood and pale creamy marble.

Ruby stood in the middle of the living area, mouth open, taking it all in. 'I was expecting something a little more… traditional,' she said to Max as she dropped her rucksack on the floor and let Sofia down from where she'd been carrying her. Sofia instantly thrust her arms upwards, demanding to be picked up again.

Ruby sighed and did as commanded. She needed a moment to get her bearings and having a wailing child wouldn't help. So far she'd felt totally at sea, and she had no idea whether she was looking after Sofia the right way. For all she knew, she could be mentally scarring the child for life.

Her uncle might not have noticed, but she needed to start acting, and thinking, like a real nanny. Tomorrow they'd be meeting Sofia's grandmother, and, if she was anything like her son, she'd be sharp as a tack, and she definitely wouldn't be oblivious to Ruby's shortcomings. The last thing she wanted was to lose this job before it had even started.

'I don't like clutter,' Max said. He took a moment to look around the suite, as if he hadn't really taken it all in before. 'While it's not exactly minimalist, it's as unfussy as this city gets.'

Sofia began to grizzle again, so Ruby carried her across to one of the bedroom doors and looked inside. There was a huge bed, with a sofa with burnt orange velvet cushions at the foot, and large windows draped in the same heavy fabric. Obviously the boss's room. She retreated and checked the door on the opposite side of the living area. It led to a spacious room with twin beds, decorated in brown and cream with colourful abstract prints on the walls. She assumed she'd be sharing with Sofia, at least for tonight.

She was relieved to see each room had its own en suite. It was odd, this nannying lark. Being part of a family, but not really being part of a family. There were obviously boundaries, which helped both family and employee, but Ruby had no idea where to draw those lines. Still, she expected that sharing a bathroom, trying to brush your teeth in the sink at the same time as your pyjama-clad boss, was probably a step too far.

Not that she wanted to see Max Martin in his pyjamas, of course.

For some reason that thought made her cheeks heat, and she distracted herself by lugging Sofia back into the living room, where her new boss was busy muttering to himself as he tried to hook up his laptop at a dark, stylish wooden desk tucked into the corner between his bedroom door and the windows.

'I'm going to put Sofia to bed now,' she told him. 'She ate on the plane, and she's clearly dog-tired.'

Max just grunted from where he had his head under the desk, then backed out and stood up. He looked at Sofia, but didn't move towards them.

'Come on, sweetie,' Ruby cooed. 'Say night-night to Uncle Max.'

Sofia just clung on tighter. Eventually he walked towards them and placed an awkward kiss on the top of the little girl's head. Ruby tried not to notice the smell of his after-shave or the way the air seemed to ripple around her when he came near, and then she quickly scurried away and got Sofia ready for bed.

She put Sofia to bed in one of the twin beds in their room. In the bag her mother had packed for her, Ruby found a number of changes of clothes, the usual toiletries, a few books and a rather over-loved stuffed rabbit.

'Want Mamma,' the little girl sniffed as Ruby helped her into her pyjamas.

Ruby's heart lurched. She knew exactly how that felt, even though her separation from her mother was permanent and at least Sofia would see hers again very soon. But at this age, it must feel like an eternity.

She picked Sofia up and sat her on her lap, held her close, and pulled out a book to read, partly as part of the bedtime ritual, but partly to distract the child from missing her mother. She also gave her the rabbit. Sofia grabbed on to the toy gratefully and instantly stuck her thumb in her mouth and closed her eyes, giving out one last shuddering breath before going limp in Ruby's arms.

Not even enough energy for a bedtime story. Poor little thing.

Ruby put the book on the bedside table and slid Sofia under the covers before turning out the light.

Ruby knew what it felt like to be carted from place to place, often not knowing where you were or who you'd been left with. She was tempted to reach across and smooth a dark curl away from Sofia's forehead, but she kept her hand in her lap.

Usually, she threw herself into each new job with gusto, immersing herself completely in it, but she had a feeling it would be a bad idea for a travelling nanny. This was a two-week job at most. She couldn't get too attached. Mustn't. So she just sat on the edge of the bed watching Sofia's tiny chest rise and fall for what seemed like ages.

When she was sure her charge was soundly asleep, and she wouldn't disturb her by moving, she crept out and closed the bedroom door softly behind her. The living room of the suite was steeped in silence and the large gurgle her stomach produced as she tiptoed towards the sofa seemed to echo up to the high ceilings. It was dark now, and the heavy red curtains were drawn, blocking out any view of the canal. Ruby longed to go and fling them open, but she supposed it wasn't her choice. If her boss wanted to shut himself away from the outside world, from all that beauty and magnificence, then that was his decision.

She could hear her employer through his open bedroom door, in a one-sided conversation, talking in clipped, hushed tones. She glanced over at the desk, where he'd already made himself quite at home. The surface was covered in sheets of paper and printouts, and a laptop was silently displaying a company name that floated round the screen.

Martin & Martin.

Ruby changed direction and wandered over to take a better look. Amongst the printed-out emails and neat handwritten notes there were also half-rolled architectural plans—for something very big and very grand, by the looks of it.

So Max Martin was an architect. She could see how that suited him. He was possibly the most rigid man she'd ever met. Anything he built would probably last for centuries.

She couldn't help peering over the plans to get a better look at the writing on the bottom corner of the sheet.

The National Institute of Fine Art.

Wow. That was one of her favourite places to hang out in London on a rainy afternoon. And she'd seen a display last time she'd visited about plans for a new wing and a way to cover the existing courtyard to provide a central hub for the gallery's three other wings.

Max's voice grew louder and Ruby scuttled away from the desk. She'd just reached the centre of the room when he emerged from his bedroom, mobile phone pressed to his ear. She did a good job of trying not to listen, pretending to flick through a magazine she'd grabbed from the coffee table instead, but, even though she was trying to keep her nose to herself, it was obvious that Max was the front-runner for the institute's new wing, but the clients had reservations.

She finished flipping through the glossy fashion mag and put it back down on the table. To be honest, she wasn't sure what to do now. Did being Sofia's nanny mean she just had to hole herself up in the bedroom with her, never to be seen or heard without child in tow? Or was she allowed to mingle with other members of the family? Seeing as this was her first experience of being a nanny she had absolutely no clue, and seeing as this was Max's first experience of hiring one—even if he had been the kind of person to dole out information without the use of thumb-screws—he probably didn't know, either.

He turned and strode towards her, frowning, listening intently to whoever was on the other end of the phone.

Ruby looked up at him, expecting maybe a nod, or even a blink of recognition as he passed by, but she got none. It was as if he'd totally forgotten she existed. So she became more comfortable studying him. He looked tired, she thought as she watched him pace first in one direction and then another, always marking out straight lines with precise angles. The top button of his shirt was undone and his tie was nowhere to be seen.

It was odd. All day so far, he'd just seemed like a force of nature—albeit in a pristine suit—and now that just the tiniest part of that armour had been discarded she was suddenly confronted by the fact he was a man. And a rather attractive one at that.

His dark hair was short but not severe, and now she knew he had Italian blood in him, she could see it in the set of his eyes and his long, straight nose. The mouth, however, was totally British, tightly drawn in, jaw tense as he grimaced at some unwelcome news and hung up on the caller without saying goodbye. He brought the phone down from his ear and stared at it so hard that Ruby thought it might burst into flames.

That was when he looked up and spotted her sitting where she'd been for the last ten minutes, and it took him by total surprise. She allowed her lips to curve into the barest of smiles and held his gaze. For some reason she liked the fact her presence sometimes ruffled him.

He shoved his phone back in his pocket. 'Is there anything you need?'

His tone wasn't harsh, just practical.

'I was wondering what to do about food.' Her stomach growled again, just to underline the fact. She refused to blush.

He had only just stopped frowning at his phone call, and now his features crumpled back into the same expression, as if he'd forgotten hunger was an option for him, and he was taking time to remember what the sensation was like. Eventually, he indicated a menu on the sideboard. 'Have what you want sent up.'

Ruby nodded. She'd been hoping he'd say that. 'Do you want anything while I'm ordering?'

'No...' His gaze drifted towards the array of papers on the desk and he was drawn magnetically to it. He picked up a sheet and started reading a page of dense text.

Ruby wasn't quite sure if he'd finished saying everything he'd been going to say, but she guessed he'd forgotten he'd actually started talking, so she went and fetched the menu. When she ordered her club sandwich she did it discreetly, so as not to disturb him, and just before she put the phone down she quietly ordered another. He hadn't touched the food on the plane, and she hadn't seen him eat anything all afternoon. He had to get hungry some time, didn't he?

If he did, he showed no sign of it. His eyes stayed on his papers while his fingers rapped out email after email on his laptop. She watched him out of the corner of her eye, slightly fascinated. He was so focused, so intense. He seemed to have an innate sense of confidence in his own ability to do what needed to be done.

To be honest, she was a little jealous.

She'd tried a number of jobs since dropping out of university but none of them had stuck. She wanted what Max had. A purpose. No, a calling. A sense of who she was in this world and what she was supposed to be doing while she was here.

A knock on the door a few minutes later heralded the

arrival of her dinner. She opened the door and tipped the room-service guy, then wheeled the little trolley closer to the sofa.

What she needed to do right now was stuff her face with her sandwich, before her stomach climbed up her throat and came to get it. That was the problem, maybe. She could always see the step that was right in front of her, the immediate details—like taking the job this afternoon—but when it came to the 'big picture' of her life it was always fuzzy and a bit out of focus.

She poured a glass of red wine from a bottle she'd ordered to go along with the food and took it, and the other sandwich, over to her boss. He didn't look up, so she cleared a little space at the corner of papers and put the plate down. The wine, however, was more tricky. The last thing she wanted to do was put it where he'd knock it over. Eventually, she just coughed lightly, and he looked up.

'Here,' she said, handing him the glass. 'You looked like you could do with this.'

For a moment he looked as if he was going to argue, but then he looked longingly at the glass of Pinot Noir and took it from her. As he did, just the very tips of their fingers brushed together.

'Thank you,' he said.

Ruby held her breath, then backed away silently. Her face felt hot and she had the sudden urge to babble. She always did that when she was flustered or nervous, and suddenly she was both.

Max, however, didn't notice. It was obvious he was as cool and calm and focused as he'd always been. He put the glass down near the back of the desk and carried on typing the email he'd been working on. Her cheeks flushed, Ruby retreated to the far end of the large sofa and ate her sandwich in silence.

When she'd finished her dinner, she stood up and replaced the empty plate on the trolley, then she hovered for a moment. He hadn't touched either the food or the wine. She wanted to say something, but she didn't know what; then she interrupted herself with a yawn. It was almost ten and it had been a long day. Maybe she should just go and get ready for bed.

Still, as she made her way towards her bedroom door she lingered, fingers on the handle, her eyes drawn to the silent figure hunched over his laptop in the corner. It was a long while before she pressed down on the metal fixture and pushed the door open.

As she got undressed in the semi-dark, careful not to wake the sleeping child, she thought about Max and all his quiet dedication and commitment. Maybe he was rubbing off on her, because suddenly she wanted to rise to the challenge in front of her.

She knew it seemed as if she'd come by this job almost by accident, but maybe that was just fate sending her a big, flashing neon sign? *This way, Ruby...* Maybe being a nanny was what she was meant to do. Hadn't Max said she was exactly what he needed? And Sofia already seemed very attached to her.

She held her breath as she slid in between the cool cotton sheets and pulled the covers up over her chest. Maybe this was her calling. Who knew? But for the next week— possibly two—she'd have her chance to find out.

Max looked up from his plans and papers and noticed a club sandwich sitting on the edge of the desk. How long had that been there? His stomach growled and he reached for it and devoured it in record time.

Ruby must have put it there. He frowned. Something about that felt wrong.

And not just because taking care of him wasn't part of her job description. He just wasn't used to being taken care of full stop, mainly because he'd carefully structured his life so he was totally self-sufficient. He didn't need anyone to look after him. He didn't need anyone, at all. And that was just as well. While his father had been his rock, he hadn't been the touchy-feely sort, and work had always kept him away from home for long hours. And his mother...

Well, he hadn't had a mother's influence in his life since he'd been a teenager, and even before the divorce things had been...explosive...at home.

A rush of memories rolled over him. He tried to hold them at bay, but there were too many, coming too fast, like a giant wave breaching a sea wall in a storm. That wall had held fast for so many years. He didn't know why it was crumbling now, only that it was. He rubbed his eyes and stood up, paced across the living room of the suite in an effort to escape it.

This was why he hated this city. It was too old, full of too much history. Somehow the past—anyone's past—weighed too heavily here.

He shook his head and reached for the half-drunk bottle of wine on the room-service trolley and went to refill his glass. The Pinot had been perfect, rich and soothing. Just what he'd needed.

He didn't want to revisit any of those memories. Not even the good ones. Yes, his mother had been wonderful when she'd been happy—warm, loving, such fun—but the tail end of his parents' marriage had been anything *but* happy. Those good times were now superimposed with her loud and expressive fits of rage, the kind only an Italian woman knew how to give, and his father's silent and stoic sternness, as he refused to be baited, to be drawn into the game. Sometimes the one-sided fights had gone on for days.

He took another slug of wine and tried to unclench his shoulder muscles.

His relationship with his mother had never been good,

not since the day she'd left the family home in a taxi and a cloud of her own perfume. He hadn't spoken to her in at least a year, and hadn't seen her for more than three.

He looked down at his glass and noticed he'd polished it off without realising. There was still another left in the bottle....

No. He put his glass down on the desk and switched off his laptop. No more for tonight. Because if there was one thing he was certain of, it was that he'd need a clear head to deal with his mother come morning.

CHAPTER FOUR

MAX WALKED OUT of his bedroom then stopped, completely arrested by the sight in front of him. *What the heck?*

And it wasn't the spray of cereal hoops all over the coffee table or the splash of milk threatening to drip off the edge. Nor was it the sight of his niece, sitting cross-legged on the carpet and eating a pastry, no sign of a tantrum in sight. No, it was the fact that the nanny he'd hired yesterday bore no resemblance to the one who was busily trying to erase the evidence of what had obviously been a rather messy breakfast session.

She froze when she heard him walk in, then turned around. Her gaze drifted to the mess in the middle of the room. 'Sofia doesn't like cereal, apparently,' she explained calmly. 'And she felt the need to demonstrate that with considerable gusto.'

He blinked and looked again.

The voice was right. And the attitude. But this looked like a different girl.... No—woman. This one was definitely a woman.

Gone was the slightly hippy-looking patchwork scarecrow from the day before, to be replaced by someone in a bright red fifties dress covered in big cartoon strawberries. With the full skirt and the little black shoes and the short hair swept from her face, she looked like a psychedelic version of Audrey Hepburn.

Hair! That was it!

He looked again. The purple streaks were still there, just not as apparent in this neater style. Good. For a moment there, he'd thought he'd been having a particularly vivid dream.

'Good morning,' he finally managed to mutter.

She raised her eyebrows.

Max covered up the fact that the sight of all those strawberries had made him momentarily forget her name by launching in with something she'd like—details. 'After breakfast we're going to visit Sofia's grandmother.' He paused and looked at the slightly milk-drenched, pastry-flake-covered child in front of him. 'Would you be able to get her looking presentable by ten?'

The nanny nodded. 'I think so.'

'Good.' Max felt his stomach unclench. 'My mother is not someone who tolerates an untidy appearance.' And then he turned to go and fire up his laptop, but he could have sworn he heard her mutter, *'What a shocker...'* under her breath.

The water taxi slowed outside a large palazzo with its own landing stage leading up to a heavy front door. They'd travelled for maybe fifteen minutes, leaving the Grand Canal behind and heading into the Castello district of the city.

The building was almost as large at the hotel they'd just left, but where its plaster had been pristine and smooth, this palace was looking a little more tired round the edges. Green slime coated the walls at the waterline, indicating the height of the high tide. Some of the pink plasterwork had peeled off at the bottom of the structure leaving an undulating wave of bare bricks showing.

There were grilles over the ground-floor windows, and the plaster was peeling away there, too, but up above there were the most wonderful stone balcony and window boxes overflowing with ivy and white flowers. The overall effect was like that of a grand old lady who'd had a fabulous time at the ball but had now sat down, a little tired and flustered, to compose herself.

Ruby's eyes were wide as she clung onto Sofia to stop her scrambling ashore before the boat was properly secured.

Max must have read her mind. 'This is Ca' Damiani and, yes, my mother lives here. But she doesn't occupy the whole thing, just the *piano nobile*.'

Ruby nodded, even though she had no idea what that meant.

'A lot of these grand old buildings have been split up into apartments,' he explained as he hopped from the boat and offered to take Sofia from her. 'In buildings like these the floor above ground level was the prime spot, where the grandest rooms of the house were situated—the stage for all the family's dramas.' He sighed. 'And there's nothing my mother likes more than a grand drama.'

His voice was neutral, expressionless even, but she could see the tension in his jaw, the way the air around him seemed heavy and tense. This was not a joyful home-coming, not one bit.

Ruby clambered out of the boat and reached for Sofia's hand, and then the three of them together walked off the dock and up to a double door with a large and tarnished brass knocker. Ruby swallowed as Max lifted it. When it fell the noise rang out like a gunshot, and she jumped. She did her best not to fidget as they waited.

After a short wait the door swung open. Ruby would have expected it to creak, from the age of it, but it was as silent as a rush of air. The woman who was standing there was also something of a surprise. Ruby had expected her to be tall and dark, like Max, but she was petite and her blond hair was artfully swept into a twist at the back of her head. She wore a suit with a dusky pink jacket and skirt and, just like every other Italian woman Ruby had ever met, carried with her an innate sense of confidence in her own style. Not a hair on her head was out of place.

Ruby looked down at her strawberry-patterned skirt. She'd chosen her best vintage dress for today in an attempt to emulate that effortless style, but now she feared she just looked like a sideshow freak instead of *la bella figura*. She held back, hiding herself a little behind Max's much larger frame.

His mother looked at him for a long moment.

No, Ruby thought, she didn't just look. She drank him in.

'Well, you have finally come, Massimo,' she said in Italian, her voice hoarse.

'I've told you I prefer Max,' he replied in English. 'And it was an emergency. Gia needed me. What else could I do? I wasn't going to run out on her, on my family, because things got a little difficult.'

The words hung between them like an accusation. Ruby saw the older woman pale, but then she drew herself taller.

'Oh, I know that it is not on my account that you are here,' she said crisply. 'As for the other matter, I named you, Massimo, so I shall call you what I like.' She glanced down and her face broke into a wide and warm smile. 'Darling child! Come here to your *nonna*!'

Sofia hesitated for a second, then allowed herself to be picked up and held. Ruby guessed that Max's sister must be a more frequent visitor here than he was. After a couple of moments Sofia was smiling and using her chubby fingers to explore the gold chain and pendant around her grandmother's neck. She seemed totally at ease.

When she'd finished fussing over her granddaughter, Max's mother lifted her head and looked at him. 'You'd better come inside.'

She retreated into a large hallway with a diamond-tiled floor and rough brick walls. There were hints of the plaster that had once covered them, and most of the moulded ceilings were intact. However, instead of seeming tumbledown, it just made the palazzo's ground floor seem grand and ancient. There were a few console tables and antiques, and a rather imposing staircase with swirling wrought iron banisters curved upwards to the first floor.

His mother started making her way up the staircase, but when she turned the corner and realised there was an extra body still following them, and it wasn't just someone who'd helped them unload from the boat, she stopped and walked back down to where Ruby was on the floor, ballet-slippered foot hovering above the bottom step, and let Sofia slide from her embrace.

'And who do we have here?' she asked, looking Ruby up and down with interest. Ruby's heart thudded inside her ribcage. Not the sort of girl who usually trailed around after her son, probably. Well, almost definitely.

'This is Sofia's nanny,' Max said, this time joining his mother in her native language. 'I hired her especially for the trip.'

'Ruby Lange,' Ruby said and offered her hand, hoping it wasn't sticky, and then continued in her best Italian, 'It's lovely to meet you.'

Max's mother just turned and stared at her son, tears filling her eyes, and then she set off up the staircase again, this time at speed, her heels clicking against the stone. 'You have insulted me, Massimo! Of all the things you could have done!'

Max hurried up the stairs after his mother. 'I've done nothing of the sort. You're making no sense at all.'

He'd reverted to English. Which was a pity, because when he spoke Italian he sounded like a different man. Oh, the depth and tone of the voice were the same, but it had sounded richer, warmer. As if it belonged to a man capable of the same passion and drama as the woman he was chasing up the stairs.

Ruby turned to Sofia, who was looking up the stair-case after her uncle and grandmother. Once again, she'd been forgotten. Ruby wanted to pull her up into her arms and hug her hard. She knew what it was like to always be left behind, to always be the complication that stopped the adults in your life from doing what they wanted. 'What do you say, kiddo? Shall we follow the grown-ups?'

Sofia nodded and they made their way up the stairs. It was slow progress. Sofia had to place both feet on a step before moving to the next one. Her little legs just weren't ca-pable of anything else. When they got halfway, Ruby gave up and held out her arms. The little girl quickly clambered up her and let her nanny do the hard work.

Well, that was what she was here for. Or she would be if Signora Martin didn't think she was so much of an in-sult that she threw Ruby out on her ear. Max hadn't been wrong when he'd mentioned drama, had he?

When she got to the top of the stairs the decor changed. There was wood panelling on the walls and the ceilings were painted in pastel colours with intricate plasterwork patterns. Every few feet there were wall sconces, dripping with crystals. If this explosion of baroque architecture and cluttered antique furniture was what Max had meant when he'd called Venetian style 'fussy', she could see his point.

The 'discussion' was still raging, in a room just off the landing. The space must have been huge, because their voices echoed the same way they would in a church or a museum. His mother's was emotive and loud, Max's steady and even. Ruby was glad her soft shoes didn't make much noise and she crept in the direction of the raised voices, Sofia resting on her hip.

'You're never going to forgive me, are you?' his mother finally said softly.

Ruby crept a little closer. The room had double doors, which were still standing where they'd been flung open, and she peeked at the interior through the gap next to the hinges.

Max's mother closed her eyes and sadness washed over her features. 'That's why you brought the nanny, wasn't it? You think I'm not fit to look after my granddaughter on my own. Was I really such a terrible mother?'

This was getting too personal, Ruby realised. It was time to back away, leave them to it. She'd just have to find somewhere to hide out with Sofia until the whole thing blew over. Surely there must be a kitchen in this place somewhere?

She retreated a couple of steps, but she'd forgotten that she was much less nimble with Sofia increasing her bulk and she knocked into a side table and made the photo frames and lamp on it jangle.

There was silence in the room beyond. Ruby held her breath. A moment later Max appeared in the doorway and motioned for her to come inside. Ruby would rather have drunk a gallon of lagoon water, but she really didn't have much choice. She hoisted Sofia up into a more comfortable position, tipped her chin up and walked into the room.

It was a grand Venetian salon, with a vast honey-coloured marble fireplace and trompe l'oeil pillars and mouldings painted on the walls in matching tones, with mythic scenes on the walls in between. A row of arched windows leading onto a stone balcony dominated the opposite side of the room, and three large green sofas were arranged in a C-shape, facing them. But the sight that Ruby was most interested in was the stiff figure in the pink suit standing in the middle of the room.

'Ruby isn't here to usurp you, Mamma. I hired her partly to help me bring Sofia over here with minimum fuss, but also because I thought she could help you. Why should you have to cancel your social engagements, alter your plans, for the next couple of weeks because of Gia's work problems?'

The other woman's features softened a little, and she looked a little ashamed. She turned to face Ruby and held out her hand. Ruby let Sofia down and the little girl ran to the window to look at a speedboat that had just shot down the medium-sized canal beyond.

'Serafina Martin.' She smiled warmly and shook Ruby's hand firmly but very briefly. 'But everybody calls me Fina. I apologise most sincerely for not welcoming you to Ca' Damiani when you first arrived, but I do so now.'

Ruby replied in her best Italian. 'Thank you, Signora Martin, for your welcome and for opening your home to me, if you do decide you could do with my help. I'm afraid this is my first job as a nanny so I've been thrown in at the deep end.' She glanced at Max, who was watching her carefully. 'You'll probably have to help me more than I'll help you.'

A small flicker of approval, and maybe relief, passed across the other woman's features. Fina tilted her head. 'Your Italian is very good.'

Ruby kept her smile demure. 'Thank you.'

Fina's gaze swept over her dress and then up to her head. 'But your hair is not. Purple?'

She shrugged. 'I like it.'

For the longest moment Fina didn't move, didn't say anything. She didn't even blink, but then she smiled. It started in her eyes and moved to just lift the corners of her mouth. '*Bene*. What do I know? I am old and out of touch, probably, and I like a woman who follows her own path.' And then she turned and swept out of the room. 'Come, Massimo! We have to decide what you are going to do about this child.'

Max stared at his mother. 'What do you mean you want me to stay here, too?'

That hadn't been the plan at all. The reason he'd brought

Sofia here was because now was definitely not the moment to take an impromptu holiday. He couldn't let everything he and his father had worked for slide.

His mother did that infuriating little wave of her hand, suggesting he was making a mountain out of a molehill. 'You made a very good point,' she said airily. 'I do have plans this week, including earning a living. I can't take time off at this short notice.'

Max's jaw dropped. 'You have a *job*?'

She turned her head to look at him. 'Why is that so hard to believe? Yes, I have a job. I work for a real estate company in the mornings, helping them dress and present their luxury properties.'

He shook his head, hardly able to believe it.

'You are straying from the point, Massimo. It is not important where I work, but how we are going to do the best for Sofia.'

He frowned. 'I know that, Mamma. That's why I came to you in the first place. It just isn't possible to keep her in London with me. There's a work issue that's at a very crucial point and I can't give her the time and attention she deserves.'

'You know I adore having Sofia with me, but do you think I keep this place running because money falls from the sky? I also have urgent work to do.'

He shot a glance across at his travelling nanny. She was kneeling on the carpet, helping Sofia build a house out of colourful blocks. Max didn't know where they'd come from. His mother must have had them stashed away somewhere. 'But that's why I brought Ruby.' He'd thought of everything, made it simple and easy. Why was his mother turning this into a problem when there was none?

'The poor child is upset and away from her mother. When I'm not here, she needs to be with someone she knows.'

She looked the picture of innocence, perched on the edge of a green damask sofa. The high windows let in the soft light of the May morning, basking her in an almost saintly glow.

'But she doesn't know me, either.'

His mother frowned. 'I thought Gia had said that you were in regular contact now.'

'We text, mainly,' he mumbled. 'And she comes into the city to have lunch every couple of months, but she doesn't usually bring Sofia with her.'

He rather suspected she deliberately chose the days Sofia was at nursery, so she could come up to town and have a few hours to herself. She very kindly always picked the best places, and always let her brother pay.

'Texting is not communicating! It is not the same as a smile or a hug or a warm word. One cannot build relationships through one's phone.'

He shrugged and his mother did another one of her famous hand gestures. Not the little elegant hand-flap, this one. Both arms flew above her head and she stood up and walked over to stare out of the windows onto the canal below. 'Then this is the perfect opportunity for you to get to know her. You really should. She is your only niece, after all.'

If that wasn't an example of his mother's own brand of circular logic, he didn't know what was.

'But she cries every time I look at her,' he said, more than a little exasperated. 'I try to talk nicely to her but it doesn't seem to make any difference. I'd stay if it were different, but it's hardly the best thing for Sofia to leave her with me on my own if that's the case.'

'But you won't be on your own,' his mother said, far too silkily for his liking. 'You'll have Ruby.'

They both transferred their gazes to the travelling nanny. Ruby, who must have sensed two pairs of eyes on her, stopped what she was doing and looked up at them from under her fringe. Max had a lightning stab of revelation. Ruby had already proved very useful when it had come to Sofia, perhaps she could be more useful still. Perhaps he could enlist her as an ally. He sent her a silent message with his eyes.

Ruby's lips twitched. 'It's true,' she said, looking at his mother. 'She does cry most of the time when she's near him. They don't know each other at all. He's not even sure how old she is.'

His mother reached across and slapped his leg. Quite hard, actually. 'Massimo! Honestly!'

She turned to look at Ruby, and Max had the feeling he was being pointedly ignored for the moment. 'She'll be three in a month,' his mother said in Italian, and then she and Ruby had a brief exchange about when Sofia's birthday was and what sort of things she liked to do. He was quite surprised at how good the nanny's Italian was, to be honest. He hadn't even known she spoke it. Just went to show his instincts about her had been right, even if she did make each day look as if she'd raided a different fancy dress shop.

However, when Ruby and his mother started getting into what time was bedtime and favourite snacks, he decided that enough was enough. He stood up and walked closer to them. 'Can we just get back to the matter in hand?' he said, maybe a little abruptly.

Both women stopped talking and looked at him. They wore identical expressions. Max had the horrible sinking feeling that maybe he'd been right about Ruby being a good ally. He just wasn't sure she was his.

'I need to know this kind of stuff, actually,' she told him. 'And you weren't much help.'

Details.

He could almost hear Ruby's mental whisper that followed.

That was enough to set his mother throwing her hands in the air again. When she'd calmed herself down by walking over to the fireplace and back again, she fixed him with a determined expression. Max knew that look. It meant she'd made up her mind about something, and budging her from that viewpoint was going to be about as easy as asking the whole of Venice to pick up her skirts and move a little further out into the lagoon.

'I have made a decision,' she announced. 'I would like nothing more than to have my lovely granddaughter here for a visit.'

He let out a breath he hadn't been aware he'd been holding. 'Thank you, Mamma.'

His mother drew herself up and put on her most regal air. 'But I will allow it on one condition.'

What?

'I won't take Sofia unless you stay, too,' his mother told him, folding her arms across her chest. 'You cannot live your life cloistered away in that stuffy office of yours, communicating to those you love through bits of technology. It's high time you lived up to your family responsibilities, Massimo.'

Max almost choked. *His* family responsibilities? That was rich!

He opened his mouth to argue, but didn't get very far. He became aware of a small but insistent tugging on the left leg of his trousers and looked down to find his niece standing there. She was trying to pull him in the direction of the pile of blocks on the rug near the fireplace.

His mother just smiled at him. 'She's not crying now, my darling son, and you said you'd stay if she stopped.' She looked over at her granddaughter. Warmth and joy flared in her eyes. 'It seems I am not the only one who has made my mind up about this—Sofia has, too.'

CHAPTER FIVE

MAX AND HIS MOTHER had had a long conversation out on the balcony, ironing out the details of her ultimatum. When they returned, Fina knelt down on the carpet beside Ruby and Sofia and joined in their game of piling up bricks into tall towers for Sofia to knock down again.

Fina smiled and laughed, totally absorbed in her grand-daughter, while her son stood, towering and silent on the fringes of the room. Ruby shot him a sideways look and found him staring back at her. She swallowed. She felt a little guilty that she'd ended up unwittingly providing Fina with leverage to use against him, but not guilty enough to regret she'd done it.

Despite Fina's superior manner and haughty words, Ruby had seen the way she'd looked at Max. That was a mother hungry for her son's company and, just like a child who'd settle for negative attention when they couldn't get praise, in desperation she'd taken whatever she could get.

Funnily, Ruby warmed to Fina for that. She wished her own father looked at her that way sometimes, but she'd never once got the impression from him that he was hun-gry for more of her company. No, he'd seemed perfectly content to push her out of the nest at an early age.

'I'd better go and check out of the hotel and get our bags,' Max finally growled.

Ruby stood up and brushed her skirt down. 'I'll help you.' That was the least she could do.

He scowled at her, indicating she'd done enough already. She ignored it and followed him as he headed out of the door. She had to trot to keep up with him as he marched down the corridor and down the sweeping staircase.

'So, what's going on?' she finally asked. 'I presume we're staying, for a short while, at least.'

Max sighed. 'My mother and I have come to an...arrangement.' He shuddered slightly, as if the idea of compromise was an abhorrent concept.

He was doing it again: failing to fill her in on the important stuff. 'Which is?'

Max stopped on the stairs and turned, hands still in pockets. 'My mother has agreed she will care for Sofia when she's free, with your help, of course, but only if I stay for a minimum of seven days. Otherwise she's happy to escort us all to the airport where we can catch the next plane back to London.'

Ruby's face crumpled into a bemused smile. 'She'd really do that?'

He grunted and set off again. 'You have no idea how stubborn my mother can be when she puts her mind to it.'

Ruby didn't reply to that. The only response that came to mind was that maybe he was more like his mother than he realised, and she'd got herself into enough trouble already with him this morning.

She studied the back of his head carefully as she followed him down the stairs. Did he really not get that this ultimatum had nothing to do with his sister's childcare issues and everything to do with Fina wanting to repair the gaping breach in her family? Ruby had also gone to extreme lengths to get just a crumb of her father's attention in her teenage years, and she understood completely why Fina had done it.

'And what about the Institute of Fine Art? The plans?'

He turned as he reached the ground floor, looking surprised.

'Couldn't help overhearing you on the phone last night. And then there are the drawings littered all over the suite...'

Max ran a hand through his hair as they emerged from the palazzo onto the dock and wearily took in the grand and crumbling buildings around them. 'I'm in Venice...' he said, and she sensed he was quoting his mother verbatim. 'The most beautiful city in the world. What better inspiration could I have?'

Thankfully, Max discovered his mother hadn't disposed of the little motor launch that had once been his grandfather's. By the looks of it, she'd kept it in immaculate condition. The varnish wasn't peeling and the navy paint on the sides was fresh and thick. He jumped in, stood behind the small windscreen and slid the key into the ignition to start it up. Ruby, unmissable in that damn strawberry dress, clambered in hesitantly then plopped down on the seat at the back. He put the boat in gear and set off through some of the narrower canals.

He'd spent every summer here as a boy, even before his parents' divorce, and it amazed him that, even though he hadn't driven a boat here in more than two decades, the old routes and back-doubles came to him easily. His passenger didn't say much. She spent most of the journey to the Lagoon Palace looking up at the tall buildings, her mouth slightly open, eyes wide. It was only when they moored the boat a short distance from the hotel's private jetty, where only the dedicated shuttles from the bus and train stations were allowed to dock, that Ruby began to talk again.

'So, what are the finer points of your agreement with your mother? You can't have spent that long arguing about it without going into details.'

He sighed as he led her up a narrow cobbled *calle* between buildings and out onto a wider one that led to the foot entrance of the hotel. He'd known he wouldn't be able to win his mother over to his plan from the moment he'd stepped out onto the balcony with her. He had, however, managed to broker a deal that meant his stay here would be on his terms.

'I have conceded to spend a couple of hours each morning with Sofia while my mother is at work and to attend a family dinner each evening.' He couldn't help the slight tone of disgust in his voice at the word 'family'.

She kept up pace, slightly behind him. 'And what did she concede?'

'That I should have the rest of the time to work on my design and do my business.'

'Will that do?'

He stared straight ahead and looked grim. 'It will have to.' As they entered the hotel through the street entrance he sighed. 'What's the alternative? At least this way I'm only tied up for seven days, instead of two weeks or more in a totally unsuitable apartment. Aside from the fact you'd be trying to stop Sofia breaking her neck every moment of the day, I've only got one bedroom.'

Ruby swallowed and her face grew just a little closer to the shade of her dress. 'No, I can see that would be a…' she swallowed again '…problem.'

'I don't know why she does these things. For some reason my mother isn't happy unless she's creating havoc in everyone else's lives as well as her own.' He shook his head.

They'd arrived at the suite now, and the next quarter of an hour was spent packing up their belongings. And then they checked out and headed back to the boat. Max carried his bag, his laptop case and his document tube, and she took care of her own rucksack and Sofia's bag.

He decided to take a less direct, but maybe more scenic,

route back. If she'd liked the little crumbling buildings of
the back canals, she'd love some of the palazzos on the
Grand Canal. He pointed a few of them out to her, telling
her a few of the famous stories connected with them, many
of which he guessed had been embellished over time with
a healthy drop of the Venetian love for drama and specta-
cle. She chatted back, asking him questions and laughing
at the more ridiculous tales, so it kind of took him by surprise when she suddenly said, 'I don't think she's done this
to cause trouble, you know. I think she just wants to spend
time with you and, yes, she's gone about it a back to front
kind of way, but she's not asking anything terrible, is she?'

He didn't say anything. Just stared straight ahead. Suddenly he didn't feel like playing tour guide any more.

He should have remembered this one was different, that
she wasn't like his employees at the firm, that she liked to
say things she shouldn't and be inquisitive. None of them
had ever dared to comment on his personal life. But then
he'd never given any of them a personal tour of Venice,
either.

He thought about what she'd said and let out a low growl
of a laugh.

'What?' she asked, never one to miss an opportunity to
stick her nose in.

'Now, maybe, my mother seems like that,' he said
gruffly, 'but she's a hypocrite.'

Despite the bustle and noise of the city—the purr of out-
board motors, the noise of the seagulls and pigeons and the
ever steady hum of a million tourists' exclamations—the
air around them went very still. He'd shocked her into silence, had he? Well, good.

'She deserted my father and left him broken-hearted. He
never got over it. So don't talk to me about family loyalty.'

He turned to look over his shoulder, wanting some grim
satisfaction in seeing her squirm, but instead he found

her looking at him, her eyes large and warm. He looked away again.

'How old were you when she left?' she asked softly, almost whispering.

He forgot to ask how she'd guessed, too caught up in a sideswipe of memories that left him gripping the steering wheel so hard it burnt his fingers. 'Fourteen,' he answered hoarsely. 'She said she didn't want to disrupt my education, so she took Gia and left me in London.'

There was a hint of uncertainty in her voice this time. 'That was thoughtful, wasn't it?'

He made that same almost animalistic sound that could pass as a laugh again. 'It was an excuse. I'm too like my father, you scc. Or I was. He died five months ago.'

There was a shuffling noise behind him. He couldn't resist a quick glance. Now he'd got what he'd wanted. Her cheeks were flushed red and she was looking down at her flat little black ballet pumps.

'Don't get sucked in,' he warned her. 'She's not what she seems. Nothing is what it seems in this city.'

Nothing is what it seems in this city.

Ruby heard the words inside her head as she stood outside the library door.

It was pure Venice, wasn't it? To have a proper room designated as a library in your palazzo, not just a flat-pack bookcase stuffed under the eaves in your poky little attic flat. Max had decided to use it as his office while he was here, and he was inside now. She could hear him tapping away on his laptop keyboard, along with the odd rustle of paper.

Not even you, Max Martin, she thought, as she knocked softly on the door. Or should that be *Massimo*?

All she got in response was a grunt. She took it as an invitation.

Max didn't look up straight away when she pushed the door open and slid inside to stand with her back pressed against the wall, hands tucked behind her. The library was small compared to some of the other rooms in the apartment, but it shared the same high ceilings and leaded windows. Two of the four walls were filled with bookshelves, and Max sat at a desk placed up against the dark green silky wallpaper of one of the other walls.

It had been a whole twenty-four hours since she'd seen him doing exactly the same thing in the hotel suite, but somehow she felt as if she were looking at a completely different man.

She'd thought him a robot, a machine, but she'd seen the bleakness in his eyes when he'd talked about his family that morning. There was a lot more inside there than met the eye. Maybe even a man with true Italian blood coursing through his veins, a man capable of revenge and passion and utter, utter devotion. The fact that the wounds of his childhood still cut deep, that he could neither forgive nor forget, showed he was capable of more than this grey, concrete existence. But like some of the crumbling buildings of this city, all that emotion was all carefully hidden behind a perfectly built façade.

He pressed the enter key with a sense of finality and turned to face her.

'I've just put Sofia to bed, and I wondered if you'd like to go and say goodnight? She's asking for you.'

His chair scraped and he moved to get up. Ruby pushed away from the wall and clasped her hands in front of her. She cleared her throat. 'I have something to say before you go.'

He stopped moving and looked at her.

She inhaled and let it out again. 'I'd like to apologise for what I said earlier. I didn't mean to butt in.'

She'd expected his face to remain expressionless, but she saw a subtle shift in his features, a softening. 'Thank you.'

He made to go forward and her mouth started off again before she could ask herself if it was a good idea or not. 'I know what it's like, you know. My relationship with my father has always been difficult. But I pretend I don't care, that it doesn't get to me. That it shouldn't matter after all these years...but it does.'

She was rambling, she knew she was. But she couldn't seem to shut up.

'So I just wanted to say that I won't comment on your family any more and that I'll try and be a little bit more professional in the future.'

He'd been right. She should keep her nose out. Not in the least because this silent, dedicated man was starting to tug at her heartstrings, but also because she was just the nanny, and getting sucked in definitely wasn't part of her job description.

He nodded and glanced towards the door. 'I'd better go and see Sofia before she falls asleep.' And then he walked down the wide corridor without looking back.

Ruby sagged back against the library wall and looked up. She hadn't noticed before, but painted cherubs were dancing on the ceiling, blowing flutes and twanging harps. For some reason, she got the feeling they were mocking her.

If there was one room Max hated more than any other in his mother's house, it was the dining room. Most people were left speechless when they walked inside for the first time, at least for a few moments, then the exclaiming would begin.

Apparently, his great-grandfather had had a fondness for whimsy, and had commissioned an artist to paint the whole room so it resembled a ruined castle in a shady forest glade. Creepers and vines twined round the doorway and round the fireplace. Low down there were painted stone blocks, making the tumbledown walls, and above, tree trunks and leaves, giving glimpses of rolling fields beyond. It even carried up onto the ceiling, where larks peered down and a pale sun shone directly above the dining table. It was all just one big lie.

The table only filled a fraction of the vast space, even though it seated twelve. Max sat down at one of the three places laid at one end and scowled as his mother sat at the head and Ruby sat opposite him. He hadn't liked being manoeuvred into this whole arrangement and he wasn't going to pretend he liked it any more than he was going to pretend they were sitting in a real forest glade enjoying the dappled sunshine. He was just going to eat and get out of here. The plans he'd left on the desk only a few minutes ago were already calling to him.

'My family were successful merchants here in Venice for five hundred years,' his mother told Ruby as they tucked into their main course. 'But now I live more simply and rent the other parts of the house out.'

Max saw Ruby's eyes widen at the word 'simply'. As always, his mother had no grip on reality, and no awareness of how other people carried on their lives. He tuned the conversation out. His mother was busy regaling Ruby with stories from the annals of their family history, both triumphant and tragic. He'd heard them a thousand times, anyway, and with each telling the details drifted further and further from the truth.

Then his mother ran out of steam and turned her attention to their guest. Well, not guest…employee. But it was hard to think of Ruby that way as she listened to his mother with rapt attention, eyes bright, laughter ready.

'So, tell me, Ruby, why did you decide to become a nanny?'

Ruby shot a look in his direction before answering. 'Your son offered me a job and I took it.'

Fina absorbed that information for a moment. 'You didn't want to be a nanny before that?'

Ruby shook her head.

'Then what were you?'

Max sat up a little straighter. He hadn't thought to ask her that during their 'interview'. Maybe he should have. And maybe Ruby was annoyingly right about *details* being important on occasion.

Ruby smiled back at his mother. 'Oh, I've been lots of things since I left university.'

He leaned forward and put his fork down. 'What course did you take?'

'Media Studies.'

Max frowned. 'But you don't want to work in that field, despite having the qualification?'

She pulled a face. 'I didn't graduate. It was my father's idea to go.' She shook her head. 'But it really wasn't me.'

His mother shot her a sympathetic look. 'Not everyone works out the right path first time.'

Max snorted. If these dinners had been his mother's plan to soften him up, it was backfiring on her. Every other word she uttered just reminded him of how she'd selfishly betrayed the whole family. She might not have been a Martin by birth, but she'd married into the institution, and if there was one rule the family lived by it was this: loyalty above all else.

If his mother had heard the snort, she ignored it. 'You must have had some interesting jobs,' she said to Ruby, smiling.

Ruby smiled back. 'Oh, I have, and it's been great. I've made jewellery and I worked in a vineyard.'

'In France?' Fina asked.

Ruby shook her head. 'No, in Australia. I did that the year after I left university. And then I just sort of travelled and worked my way back home again. I tended bar in Singapore, worked on a kibbutz in Israel. I did a stint in a PR firm, I joined an avant-garde performance company—that was too wacky, even for me—and I've also busked to earn a crust.'

His mother's eyebrows were practically in her hairline. 'You play an instrument?' she asked, taking the only salvageable thing from that list.

Ruby gave her a hopeful smile. 'I can manage a harmonica and a bit of tap dancing.'

Lord, help them all! And this was who he'd thought was exactly what he needed? No wonder his sensible plan was falling to pieces.

'And will you stay being a nanny after this? Or is it on to the next thing?' he asked.

She shook her head. 'I don't know. I know this sounds stupid, but I see the way my father loves his work, and I want to find something that makes me feel like that.'

His mother leaned forward. 'What does your father do?'

Ruby froze, as if she realised she'd said something she shouldn't. She looked up at them. 'Oh, he makes nature programmes.'

'What? Like Patrick Lange?' his mother exclaimed, clapping her hands. 'I loved his series on lemurs! It was fascinating.'

'Something like that,' Ruby mumbled.

Now it was Max's turn to freeze. *Lange?*

'Your father's Patrick Lange?' he asked, hardly able to keep the surprise from his voice. The man seemed such a steady kind of guy. Max could hardly believe he had a daughter like Ruby.

She nodded and returned to eating her pasta.

'How marvellous,' his mother gushed and then the smile disappeared from her face. 'Oh, I'm so sorry about your mother, Ruby. It was such a tragedy. She was such a wonderful woman.'

Ruby kept her head down and nodded.

Max racked his brains. There had been a news story... Oh, maybe fifteen years ago? That was it. Martha and Patrick Lange had always presented their nature documentaries together until she'd contracted some tropical disease in a remote location while filming. She'd reassured everyone she was fine, that it was just a touch of flu, and had carried on, reluctant to abandon the trip. By the time they'd realised what it was, and that she'd needed urgent treatment, it had been too late. She'd died in an African hospital a week later.

Max watched Ruby push her pasta around her plate. He knew what it was like to lose a parent, and it had been bad enough in his early thirties. Ruby could have only been... what? Nine or ten?

'Anyway,' Ruby suddenly said, lifting her head and smiling brightly. 'I'd like to find my perfect fit. My niche.'

His mother, who had finished her meal, put her knife and fork on her plate and nodded. 'There's no sense in doing something if your heart isn't in it.'

There she went again. He'd just about forgotten about being angry with her for a moment, distracted by Ruby's sad story, but she had to dig herself another hole, didn't she? It just proved she would never change.

His mother must have noticed the expression on his face, because she stopped smiling at Ruby and sent him a pleading look. He carried on eating his pasta. She tried to smile, even though her eyes glistened in the light from the chandelier.

'Well, maybe being a nanny will be your niche. You're a natural with Sofia.'

'Thank you, Fina.' Ruby smiled, properly this time, and the gloom of her previous expression was chased away. How did she do that? How did she just let it all float away like that, find the joy in life again?

'Massimo wanted to be an architect since he'd got his

first set of building blocks,' his mother said. Her face was clear of the hurt he'd seen a few moments ago, but he could hear the strain in her voice. 'He always wanted to follow in his father's footsteps.' She turned to him. 'He would have been so proud to know you'd secured the commission for the Institute of Fine—'

Max's chair shot back as he stood to his feet. 'Don't you dare presume to speak for my father,' he said through clenched teeth. His insides were on fire, yet his skin felt as cold as ice. 'In fact, I'd rather you didn't mention him at all in my presence.'

And then he turned and strode from the room.

CHAPTER SIX

MAX STARED AT SOFIA, who was currently sitting on one of his mother's sofas, staring at him expectantly. Gone was the sunshine of the previous day, replaced by a low, drizzly fog. It would probably clear up by the afternoon, but that didn't help him now.

There would be no walk this morning, no playing ball games in the street or a nearby square. Unsurprisingly, there weren't many parks in Venice, so children had to make do with whatever outside space the city presented to them. He tried to rack his brains and think what he'd done as a boy on his visits here, but most of his memories were of when he was older, involving boats or other children.

Ruby walked into the room. He hadn't seen her since last night, and had almost got used to the bright strawberry-covered dress. Her attire was once again completely different, but somehow it seemed less of a jump this morning. Today she looked like a groupie from a rock band, with skinny jeans, a black T-shirt and a multitude of necklaces and bangles. Her dark, purple-streaked hair also seemed to be standing up a little more than usual.

'Good morning,' she said.

Max nodded.

Ruby must have seen the panic in his eyes, because she smiled that soft little I'm-trying-not-to-make-it-look-as-if-I'm-laughing-at-you smile. He gave up any pretence of competence.

'What do I do?' he asked, gesturing towards the windows.

She shrugged. 'Do something she likes to do.'

Marvellous suggestion. Great. That was the whole point. 'But I don't *know* what she likes to do.'

He searched around the room. His mother didn't have many toys, just a few in the bottom section of an antique sideboard. He opened the door and started to rummage. When he was halfway through pulling things out, most of them puzzles and board games far too old for his niece, he felt a light touch on his shoulder. He twisted his head and found Sofia grinning at him. 'Dat!' she announced firmly, pointing to a cardboard box.

Max reached for it and opened the lid. It contained the brightly coloured wooden blocks that Sofia had been playing with yesterday. As he stared at them, the way they were worn, how the paint had been knocked off some of the corners and edges, he realised they'd once been his. Sofia nodded, walked over to the large rug that filled the middle of the room and sat down on it, waiting.

Well, at least he knew what to do with bricks, even if they were this small. He started arranging them into a small structure, but Sofia wasn't happy with that. 'Build pinsess!' she said firmly, tugging at his shirtsleeve.

Max looked at her. 'Huh?'

'Build pinsess,' she repeated, looking at him as if he should have no trouble obeying her command. He looked up at Ruby helplessly.

'I think she's saying "build princess".'

He was still lost.

Ruby chuckled. 'I think she wants you to build her a fairy-tale castle.'

Max looked down at his rather square, half-finished

house. Great. Now the Institute of Fine Art weren't the only ones who weren't pleased with an original Martin design.

'What does a fairy-princess castle look like?'

Ruby got down on the rug beside them and started gathering bricks. 'The basics are there,' she said. 'You just need to embellish a little.'

She leaned forward to pick up another brick and Max caught the scent of her perfume. He would have expected her to wear something bold and eye-watering, like too-sweet vanilla or pungent berries, but it was a subtle mix of flowers and spices. It made him forget where he'd been about to place the next brick.

He shook himself and found somewhere, even though he was sure he'd had a different spot in mind when he'd picked the thing up.

They finished the main structure then added turrets and a drawbridge. Ruby even went and found a blue scarf from her luggage and they circled it round the castle like a moat. Sofia took a role as site manager, instructing the adults where she wanted the next tower built and letting them know in no uncertain terms when their efforts didn't meet her expectations.

'She's reminding me of someone else I know,' Ruby muttered under her breath.

Max hid a smile. Seriously, he was not that bad.

She reached for a red triangular brick at the same time he did and their hands bumped. She pulled back and rested her bottom on her heels. 'No, you have it. You're the expert.'

He picked it up and dropped it into her hand. 'This isn't a job I can accomplish on my own. I think the finishing touches require some definite feminine input to come up to our patron's high standard.'

She grinned back at him. 'She is a bit of a slave driver.' And then she put the brick above the main gate, making a porch, instead of the obvious place where he would have put it on top of the central turret. When she'd finished she stood up and brushed the carpet fibres off her black jeans.

'Where are you going?' he asked, realising he was disappointed she was leaving.

He told himself it was because he needed her there as backup, that he didn't want to be left alone with Sofia. What if she started crying again?

'It's lunch time,' she said, smiling. 'I think Sofia is getting hungry.'

Max checked his watch. So it was. He'd forgotten how much he'd loved these blocks as a boy, how many rainy days just like this one he'd spent in this room, building forts and skyscrapers and alien space stations.

He stood up and surveyed the creation they'd made together. Despite its flouncy, OTT design, he was quite proud of himself. And Ruby and Sofia, obviously. This really was a spectacular castle. He'd enjoyed himself, remembered just how much joy could be had from building and creating when the pressure wasn't on. And he'd enjoyed the good-natured banter and arguments about which door should go where and just how ridiculously high Sleeping Beauty's tower should be. Instead of feeling burdened and irritated, he felt…

It took him a while to name the sensation. Probably because it had been absent from his life for so long.

He felt relaxed.

'That's you relieved of duty for the morning, then,' Ruby said and held out her hand for Sofia and asked her if she'd like lunch in Italian. Sofia nodded vigorously and began to tell Ruby exactly what she'd consent to eat. The list consisted of mainly chocolate and flavours of ice cream. Ruby just smiled and led her away and Max was left staring at Sofia's castle.

The smile slowly slid from his face. The tiny rainbow-coloured castle might have turned out well, but he still had no idea how to add the same flair to his design for the institute. He stuffed his hands in his pockets and trudged back to the library. For some reason, he didn't think turrets and a moat would be a hit with his clients.

Rather than the pearly mist of the day before, which had draped the whole city in soft, off-white tones, the next morning was bright and loud and colourful. Instead of setting the blocks up in the living room, Max led Ruby and Sofia outside to the dock.

A minute later they were zipping through canals heading for somewhere Max said was a prime spot for what he had in mind. Ruby stared at the 'equipment' he'd brought with them that sat in the bottom of the boat. She guessed they must be doing fishing of some kind, because there were a couple of buckets, some nets and a line of dark wire, wrapped round a plastic reel, with a weight and a hook at one end.

She looked down at the toddler in her arms. Didn't fishing require patience and silence? She wasn't sure how much of a good idea this was.

She didn't have the heart to mention that to Max, though. All traces of the frown that had been permanently etched into his forehead since she'd first met him had disappeared, and he looked calmer, more relaxed, as he drove the little boat through narrow and wide canals, manoeuvring it expertly with only a slight twist of the wheel here and there.

They moored alongside a wide path beside a smallish canal. They were deep in the heart of the city, far enough off the beaten track to have left most of the tourists behind. Max hopped out of the boat and held out his hands for the tackle. Ruby passed him Sofia first, and reminded him to hold her hand tightly. She then picked the buckets and nets up and placed them on the edge of the stone path before clambering out herself.

'What now?' she asked, slightly breathlessly.

Max stared at the opaque green water. 'Now we put our line down and see if we can catch any crabs.'

'Crabs?' That wasn't what she'd been expecting at all.

He nodded. 'Every Venetian child knows how to fish for crabs. At certain times of year, when young ones have shells that are still soft, they are considered a local delicacy.'

'Are you sure Sofia's going to—?'

'I don't know,' he said frankly. 'But why don't we give it a try?'

There wasn't much Ruby could say to that, so she stood by and lent a helping hand where she could, holding on to Sofia while Max carefully explained to her what they were going to be doing and started to put some bait on the hook. He didn't let Sofia touch that bit of the line, but lowered it slowly into the dark water, allowing her to hold on to the plastic reel, but keeping his hands over hers.

They waited for a short while and then he slowly drew the line up again. Nothing. Ruby waited for Sofia to start fidgeting, but she seemed to be fascinated. She clumsily helped Max unreel the line again, frowning in concentration.

Ruby almost laughed looking at the pair of them. She didn't know why she hadn't seen it before, but the family similarity smacked her right between the eyes. The same dark eyes, same cheekbones. They even pursed their lips in the same manner as they stared at the dark twine hanging in the water.

After a minute or so, Max helped Sofia wind the line up again, and this time a tiny green-and-brown mottled crab was hanging from the end. It was hanging on with grim determination, as if it had decided it was *his* dinner on that hook and he wasn't giving it up for anybody.

Sofia squealed. Ruby shot forward, meaning to comfort her, but she realised when she saw the little girl's eyes shining that the noise had been one of delight, not fear. In fact, Sofia was so pleased with her catch that she reached out to grab it as Max tried to gently shake it from the line into a bucket he'd filled with canal water.

Then came another squeal. This one high-pitched and urgent. It seemed Sofia had been a little too enthusiastic, and the crab had thought her a little too tempting, because it had clutched on to her with its free pincer. Ruby quickly darted in and shook it away, but Sofia's eyes filled with tears and she looked at her hand in horror. 'Naughty!' she said vehemently. 'Bad fish!'

Ruby scooped her up and gave her a hug, then bent to kiss the red patch on her finger. The skin wasn't broken and she was probably more surprised and offended than in real pain. She pulled back and smiled at the little girl. 'He just liked you so much he didn't want to let go,' she told her.

Sofia's eyes grew wide. 'Fish *like* me?'

Ruby nodded. 'He's a crab, not a fish, and, yes, I think he thought you looked very tasty.'

Sofia screwed up her face and chuckled heartily. 'Silly fish,' she said leaning over the bucket and peering at her catch. 'No bite Sofia. Kiss.' And she puckered up her lips and bent over farther. Ruby caught her quickly before she got any other ideas.

'Why don't we see if we can find him a friend?' And she indicated where Max was waiting with the crabbing line.

Sofia grinned. 'Want lots and lots friends.'

So that was what they did for the next forty-five minutes—found lots and lots of friends for the little green-and-brown crab. Ruby and Max worked as a team, keeping a firm hold on Sofia when she got over-excited and tried to lean too far over the water, and dealt with crabs and bait when needed. After the first handful of attempts they settled into an easy rhythm, giving them lulls in the action while the bait dangled in the water.

Ruby took an opportunity to look around at the buildings. She wished she had her sketchpad with her—and a free hand—so she could draw them. 'There are so many wonderful shapes to be seen in this city,' she said, sighing. 'What's that called?' She showed Max the building on the far side of the canal, where the stonework around a window curved to a point at the top.

'It's an inflected arch,' he said.

'It makes me think of far-off lands and tales of Arabian nights.'

'It's interesting that you say that, because a lot of Venetian architecture has Eastern influences. Merchants travelled to the Byzantine Empire and traded with the Moors and they came back and combined those shapes with the European gothic architecture to create a unique style.'

She pointed to another building. 'And what about those ones? They're beautiful. At first it just looks like intricate shapes, but then you can see that the fussier patterns are actually made up of intersecting circles.'

He turned to look at her and didn't say anything for a few moments. 'You have a good eye for shapes.'

She shrugged and then bent down to help Sofia shake another crab off her line into the bucket. 'Thank you. I like to draw sometimes. I suppose it's just something I've picked up.'

Max took the line from his niece for a moment and worked out a few tangles before giving it back to her. 'Is that what you've been doing when I've seen you scribbling away in that notebook of yours?'

She nodded. She hadn't realised he'd noticed. 'It's just a hobby. Nothing impressive, really.'

'You haven't thought of making a career out of it?' He gave her a dry smile. 'Seeing as you've tried everything else?'

'Ha, ha. Very funny. Go for the easy target, why not?'
Everyone else did.

'Seriously, if you love it so much, why don't you do
something with it?'

She tipped her head to one side. 'You mean, like you
did?'

'I suppose so.'

She looked down at the water below them, at the way
the light bounced off the surface, moving constantly. 'I
don't think I'd be able to do what you do. It's very structured and disciplined. When I draw, I just go with the flow.
I see something that interests me and I capture it. I'm not
sure you can make a career out of that.'

'You have plenty of discipline,' he said. 'Look at the way
you are with Sofia. And sometimes you need that creative
spark to liven all that structure up.' He let out a long sigh
and stared at the buildings across the water.

'More fish! More fish!' Sofia shouted, jumping up and
down so hard she almost toppled into the canal. Ruby kept
a firm hand on her as she shook the most recent catch into
the bucket to join his friends. Sofia did it so vigorously
that Ruby was sure the poor thing must have a concussion.

When Sofia was happily dangling the line in the canal
again, Ruby looked at Max. 'What's up?' she asked. 'Was
it something I said?'

He sighed again and crouched down to look at where
Sofia was pointing at some silvery fish swimming near the
surface of the water. 'No. It's something I said.'

She waited for him to stand again.

'It's a commission for the Institute of Fine Art,' he told
her. 'I've worked for months on a preliminary design that
I'm really proud of, but the board say they're not sure about
it.'

Ruby shook her head. She couldn't believe that. The
designs she'd glimpsed were amazing. They were totally

Max, of course. No frills. No fuss. Nothing ostentatious. But there was an elegance to the simplicity. A pared-back beauty. 'Why on earth not?'

He shrugged. 'I think the actual phrase they used is that they want more "wow factor".'

A screech from around knee level interrupted their conversation. Ruby hadn't noticed it while she'd been talking to Max, but the bucket was now almost full and the crabs were scrambling over each other in an attempt to climb out.

Max knelt down next to his niece. 'It's time to put them back now,' he said matter of factly and tipped the bucket over to let a stream of crustaceans, legs flailing, fall back into the salty lagoon water.

'No!' The exclamation was loud and impassioned and followed immediately by a stream of hot tears. 'Want friend! Want friend!'

Ruby grabbed for the bucket and righted it. Only three crabs remained in the bottom.

Sofia stopped shouting and sniffed. 'Want take fish home.'

Ruby crouched down beside her, put an arm round her shoulders and joined her in looking into the bucket. She might be wrong, but she thought one of the three crabs left might be the little one they'd caught first. 'We can't take them back to Grandma's, sweetie. They belong here in the water. It's their home. We just picked them out to say hello for a little bit.'

Sofia let out a juddering sigh.

'Why don't we put the last ones back one by one and say a nice goodbye to them?'

Sofia frowned. 'Come back 'morrow say hello?'

Ruby smiled. 'If you want.'

The little girl nodded. Ruby looked inside the bucket and then up at Max. 'How do we…?'

Quick as anything his hand plunged into the bucket and

he pulled out a crab. 'There's a trick to it. If you hold them at the back of the shell like this, they can't reach to pinch you.'

He held the crab up for Sofia to see. She puckered up her lips. 'Kiss fish?' she asked.

Ruby's heart just about melted.

'Not too close,' she said softly, imagining what Fina would say if her precious granddaughter came home with pincer holes in her lips. 'Just blow a kiss.'

Sofia blinked then puffed heartily on the crab, who was so shocked it stopped waving its legs around angrily and went still. A deep rumble started in Max's chest then worked its way up out of his mouth in the most infectious of chuckles. Ruby looked up at him, eyes laughing.

'That's a first,' he said, smiling, and then he gently plopped the crab back into the canal.

They followed the same routine with the next crab, too, but when they came to the last one, Ruby asked, 'Can I pick it up?'

Max nodded. He put the bucket down on the cobbles and took hold of Sofia while Ruby took off her watch and stuffed it in her jeans pocket. She inhaled, then dipped her hand into the cold water and aimed her forefinger and thumb for the parts of the shell the way she'd seen Max do it. It wriggled away a couple of times, but then she gripped more firmly and lifted the crab out of the water.

'I did it!' she exclaimed. 'For a moment there I didn't think I was— *Ow!*'

A searing pain shot through her finger, making her eyes water. She blinked the moisture away, slightly breathless, to find an angry little crab attached to her hand. She was sure it was scowling at her.

'Ow, ow, ow...' she yelped and started shaking her hand backwards and forwards. Anything to make it let go!

Eventually the force of the swinging must have got the crab, either that or it lost its grip on her wet hands, because it shot off, landed on the paving stones a couple of feet away then scuttled to the edge and flung itself into the canal.

'Ow,' Ruby said again, just to make her point, even though her attacker probably neither heard nor cared.

She looked down as her finger started to throb. That had definitely *not* been the original crab with the delicate little pincers that hadn't punctured Sofia's finger. This one had been mean and angry, and blood was now seeping from a hole in her skin.

'Here, let me look,' Max said and swiftly caught up her hand.

Ruby would have expected his examination to be practical and thorough, and it was, but she hadn't expected it to be so gentle. She looked at him, head bowed over her hand as he ran his fingers over the area surrounding her war wound, and for some reason the sight of his dark lashes against his cheek made her feel a little breathless.

Sofia hugged her left leg. 'No cry, Ruby. Fish no want let go.'

Despite the thudding of her pulse in her index finger, Ruby couldn't help but smile. She looked up to find Max doing the same, but his face was very close. She blinked and sucked in a breath.

'Kiss better!' Sofia commanded.

Ruby would have been okay if she hadn't realised he was holding his breath, too, that he seemed to be stuck looking at her the same way she was looking at him.

'Go on, Uncle Max! Kiss better.'

Slowly Max raised her hand, not taking his eyes off her until the moment he bent his head and softly pressed his lips to where Ruby's finger was throbbing. The sensation spread out from that finger, through the rest of her body, until she couldn't breathe, couldn't move. Max seemed to be similarly affected, because even though he'd lowered her hand again he still held it between his warm fingers.

Sofia tugged Ruby's trouser leg, seeking a response she hadn't yet got. 'Him no want let go.'

Ruby swallowed. 'I know, sweetheart.' And as she spoke the words she slid her hand out of Max's and looked away to where the crab had plopped into the water.

'I think it'll be fine,' he mumbled, then busied himself collecting up the fishing equipment and putting it back in the boat.

CHAPTER SEVEN

MAX SPENT THE REST of the afternoon in the library with the door shut. He tinkered with his plans for the institute until his eyes were gritty and his brain was spinning. It didn't help that every time he wasn't 100 per cent immersed in what he was doing he kept having strange flashbacks.

He kept seeing Ruby's slightly swollen and bleeding finger. Inevitably that led to memories of looking up into her eyes. He hadn't noticed their colour before. Warm hazel. Not green. Not brown. But a unique pairing of the two that was slightly hypnotic. He hadn't been able to look away, hadn't been able to let go. And then he'd gone and kissed her finger. What had all that been about?

Okay, he knew *exactly* what that had been about. He might not have been in the mood to date since his father's death, finding himself drawn to his own company, filling his hours with work, but he was no stranger to desire.

He stopped tweaking a design for a staircase he had up on his computer screen and deleted all the last fifteen changes he'd made. It had been better before. Now it was *more* boring, if that was even possible. He'd seen a hundred different staircases like it in a hundred different buildings.

He pushed back from the desk, stood up, began to pace.

He needed something different. Something unique.

Like those eyes...

No. Not like those eyes. They had nothing to do with it.

For heaven's sake! It wasn't even as if Ruby was anything like the kind of women he usually went out with, the kind he'd hardly noticed he'd stopped seeing: cultured, sophisticated, beautiful.

He sighed. And next to Ruby they seemed like clones churned out by a production line.

In comparison, she was strangely easy to be with. There was no game-playing. No second-guessing whether he'd accidentally said the wrong thing because he was being subjected to some secret test. If Ruby thought he'd overstepped the mark, she just told him in no uncertain terms.

There was a knock at the door and he stopped pacing and faced it, grunted his permission to enter. A moment later his travelling nanny popped her head round the door. 'Your mother wanted me to let you know that dinner is served.'

She looked down and away, as if she was feeling awkward. When she looked up again, a faint blush stained her cheeks.

The air grew instantly thick. Max nodded. 'Thank you,' he managed to say. 'I'll be along in a minute.'

She smiled hesitantly and shut the door again.

Max ran a hand through his hair and swore softly. Was he imagining it, or had she got prettier since that afternoon?

He went over and sat back down at his desk. He clicked over to his email and read a few messages to distract himself, although what they contained he couldn't have said. When he felt a little more his usual self, he rose and went to the dining room, lecturing himself en route.

You have no business noticing her eyes, warm hazel or otherwise. She's your employee. Get a grip and get over it.

Thankfully, he was sitting opposite his mother this evening at dinner, and Ruby was off to one side, so he didn't catch her gaze while they ate their...whatever it was they ate. He kept his concentration on his plate as his mother once again pounced on their guest as both willing audience and source of conversation.

'Maybe being a nanny will be your niche after all,' she told Ruby. 'You're a natural with Sofia, and she's already very fond of you.'

Ruby smiled at her. 'Thank you. I'm loving spending time with her, too, and spending time in Venice. This really is the most remarkable place.'

Fina's chest puffed up with pride in her home. 'You've never visited before?' she said.

'No. I always wanted to, though.'

Fina clapped her hands. 'Well, then we must make sure we don't work you too hard, so you get time to see some of the sights! But the best time of day to see the city is the hour leading up to sunset, don't you think, Massimo?'

Max let out a weary sigh. 'I suppose so.'

Ruby smiled and sipped her glass of water. She'd refused wine, seeing as she was still on duty. 'I'm sure it is, but I may have to wait until my next visit for that. By the time I've got Sofia bathed and in bed, it's nearly always dark.'

Fina rose from the table to go and fetch the dessert from the sideboard. 'Then Massimo must take you before he goes back to London. Don't worry about Sofia. I'm sure her *nonna* can manage bedtime alone for one night.'

They both turned to look at him.

He should say no. Make an excuse that he had too much work to do, or tell his mother to drive the boat herself, but he looked back at Ruby, her eyes large and expectant, and found himself saying, 'Okay, but later in the week. And as long as we're not out too long. I have work to do.' And then he returned to attacking his vegetables.

The women went back to chatting again but a while later Ruby piped up, 'Oh! I almost forgot. Before Sofia went to bed, she insisted I give this to you.' She pushed a piece of paper in his direction. 'I was going to let her do it herself, but you seemed to be so busy, so I just…didn't.' She shrugged. 'Well, here it is, anyway.'

He reached out and pulled the scrap towards him, careful not to brush her fingers. From the thick, riotous turquoise crayon that graced the sheet of paper, he could tell the colouring was Sofia's, but the drawing, that was all Ruby's. He smiled as he looked at it.

She'd drawn one of the crabs they'd caught that afternoon in dark ink. The little crab hanging on the end of the fishing line looked full of personality, feisty and ready to take on the world if anyone dared try to catch him and tame him. It really was rather good.

'I think you caught him perfectly,' he said, and made the mistake of looking up at her. 'You've got that devilish expression down pat.'

She didn't say anything. Just smiled. And her eyes warmed further.

Max returned his attention to his plate.

He forced himself to remember the conversation that had taken place round this dinner table only a few evenings ago. It didn't matter how nice her eyes were, or how relaxed he felt around her, it would be foolishness in the highest degree to be bewitched by that.

Ruby Lange was a drifter. She'd said so herself. She didn't finish what she started, always tempted to run after something better and brighter and shinier.

He didn't need a woman like that in his life. He'd seen what his mother had done to his father, hadn't he?

He returned his gaze to his plate.

Pork. They were eating pork.

He'd do well to keep his mind on concrete things like that. On his work. On his commission, his final gift to the parent who'd stuck around to raise him.

No more distractions, no matter how tempting.

* * *

The following evening Ruby approached dinner with a plan. Max was going home in just under forty-eight hours and still he was treating his mother like the enemy.

However, he'd softened up with Sofia nicely. He no longer held her as if she were an unexploded bomb, and interacted quite easily with her now. Sofia, who maybe had been lacking a positive male role model in her life, simply adored him. It was clear a bond was forming between them.

Surely the potential was there with Fina, too? All he needed was to be thrown in the deep end a bit, as he had been with Sofia.

So Ruby deliberately decided not to natter on at dinner time this evening, hoping it would encourage mother and son to converse. But as they waded their way through the main course, the only sound in the cavernous dining room was the clinking of cutlery and the dull thud of glasses being picked up and set down again.

Fina kept looking at him, willing him to glance her way, but mostly, unless he was reaching for the salt or refilling his glass, Max refused. As the meal wore on Ruby could sense more and more nervous energy in the woman sitting beside her. Fina must sense her chance for reconciliation ticking away with the hours and seconds until Max's flight back to London. It didn't seem as if he'd be in a hurry to return any time soon, either.

Eventually, Fina cracked. She put down her knife and fork and stared at him for a few seconds before opening her mouth. 'Massimo. You've been having such a wonderful time here with Sofia these last few days.'

Max glanced up so briefly Ruby doubted he'd even had time to focus on Fina. He grunted then turned his attention to his plate.

Fina shot a nervous look at Ruby and Ruby nodded her encouragement.

'Ruby's been telling me all about your crabbing expeditions.'

Another grunt. This time without eye contact.

Fina swallowed. 'I was thinking that maybe I'd invite the whole family to visit for the festival of San Martino in November. You used to love decorated biscuits of Martino on his horse, remember?' She laughed. 'You once asked me if we were cousins of the saint, because our last names were so similar.'

Max carried on cutting his chicken, and only when he'd precisely severed a chunk, put it in his mouth and chewed and swallowed it thoroughly, did he answer his mother. 'I don't think I'm going to be able to spare the time from work. If this commission goes through it'll be full steam ahead until the new year.' And then he went back to dissecting his meal.

Fina nodded, even though her son wasn't watching, and hung her head over her plate.

Ruby glared at him. She wanted to fish that little crab they'd met the other day out of the canal and attach it to his nose! He was being so stubborn.

Didn't he know what a gift this was? Maybe Fina hadn't been the perfect mother, but she was trying to make up for it now. Surely that had to mean something? And there had to be good reasons why a woman as warm and caring as Fina had walked away from her marriage. She might try and act blasé, but Ruby couldn't believe she'd done it on a whim, whatever Max might think.

Fina rose from her seat. 'I promiséd Renata upstairs that I would look in on her. She's not been feeling very well,' she said, and walked stiffly from the room.

Max pushed his plate away. Ruby glared at him. 'Couldn't you just even give her a chance?'

He lifted his head and looked at her. His eyes were empty, blank like the statues topping so many of the palazzos nearby. 'It's not your business, Ruby. What happens in my family is my concern.'

She stared back at him, words flying round her head. But she released none of them, knowing he was speaking the truth and hating him for it. So much for the bond she'd thought they'd forged over the last few days.

She rose and followed Fina out of the room. 'Thank you,' she said as she reached the doorway, 'for putting me firmly in my place.'

At least an hour passed before Max emerged from the library. The apartment was totally quiet. Sofia must be fast asleep and he hadn't heard his mother return from visiting her neighbour.

Everything was dark—well, almost. A few of the wall sconces were lit at the far end of the corridor near the salon. His footsteps seemed loud as he walked down it and entered the large room. In here it was dark, too, with just one lamp turned on near the sofas, making the cavernous space seem smaller and more intimate. He looked for Ruby's dark head against the cushions, for a hint of a purple streak, but there was no one there.

He was about to turn and leave the room, but then he heard a shuffling noise and noticed the doors to the balcony were open. He could just make out her petite form, leaning on the stone ledge, staring out across the water. Taking in a deep breath, he walked over to the open door and stood in the threshold.

'I can hear voices,' she said, her tone bland, 'and I think it must be someone close by, but there are no windows open upstairs and no boats going by.'

'It's just another quirk of this city,' he said. 'Sounds seem oddly hushed at some times and magnified at others. Even a whisper can travel round corners.'

She nodded. Whoever had been talking had stopped now and silence grew around them.

What a pity it wasn't silent inside Max's head. He could hear another whispering voice now, one telling him to apologise. It wasn't the first time he'd heard that voice, but he usually managed to outrun it when it prompted him to do anything as dangerous as letting down his guard, admitting he was wrong, but Venice was amplifying this sound, too, making it impossible to ignore.

Or maybe it was Ruby who did that to him.

Sometimes she looked at him and he felt as if all the things he'd held together for so long were slowly being unlaced.

He should go, retreat back to the library, to the safety of his plans and emails. That was where he'd built the fortress of his life, after all—in his work. Just like his father before him.

Ruby didn't ask anything of him. Didn't demand as his mother would have done. Instead she kept staring out into the night, a faint breeze lifting her feathery fringe.

Max stepped forward. 'I was rude earlier on,' he said. 'I'm sorry.'

She kept her elbows resting on the stone balustrade and turned just her head, studied him. 'I accept your apology, but you spoke the truth.'

She was right, he realised. That was something they always did with each other, whether they wanted to or not. 'Even if it was, I shouldn't have said it the way I did.'

Ruby's cheeks softened and her smile grew. 'Thank you.' She straightened and looked back inside. 'Sofia's appetite for things to colour in is insatiable. I was going to get some outlines done to give me a head start in the morning, but I couldn't resist slipping out here for a moment.'

She moved to go back inside, and his arm shot out across the doorway, blocking her. He didn't know why he'd done that. He should have let her go. Ruby tipped her head and frowned at him, her delicate features full of puzzlement, her eyes asking a question. A question he didn't know the answer to.

But other words found his lips, words he hadn't even realised were his. 'I find it hard to be here... This is the first time I've seen her since my father died.'

She looked back at him, understanding brimming in her eyes.

'She broke him, you know, when she left. Everyone always said he was the same old Geoffrey, hard as steel, never letting anything get to him, but they didn't know him the way I did.'

She moved a little closer, placed a hand on the arm that wasn't blocking her exit, the one that was braced against the rough stone of the balustrade. 'You're angry with her,' she said in a low voice. It wasn't a question.

He nodded. He'd been angry with her for years. It had started as a raging fire that only the indignation and passion of a teenage boy knew how to fan, and had solidified into something darker and deeper. 'Since the day of his funeral I haven't been able to ignore it any longer. I want to but I can't.'

He broke away from her and walked a few steps down the balcony, away from the doors. Ruby, of course, followed him. He heard the soft pad of her ballet pumps on the stone. 'You have to know that it's illogical, that his death wasn't her fault. They've been separated for years.'

He twisted to face her abruptly, his face contorting. 'But that's just it. It *is* her fault. You should have heard some of the things she used to scream at him.' He shook his head. 'And he never once lost his temper. It was the effort of living with her, then living without her, that brought on his high blood pressure.'

Ruby stepped closer. 'Is that how he died?'

He nodded. 'He had a stroke—a little one at first, but while he was in the hospital a bigger one struck, finishing him off.'

He felt the rage boiling inside him now. It was all so perilously close to the surface that he was scared he would punch straight through the five-hundred-year-old wall into the salon.

'She's hurting, too,' Ruby said.

He forced himself to focus on her. For a moment the red haze behind his eyes had blurred his vision.

'Can't you forgive her?'

He shook his head, unable to articulate his answer. No, he didn't think he could. He didn't even know if he'd be able to contain it again, let alone quench it.

She must have seen the tension in his expression, because she stepped even closer, this time so he could smell that maddening elusive perfume. 'You've got to let it go, Max. You can't bury it all inside.' Her eyes pleaded with him. 'If you do it might damage you the same way it damaged him.'

He knew she was right. He just didn't know if he knew how. Or even wanted to.

There was the tiniest noise in the back of his head, something snapping. But instead of releasing his anger he'd unleashed something else. It was also something he couldn't keep buried any longer, and it had nothing at all to do with his mother and everything to do with the firecracker of a woman standing in front of him.

Slowly he leaned forward, and watched Ruby's eyes widen. Darken. He slid his hand behind her neck, relishing the feel of her bare skin, the soft wisps of her hair, until he cupped her head and drew her to him. And then he unleashed the full force of all he was too weary to hold back any longer in one scorching kiss.

Ruby knew she should have frozen, knew she should have slipped out of his arms and retained some degree of decorum. Unfortunately, she wasn't that sensible. Instead of reminding him of the barrier between them, the one that no proper nanny would cross, she let him sledgehammer through it as he ran hot kisses down the side of her neck.

She'd never been one for holding back and she certainly didn't do so now. She ran her hands up his chest, grabbed his shirt collar and lifted herself closer, abandoning herself to the feel of his skin upon hers, his body pressed so tight against her own she felt breathless.

He slid his hands down the curve of her back to her waist, emphasising her femininity against his hard, straight masculinity. He kissed her again and she felt them both teeter on the edge of something, threatening to topple headlong into goodness knew what.

Oh, sweet heaven. She'd been right. When Max Martin let loose there was sizzle and passion and consuming fire, and all of that force was concentrated on her now, at the point where his lips were urgently seeking hers again. It was glorious.

It was also very stupid.

Max must have had an identical revelation at the same time, because he froze, his hands circling her waist, and then he stepped back, effectively dropping her back from her tiptoes onto her flat feet. She swayed, the sudden lack of solid, Max-shaped support and the cold air rushing between their bodies putting her off balance.

'I'm so sorry,' he almost stuttered, a look of complete horror on his face. 'That was totally inappropriate.'

Ruby's lips were still throbbing and her hormones still singing the 'Hallelujah Chorus'. She blinked and stared back at him. *Inappropriate?* That was not a word a girl wanted to hear after the hottest kiss of her life.

He shook his head and strode past her and back into the salon. She watched him go, a gnawing feeling growing in her stomach. She couldn't let him leave like this. This wasn't his fault. She had to let him know that she'd been just as much a part of it as he had been. She heaved in a much-needed lungful of night air and ran after him. 'Max!'

He turned as he passed through the double doors into the corridor.

'You don't have to… I mean, it wasn't just…' She trailed off, unable to find the words. He looked so thoroughly wretched. Part of her sank, but another part wanted to reach out to him, to soothe that crumpled expression from his face.

She'd pushed him too far, when he'd been feeling too raw, and he'd lost control. She got that. But maybe it was a good thing. Maybe loosening up in one area of his life would have a knock-on effect?

But it wasn't just that. The way he'd kissed her, hard and hungry, verging on desperate. He had to feel it, too, this weird attraction, crush…whatever. She wasn't alone in this.

She opened her mouth to speak, hardly knowing how to form the question, but at that moment Fina appeared at the top of the stairs and spotted them farther down the corridor. The atmosphere had been thick around her and Max anyway, but now it became so dense it turned brittle.

Fina walked up to them and looked at her son. Any hint of the distress she'd shown earlier was gone, replaced by a brisk and prickly demeanour. 'It's your last night tomorrow, Massimo.'

With what looked like supreme effort, Max dragged his gaze from Ruby and turned it to Fina. 'I know that,' he replied.

Ruby looked between mother and son. In an earlier cen-

tury, an atmosphere like this would have been dispersed
by cocking pistols and marching twenty paces in opposite
directions. She hoped that Fina would say something conciliatory, forgiving her son his outburst instead of nursing
her own pain into hardness.

Tell him you love him, Ruby wanted to yell. *Tell him he's
everything in the world to you.* Max might not see it, but
she did. It was evident in every breath Fina took.

But Fina stared back at her son. It seemed she'd learned
a thing or two from her buttoned-up husband about staying
granite-like in the face of pain. She nodded. 'Good. Just
don't forget you promised to take Ruby out to see the city
at sunset. It's her last chance.'

And then she turned and walked down the corridor to
her bedroom.

CHAPTER EIGHT

RUBY WAITED IN THE SALON in her carefully chosen outfit. She'd changed three times, veering between 'boating casual', which made her look as if she were going out for a country walk with her grandparents, and *Roman Holiday*, which made her look as if she was trying a little bit too hard. Maybe it had been the thick liquid liner and the red lipstick.

In the end she'd settled for a boat-necked navy cotton dress with a full enough skirt for clambering, her ballet pumps and a little black cardigan. The eyeliner stayed, but the lipstick was replaced by something in a more natural colour. Something that didn't scream 'Come and get me!', because she had a feeling there was no way Max was going to, even if it did.

While he hadn't answered the question she'd wanted to ask last night in words, his actions had done a pretty effective job for him. He wasn't in the grip of the same fairy-tale crush she had been, that was for sure.

If he had been, he wouldn't have avoided her all day. He certainly wouldn't have taken Sofia out for ice cream on his own that morning, saying that even trainee travelling nannies needed some time off. She knew a brush-off when she heard one. She'd been getting them from her father all her life.

She checked the ornate gold clock on the marble mantelpiece. Ten to seven. Fina had decreed they should leave here on the hour to catch the whole glory of the sunset, which was supposed to be closer to eight.

She wandered over to the long windows and took in the golden light hitting the front of a pink and white palazzo on the other side of the canal. Max had been right. This city spun a spell, making you believe things that weren't real, making you hope for things that could never be. She understood why so many people loved it now. And why he hated it.

She stayed there, watching the light play on the water, for what seemed like only a few minutes, and Fina startled her when she swept into the room and turned on the light. Ruby hadn't realised it had got that dark yet.

'Where's Max?' Fina asked, looking round, her brows drawn together.

Ruby shrugged. 'I don't know. We're supposed to be leaving at—'

The clock on the mantelpiece caught her eye. It was five past seven. He'd be here soon, though, she didn't doubt that. Whatever else Max was, he was a man of his word.

She almost wished he weren't. It was going to be awkward. She'd back out if she could, but she sensed Fina would blame Max somehow if she did, and the last thing Ruby wanted was to cause more trouble between mother and son.

Fina tutted and swept from the room before Ruby could say anything else.

Ruby walked over to an armchair at the edge of the seating area and dropped into it. It was one of those old seats that accepted her weight with a 'poof' then slowly sank until her bottom rested fully against the cushion.

She stared into the empty fireplace and waited. A few moments later she heard Fina clip-clopping back up the corridor. She entered the room and sighed dramatically. 'He has a very important phone call, apparently. The whole of London will fall down if he doesn't speak to this man at this precise minute.' She shook her head. 'I shall go and read to Sofia, but he says he will be out in only a few minutes.'

Ruby nodded, and placed her hands in her lap. She rested back against the armchair instead of sitting up poker straight. No point in getting a stiff back waiting for him.

There was a squeal and the sound of two pairs of footsteps—one small and slippered, the other bigger and harder—and a moment later Sofia ran into the room in her pyjamas, her grandmother in hot pursuit. She launched herself at Ruby and landed on her lap.

Fina pressed a hand to her chest, and said breathlessly, 'She's full of beans tonight, and she wanted to come and see you.'

'That's okay.' Then she turned to Sofia. 'Perhaps doing something quiet together for a few minutes will help you get ready for bed. What do you say, young lady?'

'Daw!' said Sofia loudly and pointed to the crayons and scrap paper that had been left out after their earlier colouring session.

Ruby chuckled and let Sofia slip off her lap before she joined her kneeling by the coffee table. 'And what would you like to draw this evening?'

Sofia thought for a moment. 'Naughty fish!'

Of course.

Ruby couldn't remember how many mischievous crabs she'd sketched since that first one: on the bottom of the lagoon, in a carnival mask, and Sofia's favourite—clinging determinedly to her uncle's big toe with a pair of razor-sharp pincers. She quickly did an outline in black pen, a gentler scene this time, something more in keeping with bedtime. She drew the cheeky crab in the back of a gondola with his equally cheeky crustacean girlfriend, being punted along by a singing gondolier in the moonlight.

When she realised what she'd done, how romantic she'd made the scene, she sighed and pushed it her charge's way.

There Venice went again…messing with her head.

'Here you go. And make sure you colour nicely. I don't want it all scribbled over in two seconds flat.'

Sofia nodded seriously, then set to work giving the lady crab a shock of purple hair, which Ruby approved of most heartily.

The sun was down behind the buildings now. Ruby stood and walked to the window, drawn closer by a patchwork sky of yellows and pinks and tangerines, sparsely smeared with silvery blue clouds. Venice, which often had an oddly monochrome feel to its palette, was bathed in golden light.

She walked back over to where Sofia was colouring and complimented her on her hard work, even though the cartoonish drawing she'd provided her with was almost entirely obliterated with heavy strokes of multicoloured crayon. She pulled out a piece of paper for herself. Most of the sheets had writing on the back. They'd gone through Fina's meagre stash of drawing paper and now were wading through documents Max had discarded, using them as scrap. Ruby flipped it over and looked at what was on the printed side.

It was a detail for an interior arch in one of the galleries of the National Institute of Fine Art. The shape was square with no adornment, and Ruby could see where the metal and studs of a supporting girder were left unhidden, giving it a textured, yet industrial air. She thought of the buildings Max had shown her up and down the canal, how he'd explained the Venetians had taken styles from the countries they visited with their own to make something unique, and, instead of turning the sheet back over again and drawing another princess, she picked up a pen and began to embellish.

She sighed, her heart heavy inside her chest. She might as well occupy herself while she waited.

'You need to get back here right away,' Alex, Max's second-in-command at Martin & Martin insisted, more than a hint of urgency in his tone.

Max closed his eyes to block out the dancing cherubs above his head. He'd been pacing to and fro in his mother's library and he was starting to get the uncanny feeling they were watching him. 'I know.'

'Vince McDermot wants the institute commission and he wants it bad.'

Max opened his eyes and stared at the screen on his laptop. 'I know. But the institute board have committed to giving me this extra few weeks to tweak our designs. They won't go back on that.'

Alex sighed. 'True, but McDermot has been out and about wining and dining key members of the board behind our backs. Either you need to come back to London and start schmoozing this instant or we need to come up with a design that'll blow that slimy little poser out of the water.'

Max knew this. He also knew he wasn't good at schmoozing. 'You're better at buttering clients up than I am.'

Alex let out a low, gruff laugh. 'Damn right, but it's you they want, Max. It's time to stop playing happy families and get your butt back here.'

Now it was Max's turn to laugh. *Happy families? Yeah, right.*

'I've been doing what needs to be done to focus on the work, Al. You know that.'

Alex grunted. 'All I'm saying is that there's no point in

us burying our heads in the sand about this. Otherwise, the month will be up, we'll submit new designs and, even if they do have the "wow factor", the board will be more inclined to go with that flash-in-the-pan pretty boy.'

One of the reasons Max liked Alex, both as a colleague and a friend, was that he didn't mince his words. Alex had a point, though. Vince McDermot was London's new architectural wunderkind. Personally, Max thought his designs impractical and crowd-pleasing. They'd never stand the test of time.

'I'm flying back to London tomorrow afternoon, so that's that sorted,' he told Alex. 'The other stuff? Well, that's another story, but if we can keep them sweet for the next fortnight, it'll give us time to come up with what they're looking for.'

It had to come at some point, didn't it? He'd been hailed for his 'ground-breaking minimalist and elegant style', won awards for it. But that had been before. Now he couldn't come up with anything fresh and exciting. It was as if his talent had been buried with his father.

Alex made a conciliatory noise. 'Listen, I should have more of an idea of who exactly he's been sliming up to in the next fifteen minutes. Do you want me to call back, or are you going to hold?'

Max looked at the clock. It was half past seven.

He hadn't forgotten what that meant.

He was late. Really late.

'I'll hold,' he said.

His conscience grumbled. He let the relief flooding through him drown it out.

It was better this way. It was getting harder and harder to remember Ruby was his employee. Harder and harder to stop himself relaxing so much in her presence that he kept letting his guard down. He couldn't afford to do that. Not here. Not with his mother so close.

Better to put a stop to it now.

So Max made himself sit down. He made himself tinker with the designs for the institute's atrium. He made himself ignore the clawing feeling deep inside that told him he was being a heel, that he was hurting her for no reason.

Unfortunately, he didn't do a very good job of it. Probably because the lines and angles in front of him on the screen kept going out of focus, and he kept imagining what it would be like to be out in the boat with Ruby, the dark wrapping around them, enclosing them in their own little bubble while the lights of the city danced on the lagoon.

That only made him crosser.

Damn her. It was all her fault, waltzing into his neatly ordered life, turning it upside down.

You asked her. Hell, you practically commanded her to come with you.

Yeah? Well, everybody made mistakes. Even him. Occasionally.

It was only when he stood up to pace around the room again that he realised he'd put the phone down on Alex at some point in the last five minutes and hadn't even noticed. He said a word that should have made the cherubs on the ceiling put their fingers in their ears.

And all that messing around he'd done on the atrium plans was a load of rubbish! In fact, all the work he'd done on them in the last couple of days had been tired and uninspiring. What had he been thinking?

He shook his head, perfectly aware of what had been filling it. That was why it would be so much better when he was back in London. He'd be able to get his brain round it then, removed from any distractions. Any strawberry-clad, purple-streaked distractions.

Now, where was the earlier atrium design? The one where he'd pared it all back to the basics? He might as well get rid of all these silly changes and start from scratch.

He rummaged through the papers on his mother's antique desk. He'd had a printout of it. It had to be around here somewhere.

Ruby sat back on her heels and surveyed her handiwork. Not bad, even if she did say so herself. Maybe Max was right about her having some real artistic flair. Maybe she could do something with it, rather than just 'messing around', as her father called it.

There was such beauty and simplicity in Max's designs, but this one had just needed a little something—a curve here, a twirl there. By the time she'd finished, the arch on Max's discarded plan was a strange hybrid between twenty-first-century industrial and Venetian Gothic, with a little bit of Ruby thrown in for fun.

Perhaps she should be an architect?

The fact she didn't burst out laughing then roll on the floor at that thought was all thanks to Max. He'd believed in her ability to draw, seen something no one else saw, and she was starting to think she could even see it herself. She wanted to tell him that when they went out later, to thank him, but she didn't really know how to put it into words without betraying everything else she was starting to feel.

'More fish!' Sofia demanded, grinning at Ruby so appealingly that Ruby didn't have the heart to make her say please.

'I think maybe it's time Grandma tucked you into bed,' she told Sofia, smiling. Fina rose from where she'd been reading a magazine in an armchair, and held her hand out for her granddaughter. After running and giving Ruby a hug, Sofia allowed herself to be led away and Ruby was once again alone in the salon.

She tried not to look, but the gold clock on the mantelpiece drew her gaze like a magnet.

Eight o'clock.

A quick glance outside confirmed her suspicions. Compared to the brightly lit salon, the sky outside was bottomless and dark. Not helped by the heavy clouds that had started to gather over the city in the last half hour.

Max had stood her up.

She let her eyelids rest gently closed and inhaled. It didn't matter.

The heaviness in her heart called her a liar.

But it shouldn't be there. She was a paid employee. He owed her nothing more than her wages.

It was just...

She shook her head and opened her eyes again, then she got off up the floor and started piling the scattered bits of drawing up, putting the crayons back in their tub.

Just nothing.

She'd been fooling herself again, thinking this was something when it wasn't. Max hadn't seen inside her, he hadn't spotted the potential that no one else had. He'd just paid her a compliment or two, that was all. And that kiss? Heat-of-the-moment stuff that produced nothing but regrets. She'd doled out a few of those herself in her time. Nothing to sweat about.

Then why did she feel like going to her room, shutting the door behind her and bawling her eyes out?

She gathered the sheets of paper in various sizes up in her arms and headed towards the door. She wasn't quite sure where she was going to put these, but she suspected Fina wouldn't want them scattered around her most formal living space. Maybe they could find a home for one or two of the best ones on the fridge door?

She couldn't have been looking where she'd been going, because when the salon door burst open and Max came barrelling through she didn't have time for evasive manoeuvres. She stumbled sideways, the stack of paper went flying into the air and then fluttered noisily down like over-sized confetti.

Max just stood in the doorway, looking somewhat stunned.

He didn't say anything, but he shook himself slightly then bent to help her pick up the scattered drawings.

Damn him for being such a gentleman. She wanted to hate him right now.

'Here,' he said, when they'd finished gathering up the last of them, and held a sheaf of papers in her direction.

'Thanks,' she mumbled, chickening out of looking him in the eye.

Max must have been doing the same, because suddenly he got very interested in the top sheet of paper.

'What the hell?' he started to say, and then his expression grew thunderous. 'What's this?'

Ruby rolled her eyes. 'Sorry,' she said, feeling her cheeks heat. 'I didn't intend to make the cartoon of you being bitten by the crab at first, but Sofia thought it looked like you, because it was a man, probably, and then it just became a kind of joke and we—'

'I'm not talking about a silly drawing!' Max said, his voice getter louder.

His words were like a punch to Ruby's gut. 'But I—'

'I'm talking about *this*!' And he thrust a sheet of paper so close to her face that she had to step back to focus on it. It was the doodle she'd just finished: Max's arch with her little bit of decorative nonsense superimposed.

Artist? Hah! Don't kid yourself, Ruby.

'It was just… I mean, I just…' She let out a frustrated sigh and spiked her fingers through her neatly combed fringe. 'It's just a doodle, Max.'

'A *doodle*?'

Ruby's heart thudded and her stomach dived into her ballet pumps. If the heat of Max's anger hadn't been scalding her face, his expression would have been kind of funny. She nodded, feeling all the while that she was walking into an ambush that she didn't know how to avoid.

'These are my plans!' Max bellowed. 'What on earth makes you think you have the right to *doodle* on them? Are you out of your mind?'

Ruby's mouth moved and she backed away. 'But, it was there…' her gaze flicked to the coffee table, where the pile of unmolested scrap paper still sat. '…with the stuff you tossed out the other day…on the top of the pile.'

'This wasn't *scrap*!' he yelled. 'These are my original plans. You had no right to use them for Sofia. No right at all.'

Ruby was so puzzled that she couldn't even react to Max's anger at that moment. How had Max's plans got there? How? He'd given them the sheaf of papers himself yesterday and, okay, she hadn't noticed that one sitting on top then, but neither she nor Sofia had been anywhere near the library. The plans couldn't have walked here on their own.

'I don't understand,' she said, shaking her head.

Max began to laugh. But it wasn't the warm, rich sound she remembered from the the day they'd gone crabbing. It was a dark, rasping sound that made the hair on her arms stand up on end.

'Of course,' he said, shaking his head. 'I knew I shouldn't have hired you. Why I didn't listen to my gut I'll never know. What was I thinking? You have no qualifications, no experience—'

Now was the moment that the furnace of Ruby's anger decided to *whomph* into life. She went from shivery and cold to raging inferno in the space of a heartbeat.

'You're right!' she yelled back at him. 'You want to know if I'm cut out to be a nanny? Well, I can answer that right now—I'm not! Not if it means I have to like working for closed-off, emotionally constipated jerks like you.'

Max went very still and his expression was completely neutral. If anything, that was more worrying than all the bluff and fluster had been. Ruby felt herself start to shake. She knew she'd gone too far, that she shouldn't have said that. But, as the sensible side of her brain tried to tell her that, the impulsive, emotional side blocked its ears and sang *la la la*.

'I should fire you for this,' he said, and his voice was as cold as the marble floor beneath their feet.

'Don't bother,' she shot back, making enough heat and anger for both of them. 'I quit. I'm not cut out for this and I don't want to be.' And she dumped the pile of paper she'd been holding onto Max's pile and stomped off towards the door. Thank goodness she only had that one rucksack to pack. She could be out of here within the hour.

'That's right,' Max said, his voice low and infuriatingly even as she reached the door. 'Run out on another job.'

She spun round to face him. 'You know nothing about me. So don't you dare judge me.'

He stared her down. The fire from a few moments earlier was gone, doused by a healthy dollop of concrete, if his expression was anything to go by.

'I know that you bail when the going gets tough, that you've never seen a single job through to the end.'

'So? That's my business, not yours. You've made that abundantly clear.'

He stepped forward. 'I'm afraid it is my business when you're leaving before the end of your contract.'

That was when Ruby smiled. She really shouldn't, but it started somewhere deep down inside and bubbled up until it reached her lips. 'And there's your problem, Mr Hot Shot. I don't have a contract, remember?'

And, leaving him to chew on that, she stalked down the

corridor. Pity she was wearing ballet slippers, because it would have been so much more effective in heels.

'We had a verbal agreement!' he yelled after her.

Ruby's response was to keep walking but use some non-verbal communication she was pretty sure was offensive in just about any language you cared to mention.

An angry shudder ripped through her as she headed for her room, already mentally packing her rucksack. And she'd thought she was attracted to this man? She really was insane. The sooner she got out of Venice, the better.

CHAPTER NINE

MAX WAS SO FURIOUS he couldn't speak, could hardly even breathe. How dare she act as if he were in the wrong? And how dare she bail on him after only one week? What was he going to do now? Knowing his mother, she'd make an impulsive decision and say she couldn't possibly keep Sofia here on her own, and then he'd be stuck here, right when it was more urgent than ever that he leave this tangled family mess behind and concentrate even harder on his work.

He wanted to march after Ruby, to give her a piece of his mind, but he suspected she was in no mood to listen. She was stubborn as hell, that woman, and bound to dig her heels in if he went in with all guns blazing.

He'd give her half an hour. Then he'd go and find her, make her see sense.

He looked down at the stack of papers in his hands. His scribbled-on plans were on top. Just the sight of them made his temperature rise a couple of notches. He turned and headed for the library. At least he'd be able to distract himself for a short while trying to see if anything was salvageable. Once he was there, he dropped the stack of papers on the desk and sank into the chair.

It had to have been her fault. She must have come and got more paper from his makeshift office at some point, despite what she'd said, because how else could his pristine plans have ended up on Sofia's drawing-paper pile? They hadn't been outside the library all week.

A cold feeling washed through him from head to toe.

Except...

Last night, when he'd taken some papers into the salon as a cure for insomnia, and the plans had been amongst them. It had worked, too. After an hour and a half of poring over them, going over every detail, he'd woken himself up, his head lolling against his chest, and then he'd stumbled back to bed.

Oh, hell.

And he had no idea if he'd stumbled back into the library first and replaced the plans.

He stared at the clean, narrow printed-out lines of his plans, with Ruby's thicker doodlings over the top. It was his fault, wasn't it? Not hers. While he hadn't exactly put them on Sofia's paper stack by leaving them lying around in the salon he'd opened up the way for them to get muddled into it during the course of the day.

Max exhaled heavily and let his forehead drop so it rested on the pile of papers.

Damn.

And he'd lost his temper. Something he never did. He'd always hated losing control like that. Not just because when his really long fuse went, it tended to verge on apocalyptic, but because of how he was feeling right now. Raw. Open. Weak.

If it had been Sofia that had done the drawing he knew he wouldn't have reacted the same way. Oh, he'd have been cross, but he wouldn't have exploded like that, and not just because she was only two and he would have scared the living daylights out of her.

There was something about Ruby that just got under his skin.

He sat up, ran his hand through his hair and stared at the dark green wallpaper.

He should let her leave, shouldn't he?

She wanted to. It would certainly be better for him.

But he needed her.

He shook his head. No. He didn't need anyone. Especially not a woman who ran at the first sniff of trouble, which was exactly what Ruby had done, proving his point very nicely for him.

He needed a nanny. That was all.

The choice was up to her. If she still wanted to go he wouldn't stop her, but there was one thing he needed to do first—apologise.

In a bit, though. Ruby was probably still spitting fire, and if he tried to knock on her door now, he'd probably get a few more of those wonderfully eloquent hand gestures.

A smile crept across his face, even though he knew it wasn't really funny at all.

She was a pill, that one.

He sighed and turned his attention back to the plans in front of him, unfolding the paper and having a good look. It was interesting what she'd drawn. She'd taken his plain, square arch and added some traditional Venetian style to it. She really had been paying attention to the shapes and patterns of the buildings, hadn't she? Here was an ogee arch, and here a lobed one. She'd reproduced them perfectly, even when she'd only been doodling.

That was when something smacked him straight between the eyebrows.

The shapes.

Ruby had been talking about the geometric shapes, the other day, the way simple ones interlocked to make more complicated ones. All he'd been able to see when he came to Venice was the fuss, the frilliness. He'd forgotten that even the most of ornate fasciae were constructed of much simpler, cleaner elements.

If he took Ruby's idea and pared it back, using simpler shapes, overlapping and juxtaposing them to create something, not exactly elaborate, because that wasn't his style, but something more intricate that still kept that essence of simple elegance.

He grabbed one of Sofia's scrap-paper sheets and a pen and began to scribble. Semicircular arches here and here, intersecting to create a more pointed version, with slender pillar for support. His hand flew over the paper, sketching shapes and lines, at first for the arches in the atrium, but then taking the same idea and applying it to other aspects of the space, giving it all a cohesive feel.

He could see it so clearly. Just a hint of gothic style, built in glass and steel. Modern materials that echoed back to classic design. It was just what he needed to tie the new wing and the existing institute building together and make them feel like one space.

He kept going, filling sheet after sheet, until he suddenly realised he'd been at this for ages.

Ruby!

He still hadn't gone and apologised.

He shoved away from the desk, sending a stack of Sofia's colourful drawings flying, and then sprinted down the corridor in the direction of her and Ruby's rooms. He didn't bother knocking when he got there, just flung the door open and raced inside, expecting to find her shoving clothes into her rucksack, a scowl on her face.

Wrong again, Max.

She can pack in under ten minutes, remember? Sometimes five.

Where Max had expected to find Ruby stewing and

muttering insults under her breath, there was nothing but empty space.

Ruby Lange was gone.

Ruby shivered as she waited on the little creaky dock out-side Ca' Damiani. The clouds had sunk closer to the water and coloured everything a murky grey. A drop of rain splashed on her forehead. Great.

Her rucksack was at her feet, leaning against her lower legs, and she craned to see if the light bobbing towards her, accompanied by the sound of a motor, was the taxi she'd ordered. She needed to get out of here and she needed to do it right now.

This was so *not* how she'd imagined seeing Venice by water this evening.

More raindrops, one after the other. She could hear them plopping into the canal near her feet.

The approaching craft turned out to be a private boat that puttered past and stopped outside one of the buildings opposite. Ruby felt her whole body sag.

Stupid, stupid girl. You take on a job you know noth-ing about—just because some random guy says he needs you—and you think he's going to see past all of your inex-perience and believe you're something special? Get real. The only thing Max Martin believed about her was that she was a flaky screw-up, just like everyone else on this planet.

She hugged her arms tighter around her, wishing she hadn't packed her jacket in the very bottom of the rucksack.

Not everyone believes you're a screw-up.

Okay, maybe she was being a little dramatic. A number of her bosses over the years had begged her to stay when she'd realised the job wasn't for her and had given in her notice. They'd said she was competent and organised and they'd love to promote her, but she hadn't been able to ig-nore that itchy feeling once it started. The only way to stop the intense restlessness, the only way to scratch it enough so it went away, was to move on. But Max was wrong. She didn't run away. She ran *to* the next thing. There was a whole world of difference.

The rain began to fall harder now. She pushed her fringe out of her eyes. It was already damp. Where *was* that taxi?

There was a creaking behind her as the boat door that led to the dock opened. Ruby's blood solidified in her veins. She refused to turn round.

She expected another angry tirade, braced herself against it, but when his voice came it was soft and low. 'Ruby?'

'That's my name,' she said, and then grimaced, glad he couldn't see her face. What was this? High school?

'Don't go.'

She spun round to face him, arms still clutched around her middle, as if she was afraid she'd fall apart if she didn't hold herself together. 'What?'

The anger was gone. She could see none of its vestiges on his features. Part of her breathed a sigh of relief, but another, deeper part, sighed with disappointment. The anger had been horrible, but it had been a little wonderful, too.

He walked forwards. Ruby was tempted to back away, but that would mean taking a dip in the canal, so she had to stay where she was. Cold drops peppered her skin and she shivered. Off in the distance there was a muffled rumble of thunder.

'I want to apologise,' he said, looking so earnest her heart grew warm and achy inside her chest. 'I should never have let off at you like that. It was totally uncalled for.'

'Thank you,' she said in a wobbly voice. 'And I should probably apologise for the verbal—and non-verbal—assault. That wasn't very professional.'

A wry smile lifted one corner of his mouth. 'I deserved it.'

Her stony blood started to warm and melt. It danced and

shimmered and sang. *Stop it*, she told it. *You're making it very hard to leave.*

And so was he, looking at her like that.

The itchy feeling returned, stronger this time. Unable to stand still, she walked in a small circle. The falling rain multiplied the lights of the city, but a cold breeze wrapped around her, stealing her breath.

'It was my fault the plans got mixed up with Sofia's drawing paper,' he said, not breaking eye contact. 'I left them in the salon the night before. I'm sorry I accused you of that.'

She nodded, not trusting herself to say anything.

He looked down at his feet briefly before meeting her eyes again. 'Forgive me.'

Revenge, passion and utter, utter devotion. The words spun through Ruby's head.

'Okay,' she croaked.

He nodded, his expression still slightly grim. 'Then stay...please?'

Ruby blinked. Up until now, she hadn't been sure that word was part of Max Martin's vocabulary.

She looked away, even closed her eyes for good measure. She'd wanted to go so badly. So badly... It was a surprise to discover the tug to stay was just as strong. Not to stay and be Sofia's nanny, although she was sure she would enjoy another week of that, but to stay here. In Venice. With Max.

She sucked a breath in and held it. Thank goodness he had no idea about the silly things she'd been feeling. Thank goodness he probably thought she was acting out of hurt pride. And fear, yes. He'd been right about that. She did run when things got too hard. Always had. How could you save yourself the crushing pain of disappointment otherwise?

She opened her eyes and looked out across the water. The moon was rising farther away, where the clouds had not yet blotted it out. It cast a silvery glow on the far-off bell towers and roofs, spilling glitter on the still waters of this back canal, where it undulated softly. It looked like a fairy tale.

And if this were a fairy tale, she'd stay. Max would fall madly in love with her and make her his princess. In their happy-ever-after she'd soothe his pain, teach him to let it go, and they'd be gloriously happy together.

Only real life didn't work that way. It hadn't for her and her father, and it hadn't for Fina. Only a fool wouldn't escape when they had the chance rather than sentence themselves to that kind of misery.

If she stayed, she might fall for him properly, not just teeter on the brink of an *inappropriate* crush.

She pulled her rucksack up from the floor of the dock and hugged it to her before turning to face him. 'I don't know, Max. I don't think it's a good idea I stay...for anybody.'

The water taxi chose that moment to turn up. The driver, oblivious to the tense scene occurring on the little wooden dock, looped a rope round a post and called out in Italian.

Ruby wiped the rain off her face and waved to show she'd heard him, then she slipped the straps of her rucksack over her shoulders. She pressed her lips together and tried not to let her eyes shimmer. 'Goodbye. Tell Fina and Sofia I'm sorry.' And then she turned and steadied herself before stepping into the boat.

As she lifted her foot he called out again. 'Don't go.'

She turned to look over her shoulder. 'Why, Max? Why shouldn't I go?'

For a moment he didn't say anything, but then he looked her straight in the eye. 'Because I need you.'

CHAPTER TEN

IF RUBY HAD THOUGHT she'd felt a little breathless before, now she really struggled to pull oxygen into her body. Max needed her?

He doesn't mean it that way. Don't be stupid.

'No, you just need a proper nanny. It isn't me *specifically* that you need.'

No words left Max's mouth, but she discovered his eyes contradicted her quite beautifully. Her heart literally stopped beating inside her chest, just for a second. When it started up again, her pulse thundered in her ears.

She let her rucksack slip off her shoulders and it landed behind her on the dock with a thud. The rain began to fall in earnest, soaking the thin wool of her cardigan, but she didn't seem to feel the damp and cold seeping into her skin.

Him, too? It hadn't just been a physical, knee-jerk kind of thing?

That made her feel as if the world had just done a somersault around her and she needed to find solid ground again. Pity she was stranded in a city where that was in short supply.

That didn't mean she was about to commit emotional suicide by staying, though. She cleared her throat. 'I meant what I said earlier, Max. I don't think I'm cut out to be a nanny in the long term.'

He nodded. 'I agree. But I'm not asking you to be a

nanny for the rest of your life. I'm just asking you to be one for the next week or so. After that it's up to you.'

She nodded. That all sounded very sensible.

'If you don't think I'm cut out to be a nanny, why on earth do you want me to stay and look after Sofia?'

Max gave her a weary look. 'I didn't say I didn't think you could do the job.' He smiled gently. 'I said it because I didn't think you should commit yourself to something when your talent clearly lies elsewhere.'

Ruby's eyes widened. 'You think I have talent?'

He frowned. 'Don't *you*? Your drawings are fabulous, and that doodle you did on my plans set ideas firing off in my head so fast I could hardly keep up with them.' The smile grew into a grin. 'I have my "wow factor" for the Institute now, Ruby, and it's all because of you.'

She closed her eyes and opened them again, not quite able to believe what she was hearing. 'Do you... Do you think I should be an architect?'

His eyes warmed, making her forget the salty lagoon breeze that kept lifting the shorter bits of her hair now and then. 'I think you could do that if you wanted to, but there's something about your sketches that's so full of life and personality. I think you've got something there. They're quirky and original and full of...'

You. His eyes must have said that bit, because his mouth had stopped moving.

'They're captivating.'

Ruby felt the echo of his words rumble deep down inside her. Or maybe it was the crack of thunder that shook the sky over their heads.

Oh, heck. She really was in trouble, wasn't she? How could she leave now?

And maybe Max was right. Maybe it was time to stop running. She might not have to see being a nanny through to the bitter end, but she could see this job through. How could she leave them all in the lurch like this? Sofia wouldn't understand where she'd gone and feel abandoned all over again, Fina would be saddled with looking after a toddler full time, and Max wouldn't have time to work on his plans, and she really wanted him to do that.

She still didn't believe there was much in the future for them, even if some bizarre chemistry was popping between them, but she'd like to visit the National Institute of Fine Art on a rainy afternoon in a few years' time and sit under Max's atrium and feel happy—and maybe a little sad—to know that she'd had something to do with it, that in some lasting way she had a tiny connection to him.

She looked down at the rucksack threatening to pitch off the dock and into the canal. The taxi driver, whom she'd forgotten all about, coughed and mumbled something grumpily about being made to hang about in this kind of weather. She shot him a look of desperation.

He shrugged in that fatalistic Italian way, his expression saying, *Are you coming or not?*

Ruby looked back at Max. He was waiting. Not shouting. Not bulldozering. It was totally her choice and she knew he would hold no grudges if she got on this boat and told the driver to take her to the Piazzale Roma to catch a train.

She swallowed and twisted to face the driver and rummaged in her pocket and gave him a tip for his trouble. *'Mi dispiace, signore.'*

Ruby woke up to sunshine pouring into her bedroom the next morning. She stumbled over to the window, which overlooked a narrow little canal that ran down the side of the palazzo. It almost felt as if the night before had never happened. There was no hint of the storm. The sky was the clear pale blue of a baby's blanket, hardly a cloud to mar it, and where the sun hit the canal it was a fierce and glittering emerald.

Things were just as surreal at breakfast, with Fina bustling around and fussing over Sofia, never once mentioning that Ruby had packed her bags and tried to leave last night.

Max had been in the library since before she'd got up, and that had been pretty early. She half expected him to bury himself away all day, working on his plans until it was time to pack up and leave for the airport. She didn't know what would be worse: not seeing him most of the day or spending a bittersweet last few hours with him before he returned to London. She'd forgotten all about that last night when she'd agreed to stay. So when the salon door opened at ten o'clock and Max walked in, Ruby's heart leapt and cowered at the same time.

'What do you want to do this morning?' he asked his niece, glancing briefly at Ruby and giving a nod of greeting.

'Fishing!' Sofia yelled and ran off in the direction of the cupboard where the crabbing gear was kept.

Both Ruby and Max charged after her, knowing just how tightly that cupboard was packed and just how much mischief an unattended two-year-old could get up to inside it. They managed to beat Sofia to the lines and hooks, but Max gave her a bucket and a small net to carry to keep her happy. And then they bustled around, getting into the boat, coaxing Sofia into a life jacket, making sure she didn't let go of her bucket and leave it floating down a canal somewhere.

She and Max worked as a team, exchanging words when needed, passing equipment to each other, but it wasn't until they were standing at Max's favourite crabbing spot, the little boat moored up and bobbing about a short distance away, that they slowed down enough for Ruby to get a sense of his mood.

She watched him gently helping Sofia wind an empty

line back up without getting it tangled. He'd been polite this morning, almost friendly.

Had she imagined it? Had it all been some weird dream, a spell cast by this contrary city?

She let out a long sigh. Maybe it was better if that was the case. It was sheer craziness. Even if she'd seen what she'd thought she'd seen in his eyes last night, what did she think was going to happen? A wild fling in his mother's house, with a toddler running around?

Once again, get real, Ruby.

She knelt down and took interest in what Sofia was doing. She'd plopped the crab line into the water for the fourth or fifth time, but so far no luck. The little girl heaved out a sigh. 'Fish go 'way,' she said slightly despondently.

Ruby couldn't help but smile. Despite her self-contained manner, Sofia had a little bit of her grandmother's flair for drama in her. She forgot herself, looked up at Max to share the joke. He was crouching the other side of Sofia, who was sitting on the edge of the *fondamenta* where the railings parted, her little legs swinging above the water, and their eyes met across the top of her head.

Ruby almost fell in the canal.

It was all there, everything he hadn't said last night and everything he had.

Oh, heck. Just when she'd almost managed to talk some sense into herself.

And it still all did make sense. He was her boss. He was going back to London in a matter of hours. He was her total polar opposite. In what world was that anything but a recipe for disaster?

Everywhere but Venice, she discovered as a slow smile spread across her lips. She felt she must be glowing. Actually radiating something. It would probably scare the fish away.

She wanted to lean across, press her lips to his, wind

her arms around his neck and just taste him. Feel him. Dive into him.

'Fish!' Sofia yelled, and it was almost her who did the diving. She got so excited she almost toppled off the edge into the canal. It was only Max's quick reflexes that saved her.

After that they made sure they had their eyes on Sofia instead of each other at all times. It didn't matter, though. It was pulsing in the air around them, like a wonderful secret, a song carried on a radio wave that only they could tune into.

She felt it as they ended their crabbing expedition, a weary Sofia rubbing her eyes and complaining about being hungry. She felt it as they stood mere inches apart at the front of the boat, Max steering, her holding Sofia so she could see over the top of the little motorboat's windscreen. Felt it as they passed buckets and nets and bags to each other from boat to dry land.

As they pulled the last of the luggage from the boat and headed into the large downstairs hall of the palazzo Ruby turned to Max, made proper eye contact in what seemed the first time in decades. 'What time's your flight?' she asked, plainly and simply.

It was all very well dreaming on the canals, but their feet were back on solid ground now. It was time to anchor herself back in reality, remind herself of what really was happening here.

'Five o'clock,' he said.

She nodded towards the first floor. 'You'd better get going if you're going to get any work done before you have to stop and pack.' She held out her hand to take the nets from him.

Max looked at her for a long while, and an ache started low down in her belly. 'Yes,' he said, and then handed her the nets and set off up the staircase, taking the steps two at a time.

* * *

Ruby jiggled her leg while she waited for Sofia to finish brushing her teeth. Once she'd had a try herself, Ruby dived in and gave them another going-over. As mundane as the task was, she was glad of something to do. Sofia had had an extra-long sleep that afternoon. Ruby had gone into her room again and again, expecting to find her jumping on the bed, but each time Sofia had been sprawled on the mattress, her pink rabbit tucked in the crook of her arm and her thumb in her mouth.

She'd heard Max leave the palazzo around three. His plane was probably somewhere over the English Channel now.

He hadn't even said goodbye.

A stab of something hit her in the stomach, but she forced it away. She bundled Sofia from the bathroom and back to her bedroom, where she found Fina sitting on the bed, waiting for them.

'You are looking tired, *piccola*.'

Ruby ruffled Sofia's hair. 'I don't know why, after that mammoth sleep she had.'

Fina smiled and tipped her head on one side. 'I was talking about you, my darling.'

Ruby tried not to react. Was it really that obvious?

Fina waved her hand in a regal manner. 'Well, it is all for the good. I came to say I would read Sofia her story and put her to bed tonight, so you go and relax in the salon.'

Ruby shook her head. More sitting around with nothing to do—the last thing she needed. 'It's my job, Fina—'

Fina stopped her with an imperious eyebrow lift. 'But I wish to. So…off you go.' And she dismissed Ruby with a gracious smile.

There wasn't much Ruby could say to that, so she sloped off in the direction of the salon to do as she was told. The setting sun was streaming in through the windows when she entered the room, almost blinding her, and at first she didn't see the dark shape by the window, but after a moment or two the dark smudge morphed into something more solid.

Ruby's mouth dropped open. 'B-but I thought you were going back to London!'

Max turned round. He was silhouetted against the ornate arches, and she couldn't see his face, let alone read his features.

'So did I.'

She shook her head. 'What changed?'

'Nothing…and everything.'

He stepped forward out of the light and Ruby could see he wasn't wearing his suit, just dark casual trousers and a light sweater. Her heart began to beat faster.

'But this afternoon, when I carried on using the ideas from your doodle and incorporating a pared-down Venetian style into my plans for the institute, I realised I need to be here, not in London. I need to get my inspiration from the source, not just inaccurate and misleading memories. I've spent all afternoon wandering around looking at buildings I've known all my life and seeing them with completely fresh eyes.' He shook his head.

Ruby glanced over her shoulder towards the corridor, and Sofia's bedroom. She could just about hear the warm tones of Fina's voice as she read her granddaughter a fairy story. 'There's something to be said for stripping the preconceptions and prejudices of the past away and looking at things with fresh eyes.'

'Did my mother put you up to saying that?'

She turned back, expecting him to be scowling, but his face was almost neutral, save for the barest hint of a smile.

One corner of Ruby's mouth lifted. 'No. I think I'm quite capable of irritating you without outside help.'

Max laughed, and it made something rise like a balloon inside Ruby and bump against the ceiling of her ribs.

He walked towards the door in the path of a long, golden shadow. 'Come on,' he said.

Ruby frowned, but she turned to follow anyway. 'Where?'

He stopped and looked back at her. 'You missed seeing Venice at sunset last night because I had an attack of stupid. It's only right I should make it up to you tonight.'

CHAPTER ELEVEN

As THEY WALKED along the little wooden dock in front of his mother's palazzo, Max couldn't help but remember being there with Ruby the night before. He jumped down into the little speedboat, and Ruby followed him. Without even asking, she helped with the ropes and fenders.

She'd only been here a week, and no one had shown her what to do. She'd just picked it up, that quick mind of hers soaking up all the information and putting it effortlessly to use.

She sat in the stern as he drove the boat away, silent. The outfit tonight was the plainest one yet. No hippies. No rock chicks. No damn strawberries. All she wore was a cream blouse with soft ruffles, a pair of capris and a light cardigan thrown over her shoulders. He watched her drink in the way the setting sun made every façade richer and more glorious, harking back to the days when some had actually been covered entirely in gold leaf.

In fact, he found it hard to *stop* watching her.

But he needed to.

Ruby Lange seemed bright and sunny and harmless, but she was a dangerous substance. She dissolved through his carefully constructed walls without even trying. He really should keep her at a distance.

Then why did you invite her to come out with you this evening?

Because it was the right thing to do. He'd acted like a total idiot the previous evening and so he was making it up to her. And he'd given his word. He'd said he'd show her Venice at sunset and so he was going to show her Venice at sunset.

Yeah, right. You keep telling yourself that. It has nothing to do with wanting to be alone with her, with wanting her to melt those walls that have left you claustrophobic and breathless for too long.

Max steered the boat down the canal and busied himself doing what he'd come here to do—no, not spend time alone with Ruby, but offer his services as tour guide and boat driver. He beckoned for her to come up and stand beside him, pointed out a few landmarks, and they talked easily about history and architecture for at least ten minutes.

It wasn't working.

Inside there was a timer counting down, ticking away the seconds until the sun slipped below the horizon and he and Ruby would be cocooned in the dark. He couldn't stop thinking about it.

He needed to remember why this was a bad idea, remember why Ruby wasn't right for him. As alluring as she might be, last night's uproar had proved one thing quite firmly: Ruby Lange ran when things got too close, when things got too serious. And these days he was nothing but serious.

He slowed the engine a little and looked over at her. 'Why do you move from job to job?'

She tore her gaze off the city and looked at him. 'I told you the other night. I want to find my perfect fit, like my father has. Like you have.'

He took his eyes off her for a moment to steer past a boat going a little slower than they were. 'Does it have to be perfect?'

Ruby gave him a puzzled smile. 'Well, I'd like it to be.

Who wants to do a job their whole life if they have no passion for it?'

'Millions of people do.'

She shook her head. 'I want more out of life. I'm tired with settling for crumbs. I want the whole banquet.'

He nodded. That part he understood only too well, but there was something else she hadn't considered.

'Whatever my mother says, I wasn't sure about architecture, at least not when it came time to choose a profession,' he told her, returning his gaze to the canal, as they'd turned into a busier, wider stretch and he needed to pay attention, but every now and then he glanced over at her. 'I liked it. It fascinated me, but, like you, I wasn't sure it was what I wanted to do with my life. I often wondered if I'd picked it because I wanted to impress my father.'

On his next glance across her eyes were wide. 'It's not your passion?' she almost whispered. 'Because if it isn't, I'd be fascinated to see what you're like when you really get into something!'

He smiled. 'No. It is my passion, or at least it is now. What I'm trying to say is that what if there is no perfect job, not at the start? What if it's the learning, the discipline of immersing yourself in it and scaling the learning curves that makes it a perfect fit?'

She frowned and her eyes made tiny, rapid side-to-side movements as she worked that one out in her head. She frowned harder. He guessed she hadn't been able to neatly file that thought and shove it away out of sight.

'But how do you do that and not lose your heart and soul to something that might not be the right choice?' Her voice dropped to the scratchiest of whispers. 'What do you do if you choose something and it doesn't choose you back?'

He shrugged. Maybe he'd been lucky. 'But there's the irony—you may never know unless you try.'

She folded her arms, scowled and turned away to look at

the buildings as he turned the boat onto the Grand Canal. 'That's a very Italian thing to say,' she muttered darkly.

'I *am* half Italian,' he reminded her.

She shot him a saucy look. 'And there was me, thinking you'd forgotten.'

Then she turned and just absorbed the scenery. They'd come from the relative quiet and muted tones of the smaller canals onto the wide strip of water that snaked through the centre of the city. Suddenly it was all light and colour.

Sunset seemed further away here, out of the shadows of the tall buildings, where the remaining light reflected off the water onto the palazzos and back into the sky. Awnings were pulled down over restaurants that lined the water's edge, and the spaces inside were bustling, full of warm light and moving people.

She looked across at him. 'Talking of trying, your mother is very pleased you're staying on.'

He gave her a resigned look. 'I know.'

'So why won't you let *her* try, Max?'

There she went again, tapping at his walls with her little pickaxe, testing them for weak spots.

'Have you ever listened to her side of the story?' she continued. 'Or have you always gone on what your father told you?'

Ouch.

She'd found one. A chink in his perception of his life that he hadn't even realised had been there. He tried to plug it up. 'I saw enough with my own eyes,' he replied gruffly. 'And my father rarely spoke of her.'

But the damage had been done. Memories started spilling into his brain, scenes of his parents' marriage. He'd always thought he'd understood what was going on so clearly, but it was as if this was another version of the same film, and different details sprang to life, tiny things that tipped everything on its head—the look of desperation in his mother's eyes, the way she'd sobbed late into the night, the way she'd looked at his father, with such adoration, in both good times and bad.

He drowned them out by taking another, busier route with the boat, so he had to give driving it his full concentration. He steered the boat down the canal and out towards St Mark's Square. It was full of gondolas of sighing tourists here, and he felt his irritation with the city, with its over-the-topness returning. Maybe Ruby had something in her idea of not wanting to give your heart and soul to something, only to be disappointed.

'Can *you* try?' she asked softly.

As always, she took what he was prepared to give and pushed him to cough up more. The sensation was one rather akin to having a particularly sticky plaster ripped off a tender patch of skin.

'And that's what happens in your family, is it?' He glanced skyward, noticing neither the pink drifting clouds nor the orange sky behind them. 'Last I heard, you were all for keeping parents at a safe distance.'

Ruby looked at her shoes. He couldn't see her cheeks, but he'd bet they were warmer than they'd been a few seconds ago. 'I didn't think you'd remember that,' she mumbled.

'Well, I did.' She could have been right, though. He managed to tune out most people most of the time, but there was something about Ruby that made him listen, even when he'd dearly like to switch everything off and sink into blessed silence. 'So maybe you should practise what you preach before you start lecturing me.'

She shuffled her feet and looked up at him, arms still hugging herself. 'Okay, maybe I should. But I've tried over the years with my father, Max, and he always keeps me at arm's length, no matter what.'

That was hard to believe. Look at her, with her large, expressive eyes, her zest for life, which still seemed to be

threatening to burst out of her, despite her slightly sub-
dued mood. He was having trouble *maintaining* a distance
of arm's length.

'Why?' he asked, glad for a chance to swing the inter-
rogation light her way.

Ruby sat down on one of the cushioned benches. Max
slowed the motor and brought the craft to a halt, letting it
bob on the canal as the pleasure boats, *vaporetti* and gondolas drifted past. He turned to lean against the steering
wheel and looked back at her.

She shook her head, staring out across the dark green
canal, now flecked with pink and gold from the setting
sun. 'It took me years to even come close to forming a the-
ory on that one. It's partly because he's so absorbed in his
work, and it's got worse the older he gets. There are only
so many weeks and hours left to educate the world about
the unique habitats the human race is ripping through, the
species we're forcing into extinction. How can one "flighty"
child compete against all of that?'

'What's the other part?'

Ruby looked up at him. 'He has plenty of friends and
colleagues who have wild children—celebrity offspring
syndrome, I've heard him call it. Over-indulged, privileged,
reckless. I think he wanted to save me from that.'

That was understandable, but surely anyone who knew
Ruby knew she wasn't that sort. She might be impulsive,
but that came from her creativity, not out of selfishness or
arrogant stupidity.

She sighed and stood up, walked to the back of the boat,
even though it was only a few steps. 'I came to understand
his logic eventually. I think he thinks that if he rations out
the attention and approval then he won't spoil me.' She
sighed again. 'It's so sad, especially as I know he wasn't
like that with my mother. He'd have given her anything.'

Max didn't say anything, mainly because he was rubbish at saying the right thing at the right time, but he also suspected she just needed room to talk.

'I can't live on the scraps he hands out,' she said sadly. 'He doesn't understand it, but women, be they wives or daughters or sisters, need more than that.'

They both fell into silence. Max thought of his mother, and wondered if Ruby was thinking of her too. He'd never wanted for approval from his father—not that the old man had ever said anything out loud—but they'd been so alike. It had been easy to see the things beneath the surface, hear the words his father had never been able to say. For the first time ever it struck him that maybe not everyone had that ability.

They'd been so different, Geoffrey and Serafina Martin. His mother emotional and demonstrative, his father stoic and silent. He'd always thought their extreme personality types should make them the perfect complement for each other, but maybe he'd been wrong. Maybe that had been the reason for his mother's midnight tears; she'd desperately needed to reap some of the tangible demonstrations of love she'd so generously sowed.

He nodded slowly. 'I'm starting to understand that.' He caught her eye. 'And it makes sense why it's easier to run away, rather than stay.'

He didn't like to say that. It went against everything in him, but he couldn't ignore the sense in it.

Ruby read him like a book. She laughed a soft little dry laugh. 'And you think you don't?'

Max stood up, his brows bunching together. No, he didn't run. He was the one that was solid, stuck things out.

She walked towards him, until she was standing right in front of him. 'You can't be fully committed to something if you keep part of yourself back. It's cheating—a bit like this lagoon.' She stretched her arm out to encompass the water, including the tiniest glimpse of the open sea in the distance. 'It looks like the deep blue sea, smells like it, tastes like it, but when you try and jump all the way in you find out how shallow it is. Commitment is easy when it's only ankle deep.'

Max wanted to be angry with her. He wanted to tell her she was so very wrong, but he couldn't. Instead he exhaled long and hard and met Ruby's enquiring gaze. 'That makes us two very similar creatures, then.'

She stared back at him, more than a hint of defiance in her expression. 'Yes.'

On the surface he and Ruby were chalk and cheese. She was quirky and outspoken, where he was taciturn and strait-laced. She was emotional and effusive, where he…wasn't. But underneath? Well, that was a whole different story.

Her eyes softened a little, but the hard-hitting honesty in them remained. 'Okay, I admit it. I'm a coward when it comes to my family. And maybe I do flit from thing to thing because I'm nervous about committing to anything fully, but you have to face it, Max, despite all your fine words, the only thing you're truly committed to when it comes to your family is your prejudice and lack of forgiveness.'

He turned and started up the engine again. The canals— even this wide, spacious one—we're closing in on him, and the sun would slip below the horizon soon. He headed out of the end of the Grand Canal and into the lagoon, so they could see the painfully bright orange smudge settling behind the monastery on Isola di San Giorgio. Out here the salty wind soothed him. He felt as if he could breathe properly again.

Ruby hadn't said anything since they'd set off again. She'd just sat down on the bench and crossed her arms. He slowed the motor and checked on her. She didn't look happy. He had a feeling he'd have no trouble keeping her at arm's length now. He might as well dig himself in further.

'Have you forgiven *your* father?'

She chewed her lip for a while. 'I hadn't realised I needed to, but maybe I do.' She looked up and noticed the sunset for the first time. 'Oh,' she said, her face lighting up, and Max couldn't bear to tear his eyes from her and turn around.

After staring for a moment, her focus changed and he could tell she was now studying him instead. 'I'm not sure it'll change anything. He'll probably still treat me the same way, but with you and Fina... It could change everything.'

'Maybe,' he said. And then he turned to watch the sun descend into the blue-grey water. They didn't say anything as it went down, just watched in silence, the only sound the gentle waves of the lagoon slapping against the hull of the little painted boat, then he started up the engine again. 'Do you want to go round the island?'

A twinkle of mischief appeared in her eyes, totally blind-siding him. 'You know what I'd really like?'

He shook his head.

'We're always being so safe when Sofia is in the boat, puttering around, going slow down the canals. I'd like to go out onto the open water and build up some speed, see what this little vintage baby can do.'

Max set off again at a moderate speed, at least until they'd rounded the large island in front of them and faced the open lagoon. Out here there was only the occasional ferry, plenty of room to let off some steam, and he discovered he was yearning for it as much as she was.

'Ready?' he asked, and shoved the throttle forward before she had time to answer.

Ruby squealed and hung on to the woodwork in front of her as the bow of the little boat lifted, skimming through the moonlit waves, and the wind rushed through their hair. At first she was silent, her breath taken by the change in speed, but as he circled around and the boat tilted she began to laugh, then she let out a loud whoop.

Max found himself laughing too, which was insane, seeing as how serious he'd been feeling only minutes earlier. He kept the speed up, took a few unexpected turns, raced the waves out towards Lido Island and then back again until they were both windswept and breathless.

As they circled the Isola di San Giorgio again, he reluctantly slowed the engine. The sky was a velvety midnight blue above them and the lights and reflections of Venice were threatening to outnumber the stars in their brilliance and beauty.

Ruby sighed. 'Can we stop here for a moment, before we head back home? I won't get a chance to see this again.'

He didn't answer, just circled one last time then flipped the key in the ignition and cut the engine. Ruby got up and walked shakily towards him as they got caught up in their own wake. She stopped before she got too close, though. Still out of reach. Just.

Another surge hit them. Max hardly noticed it, being used to boats as he was, but Ruby lost her footing, wobbled slightly.

Her arms, which had still been loosely hugged round herself, flew out for balance. At the same time he reacted on reflex and his hand shot out and curled round her elbow, steadying her.

Not at arm's length now. Not at all.

He looked down at where they were joined and wondered how hard it would be to let go. He looked up again to find Ruby's eyes large, but her expression calm and open. Very hard, he decided. Even after the boat had rocked itself back into equilibrium he found he hadn't been able to do it.

But maybe he didn't need to.

He slipped his hand down her arm, over her wrist, until his fingers met hers, and he laced them together, reminding himself of those intersecting arches he'd stolen for his design. How simple the shapes were on their own, but how much better they were when they were joined with something similar.

He reached for her other hand, meshed it to his in the same way. She looked down at their intertwined fingers, so tangled up with each other that he couldn't tell whether he was holding her or she was holding him, and then she looked back up at him, her breathing shallow, her cheeks flushed.

This was *way* more than ankle deep.

Gently he tugged, and she came. Their hands remained joined, and he bent his head to brush his lips against hers. It wasn't enough. He kissed her again, lingering this time. Ruby sighed and leaned against him. Gently she slid her fingers from his and ran her hands up his arms, onto his neck. He could feel her fingertips on the bare skin above his collar, her thumbs along his jaw.

She pulled away and opened her eyes. He looked back at her. Her fingers continued to roam, exploring his jaw and temple, tracing his cheekbones, and then they kissed again, sinking into it.

It wasn't like their first meeting of lips. It wasn't hot and urgent, fuelled by simple physical need, but neither was it hesitant and testing. It was slow and intimate, as if they'd been lovers for years, nothing but truth flowing between them, even if he was a little fuzzy on what exactly that truth was.

As the bells of the far away *campanili* rang out across the lagoon, and Venice glittered like a jewel in the distance, Max wrapped his arms around Ruby, pulled her as close as he could get. He might be rubbish with words, but he spoke to her in the poetry every Italian knew so well.

CHAPTER TWELVE

THEY DIDN'T GET BACK to the palazzo until well after nine. Max cut the engine and stared at the hulking exterior of his mother's house. Here, his and Ruby's roles were defined for them, clearly marked out. Out there on the lagoon, there had been nothing but a delicious blurring of all the reasons they shouldn't be together.

Ruby jumped out of the boat, took the rope from him and secured it to a post. Max stayed where he was in the boat.

He didn't want to go back inside.

For the last hour he'd felt alive again, free. The grief that had been the wallpaper of his life since his father's death had evaporated briefly, but now it was back again, slamming into his chest with such force he had to draw in a breath.

Ruby smiled at him, a sweet, beguiling smile, but he found he couldn't return it. Shutters were clanging up fast inside him, like those in a bank when the panic button had been pressed, and by the time he climbed out of the boat and headed inside no chink remained.

Each step up the staircase made him feel heavier, as if gravity were increasing.

'Max?' Ruby said as they reached the top, her eyes clouded with worry. He wanted to tell her it wasn't anything to do with her, that she was the only bright spot in his life at the moment, but the words didn't even make it up his throat, let alone out of his mouth.

He did what he could: he reached for her hand, caught it in his and wove his fingers into hers the way he'd done back on the boat just before he'd kissed her.

He saw relief flood her features and the smile came back. Sweeter this time, softer. What he wouldn't give to just lose himself in that smile.

'You have returned?' His mother's voice came from inside the salon.

Ruby jumped and slid her fingers from his before his mother appeared in the doorway. His skin felt cold where hers had just been.

'Why don't you come and have a coffee with me and tell me all about it?'

His mother looked hopefully at him, and Ruby joined her.

His head started to swirl—with the memories that had assaulted him earlier, with the conversation he'd had with Ruby out on the lagoon. He knew he should try with his mother, knew he should at least let her share her side of the story, that going in for coffee now would be a tiny and harmless step in that direction, but he couldn't seem to make his feet move.

'Max?' Ruby said, her smile disappearing, her brow creasing.

He felt as if he were made of concrete. 'I'm sorry,' he said, his voice a little hoarse, 'but I need to make up the time I took away from my work.'

Ruby's face fell. His mother just stared at him.

'I'm sorry,' he said again, and strode off in the direction of the library.

Ruby and Fina watched Max go. When the library door had shut behind him, Fina sighed and turned back into the salon.

'I don't blame him, you know,' she said as she walked to the coffee table and poured espresso into delicate cups. 'When things were at their worst between me and Geoffrey, I didn't behave well. He probably has many memories that make it easy for him to hate me.'

Ruby wanted to reach out to her, put a hand on her arm. 'I'm sure that's not true,' she said softly.

Fina shook her head. 'I loved that man, even though he was just as pig-headed as his son.' Fina sighed. 'I could have handled that. It was the fact he locked himself away...here.' She thumped her chest with her palm then looked Ruby right in the eye. 'I grew tired of hungering for something I thought he wouldn't—or couldn't—give me.'

Fina didn't pick up her coffee cup, but walked over to the windows and stared out. Ruby couldn't tell if she was focusing on the moon beyond or her reflection in the glass.

'I had glimpses of the man underneath,' she said. 'Foolishly, I thought that once we were married the process of slowly unravelling all that bound him would start. I tugged, pulled at threads, but I could never find the right place to begin.'

Ruby swallowed. She knew all about glimpses. Knew all about how tantalising they could be.

'In the end I used to do anything I could to provoke emotion from him. Anger was the easiest. I told myself that if I could make him feel *something* it proved he still cared.' She shook her head and looked at Ruby. 'I pushed him and pushed him. Doing things, saying things, I shouldn't have. And each time I had to try harder, do more. I must have seemed like a monster to my son, but really I was just...' She paused, struggling for the right word.

'Desperate?' Ruby finished for her.

Fina gave her a grateful look. 'Yes.' She looked back at

her reflection in the window. 'And in the end I succeeded. I pushed him to the ultimate limit.'

Ruby held her breath for a moment. 'What did you do?'

Fina blinked. 'I left him.'

Ruby stepped closer.

'It broke him,' Fina continued, her tone taking on a ragged quality. 'I finally had my proof. But I could never go back. I'd done too much damage.'

Ruby didn't know what to say, which was just as well, because if she'd tried to speak, tears would have coursed down her face. She just nodded, letting Fina know she was listening.

'It's my fault Massimo is the way he is,' Fina added softly, 'so I cannot be angry with him. I just don't want him to harden himself further, end up like his father.' She paused a moment and heaved in a breath. Ruby sensed she was trying not to lose composure completely. 'I shouldn't have left him behind, but I thought I was doing the right thing. He had his school...and Geoffrey adored him. I couldn't rob him of his son, too.'

'Of course you couldn't,' Ruby said.

Fina suddenly turned to face her, grabbed her hands and leaned in. 'Be careful when you fall in love,' she said hoarsely. 'It is a curse to love something so much, believe it is in easy reach, and then discover it will always be kept beneath lock and key.' Fina sighed dramatically and dropped her hands.

Ruby nodded and then stepped away, walked back to the table and picked up her espresso. She finished it quickly, even though it felt like gravel going down.

'I'd better check on Sofia,' she mumbled, then fled from the room.

Fina knew. Ruby didn't know how. Maybe she'd worked out that Ruby's dishevelled appearance after the boat ride

had been down to more than a brisk twilight wind, but she
knew. And she was warning Ruby off.

The morning was clear and bright. A light mist hovered over the lagoon and the Damiani family boat carved
through it at speed as it headed away from the city and out
into the open water. Max stood at the wheel, breeze lifting
his hair, and concentrated on pinpointing their location. It
had been a long time since he'd visited this place and he
knew if he didn't pay attention that he'd miss it altogether.

'Where go?' Sofia piped up from the back of the boat.

He glanced over his shoulder and gave her a smile. Sofia
was snuggled up between Ruby and his mother and all three
of them were surrounded by a jumble of beach equipment—
an umbrella, a picnic basket, various bags containing sun-
screen and towels and changes of clothes.

He deliberately didn't catch Ruby's eye. Mainly because
he was only just hanging on to the last bit of his control.
The urge to touch her every time he saw her was quickly
becoming overpowering—and had led to a few interesting stolen moments over the few days since their sunset
trip. She was like a drug. The more he had, the more he
wanted. Needed.

He took a deep breath and forced himself to behave. His
mother and his not quite three-year-old niece were also in
the boat; that should help somewhat. And it did. Just about.

'We're going to the beach,' he told Sofia and turned back
round to concentrate on where he was going. A few moments later he slowed the motor and peered around, first at
the water directly in front of the boat and then at the horizon,
checking the location of various landmarks on the coast.

This was it. He was sure it was. He cut the motor and
let down the small anchor.

'Want beach,' Sofia said, most determinedly, and Max
threw her another smile.

'We're here.'

Ruby frowned at him. 'Don't tease her. She doesn't understand.'

'I'm not teasing,' he said. She was even adorable when she was cross with him, which was just as well, really, seeing as he was rather good at getting her in that state. He turned his attention to Sofia.

'This is a magic beach. You just wait and see.' And he stuck his thumb and forefinger in his mouth and whistled loudly. 'That's what gets the magic started,' he explained.

His mother just patted the child's hand and looked back at him with soulful eyes. This place had always been special to him, a highlight of their family holidays each year, and he knew she was experiencing the same rush of memories that he was. He'd thought it would help, bring them a sense of connection, but he managed to return her gaze for a second or so before he looked away.

He didn't have many memories of his father in Venice, especially as he'd often worked through the long summer holidays and had only joined them for snatched days and weekends, but this had been one of his favourite places. He'd been charmed by the sheer contrariness of it.

The tide had caused the boat to swing on its anchor slightly, just as he'd planned, and now he gave Sofia a salute, kicked off his shoes and jumped overboard.

'No!' screamed Ruby and stood up, but then she sat back down again with a plop when she realised he was standing and the water was only lapping round his calves. Sofia ran over to the edge of the boat and peered over the edge.

Ruby gave him an exasperated look and mouthed an insult that wasn't fit for Sofia's ears. He grinned back at her. Some primal part of him was stupidly pleased she'd been worried for him. She shook her head and smiled, rolling her eyes.

He didn't want to move, didn't want to do anything but

stand here, the water turning his toes pruney, and look at her. It was the kind of thing he'd mocked his friends for doing when they'd met someone special, and had never, ever expected to fall prey to himself. He had to force himself to look away.

'Told you it was magic,' he said, and lifted Sofia out of the boat, lifejacket and all, and put her down beside him, careful to keep a grip on her hand. Sofia squealed, at first from the surprise of the cold water, but then from delight. He walked along a short length of the hidden sandbank just under the water then back to the boat.

'It's all very well having a magic beach,' Ruby said, trying to maintain an air of superiority and failing, 'but what good is it if it stays underwater?'

'You just wait and see. Coming in?'

Ruby nodded, and began stripping off her skirt to reveal shapely legs and the bottom half of her swimming costume. His mouth dried. He turned to his mother and raised an eyebrow.

'Don't be an idiot, Massimo. I'm far too old to be wading about in the lagoon. You just carry on and I'll enjoy the sun in the boat for a while.'

He nodded and held out his hand to Ruby so she could steady herself getting out of the boat. Once she was in the shallow water, they placed themselves either side of Sofia and went exploring. The remains of what once might have been an island was tiny, maybe only thirty metres by ten, but as they splashed around in the shallows, swinging Sofia between them, the tide crept away and revealed a perfect golden sandbank.

Sofia stood on the damp sand and stared at the grains beneath her feet. 'Magic,' she whispered. 'How do, Unc Max?'

He crouched down beside her. 'I whistled and it came.'

Sofia jammed all five fingers of her left hand in her

mouth and puffed. 'No work,' she said, after she'd pulled them out again.

'That's because learning to whistle takes practice,' he told her. 'You have to do it again and again until you're good at it. When you're older, you'll be able to call the island, too. Everyone in our family can.' In the meantime, he showed her the basics—how to pucker her lips, how to blow gently. Sofia didn't manage to produce more than a raspy sound, but she seemed quite happy trying.

He looked up at Ruby. 'Can you whistle?'

She smiled and rolled her eyes. 'Not like you. In comparison my efforts seem pathetic.'

Max stood up, still holding Sofia's hand. The patch of sand was growing now, the almost imperceptible tilt of the land helping the tide to recede rapidly. 'Let's all whistle together, and perhaps the rest of the island will come.'

So they stood solemnly in a row, faced the lagoon, and blew, his whistle loud and long, Ruby's slightly throaty, with a unique little trill at the end, and Sofia's determined puffing filling out their little orchestra.

It was strange. He'd found it hard to be at the island again at first, but bringing Ruby here was changing that. Somehow she soothed the dark voices in his head away, made him believe he could be free of them one day.

When they'd finished they headed back to the boat and began unloading their beach stuff. He set up the umbrella and spread the blanket while Ruby held on to Sofia. Fina directed from the bow of the boat, and only when it was all set up to her liking did she consent to let him pull the boat closer so she could step onto dry sand.

They ate their lunch under the umbrella, a simple affair of meats and cheeses, bread and olives, and when they'd finished Ruby grabbed a towel, headed out from under the shade of the umbrella and laid it on the sand. She unbuttoned her white, Fifties-style blouse and shrugged it off, to reveal a matching swimsuit.

Not matching in colour, because it was a deep ruby red with large black roses all over it, but matching in style. It was one of those weird things he'd seen in old-fashion photos, with a wide halter-neck strap, a ruched front and a leg line that was low, completely covering her bottom and reaching to the tops of her thighs. It should have been un-flattering, and on many women it would have looked like a Halloween costume, but on Ruby it looked sensational. She reminded him of those sirens with the rosy cheeks, red lips and long legs that he'd seen painted on the side of wartime planes.

'I didn't think you'd remember the whistle,' his mother muttered beside him, her eyes a little misty.

His first reaction was to bristle, to bat the comment away and pretend he hadn't heard it. Of course he'd remembered. It had been his father's trick to call the island that way. For a man who'd had a hard time expressing his emotions, he'd been unusually imaginative. It had made him a good ar-chitect, but it had made him an even better father, soften-ing the gruff edges.

He turned and watched Ruby as she finished getting her towel just so, then lay down on top of it to face the sun.

He thought about her willingness to try and try again, even when things didn't go according to plan. She never gave up, never locked herself away from new experiences. Never locked herself away from hope that it would all turn out right one day. She wasn't weak and flaky, as he'd thought her. She was strong. Resilient.

And she was right. He needed to try with his mother. Not just for the sake of his family, but because he wanted to be the kind of man who was worthy of Ruby Lange. The kind of man who knew how to do more than just 'ankle deep'. That was what she needed, and that was what he wanted to give her.

His mother was staring out to sea, and had obviously given up on him giving her an answer. For the first time he saw it—what Ruby had been trying to tell him about— the deep pain behind her eyes. The same kind of desolation he'd seen his father wear in unguarded moments, the same one that had eaten away at him, until it had sucked the life right out of him.

Something warm flooded his chest. Something that wasn't bitterness or rage or judgement, something that made him remember how warm and kind she'd been when he'd been younger, how she'd have given anything for her children, and even more for her husband.

Words rushed around inside his head, the beginnings of sentences. The beginnings of a truce.

But none of them left his mouth. It felt as if he were looking at his mother from behind a large sheet of bulletproof glass. There was so much he wanted to say, so many questions he wanted to ask, but he found he could release none of them. It wouldn't come, even though, for the first time in almost two decades, he wanted it to. He wanted to *try*.

Eventually his mother picked up a book and began to read. Max sat there, adrenaline making his blood surge and his skin prickle, but anyone looking at him would have thought he was resting his hands on his knees, relaxing in the sun. He twisted his head and searched for a flowery red and black costume.

For most of his life he'd been proud when people had called him his father's son, when they'd remarked on the likeness, not just in looks but in temperament, but for the first time that pride chilled into fear. If he was the cookie-cutter offspring everyone always said he was, there was a real chance that he would never deserve a woman like Ruby Lange.

CHAPTER THIRTEEN

RUBY RETURNED TO THE SALON that evening after dinner to tidy some of Sofia's things away. She sorted through a stack of drawing papers, thinking she'd find one or two to present to Fina as a memento of Sofia's visit.

She reached a shortlist of seven. Some drawings that she'd done and Sofia had coloured in, and a few of her charge's own creations. They needed skilful interpretation, but the intent was there. Ruby stopped as she stared at a page that was filled with different-coloured crayon blobs, all lined up. The shocking pink blob was Fina, apparently. The smaller one next to her, a vibrant, bright yellow, was Sofia herself. The dark blue one off to the side, looking a bit like a navy, vertical thundercloud, was Max. Ruby had giggled at that when Sofia had pointed it out.

That only left the purple blob.

The purple blob so close to the blue one they practically merged at the edges, creating an indigo smudge.

It was understandable, Ruby supposed, that Sofia should put her and Max next to each other. She spent a lot of time with the pair of them, after all. Ruby had smiled when Sofia had told her the scribble of purple was her, honoured to have been included, but now she looked at it she realised just how much artistic licence Sofia had taken.

But Max didn't do that, did he? He didn't let his edges blur like that. And maybe he never would.

That was what Fina had been trying to tell her.

Was she just fooling herself?

Ruby sighed and sank onto the rug. The pieces of paper she'd collected fluttered out of her hand and fell onto the floor unseen. She was so confused.

They'd spent a lot of time together over the last five days. Not just the morning outings with Sofia, but in the evenings Fina often disappeared to visit her friend Renata after they'd eaten dinner, then Ruby would creep into the library and she'd have a glorious hour or two alone with Max.

When she was with him, everything was amazing and she couldn't think about anything else. When he kissed her, she felt as if she were touching something deep inside him. More and more he was giving her 'glimpses' of the real Max, and each time she dived deeper in she got lost a little more. One day soon there'd be no going back.

But then she'd leave him and the little doubts would start to creep in, nibbling away at her.

He had to feel the same way, didn't he? The truth of it rang between them every time they were in the same room together, and she really wanted to believe it, but...

Never once had he mentioned where this was going—or even *if* it was going—once their stay in Venice ended. Never once had he put words to how he felt about her, given her any hint about the future. Their days here were numbered; she knew that. Gia had phoned saying she needed a little longer in L.A., but the original fortnight was up in just two days' time.

She sighed and collected the pieces of paper together and put them away in the sideboard with the other drawing things, forgetting that she'd sorted out the masterpieces and jumbling them back in with the others again.

Once she was finished putting them away she headed for the library. Max was poring over his laptop, as usual, but when he saw her he got up from his chair and crossed the room to where she was standing just near the doorway. He stood close, far too close for a boss approaching his employee, then gave her an impish smile as he closed the door behind her, pressed her up against it and kissed her until her head was spinning and her lungs were convinced oxygen was just a deep and distant memory.

When he pulled back to look at her, she saw a flash of something in his eyes. Something deep. Something true. It sent her heart spinning like the waltzer at the fairground. She so wanted to forget about tomorrow and just do what felt right for now, but that was how she'd spent her whole life so far, and it was time to step back and take a more mature approach. Where Max was concerned, she really needed to pay attention to the big picture.

She wanted him to say something.

Exactly what, she didn't know. Just something. Something that she didn't have to prise out of him. Something to let her know what was happening between them, if he was as confused as she was, but Max just leaned in and stole another kiss. It made her blood dance right down to her toes.

She pulled away, looked him in the eyes. 'What are we doing?' she whispered.

Just one of Max's eyebrows hitched up a little. 'I thought we'd covered enough ground for you to be sure, but if you want a little more demonstration?'

He leaned close again, but Ruby stopped him with her hands on his chest. Hands that dearly craved a little more 'demonstration', but she forced them to stay put instead of using them to explore him further.

'I mean *us*. Is this just a holiday fling, or what?'

He frowned. She'd upset him, she could tell, but she had to know. She'd spent her whole life straining for the crumbs one man doled out to her. She'd had no choice but to accept what her father gave her, but with Max she did, and she'd be insane to follow that pattern with him. *Glimpses* were all well and good for now, but for the long term? That was like trying to nourish yourself with only a diet of canapés for the rest of your life.

'Ruby? Don't you know?'

She shook her head. All she knew was that she had a choice: dive in and hope that one day Max would shed the same chains that had bound his father, or run now before things got even more serious.

More serious? Hah. She was kidding herself. She was already half in love with him. It wouldn't take much more to push her over the precipice.

Max's hands moved to circle her waist, to pull her as close as she could possibly get without their physical boundaries blurring just as they had done in Sofia's drawing. *'Lascia che ti mostri.'*

Let me show you.

When he touched her lips with his again she just about melted clean away. She'd thought she'd experienced passion from Max before. She now realised they'd just been paddling in the shallows. But even as he unleashed the force of it on her, as the kiss continued, she got the sense that Max was a like a dam, holding back the pressure of a million gallons of water. There was still more beneath, so much more.

She wanted him to tear that last barrier down, to unleash the torrent and let it sweep her away, but the structure was solid, impenetrable. Nothing she could do could get it to crack. A tiny part of her cried out in pain as she realised that, even in this, Max was holding himself back.

He picked her up and carried her to the small love seat in the corner of the room, and they both fell onto it in a tangle of arms and legs, hot breath and pounding hearts, and as his lips found the curve of her neck and his hands smoothed down her body she discovered something did crumble after all. But it was all her good resolves, not him.

* * *

Ruby lay in bed that evening and reached for her mobile phone, which had lain untouched most of the last fortnight. Partly because it was too expensive to turn data roaming on, but also because she was avoiding communication from her father about The Job.

However, she'd started fantasising about carrying on back in London with Max, about being the kind of woman he'd consider sharing his life with. That clearly meant that the world was upside down and back-to-front, and she obviously needed a sharp dose of reality to counteract that and help her think straight. And a *What have you done now?* lecture and an exorbitant phone bill would do nicely on that front.

Just as she feared, an email from dear old dad was lurking in her inbox. She shifted position, took a deep breath and opened it.

FAO: Ruby Lange.

That was typical Dad. Other people started emails with *Hi!* or *Hey!* or just launched into the subject at hand as quickly as possible. Only Patrick Lange could make an informal communication sound like a court summons.

Dear Ruby,
I had hoped to hear from you by now on your current employment situation. I understand from your flatmate that you are in Europe somewhere, doing something, but she could not enlighten me any further. Would you care to? I'm holding the job open for you, and I'd greatly appreciate it if you could let me know if you're going to take it. There are plenty of other people who would kill for this kind of opportunity, you know.

Yes, she knew. He'd told her often enough.

You need to approach life with a more adult attitude, Ruby. You can't flit around for ever 'finding yourself'. At your age it's time you stopped running away from responsibility and started embracing it.

I need to know about the production assistant position before next Monday. Please get in contact and let me know.
Dad x

Ruby scowled at her mobile screen. No *I know I've been incommunicado for a month, but how are you doing, Ruby?* No *Great you've found yourself a new job, Ruby!* Just judgement and how much she was disappointing him, as always.

She knew she really shouldn't message angry, but she couldn't help herself.

Thanks for the vote of confidence, Dad.

Much to her surprise, her message alert went off a few minutes later.

Ruby, understand that I don't say the things I do to hurt you. You have so much potential and it's a crime to waste it drifting from thing to thing. The job offer stands. I think you might enjoy it, and I expect you will be good at it. You have just the right kind of energy the team needs. D x

Ruby flipped her phone case closed and put her mobile back on the bedside table. She didn't know whether to be angry that she'd finally forced him into giving her a back-handed compliment or just stupidly happy he thought she could be good at something. She folded her arms across her chest on top of the quilt and stared at the ceiling.

Well, she'd wanted reality, and her father had dished up some five-star fare.

But there was a difference between not being able to stick with something and not wanting to. Why didn't he understand that?

Because it looks the same, smells the same, tastes the same...

No. It wasn't the same. It was always her choice. Always her decision.

You choose to get that itchy feeling, want to feel it torment you until you have no other option but to outrun it?

She scowled at the pretty looping baroque designs on the ceiling. Now even her subconscious was ganging up on her. That wasn't true, was it? That feeling of being pinned down, of getting so close to something to feel its heat, to feel how much it could scorch and burn, that wasn't what made her seek out new and exciting things. It couldn't be.

But as she followed the patterns and shapes on the ceiling with her eyes she catalogued all the jobs she'd had over the last five years, all the people and places she'd thought she'd become attached to, and she discovered there wasn't one time that she hadn't left because, not only had her feet got itchy, but her whole being had got itchy. She used to think it was the yearning for fresh pastures that made her feel that way, but now she was staring it in the face, dissecting it and pulling it apart, she saw it for what it really was.

Fear.

Plain and simple.

You're not a free spirit, Ruby Lange. You're a coward.

There wasn't one time she hadn't succumbed to that itch, except...

Except that night almost a week ago on the dock, when it had been itching so hard she'd almost jumped into the canal to stop the burning. When Max had asked her to stay. And she had.

Ruby let out a long and shuddering breath.

She wanted to stick with Max. No matter what. She wanted that with all her heart.

The realisation shocked her. It should have made her heart race and her breathing shallow, but all she felt instead of blind panic was a strange but not unwelcome sense of peace creeping up on her.

Ruby threw the covers back, jumped out of bed and walked over to stare out of the window. For some reason, the gently lapping water soothed her, helped her think.

She had to be sure about this.

Not just about Max's feelings for her, but about her feelings for Max. If they went forward with this, and he held back from her, she knew she wouldn't be able to stay around and let her heart endlessly beg for more. Look at what that had done for Fina.

But she also knew that if she dived into this relationship, and then bailed, it might seal his fate. He would shut down completely. And that would lead to consequences, not just for her, but possibly for Fina and Sofia and the rest of his family. Max had so much to give, if he would only let himself, and she didn't want to be the reason he didn't.

She started to pace. Back and forth, back and forth she went. She finally fell into bed and tossed back and forth there too. At 3:00 a.m. she punched her pillow hard and let out a low moan of frustration.

The only thing solid she could come up with was that she'd rather be with Max than without him. And she could do it, she knew she could, but it was one thing for her to be sure of it, and another entirely to convince Max of the same.

Another realisation hit her straight between the eyebrows. Maybe that was why he was holding back! Maybe it was nothing to do with him and everything to do with her.

She wouldn't blame him if he didn't trust her not to run when things got sticky. Her track record was all hundred-metre dashes: exciting and adrenaline-inducing while they lasted, but over quickly and leaving everyone feeling burnt out and exhausted. She needed to convince him she was capable of a marathon; that she'd changed in the space of two short weeks and was ready to do more. Be more. That she was a safe pair of hands for his heart.

But how?

Words wouldn't be enough. Max was all about the concrete, the tangible evidence. She'd have to prove it to him in no uncertain terms. She went back to staring at the ceiling, familiar with its intricate patterns and leafy trails now, and after only a few moments the solution dropped into her brain with a thud.

Of course! It was perfect.

She rolled over, picked up her phone and began typing in an email with her thumbs.

CHAPTER FOURTEEN

THE PLANS FOR the institute were almost finished. It was just as well, because, although he had got up at four the last few days to put in the hours needed, the whole time he worked away at his desk there was an internal timer that clicked away within him, counting down the seconds to ten o'clock, when he could rise from his desk, shove the papers away and go and see her.

Every day was a surprise, something new. And he didn't just mean her wardrobe, although it was an endless source of fascination to him that the handful of clothes she'd stuffed into that rucksack could be combined in so many different ways to create so many different looks.

No, he meant Ruby. Every day she brought him something fresh, something exciting. When he'd first met her, he'd thought she needed to grow up and settle down, but now he realised how fearless, how magnificent she was. He didn't want her to change a thing about herself.

The timer on his watch beeped at him and he looked up from his desk. Two minutes to ten. It was time. He'd done his duty, done his hours, and now he could spend time with Ruby. He didn't even mind that Sofia was always thrown into the mix.

To be honest, he was glad to have a reason to take things slowly. Otherwise he wasn't sure he'd be able to help himself. She wanted new experiences? She wanted romance?

He wanted to show her just how amazing Venice could be, just how it could imprint itself on a soul. He wanted to talk about dreams and plans and for ever. And he would have done, if not for one thing: he didn't want to scare her off. It was only a supreme act of will that prevented him spilling it all out to her and laying it at her feet.

Breathe, Max. Give the girl time. Don't spook her.

He just needed to get the groundwork in before Gia arrived back to claim Sofia.

He slowed in the corridor that led to the salon, took a moment to inhale and exhale, and then he turned the corner and walked through the door.

As he often found them when he arrived for his morning session with his niece, she and Ruby were drawing. Sofia was colouring-in a princess in a flowing robe, having got over her 'naughty fish' obsession, and Ruby was bent over her sketchbook. He crept up behind her while she was absorbed and sneaked a look.

She was working on a drawing of a gondola floating in front of a palazzo. Her style was interesting. She often drew in black pen, but the lines were always fluid and emotive. It should have given a messy look to the sketch, but somehow she managed to get the shape and structures perfectly without making it look staid and formal, something he could never have done. And he could see she was growing, developing. There was a new confidence in her work that hadn't been there when she'd arrived.

That was the elusive 'niche' she'd been looking for, he was sure of it, but he sensed she lacked confidence to pursue it. He wondered what he could do to encourage her. She'd helped him rediscover the real excitement and passion that had been missing from his work for months now, and he'd like to return the favour.

She started, suddenly realising he was close, jumped up and turned round, smiling. 'Nosey,' she said.

The air crackled between them, and he bent down and stole a kiss. 'Guilty as charged.' He nodded at his niece, who'd almost finished obliterating her princess in a cloud of bright orange crayon so thick one could hardly see the black lines of Ruby's pen underneath.

Ruby chuckled. 'She's nothing if not thorough. I have no idea where she gets that from.'

'Shut up,' he said. 'Are you ready to go?'

She nodded. 'We're off to feed the pigeons in St Mark's Square, right?'

He didn't answer. When he'd mentioned pigeons, it wasn't necessarily feeding them he'd been thinking about, seeing as the city was trying to actively discourage it. Chasing them had been a much preferred boyhood pastime, one he thought Sofia would enjoy with equal relish, and almost verged on the side of civic duty these days, as the birds caused so much damage to the delicate buildings and statues.

When Ruby stood back, he frowned. Something was different. Something was not quite right....

And then he realised what it was. He'd seen that outfit before. It was the plain T-shirt and jeans she'd worn a couple of times before, but today it was unadorned. No loops of beaded necklaces, no vintage waistcoat, no floaty scarves. It was most odd. But since Ruby had always been one to defy expectation where her wardrobe was concerned, he supposed she was following true to form.

It should have only taken ten minutes to walk to St Mark's from Ca' Damiani, but it took Max, Ruby and Sofia closer to twenty. Mostly because they didn't bother with the buggy and had to accommodate Sofia's tiny little legs. When they were there, Sofia delighted in chasing the pigeons, which flew up in clouds as she cut a path through them, but settled back down nearby only seconds later.

He and Ruby watched on from the sidelines, smiling.

He reached over and took her hand, relished the feel of her warm skin in his. She always felt that way, never cold, always soft and inviting.

'That drawing you were doing this morning was very good,' he told her. 'I really think you should do something with it.' He thought about the overpriced prints and postcards for the tourists, the sickly, sentimental paintings in some of the shops that sold carnival masks by the bucketload. 'Your drawings of Venice are better than a lot of what's out there.'

He thought she'd be pleased at some encouraging words, but she pressed her lips together and stared out across the vast square with its arcades and hundreds of pillars. 'Nah,' she said, lifting just one shoulder in a little shrug. 'I think it's better if I keep it as a hobby for now.'

His brows drew together as he waited for her to carry on, say something more cheery and upbeat, but she just let out a huge sigh. Something really was different, and it wasn't just the wardrobe.

'Come on,' he said, 'let's walk a bit more.'

She nodded and called for Sofia, who wasn't that enthralled at the idea of leaving the pigeons alone, but she came without too much grizzling.

It wasn't just today, was it? This strange behaviour. There had been little things for the past few days. Tiny things he'd hardly noticed when they'd been random, individual occurrences, but now they were building to make something bigger, forming themselves into a pattern. She'd been quieter, more restrained. She'd laughed less. And there was something else, too, about the way she looked that was different. Something other than the lack of accessories. He just couldn't put his finger on what it was.

Was this connected to the drawing thing?

She talked about passion, about wanting to find it. It was clear to him that drawing was what she really loved to do. She couldn't *not* do it. He couldn't count the number of scraps of paper, backs of receipts, paper napkins he'd seen her sketches on in the last couple of weeks. So why did she resist it? Why did she avoid it when the thing that tugged her heart most was under her nose?

They walked out towards the Doge's Palace. He'd been going to tell her some interesting facts about it, things linked to conversations they'd had earlier in the week, but now it just felt like the wrong thing to do, so they strolled in silence to the water's edge and stared over to Isola di San Giorgio. Out on the lagoon, he could see the exact spot he'd cut the motor on their sunset trip, but there was no moonlight now, no gently flickering stars, just bright sun, beating down on them and bleaching all the shadows away.

'I've got something to tell you,' she said, after they'd been staring at the water for a couple of minutes. 'It's really great news.'

She twisted to look at him, but the smile she wore seemed hollow, like the trompe l'oeil in his mother's salon. It had the appearance of reality, but there was no depth to it.

'I've decided to take the job with my father's production company.' She looked at him, waiting for a response.

Max froze as the vague feeling that had plagued him all morning solidified into something hard and nasty, turning his insides cold. This wasn't her dream, her passion. In fact, it was the very opposite of what she'd said she'd wanted out of life.

He shook his head. 'Why?'

Her smile disappeared. '*Why?* Not "well done, Ruby. Good on you for choosing something you're going to stick to"?'

His mouth moved. He had *not* seen that coming. 'I thought it was the last thing you wanted.'

She shrugged and bent to retie Sofia's shoelace, which had come undone, then stood up again. 'I thought about what you said about finding the perfect thing by doing the hard stuff. Maybe you're right. And since my parents were both nuts about television and nature, maybe it's in my genes. Who knows?'

'Don't do it,' he said, and she turned to face him, shocked.

'Max, you are making no sense. I thought you'd be overjoyed at this. I thought you'd understand.'

He could tell she was hurt by the way she folded her arms across her middle, by the way she rubbed the toe of her shoe against the flagstones.

'It's too late, anyway' she said quietly. 'I've already formally accepted the offer.'

'When?'

The toe ground harder into the floor. 'Two days ago.'

He wanted to grab hold of her, to tell her not to turn her back on her dreams, to run with them and to hell with the consequences. He wanted to tell her to try every damn job in the universe if she liked, not to care what anybody else said, as long as she didn't give up. This was worse. This was way worse than not finishing something. For some reason he sensed Ruby was waving the white flag of defeat.

He wanted to tell her all of that and more. That he loved her. That he wanted her to brighten his day every day for the rest of his life. But he didn't. Couldn't. What if he got too intense too soon and scared her away? He didn't think he could bear it.

He opened his mouth, got ready to say something. Anything. He had to tell her something of how he felt, even if he only let a fraction of it slip, but then he realised what he'd been trying to put his finger on, what else had changed about her. He closed his mouth again and stared.

As she looked at her feet the sun glinted off her dark hair. It looked beautiful, shiny and thick, but not one hint of purple remained.

* * *

Ruby knocked softly on the library door. It was ten past ten and Max hadn't turned up for their usual session with Sofia. The day was grey and drizzly, the mist hanging so low over the whole city that the tops of the buildings seemed to melt into the white sky. A castle-building session was much needed.

'Yes?' came his reply from behind the door.

Ruby hesitated for a second. He didn't sound angry exactly, but there was a definite edge to his voice. She pushed the door and leaned in, keeping her feet on the threshold. 'It's past ten.'

He didn't turn round for a moment, just kept making deft, straight lines on a piece of paper with a pencil. When he turned round a faint scowl marred his features. It was just the concentration of working on his plans, right? As far as she was aware she hadn't done anything wrong in the last few days. In fact, she was doing her level best to do everything right, to prove to Max that she could be the kind of woman he could rely on.

'I don't think I'm going to be able to join you today,' he said, his voice neutral.

'Oh.' It took Ruby a moment to adjust to that information. They'd got into such a rhythm that it felt as if they'd missed a step and everything had jarred. And then there was the fact that he hadn't taken the opportunity to grab her, press her up against the wall and kiss her until she was breathless, a ritual she'd come to look forward to.

'But you promised your mother—'

'I promised my mother I'd stick to her terms for a week. I did that—and more. My agreement with her has ended, Ruby.'

She frowned, then nodded. She hadn't thought about it that way, but she supposed he was right. He hadn't needed to come out with her and Sofia for the last week. It should have made her happy that he'd possibly done so in order to spend time with her, but the expression on his face stopped that. It was like glass. Hard, solid, reflecting everything back at her.

He also hadn't softened one iota with his mother. That scared her. And not just for Fina's sake. Were those walls of his ever going to come fully down?

'The deadline for getting the final plans into the National Institute of Fine Art is next week,' he explained calmly. 'I have to focus on that for a while.'

'Okay,' she said slowly. For some reason she felt she was missing something here. Something big. Or was she just being paranoid? 'We'll miss you.'

Max just nodded. His body shifted, and she could tell he was itching to get back to his plans. She did her best not to take it personally, not to take it as a rejection.

'Will we see you at dinner this evening?'

A bit of the familiar, world-weary Max she'd met at the beginning of their trip returned. 'My mother has insisted I take you out to eat. She told me in no uncertain terms that it's a travesty that you've spent more than a fortnight in a city full of fabulous restaurants and haven't sampled their food yet.'

'Oh,' Ruby said again. 'That's lovely.'

Maybe Fina had decided she'd been wrong about what she'd said to her. Ruby had grown more and more suspicious that Fina's evenings out visiting Renata had quickly become an excuse to give them time alone together. Maybe she thought there was hope for her and Max after all.

Then why wasn't Ruby happy about that? Why did her stomach feel as heavy as a bowling ball?

Max just gave her a single nod.

Silence filled the space between them.

'Well…I'll just go and…' Ruby gestured in the direction of the salon. 'I'll see you this evening.'

'This evening,' Max echoed, but he'd already turned and started making swift lines on his plans.

Ruby slid her body from the space between door and frame and closed it softly behind her.

CHAPTER FIFTEEN

WHEN IT WAS TIME to leave that evening, instead of jumping in the launch via the boat door Max lead Ruby out of Ca' Damiani's tiny, almost dowdy street entrance, through a little, high-walled courtyard and out of a nondescript wooden door. There, the narrow *calle* opened onto a wider one, and within five minutes they had entered a secluded little square with a few restaurants and shops that were closed for the night.

They headed for an unremarkable-looking restaurant almost in the corner of the *campo*, with a dull, cappuccino-coloured awning and a few tables and chairs outside. The inside, however, was always a surprise after the mundane exterior. There were whitewashed brick walls and dark wood panelling. A counter stretched down one side, full of doors and drawers, reminiscent of an old-fashioned haberdashery shop. A gramophone perched on a table in the corner and glasses and bottles of wine filled what looked like a bookshelf at the far end of the space.

Ruby turned to him and grinned. He'd guessed she'd like this place. It was quirky and unique, as she was. And it didn't hurt that it served some of the best seafood in Venice.

They sat at a small table in the corner, overlooking the square, decked out in thick white linen and spotlessly shiny silverware.

It should have been romantic.

It was.

Well, it would have been, but for the conversation he knew had to come. One neither of them would like, but was totally, totally necessary. His plan to work on his designs that morning had been shot to pieces after Ruby's visit, and he'd spent the couple of hours until lunchtime mulling their situation over and over.

Ruby was changing herself. For him. He'd finally realised that when he'd noticed she'd dyed her hair. The clothes, the more sedate version of Ruby who'd appeared over the last couple of days…it all made sense now. And he hated himself for it.

He *needed* her to be the Ruby he'd fallen in love with, couldn't settle for anything less. Drastic action was needed.

He wanted to tell her that over dinner, as they ate their marinated raw fish starters, but it was as if there were a glass wall between them. Not a thin sliver, either, that could have been shattered with a ball or a fist, but one ten inches thick that repelled his words, weighed him down.

Was this what his father had felt when he'd looked at his mother? Everything swirling inside so hard and so fast he thought it might consume him with no way to let it out? He feared it was.

Geoffrey Martin had loved his vibrant Italian wife so much. Max had always known that, always respected it. But now he saw that maybe his father had grasped too hard and given too little back. Serafina had been what he'd needed to bring him out of his shell, balance him out, but he hadn't been what she'd needed. Or had chosen not to be. For the first time in his life, Max realised his father had been selfish, and that had created an imbalance in the relationship that had ultimately doomed it to failure.

The same kind of imbalance he was aware of when he thought about himself and the petite, vibrant woman sitting opposite him, eating her blackened sea bass.

He would not make the same mistake. He would not be a coward and make Ruby pay for his weakness. He wouldn't let her crush her spirit for him, deny everything she was and wanted to be. It was too high a price to pay. But there was only one way he could think of preventing that, even if it meant a colourless, bleak future ahead for himself. But he'd do it—for her.

He took a deep breath, hoping she'd answer differently this time, hoping she'd spare them both. 'Are you still determined to take that job with your father?'

Ruby looked up from her fish and met Max's gaze. When he'd mentioned going out to dinner this evening, she'd thought the conversation might have been a little more... intimate. This was a wonderful chance for them to be away from the palazzo, to be romantic with each other, and yet he wanted to talk about her father? Talk about a passion killer.

'Yes.' She was determined to show him she could stick at something, think about the big picture rather than just the details of the here and now.

He sighed. 'I wish you wouldn't.'

She put her knife and fork down and looked at him helplessly. 'Why?'

'Because it's not your passion.'

She reached for her wine glass. 'It could be my passion. Like you said, how do I know if I don't try?'

To be honest, she didn't care about the job. It was just a means to an end. What she was really passionate about was being with Max. But in his current strange mood, she wasn't sure he was ready to hear that. She'd do anything it took. Anything. Even taking that job with her father.

'And I can't say anything to change your mind?'

She shook her head. 'No.' Max wanted to see if she could stick to something? Well, she wasn't budging on this, even if it killed her.

He went back to eating his food, his expression grim. What had she said now?

They finished their meals, only punctuating the silence with odd snatches of meaningless conversation, until their espressos came, then Max sat up straighter and looked her in the eye. 'I need to talk to you about something…something important.'

His expression was so serious, but instead of making her jittery, it melted her heart. He was so earnest, so full of wanting to do the right thing, and she loved him for it. When Max's heart was in something, it was all-in, and she could allow him a little severity in return for that. She reached out and covered his hand with hers across the table. His skin felt cool and smooth.

'I told you when I hired you that this was going to be a two-week job at most and we've exceeded that now.'

This was it. This was the conversation. About where they were going when they got back to London, her stupid secret fantasies on the verge of coming true. Ruby forced herself to sit still and listen, which was hard with her heart fluttering about madly inside her ribcage like a trapped bird. She nodded, encouraging him to keep going.

'Well, I think it's time your contract came to an end.'

Ruby blinked. That wasn't what she'd expected him to say at all. Was this a particularly 'Max' way of saying their relationship was moving fully from professional to personal? 'Okay. So when are we heading back to London?'

He swallowed. 'I'm not, but you are.'

Ruby removed her hand from on top of his and sat back. 'I don't understand.'

'I can't begin to thank you for the way you've helped me change,' he said, and while his expression remained granite-like his eyes warmed. She could feel her heart reaching out to him, even as all her other instincts told her to back away. 'But it's time for me to fly solo.'

'What does that mean?'

He broke eye contact. 'I need to learn to interact with my family without having you there as both catalyst and buffer. I need to learn to do it on my own, Ruby.'

She shook her head, not really sure which bit of information she was rejecting, or why. 'But I can just keep out of the way... I can...'

He shook his head. 'You've been amazing, but now it's time for you to go home.' A gruff laugh followed. 'I'd say it was time for you to travel, to explore, to find whatever it is you're looking for in life, but you're determined to take that damn job with your father.'

She frowned. 'Yes, I am. But what has that got to do with anything?'

He just looked at her, as if he was trying to send a message with his eyes, but she got nothing. Those walls were back up, weren't they? He was shutting her out. Her stomach dropped as she realised that was what this had all been about. He'd been pulling away slowly for the last couple of days, hadn't he? She'd just been too stupidly in love with him to notice.

You've finally done it, Ruby. Brava. You've jumped in with your heart, given it wholly and completely, and the man you've given it to doesn't want it. He's handing it back to you on a plate. Thanks, but no, thanks.

Part of her couldn't quite believe it.

'But when you get back to London, will we...?'

Now the message from his eyes got through. Loud and clear.

No.

There would be no London.

There would be no Max for her. All they would ever have was what had happened here in Venice.

'Max?' she croaked.

He shook his head. 'I'm sorry, Ruby. Professionally speaking, I don't need you any longer.'

She swallowed. 'And personally?'

Max didn't say anything, just sat ramrod straight in his chair, jaw tense, eyes empty.

That was when the bird inside stopped fluttering madly. In fact, Ruby wasn't sure there was any movement at all any more.

She'd never been fired from a job—mainly because she always left before that kind of eventuality arose—but Max had managed to make her first experience of it a real doozy.

I don't need you.

Professional and personal rejection in one go. Nice shot.

She got up, threw her napkin down and walked out of the restaurant.

Thankfully, the fact they'd walked here meant she could find her way back to the palazzo on her own, and once there she'd pack. In *three* minutes. And then she'd be out of here, and there was no way Max Martin would stop her this time.

He caught up with her not long afterwards, as she was leaving a wider street and turning into a narrow, cobbled one.

'Ruby!'

Heavy footsteps pounded behind her, getting closer. She kept walking.

'Where are you going?' He didn't sound flustered or bothered at all, just slightly out of breath from the running. It made her want to scream.

Home, she almost said, but then she realised just how stupidly inaccurate that was. 'Back to the palazzo,' she said. 'I thought that was obvious.'

He fell into step beside her, and the narrowness of the *calle* meant he was far too close. 'You don't have to leave straight away. Wait until the morning.'

That sounded so generous, so reasonable. She regretted not having that contract now, because maybe, just maybe, she could have found something in it so she could sue his sorry hide for breaching it, for false advertising...*something*. There was no way she was staying here overnight. What did he want her to do? Lie in bed and cry over him? She wasn't that girl. It was time to move on. Onwards and upwards, remember?

She stomped down the street, glad she was wearing her ballet flats. They might not produce a satisfying echo, but they did make for a quick getaway. How could she have read him so wrong?

A series of images flashed through her head: kissing on the boat as the sun set over the lagoon, watching him building castles with Sofia the very first time, the moment that stupid little crab had bit her on the finger, and, last, the way he'd whistled for an island to appear out of the sea.

She stopped walking.

That was the real Max. She was sure of it.

He froze beside her, but she kept staring straight ahead.

She'd lived in the same house as this man for two weeks, and one thing she knew: he wasn't that good of a liar. He might keep things locked away, but he wasn't a man to kiss and run, to promise one thing with his eyes and smiles and lips and then deliver another. Was he?

She turned to face him. His features gave nothing away.

That should have made her angry, but it didn't. Instead, the fire she'd been ready to unleash on him flickered out. This was the façade, wasn't it? The face he showed when he wanted to pretend to the world that nothing got to him. The face he was showing to her to let her know the same. If there was a lie Max Martin told, this was it. The only one.

She searched his face, desperately looking for some hint she was right. His expression remained blank, but his jaw tightened. She started walking again, until they reached the little wooden door that led to the palazzo's tiny courtyard. Once there, she pushed the gate open and walked inside. She waited while he closed it behind him.

Nothing about this evening made sense, except the one truth she kept coming back to. Max Martin did the right thing, even if it killed him, even if it cost all that he had. So what about sending her away was 'right', and how on earth did she go about changing his mind?

Something drastic. Something shocking. Something he couldn't ignore. She was usually good at that. She dug down inside herself, poking in the dark corners of her imagination, to see if she could find anything to help, and came away empty, save for one thing—the only thing she'd been able to think about for the last few days.

'I love you,' she blurted out, and waited for his reaction.

He seemed to grow another layer of cement. 'I know.'

'Is that why you're sending me away?' she asked, a small wobble in her voice betraying her.

He nodded.

No breaking ranks and pulling her into his arms as he had done countless times since that evening on the lagoon. No echoed protestations of love. The silence grew around them. Here in the tiny courtyard with its high wall, it was complete.

So I tried to make him angry...

Fina's words floated through her head. It wasn't a great plan, but telling him she loved him had been a worse one. If at least she could get him to show *some* emotion, those walls might start to crack; she might be able to tell if he really felt anything for her at all, or whether it had just been another mirage this city had thrown up. Her heart was telling her one thing and her brain another and she had to stop the Ping-Pong match between them and just *know*.

It shouldn't be too hard. She seemed to have a special talent for lighting Max's fuse.

'You paint yourself as this big, strong man, who can rule the universe and isn't scared of anything, but underneath it you're nothing but a coward.'

He blinked. Very slowly.

Ruby felt the air pulse around her head. It had felt good to say those words. She hadn't anticipated how much.

'No wonder you can't get that design for the institute right, no wonder they had reservations about going with you. Because to create something stupendous, first you'd have to *feel*, to dream, but you don't have the courage.'

This time he didn't move at all. Now the air in the whole courtyard throbbed.

She was running out of things to say, things she thought might wound him, provoke some kind of a reaction. He might seem to be made of stone, but her blood was rushing round her veins, her cheeks heating. Feigned anger was quickly becoming the real deal.

He had to feel something for her—he had to. She drew in a deep breath, then gave it her best shot. 'Your father dug his own grave, you know. He finally imploded with the effort of keeping himself under lock and key, and you're going to end up the same way. He didn't deserve your mother, who's more patient and loving and forgiving than you will ever realise, and you're going to turn out just the same if you're not careful.'

She was on a roll now, couldn't stop herself if she wanted to. Hot tears began to stream down her face and her throat grew tight, making her voice scratchy. 'And you know what? Maybe it is better if I go, if I get as far away from you as I can, because I don't think I could stand being with a man like you anyway. I need someone who actually knows how to live and breathe, who knows how to love and be loved. Who, when he feels something for a woman, comes out and says so—not just stands there like a lump of stone doing nothing!'

And he was like stone. Still.

She had no volume left now, only a hoarse whisper that only just made it past her lips. She started walking backwards towards the door. 'Well, you've got your wish. I'm leaving. And not because you're telling me to, but because I want to. I know you feel something for me!' She thumped her chest with her closed fist. 'I know it! But you can't—or won't—bring yourself to show it. And that means you don't deserve me, Max Martin, and you never will.'

Max stood in the courtyard long after Ruby had left him. It had taken all his effort to take what she'd thrown at him, every last ounce of his strength, and he had none left to open the door and follow. He'd wanted to kiss her fiercely, deeply, as if his very life depended on it—which it well might—and tell her just how much he cared, but he couldn't. Wouldn't.

He wondered if he was actually dripping blood, because that was what it felt like. Her words had stabbed him in the heart. This was what he'd always tried to avoid, what he'd always protected himself against. Did she think he didn't know that he didn't deserve her, that *he* wasn't what *she* needed? That was why he hadn't answered her question, had just let her assume the worst. He was letting her go, setting her free.

It felt as if he hadn't taken a breath in minutes, and he dragged one in now, the cool night air burning his lungs. He could see the lights on in the *piano nobile* of Ca' Damiani, could imagine her shoving clothes into her scruffy little rucksack, calling him every name under the sun.

A foolish part of him hoped that this wasn't it. That one day they'd meet again, and it would be the right time, that they'd both be ready, but he knew it was probably impossible. He didn't think she'd ever forgive him. And she had every reason not to.

But he'd had to do it this way. Otherwise she wouldn't have left, she'd have just kept trying, killing herself off piece by piece in the process. Damn her resilience.

He closed his eyes and swore out loud. In Italian. And then he walked through the ground floor of the palazzo, the space that used to be the merchants' warehouse when the Damiani family had been part of the city's elite, and out of the boat door.

He needed to get out of this place, out of this glittering city that promised with one hand then took away with another.

He knew of somewhere much more appropriate. There were a number of deserted islands scattered across the lagoon that had once been quarantine islands, places where those with the plague had been imprisoned to stop them infecting the city, places where forgotten souls were still supposed to howl on a moonless night like this.

As the mist descended across the lagoon he started up the launch and headed away from the deceptive lights of the city, fully intending to join the dead in their howling.

Ruby flung all her belongings in her rucksack, but it took her considerably longer than three minutes. More like twenty. Maybe because she had to keep stopping to either wipe her eyes so she could see what she was doing or shout at the painting of the old man in a large black hat on the wall about what a pig-headed idiot his descendant was being.

When she was finally finished she crept next door to Sofia's room and watched the little girl sleeping, legs and arms flung carelessly over the covers. She pressed the gentlest of kisses to her temple, then quickly left, before she dripped tears on her and woke her up.

She met Fina in the hallway. 'You're back early!' she said, smiling, and then she stopped smiling. 'What has that fool of a son of mine done now?'

Ruby shrugged. 'He fired me.'

Fina went pale. *'What?'*

'Maybe "fired" is a little dramatic.' She sighed. 'It's the end of my contract. I knew it was only going to be a couple of weeks, but—' The tears clogging her throat prevented her from saying more.

Fina just walked forward and drew her into a hug. The kind of hug Ruby's mother used to give her when she was small and she hadn't realised she'd missed quite so badly. Ruby's torso shuddered and she clung on to Fina for a few long minutes before pulling away, putting the pieces of herself back together.

'You must come again,' Fina said, her eyes shining and her voice husky.

Ruby looked at her helplessly. She didn't know if she could return to this place. Somehow it had burrowed under her skin and she feared she'd always be reminded of what she'd almost had, of what it had snatched away from her on a fickle whim.

Fina must have understood that look, because she smiled softly. 'Well, when I come to London, then… You must take me out for tea and scones.'

A watery giggle escaped Ruby's lips. 'It's a deal.' She could just imagine Fina at the Ritz tea room, holding court and charming all the waiters, while the pianist played and the china clinked.

She checked her watch. 'I've ordered a taxi, so I really should go and get my things.'

'So soon?' Fina asked, looking a little forlorn.

Ruby nodded, and then Fina did, too. She was a woman who understood that when the time came a swift exit was the cleanest, if not the least painful, method of departure. Ruby was grateful for that.

She went and fetched her rucksack, hugged Fina once more, then descended the stone staircase for the last time and pushed the boat door open to walk onto the dock. The water taxi arrived only a few minutes later and Ruby climbed inside and looked steadfastly at the buildings on the other side of the canal as it turned around and pulled away.

She kept staring like that, stiff and unseeing, all the way to the train station. She didn't want to see any more of Venice. Not the details, anyway. Not the shapes of the arches or the patterns in the lace-like gothic façades. She was happier if it all just blurred into one big pool of light before her eyes.

CHAPTER SIXTEEN

'No, I'm afraid the four o'clock flight won't do. The crew need to catch another connection out of Paris to Antananarivo at five. We need them on the two forty-five.'

The travel agent on the other end of Ruby's phone huffed.

She lowered her voice, made it softer. 'Mr Lange would be ever so grateful if you could swing it. I'd even arrange to have a box set of his last series sent round as a thank-you.'

She could tell he'd just opened his mouth to give her an excuse, but he paused. 'My mum really does love his programmes. Have you got the one with the penguins in it?'

'*The Ice World of Antarctica?*' Ruby asked, drawing a little black-and-white penguin with a bobble hat on in the corner of her office pad. Now, they'd make a great subject for a series of drawings. What was not to like? They were cute and walked funny.

'That's the one,' the man said, then chortled most unappealingly. 'And I'd have one less Christmas present to buy come December.'

Ruby pulled a face at the phone. Cheapskate. 'So can you help me?' she asked, almost purring down the line.

'Leave it with me,' he said, sounding a bit chirpier than when she'd first started talking to him. 'What did you say your name was again?'

'Ruby,' she said with a sigh in her voice. 'Ruby Lange.'

'Wow! You related?'

She resisted the urge to say *I'm his grandmother.*

'Yep. He's my dad.'

Ruby wilted a little further towards her desk. Just about every conversation she had these days ended up like this one. And she made hundreds of calls a week.

'It must be really cool to be Patrick Lange's daughter!' he said. 'What's it like working for him?'

Okay, *now* he wanted to be friendly and chatty, after making the last twenty minutes trying to get the flights for the next filming trip booked like squeezing blood from a stone.

'It's a blast,' she said as she drew a jagged crevice that her cartoon penguin was about to fall into. Still, she said her thank-yous and goodbyes politely and sweetly. No point zinging him until after the flights were booked.

The phone on her desk rang. She picked it up, half expecting it to be the travel guy again, and prepared herself to tell him, yes, she could send an autographed photograph to go with the DVDs, he just needed to let her know who her dad should make it out to, but it turned out to be Lucinda, her father's secretary.

'Mr Lange would like to see you in his office,' she said, then hung up.

Ruby stuck her tongue out at the phone. Lucinda always called Dad 'Mr Lange' in her presence; it was most weird. She was laced up as tight as the man in question was, so no wonder they'd been working well together for the last ten years.

Ruby shoved her chair away from her desk and picked up her pad and pencil. She ripped off the top sheet and hid it in her letter tray. Dad didn't really 'get' the doodling. Drawing while she was on the phone always helped her think, but if he saw it he'd only think she'd been slacking off, which she so hadn't.

She walked through the open-plan office and knocked on her father's door.

'Come!' he shouted.

Ruby obeyed.

'You wanted to see me?' she asked, choosing not to sit down. She had rather a lot to do today, what with the trip coming up. One of the crew wasn't British and needed an extra visa, and the paperwork was a nightmare.

Her father looked up from his desk. He was approaching sixty, but he was still fit and healthy, if a little weathered round the edges from all his travelling. 'Have you managed to source that special lens Cameron was after?' he asked.

She nodded. Their top cameraman had a brochure sitting on his desk and an appointment at one of the best video equipment suppliers to test it out in a few days' time.

'And how are we on getting that actress to do some of the voiceovers?'

Ruby hid a smile. 'That actress' was a multi-Oscar winner, who'd gone all fangirly when Ruby had called her people and asked if she'd like to work on the next series of Patrick Lange documentaries. 'Her office has just confirmed, but she won't be available for recording during September and October because she's shooting in Bulgaria.'

'Great.' Her father steepled his fingers and looked at her. 'And what about the tea?'

'In the kitchen,' she answered. Seriously, you'd have thought that finding a tin of his fresh leaf lapsang souchong when it had run out had been a national emergency. Thankfully, there was a little tea shop round the corner in Wardour Street that stocked just what she'd wanted.

'Do you want a cup?'

'Yes,' he said, and Ruby turned to go. 'But in a minute.'

She turned back again.

'Why don't you sit down?'

Uh-oh. He wasn't going to fire her, was he? She thought

she'd been doing okay for the two months she'd been working here, and that incident with the delivery guy and the
ten-thousand-pound camera really hadn't been her fault.

She sidled round the chair sitting opposite his desk and
slid into it.

'I think we need to talk about your future here, Ruby.'

Oh, Lord. Here it came.

'Lucinda has let me know that she's going to have to take
maternity leave in the autumn, and I wondered if you'd be
interested in filling in for her.'

Ruby's mouth dropped open. Whether it was because
her father was offering her what was, in fact, a temporary
promotion, or the idea of someone actually knocking frosty
old Lucinda up, she didn't know.

'You've made quite an impression since you've been
here,' he continued. 'I think it could be a nice step up for
you.'

Ruby closed her eyes and opened them again. She'd
obviously been transported into a parallel universe. 'I beg
your pardon?'

Her father smiled at her, actually smiled! 'You've been
doing a great job. Everyone thinks so.'

Ruby couldn't help the next words that fell out of her
mouth. They just popped out before she had a chance to
edit herself. 'Do *you*?'

He gave her a bemused smile, as if what she was asking was confusing or funny in some way. 'Of course I do.
I always knew you could be good at something if you just
settled to it.'

Yes, she was definitely in a parallel universe. It must
have happened when she'd crossed the threshold into his
office, because before then everyone and everything had
been behaving as normal.

She looked back at him, searching his face. Was he really being serious?

What she saw shocked her.

Well, at least her time with Max had given her something more than bittersweet memories of a city she could probably never bear to visit again, because, just as she'd been able to look at Max, see the shell, know of its existence, but still catch glimpses of what was underneath, suddenly she could do the same with her father.

What she saw was different, of course. A little bit of paternal pride, more than a smidge of affection. Why had she never seen this before?

To be honest, she didn't know and she didn't care.

'What do you think?' her father said.

'I don't know,' she said truthfully. 'I've enjoyed the challenge of working here, and I'm not about to quit any time soon, but I'm just not sure it's...'

'You're not sure it's for you,' he finished for her softly.

She shook her head, afraid words would make the 'glimpses' disappear.

'Neither am I,' he said, standing up. 'But I thought I should offer you the opportunity.'

Ruby stood up, too. On a burst of emotion she ran over to her father and flung her arms around his neck. 'Thanks, Dad.'

He hugged her back, but muttered something about not making a fuss and nonsense at work.

Ruby pulled back and grinned at him. 'Sorry, I forgot. Lucinda would flay me alive if she heard me talking that way. I meant to say, "Thanks, Mr Lange".'

Real humour sparkled in his eyes, but he shooed her away. 'Go and get me that tea,' he said. 'And then it's probably about time you took your lunch break.'

Ruby looked at the clock. It was quarter to three already. No wonder her stomach was gurgling. She'd just been so busy that she'd forgotten to even think about lunch.

Ten minutes later she emerged from the Soho offices of

One Planet Productions and turned left, her large slouchy patchwork bag tucked under her arm. She hadn't used it since that day she'd tried to blag a job in Thalia Benson's office, and she'd made herself bring it out today. One couldn't spend all one's life hiding from half the contents of one's wardrobe because of the memories they conjured up. Sometimes one had to suck it up and keep moving. Onwards and upwards. Her motto was still keeping her strong.

First stop was her favourite coffee shop for a latte and a wrap, and then she headed for the little park on Golden Square. She sat on her favourite bench on the south-west corner, under a tree, and ate her lunch. Once that was disposed of, she opened her bag and pulled out a large A4 sketchpad. She flipped the cover open and turned to the first blank page and began to draw.

Not a cheeky crab. She'd given up on those. Instead a grumpy pigeon.

Her whole sketchbook was filled with Grumpy Pigeon drawings. Pigeon on Nelson's Column, Pigeon at the palace with the Queen, Pigeon on the Tube…

Max had been right. This was her passion. She drew when she got up in the mornings now. She drew during her lunch break and she drew when she got home from work. Her flatmate was threatening to use the accumulated stack of papers in their flat to wallpaper the toilet.

Drawing also had another benefit. While she was throwing herself into it, she didn't think of Max.

Well, okay, she did, but the memories got pushed to the back instead of jostling themselves to the front, where they were sharp and painful.

She hadn't heard anything from him since her return to London or, presumably, at some point, his. At first she'd hoped it had all been some Venice-induced hysteria, that everything would right itself and he'd come and see her, make contact somehow. She should have remembered that Max wasn't big on communication.

But she had other things to concentrate on now. She was finally laying the path for her own future, rather than wandering around in the dark. Not only did she know her next step, she knew where she wanted to be in six months' time, and five years' time.

She had a big picture.

How sad there was a dark hole in it that should have been filled by someone, but he'd decided it wasn't his perfect fit.

She sighed and carried on drawing. She had a meeting with a young, funky greetings-card firm that had offices in Shorcditch. They loved the grumpy little pigeon and she was talking to them about trialling a series of cards. And the owner of the vintage fashion shop she'd worked at wanted her to do some drawings for their new publicity drive—too fabulous to be true fifties divas in sunglasses and headscarves. Then there was a friend of a friend who said he might be able to put her in touch with people who did book jackets. All in all, things were looking promising.

Oh, she knew she'd have to keep working at One Planet for at least another year or two, maybe more. But she enjoyed it and it was a way to pay the bills. That was what grown-ups did, didn't they? They dug in and worked hard for what they wanted instead of drifting around and waiting for the universe to drop it into their laps.

When her hour was up, she packed her stuff away and headed back to the office. When she walked up to her desk, Jax, one of the other production assistants, leaned over the partition between their desks.

'You had a telephone call while you were out,' he said.

'Oh?' Her heart did a little flip. *Stop it*, she told it. *You can't keep doing this every time the darn thing rings. It's pointless... Hopeless... Give it up, already.*

'Yeah. It was some guy from a travel company.'

Ruby sank into her chair and laid her head on her desk.

'He wants to know if you can get a set of DVDs for his nan, too.'

Serafina Martin glided into the high-rise offices of Martin & Martin, her sunglasses on and a scarf tied round her neck. Her son resisted the urge to roll his eyes as he watched her from the confines of his glass office. She wafted through the main floor in his direction, bestowing regal smiles on his employees.

He'd finally gone to his mother at the end of his stay in Venice, had given her the space and time to tell her side of the story. It hadn't been easy to hear it, but he'd done it. And upon his return to London he'd remembered what she'd said about never having seen his flat, so he'd invited her over.

Not that she'd consented to actually stay with him, but she'd very kindly let him foot the bill for a room at the Dorchester. It was probably worth it, anyway. If they were under each other's feet twenty-four-seven, they'd probably drive each other crazy and undo all the progress that they'd made.

They'd had a long heart-to-heart the night before over dinner. He'd been aware that he'd listened to her side of the story in Venice, but he'd finally managed to release the things he'd needed to say, too. Like how he was sorry that he'd pushed her away for most of his life. He should have been loyal to both parents, not barricaded the doors against her as if she were the enemy. And he'd done it without Ruby there to egg him on, prod him when he was being stubborn. She would have been proud of him.

He ignored the stab of pain in his chest at the thought of her. That particular wound still hadn't closed, still dripped and weeped every day.

Neither he nor his mother were exactly sure what was going to happen from here on, but at least they were willing to try. He'd attempted to explain it to her. In actual words. The best he'd been able to do was tell her he wasn't sure how to deconstruct a relationship back to where it had been almost twenty years ago and start again, build it up in a different shape, with a different foundation.

Yes, he'd used a lot of building metaphors. He couldn't help it. He was new at this talking stuff, and it was the only way the words would come.

Fina had just leaned across the table and patted his hand. 'You're the best architect I know, Massimo. You'll work it out.'

His mother finally reached his office door and entered without knocking, then collapsed gracefully into a leather chair and smiled. 'Shopping is so tiring, don't you think?'

Max frowned. If it was that tiring, you'd think she'd do less of it.

'I thought you said you'd be back at two. It's past four.'

She waved a hand, as if minutes and seconds were of no consequence. 'I was otherwise engaged.'

'Oh, yes?'

She fidgeted with her handbag. 'I met Ruby for after-noon tea at the Ritz.'

It was a warm August day outside, and the sun was glint-ing off the skyscrapers in the City of London, but Max's skin chilled and his heart lumbered to a stop.

'She showed me this,' she said, and handed him a small rectangular card in a cellophane sleeve. He turned it over to discover it was a greetings card. He hadn't seen the design before—a rather fierce-looking pigeon, who was stand-ing guard at the Tower of London—but he recognised the style instantly.

She'd done it? She'd really done it?

His mother took the card back from him and tucked it in her handbag. 'I told her I thought the pigeon reminded me of someone we both knew, but she said she couldn't see it.'

'I do *not* scowl like that.'

'Darling,' she said sweetly, 'you're doing it now.'

He shook his head and walked back round the other side of his desk. 'How was she?' he asked, keeping his tone light, neutral, and messing with some bits of paper on his desk.

It had been hard knowing he was in the same city as her. He'd have considered moving back to Venice if the institute commission hadn't been ploughing ahead at full steam. They'd loved his new designs. Had eaten them up, and Vince McDermot had scurried off with his tail between his legs.

And it was all because of Ruby. He wished he could see her to tell her that.

Hell, he wished he could see her full stop. He looked up, realising his mother hadn't answered him.

'Honestly, Massimo,' she said, giving him that same look she'd used to give him as a boy when he'd been caught stealing the family launch to go racing with his friends. 'When are you going to give up and admit you're head over heels for that girl?'

He stared back at her. Admitting it wasn't the problem. Forgetting it was.

And now he'd seen her drawings he knew he'd done the right thing. He'd only have weighed her down, held her back.

'Sometimes it's better to walk away. I thought you'd understand that better than anyone.'

His mother threw her hands in the air, indicating she did not know what to do with him. 'For a very intelligent man, my darling son, you can be incredibly stupid.'

'Thanks, Mamma,' he said between gritted teeth.

She stood up and walked over to him, her eyes warm and full of compassion. 'You are not your father, Massimo.'

He opened his mouth, but she held up her hand.

'Yes, you are very like him, but you are not a carbon copy.' She gave him a heartfelt look. 'You have a chance, darling, to make this right, to be happy. You can be what your father could not. I know it.'

It was surprising to discover just how much her faith warmed him. 'How can you be so sure?'

'Because I gave birth to you, because I know you. Because I've seen the way you've changed this summer.'

'I don't know how to tell her.'

She kissed him on the cheek and patted his arm. 'Skills like that are just like muscles. The more you use them, the stronger they get, and you've already made a start.'

Max thought of all the things he'd said to Ruby that last night in Venice. The way he'd seen her crumble in front of him. He wasn't sure words would ever be enough to repair that damage.

'Anyway,' she said, regaining some of her usual breezy air and heading for the door, 'I've got a taxi waiting downstairs and I need someone to carry my bags.'

Max raced after her. A taxi? They'd been talking for at least five minutes!

'What bags?' he said, sounding more like his usual self.

'Oh, I paid a little visit to Harrods before the Ritz.'

Four large bags were waiting for him in the back of the cab. He climbed in and passed them to his mother. The cabby smiled. He'd seemed quite happy to wait, with the meter ticking over at the speed of light. When the last one had hit the pavement, his mother gave him a gentle shove so he lost his balance and landed on the back seat.

'Go! Go and see Ruby.'

He looked back at her helplessly. He'd had no time to prepare, no time to think up any building-related images to help him explain. 'What will I say?'

'Just start, Massimo,' she said as she shut the door. 'The rest will come.'

And then she thumped the taxi on the roof and it sped off into the London traffic.

Ruby was supposed to be working, but she'd drifted off, staring out of the window. It wasn't something she usually did, but she'd looked up at the sky between the narrow buildings. It was exactly the same colour as the day they'd taken the speedboat out into the lagoon and found the secret beach, and for some reason she'd just ground to a halt.

She supposed she could call it a coffee break, but she usually filled her breaks with sketching, because when they were filled with sketching it blocked out other things she didn't want to think about.

A large, heavy sigh deflated her ribcage.

She hadn't let herself look back much, but some of the memories were so lovely, even if it hurt like hell to think about them.

If only whistles were really magic...

Then she could put her lips together and let out that breathy little sound and everything she wanted would just rise from the London street to meet her.

She pursed her lips, and the noise that came out was both pathetic and forlorn.

Nothing happened. But why would it? This was London, not *La Serenissima*.

She shook herself. This was no way to live. *Come on, Ruby. Find yourself something to do, something to keep yourself occupied.* In this madhouse, it shouldn't be hard enough.

And, right on cue, a commotion erupted near the foyer. It was probably that clumsy motorbike delivery guy again. Thank goodness she was nowhere nearby to get blamed for his mishaps again.

The noise got louder. It was coming closer.

The One Planet office was large, but full of clutter and equipment, and the desks were separated by low screens to make cubicles. Ruby half stood and peered round the edge of hers to see what was going on.

There was a man walking down the central aisle, looking terribly grim, terribly stern. Everyone else cleared out of the way, but Ruby found she couldn't do anything but freeze as her pulse went crazy. If it got any faster, she was either going to have a stroke or shoot straight through the ceiling.

That was Max. Here in the office.

He spotted her—half crouching, half leaning out of her cubicle—and his trajectory changed.

Jax, who fancied himself a bit as the office bouncer, was on his heels. 'Hey, mate! Where d'you think you're going?'

'I'm going to see Ruby Lange,' Max replied, not taking his eyes off her.

Ruby stood up, and the folds of the skirt of her strawberry dress fell around her knees.

He stopped when he was about ten feet away. 'Wh-what do you want?' she stammered.

Faces appeared above partitions and some of those who worked down the other end of the office drew closer to see what was going on.

Max just stared at her.

My, he looked amazing. All tall and gruff and…Max. She wanted to smile, to run to him, but she held back. Wasn't he going to say anything?

He stopped looking quite so stern. She saw him swallow.

He wasn't going to be able to do it, was he? He found saying what needed to be said impossible at the best of times. That was why she'd left him in Venice. Not because he hadn't cared, but because he'd been too much of a coward to show it. How was he going to do it with all these people looking on, all these strangers?

But then he straightened, grew even taller and smiled at her.

'I need you.'

The words hit her heart like an arrow, but this time she would not be wooed by them so easily. She needed to test them, to know their strength.

'I'm not a nanny any more,' she answered softly.

The heads of the onlookers swivelled back to look at Max.

The smile disappeared. 'I don't need a blasted nanny,' he told her. 'I need *you*, Ruby.'

'Why?' she almost whispered. Her heart thudded madly inside her chest, blood rushed in her ears. The seconds ticked by.

Details, Max. I need details.

He took a step forward. He was so close now that she could have reached out and touched him if she'd wanted to. The crowd shuffled closer. Someone walked in the door, back from a meeting and talking loudly on their mobile phone, and was shushed by at least five others.

'Because,' Max said, 'you are bright and beautiful and talented.'

She let out a shaky breath.

But he wasn't finished yet. 'Because you brought joy back into my dull, structured life.'

She felt a lump rise in her throat. She started to speak anyway, but he stopped her with a look.

'Because you challenge me, contradict me and generally drive me crazy.'

There was a rough laugh from behind her. 'Yes, but isn't she wonderful?'

Ruby turned to see her father standing at the end of the room. He was smiling. She looked back at Max, hardly knowing whether to laugh or cry.

'I wouldn't have it any other way.'

And then he was reaching for her, pulling her to him and his lips were on hers and his arms crushed her to him.

'And because I love you,' he whispered in her ear, but she didn't mind that. These words were hers and hers alone. 'More than anything in this world, more than designing or building or even breathing. I promise you I am no longer ankle deep. I am in way, way, way over my head.'

She pulled back to look at him. 'Good answer,' she said, grinning. 'Because so am I.'

Max just laughed and kissed her again.

* * * * *

THE
UNCOMPROMISING
ITALIAN
CATHY WILLIAMS

To my wonderful daughters.

Cathy Williams is originally from Trinidad, but has lived in England for a number of years. She currently has a house in Warwickshire, which she shares with her husband Richard, her three daughters, Charlotte, Olivia and Emma, and their pet cat, Salem. She adores writing romantic fiction, and would love one of her girls to become a writer – although at the moment she is happy enough if they do their homework and agree not to bicker with one another!

CHAPTER ONE

LESLEY FOX SLOWLY drew to a stop in front of the most imposing house she had ever seen.

The journey out of London had taken barely any time at all. It was Monday, it was the middle of August and she had been heading against the traffic. In all it had taken her under an hour to leave her flat in crowded Ladbroke Grove and arrive at a place that looked as though it should be plastered on the cover of a *House Beautiful* magazine.

The wrought-iron gates announced its splendour, as had the tree-lined avenue and acres of manicured lawns through which she had driven.

The guy was beyond wealthy. Of course, she had known that. The first thing she had done when she had been asked to do this job had been to look him up online.

Alessio Baldini—Italian, but resident in the UK for a long time. The list of his various companies was vast and she had skipped over all of that. What he did for a living was none of her business. She had just wanted to make sure that the man existed and was who Stan said he was.

Commissions via friends of friends were not always to be recommended, least of all in her niche sideline business. A girl couldn't be too careful, as her father liked to say.

She stepped out of her little Mini, which was dwarfed in the vast courtyard, and took a few minutes to look around her.

The brilliance of a perfect summer's day made the sprawling green lawns, the dense copse to one side lush with lavender and the clambering roses against the stone of the mansion facing her seem almost too breathtakingly beautiful to be entirely real.

This country estate was in a league of its own.

There had been a bit of information on the Internet about where the man lived, but no pictures, and she had been ill-prepared for this concrete display of wealth.

A gentle breeze ruffled her short brown hair and for once she felt a little awkward in her routine garb of lightweight combat trousers, espadrilles and one of her less faded tee-shirts advertising the rock band she had gone to see five years ago.

This didn't seem the sort of place where dressing down would be tolerated.

For the first time, she wished she had paid a little more attention to the details of the guy she was going to see.

There had been long articles about him but few pictures and she had skimmed over those, barely noting which one he was amidst the groups of boring men in business suits who'd all seemed to wear the identical smug smiles of people who had made far too much money for their own good.

She grabbed her laptop from the passenger seat and slammed the door shut.

If it weren't for Stan, she wouldn't be here now. She didn't need the money. She could afford the mortgage on her one-bedroom flat, had little interest in buying pointless girly clothes for a figure she didn't possess to attract men in whom she had scant interest—or who, she amended with scrupulous honesty to herself, had scant interest in *her*—and she wasn't into expensive, long-haul holidays.

With that in mind, she had more than enough to be going on with. Her full-time job as a website designer paid well and, as far as she was concerned, she lacked for nothing.

But Stan was her dad's long-time friend from Ireland. They had grown up together. He had taken her under his wing when she had moved down to London after university and she owed him.

With any luck, she would be in and out of the man's place in no time at all.

She breathed in deeply and stared at the mansion in front of her.

It seemed a never-ending edifice of elegant cream stone, a dream of a house, with ivy climbing in all the right places and windows that looked as though they dated back to the turn of the century.

This was just the sort of ostentatious wealth that should have held little appeal, but in fact she was reluctantly charmed by its beauty.

Of course, the man would be a lot less charming than his house. It was always the way. Rich guys always thought they were God's gift to women even when they obviously weren't. She had met one or two in her line of work and it had been a struggle to keep a smile pinned to her face.

There was no doorbell but an impressive knocker. She could hear it reverberating through the bowels of the house as she banged it hard on the front door and then stood back to wait for however long it would take for the man's butler or servant, or whoever he employed to answer doors for him, to arrive on the scene and let her in.

She wondered what he would look like. Rich and Italian, so probably dark-haired with a heavy accent. Possibly short, which would be a bit embarrassing, because she was five-eleven and a half and likely to tower over him—never a good thing. She knew from experience that men hated women who towered over them. He would probably be quite dapper, kitted out in expensive Italian gear and wearing expensive Italian footwear. She had no idea what either might look like but it was safe to say that trainers and old clothes would not feature on the sartorial menu.

She was fully occupied amusing herself with a variety of mental pictures when the door was pulled open without warning.

For a few seconds, Lesley Fox lost the ability to speak. Her lips parted and she stared. Stared in a way she had never stared at any man in her life before.

The guy standing in front of her was, quite simply, beautiful. Taller than her by a few inches, and wearing faded jeans and a navy-blue polo shirt, he was barefoot. Raven-black hair was combed back from a sinfully sexy face. His eyes were as black as his hair and lazily returned her stare, until she felt the blood rush to her face and she returned to Planet Earth with a feeling of sickening embarrassment.

'Who are you?'

His cool, rich, velvety voice galvanised her senses back into working order and she cleared her throat and reminded herself that she wasn't the type of girl who had ever been daunted by a guy, however good-looking he was. She came from a family of six and she was the only girl. She had been brought up going to rugby matches, watching the football on television, climbing trees and exploring the glorious countryside of wild Ireland with brothers who hadn't always appreciated their younger sister tagging along.

She had always been able to handle the opposite sex. She had lived her life being one of the lads, for God's sake!

'I'm here about your... Er...my name's Lesley Fox.' As an afterthought, she stuck out her hand and then dropped it when he failed to respond with a return gesture.

'I wasn't expecting a girl.' Alessio looked at her narrowly. That, he thought, had to be the understatement of the year. He had been expecting a Les Fox—Les, as in a man. Les, as in a man who was a contemporary of Rob Dawson, his IT guy. Rob Dawson was in his forties and resembled a beach ball. He had been expecting a forty-something-year-old man of similar build.

Instead, he was looking at a girl with cropped dark hair, eyes the colour of milk chocolate and a lanky, boyish physique, wearing...

Alessio took in the baggy sludge-green trousers with awkward pockets and the faded tee-shirt.

He couldn't quite recall the last time he had seen a woman dressed with such obvious, scathing disregard for fashion.

Women always tried their very hardest when around him to show their best side. Their hair was always perfect, make-up always flawless, clothes always the height of fashion and shoes always high and sexy.

His eyes drifted down to her feet. She was wearing cloth shoes.

'I'm so sorry to have disappointed you, Mr Baldini. I

take it you *are* Mr Baldini and not his manservant, sent to chase away callers by being rude to them?'

'I didn't think anyone used that term any more...'

'What term?'

'*Manservant*. When I asked Dawson to provide me with the name of someone who could help me with my current little...problem, I assumed he would have recommended someone a bit older. More experienced.'

'I happen to be very good at what I do.'

'As this isn't a job interview, I can't very well ask for references.' He stood aside, inviting her to enter. 'But, considering you look as though you're barely out of school, I'll want to know a little bit about you before I explain the situation.'

Lesley held on to her temper. She didn't need the money. Even though the hourly rate that she had been told about was staggering, she really didn't have to stand here and listen to this perfect stranger quiz her about her experience for a job she hadn't applied for. But then she thought of Stan and all he had done for her and she gritted back the temptation to turn on her heel, climb back into her car and head down to London without a backward glance.

'Come on in,' Alessio threw over his shoulder as she remained hovering on the doorstep and, after a few seconds, Lesley took a step into the house.

She was surrounded by pale marble only broken by the richness of a Persian rug. The walls were adorned with the sort of modern masterpieces that should have looked out of place in a house of this age but somehow didn't. The vast hall was dominated by a staircase that swept upwards before branching out in opposite directions, and doors indicated that there was a multitude of rooms winging on either side, not that she wouldn't have guessed.

More than ever, she felt inappropriately dressed. He might be casual, but he was casual in the sort of elegant, expensive way of the very wealthy.

'Big place for one person,' she said, staring around her, openly impressed.

'How do you know I haven't got a sprawling family lurking somewhere out of sight?'

'Because I looked you up,' Lesley answered truthfully. Her eyes finally returned to him and once again she was struck by his dark, saturnine good looks. And once again she had to drag her eyes away reluctantly, desperate to return her gaze to him, to drink him in. 'I don't usually travel into unknown territory when I do my freelance jobs. Usually the computer comes to me, I don't go to the computer.'

'Always illuminating to get out of one's comfort zone,' Alessio drawled. He watched as she ran her fingers through her short hair, spiking it up. She had very dark eyebrows, as dark as her hair, which emphasised the peculiar shade of brown of her eyes. And she was pale, with satiny skin that should have been freckled but wasn't. 'Follow me. We can sit out in the garden and I'll get Violet to bring us something to drink… Have you had lunch?'

Lesley frowned. Had she? She was careless with her eating habits, something she daily promised herself to rectify. If she ate more, she knew she'd stand a fighting chance of not looking like a gawky runner bean. 'A sandwich before I left,' she returned politely. 'But a cup of tea would be wonderful.'

'It never fails to amuse me that on a hot summer's

day you English will still opt for a cup of tea instead of something cold.'

'I'm not English. I'm Irish.'

Alessio cocked his head to one side and looked at her, consideringly. 'Now that you mention it, I do detect a certain twang...'

'But I'm still partial to a cup of tea.'

He smiled and she was knocked sideways. The man oozed sex appeal. He'd had it when he'd been unsmiling, but now...it was enough to throw her into a state of confusion and she blinked, driving away the unaccustomed sensation.

'This isn't my preferred place of residence,' he took up easily as he led the way out of the magnificent hall and towards sprawling doors that led towards the back of the house. 'I come here to give it an airing every so often but most of my time is spent either in London or abroad on business.'

'And who looks after this place when you're not in it?'

'I have people who do that for me.'

'Bit of a waste, isn't it?'

Alessio spun round and looked at her with a mixture of irritation and amusement. 'From whose point of view?' he asked politely and Lesley shrugged and folded her arms.

'There are such extreme housing problems in this country that it seems crazy for one person to have a place of this size.'

'You mean, when I could subdivide the whole house and turn it into a million rabbit hutches to cater for down and outs?' He laughed drily. 'Did my guy explain to you what the situation was?'

Lesley frowned. She had thought he might have been

offended by her remark, but she was here on business of sorts, and her opinions were of little consequence.

'Your guy got in touch with Stan who's a friend of my dad and he… Well, he just said that you had a sensitive situation that needed sorting. No details.'

'None were given. I was just curious to find out whether idle speculation had entered the equation.' He pushed open some doors and they emerged into a magnificent back garden.

Tall trees bordered pristine, sprawling lawns. To one side was a tennis court and beyond that she could see a swimming pool with a low, modern outbuilding which she assumed was changing rooms. The patio on which they were standing was as broad as the entire little communal garden she shared with the other residents in her block of flats and stretched the length of the house. If a hundred people were to stand side by side, they wouldn't be jostling for space.

Low wooden chairs were arranged around a glass-topped table and as she sat down a middle-aged woman bustled into her line of vision, as though summoned by some kind of whistle audible only to her.

Tea, Alessio instructed; something cold for him, a few things to eat.

Orders given, he sat down on one of the chairs facing her and leaned forward with his elbows resting on his knees.

'So the man my guy went to is a friend of your father's?'

'That's right. Stan grew up with my dad and when I moved down to London after university… Well, he and his wife took me under their wing. Made room for me in their house until I was settled—even paid the three months' deposit on my first rental property because they knew that it would be a struggle for my dad to afford it. So, yeah, I owe Stan a lot and it's why I took this job, Mr Baldini.'

'Alessio, please. And you work as…?'

'I design websites but occasionally I work as a freelance hacker. Companies employ me to see if their firewalls are intact and secure. If something can be hacked, then I can do it.'

'Not a job I immediately associate with a woman,' he murmured and raised his eyebrows as she bristled. 'That's not meant as an insult. It's purely a statement of fact. There are a couple of women in my IT department, but largely they're guys.'

'Why didn't you get one of your own employees to sort out your problem?'

'Because it's a sensitive issue and, the less my private life is discussed within the walls of my offices, the better. So you design websites. You freelance and you claim you can get into anything.'

'That's right. Despite not being a man.'

Alessio heard the defensive edge to her voice and his curiosity was piqued. His life had settled into a predictable routine when it came to members of the opposite sex. His one mistake, made when he was eighteen, had been enough for him to develop a very healthy scepticism when it came to women. The fairer sex, he had concluded, was a misconception of stunning magnitude.

'So if you could explain the situation…' Lesley looked at him levelly, her mind already flying ahead to the thrill of solving whatever problem lay in store for her. She barely noticed his housekeeper placing a pot of tea in front of her and a plate crammed with pastries, produced from heaven only knew where.

'I've been getting anonymous emails.' Alessio

flushed as he grappled with the unaccustomed sensation of admitting to having his hands tied when it came to sorting out his own dilemma. 'They started a few weeks ago.'

'At regular intervals?'

'No.' He raked his fingers through his hair and looked at her earnest face tilted to one side... A small crease indented her forehead and he could almost hear her thinking, her mind working as methodically as one of the computers she dealt with. 'I ignored them to start with but the last couple have been...how shall I describe them?...a little *forceful*.' He reached for the pitcher of homemade lemonade to pour himself a glass. 'If you looked me up, you probably know that I own several IT companies. Despite that, I confess that my knowledge of the ins and outs of computers is scant.'

'Actually, I have no idea what companies you own or don't own. I looked you up because I wanted to make sure that there was nothing dodgy about you. I've done this sort of thing before. I'm not looking for background detail, I'm generally looking for any articles that might point a suspicious finger.'

'Dodgy? You thought I might be *dodgy*?'

He looked so genuinely shocked and insulted that she couldn't help laughing. 'You might have had newspaper cuttings about suspect dealings, mafia connections...you know the sort of thing. I'd have been able to find even the most obscure article within minutes if there had been anything untoward about you. You came up clean.'

Alessio nearly choked on his lemonade. 'Mafia dealings...because I'm Italian? That's the most ridiculous thing I've ever heard.'

Lesley shrugged sheepishly. 'I don't like taking chances.'

'I've never done a crooked thing in my entire life.' He flung his arms wide in a gesture that was peculiarly foreign. 'I even buck the trend of the super-rich and am a fully paid-up member of the honest, no-offshore-scams, tax-paying club! To suggest that I might be linked to the Mafia because I happen to be Italian...'

He sat forward and stared at her and she had to fight off the very feminine and girlish response to wonder what he thought of her, as a woman, as opposed to a talented computer whizz-kid there at his bidding. Suddenly flustered, she gulped back a mouthful of hot tea and grimaced.

Wondering what men thought of her wasn't her style. She pretty much *knew* what they thought of her. She had lived her whole life knowing that she was one of the lads. Even her job helped to advance that conclusion.

No, she was too tall, too angular and too mouthy to hold any appeal when it came to the whole sexual attraction thing. Least of all when the guy in question looked like Alessio Baldini. She cringed just thinking about it.

'No, you've been watching too many gangster movies. Surely you must have heard of me?' He was always in the newspapers. Usually in connection with big business deals—occasionally in the gossip columns with a woman hanging onto his arm.

He wasn't sure why he had inserted that irrelevant question but, now that he had, he found that he was awaiting her answer with keen curiosity.

'Nope.'

'No?'

'I guess you probably think that everyone's heard of you, but in actual fact I don't read the newspapers.'

'You don't read the newspapers…not even the gossip columns?'

'Especially not the gossip columns,' she said scathingly. 'Not all girls are interested in what celebs get up to.' She tried to reconnect with the familiar feeling of satisfaction that she wasn't one of those simpering females who became embroiled in silly gossip about the rich and famous, but for once the feeling eluded her.

For once, she longed to be one of those giggly, coy girls who knew how to bat their eyelashes and attract the cute guys; she wanted to be part of the prom set instead of the clever, boyish one lurking on the sidelines; she wanted to be a member of that invisible club from which she had always been excluded because she just never seemed to have the right code words to get in.

She fought back a surge of dissatisfaction with herself and had to stifle a sense of anger that the man sitting opposite her had been the one to have generated the emotion. She had conquered whatever insecurities she had about her looks a long time ago and was perfectly content with her appearance. She might not be to everyone's taste, and she certainly wouldn't be to *his*, but her time would come and she would find someone. At the age of twenty-seven, she was hardly over the hill and, besides, her career was taking off. The last thing she needed or wanted was to be side-tracked by a guy.

She wondered how they had ended up talking about something that had nothing at all to do with the job for which she had been hired.

Was this part of his 'getting to know her' exercise? Was he quietly vetting her the way she had vetted him, when she had skimmed over all that information about him on the computer, making sure that there was nothing worrying about him?

'You were telling me about the emails you received...' She brought the conversation back to the business in hand.

Alessio sighed heavily and gave her a long, considering look from under his lashes.

'The first few were innocuous enough—a couple of one-liners hinting that they had information I might be interested in. Nothing worrying.'

'You get emails like that all the time?'

'I'm a rich man. I get a lot of emails that have little or nothing to do with work.' He smiled wryly and Lesley felt that odd tingling feeling in her body once again. 'I have several email accounts and my secretary is excellent when it comes to weeding out the dross.'

'But these managed to slip through?'

'These went to my personal email address. Very few people have that.'

'Okay.' She frowned and stared off into the distance. 'So you say that the first few were innocuous enough and then the tenor of the emails changed?'

'A few days ago, the first request for money came. Don't get me wrong, I get a lot of requests for money, but they usually take a more straightforward route. Someone wants a sponsor for something; charities asking for hand-outs; small businesses angling for investment...and then the usual assortment of nut cases who need money for dying relatives or to pay lawyers before they can claim their inheritance, which they would happily share with me.'

'And your secretary deals with all of that?'

'She does. It's usually called pressing the delete button on the computer. Some get through to me but, in general, we have established charities to which we give healthy sums of money, and all requests for business investment are automatically referred to my corporate finance division.'

'But this slipped through the net because it came to your personal address. Any idea how he or she could have accessed that information?' She was beginning to think that this sounded a little out of her area of expertise. Hackers usually went for information or, in some cases tried to attack the accounts, but this was clearly... personal. 'And don't you think that this might be better referred to the police?' she inserted, before he could answer.

Alessio laughed drily. He took a long mouthful of his drink and looked at her over the rim of the glass as he drank.

'If you read the papers,' he drawled, 'you might discover that the police have been having a few off-months when it comes to safeguarding the privacy of the rich and famous. I'm a very private man. The less of my life is splashed across the news, the better.'

'So my job is to find out who is behind these emails.'

'Correct.'

'At which point you'll...?'

'Deal with the matter myself.'

He was still smiling, with that suggestion of amusement on his lips, but she could see the steel behind the lazy, watchful dark eyes. 'I should tell you from the offset that I cannot accept this commission if there's any suggestion that you might turn...err...*violent* when it comes to sorting out whoever is behind this.'

Alessio laughed and relaxed back in his chair, stretching out his long legs to cross them at the ankle and loosely linking his fingers on his stomach. 'You have my word that I won't turn, as you say, violent.'

'I hope you're not making fun of me, Mr Baldini,' Lesley said stiffly. 'I'm being perfectly serious.'

'Alessio. The name's Alessio. And you aren't still under the impression that I'm a member of the Mafia, are you? With a stash of guns under the bed and henchmen to do my bidding?'

Lesley flushed. Where had her easy, sassy manner gone? She was seldom lost for words but she was now, especially when those dark, dark eyes were lingering on her flushed cheeks, making her feel even more uncomfortable than she already felt. A burst of shameful heat exploded somewhere deep inside her, her body's acknowledgment of his sexual magnetism, chemistry that was wrapping itself around her like a web, confusing her thoughts and making her pulses race.

'Do I strike you as a violent man, Lesley?'

'I never said that. I'm just being…cautious.'

'Have you had awkward situations before?' The soft pink of her cheeks when she blushed was curiously appealing, maybe because she was at such pains to project herself as a tough woman with no time for frivolity.

'What do you mean?'

'You intimated that you checked me out to make sure that I wasn't *dodgy*…and I think I'm quoting you here. So are you cautious in situations like these… when the computer doesn't go to you but you're forced to go to the computer…because of bad experiences?'

'I'm a careful person.' Why did that make her sound like such a bore, when she wasn't? Once again weirdly conscious of the image she must present to a guy like him, Lesley inhaled deeply and ploughed on. 'And yes,' she asserted matter-of-factly, 'I *have* had a number of poor experiences in the past. A few months ago, I was asked to do a favour for a friend's friend only to find that what he wanted was for me to hack into his ex-wife's bank account and see where her money was being spent. When I refused, he turned ugly.'

'Turned ugly?'

'He'd had a bit too much to drink. He thought that if he pushed me around a bit I'd do what he wanted.' And just in case her awkward responses had been letting her down, maybe giving him the mistaken impression that she was anything but one hundred per cent professional, she concluded crisply, 'Of course, it's annoying, but nothing I can't handle.'

'You can handle men who turn ugly.' Fascinating. He was in the company of someone from another planet. She might have the creamiest complexion he had ever seen, and a heart-shaped face that insisted on looking ridiculously feminine despite the aggressive get-up, but she was certainly nothing like any woman he had ever met. 'Tell me how you do that,' he said with genuine curiosity.

Absently, he noticed that she had depleted the plate of pastries by half its contents. A hearty appetite; his eyes flicked to her body which, despite being well hidden beneath her anti-fashion-statement clothing, was long and slender.

On some subliminal level, Lesley was aware of the shift in his attention, away from her face and onto her body. Her instinct was to squirm. Instead, she clasped her hands tightly together on her lap and tried to force her uncooperative body into a position of relaxed ease.

'I have a black belt in karate.'

Alessio was stunned into silence. 'You do?'

'I do.' She shrugged and held his confounded gaze. 'And it's not that shocking,' she continued into the lengthening silence. 'There were loads of girls in my class when I did it. 'Course, a few of them fell by the wayside when we began moving up the levels.'

'And you did these classes…when, exactly?'

In passing, Lesley wondered what this had to do with her qualifications for doing the job she had come to do. On the other hand, it never hurt to let someone know that you weren't the sort of woman to be messed with.

'I started when I was ten and the classes continued into my teens with a couple of breaks in between.'

'So, when other girls were experimenting with make-up, you were learning the valuable art of self-defence.'

Lesley felt the sharp jab of discomfort as he yet again unwittingly hit the soft spot inside her, the place where her insecurities lay, neatly parcelled up but always ready to be unwrapped at a moment's notice.

'I think every woman should know how to physi-cally defend herself.'

'That's an extremely laudable ambition,' Alessio murmured. He noticed that his long, cold drink was finished. 'Let's go inside. I'll show you to my office and we can continue our conversation there. It's get-ting a little oppressive out here.' He stood up, squinted towards his gardens and half-smiled when he saw her automatically reach for the plate of pastries and what-ever else she could manage to take in with her.

'No need.' He briefly rested one finger on her out-stretched hand and Lesley shot back as though she had been scalded. 'Violet will tidy all this away.'

Lesley bit back an automatic retort that it was il-luminating to see how the other half lived. She was no inverted snob, even though she might have no time for outward trappings and the importance other people sometimes placed on them, but he made her feel defen-sive. Worse, he made her feel gauche and awkward, sixteen all over again, cringing at the prospect of having to wear a frock to go to the school leaving dance, knowing that she just couldn't pull it off.

'I'm thinking that your mother must be a strong woman to instil such priorities in her daughter,' he said neutrally.

'My mother died when I was three—a hit-and-run accident when she was cycling back from doing the shopping.'

Alessio stopped in his tracks and stared down at her until she was forced uncomfortably to return his stare.

'Please don't say something trite like *I'm sorry to hear that*.' She tilted her chin and looked at him unblinkingly. 'It happened a long time ago.'

'No. I wasn't going to say that,' Alessio said in a low, musing voice that made her skin tingle.

'My father was the strong influence in my life,' she pressed on in a high voice. 'My father and my five brothers. They all gave me the confidence to know that I could do whatever I chose to do, that my gender did not have to stand in the way of my ambition. I got my degree in maths—the world was my oyster.'

Heart beating as fast as if she had run a marathon, she stared up at him, their eyes tangling until her defensiveness subsided and gave way to something else, something she could barely comprehend, something that made her say quickly, with a tight smile, 'But I don't see how any of this is relevant. If you lead the way to your computer, it shouldn't take long for me to figure out who your problem pest is.'

CHAPTER TWO

THE OFFICE TO which she was led allowed her a good opportunity to really take in the splendour of her surroundings.

Really big country estates devoured money and consequently were rarely in the finest of conditions. Imposing exteriors were often let down by run-down, sad interiors in want of attention.

This house was as magnificent inside as it was out. The pristine gardens, the splendid ivy-clad walls, were replicated inside by a glorious attention to detail. From the cool elegance of the hall, she bypassed a series of rooms, each magnificently decorated. Of course, she could only peek through slightly open doors, because she had to half-run to keep up with him, but she saw enough to convince her that serious money had been thrown at the place—which was incredible, considering it was not used on a regular basis.

Eventually they ended up in an office with book-lined walls and a massive antique desk housing a computer, a lap-top and a small stack of legal tomes. She looked around at the rich burgundy drapes pooling to the ground, the pin-striped sober wallpaper, the deep sofa and chairs.

It was a decor she would not have associated with

him and, as though reading her mind, he said wryly, 'It makes a change from what I'm used to in London. I'm more of a modern man myself but I find there's something soothing about working in a turn-of-the-century gentleman's den.' He moved smoothly round to the chair at the desk and powered up his computer. 'When I bought this house several years ago, it was practically derclict. I paid over the odds for it because of its history and because I wanted to make sure the owner and her daughter could be rehoused in the manner to which they had clearly once been accustomed. Before, that is, the money ran out. They were immensely grateful and only suggested one thing—that I try and keep a couple of the rooms as close as possible to the original format. This was one.'

'It's beautiful.' Lesley hovered by the door and looked around her. Through the French doors, the lawns outside stretched away to an impossibly distant horizon. The sun turned everything into dazzling technicolour. The greens of the grass and the trees seemed greener than possible and the sky was blindingly turquoise. Inside the office, though, the dark colours threw everything into muted relief. He was right; the space was soothing.

She looked at him frowning in front of the computer, sitting forward slightly, his long, powerful body still managing to emanate force even though he wasn't moving.

'There's no need to remain by the door,' he said without looking at her. 'You'll actually need to venture into the room and sit next to me if you're to work on this problem. Ah. Right. Here we go.' He stood up, vacating the chair for her.

The leather was warm from where he had been sitting, and the heat seemed to infiltrate her entire body as she took his place in front of the computer screen. When he leaned over to tap on the keyboard, she felt her breathing become rapid and shallow and she had to stop herself from gasping out loud.

His forearm was inches away from her breasts and never had the proximity of one person's body proved so rattling. She willed herself to focus on what he was calling up on the screen in front of her and to remember that she was here in a professional capacity.

Why was he getting to her? Perhaps she had been too long without a guy in her life. Friends and family were all very good, but maybe her life of pleasant celibacy had made her unexpectedly vulnerable to a spot of swarthy good looks and a wicked smile.

'So...'

Lesley blinked herself back into the present to find herself staring directly into dark, dark eyes that were far too close to her for comfort.

'So?'

'Email one—a little too familiar, a little too chatty, but nothing that couldn't be easily ignored.'

Lesley looked thoughtfully at the computer screen and read through the email. Her surroundings faded away as she began studying the series of emails posted to him, looking for clues, asking him questions, her fingers moving swiftly and confidently across the key board.

She could understand why he had decided to farm out this little problem to an outside source.

If he valued his privacy, then he would not want his IT division to have access to what appeared to be vaguely menacing threats, suggestions of something that could harm his business or ruin his reputation. It would be fodder for any over-imaginative employee, of which there were always a few in any office environment.

Alessio pushed himself away from the desk and strolled towards one of the comfortable, deep chairs facing her.

She was utterly absorbed in what she was doing. He took time out to study her and he was amused and a little surprised to discover that he enjoyed the view.

It wasn't simply the arrangement of her features that he found curiously captivating.

There was a lively intelligence to her that made a refreshing change from the beautiful but intellectually challenged women he dated. He looked at the way her short chocolate-brown hair spiked up, as though too feisty and too wilful to be controlled. Her eyelashes were long and thick; her mouth, as he now saw, was full and, yes, sexy.

A sexy mouth, especially just at this very moment, when her lips were slightly parted.

She frowned and ran her tongue thoughtfully along her upper lip and, on cue, Alessio's body jerked into startling life. His libido, which had been unusually quiet since he'd ended his relationship with a blonde with a penchant for diamonds two months ago, fired up.

It was so unexpected a reaction that he nearly groaned in shock.

Instead, he shifted on the chair and smiled politely as her eyes briefly skittered across to him before resuming their intent concentration on the computer screen.

'Whoever's sent this knows what they're doing.'

'Come again?' Alessio crossed his legs, trying to maintain the illusion that he was in complete control of himself.

'They've been careful to make themselves as un-traceable as possible.' Lesley stretched, then slumped back into the chair and swivelled it round so that she was facing him.

She stuck out her legs and gazed at her espadrilles. 'That first email may have been chatty and friendly but he or she knew that they didn't want to be traced. Why didn't you delete them, at least the earlier ones?'

'I had an instinct that they might be worth hang-ing onto.' He stood up and strolled towards the French doors. He had intended this meeting to be brief and functional, a blip that needed sorting out in his hectic life. Now, he found that his mind was stubbornly re-fusing to return to the matter in hand. Instead, it was relentlessly pulled back to the image he had of her sit-ting in front of his computer concentrating ferociously. He wondered what she would look like out of the unap-pealing ensemble. He wondered whether she would be any different from all the other naked women who had lain across his bed in readiness for him.

He knew she would—instinct again. Somehow he couldn't envisage her lying provocatively for him to take her, passive and willing to please.

No. That wasn't what girls with black belts in karate and a sideline in computer hacking did.

He played with the suddenly tempting notion of prolonging her task. Who knew what might happen between them if she were to be around longer than originally envisaged?

'What would you suggest my next step should be? Because I'm taking from the expression on your face that it's not going to be as straightforward as you first thought.'

'Usually it's pretty easy to sort something like this

out,' Lesley confessed, linking her hands on her stomach and staring off at nothing in particular. The weird, edgy tension she had felt earlier on had dissipated. Work had that effect on her. It occupied her whole mind and left no room for anything else. 'People are predictable when it comes to leaving tracks behind them, but obviously whoever is behind this hasn't used his own computer. He's gone to an Internet café. In fact, I wouldn't be surprised if he goes to a variety of Internet cafés, because we certainly would be able to trace the café he uses if he sticks there. And it wouldn't be too much of a headache finding out which terminal is his and then it would be a short step to identifying the person... I keep saying *he* but it might very well be a *she*.'

'How so? No, we'll get to that over something to drink—and I insist you forfeit the tea in favour of something a little more exciting. My housekeeper makes a very good Pimm's.'

'I couldn't,' Lesley said awkwardly. 'I'm not much of a drinker and I'm...err...driving anyway.'

'Fresh lemonade, in that case.' Alessio strolled towards her and held out his hand to tug her up from the chair to which she seemed to be glued.

For a few seconds, Lesley froze. When she grasped his hand—because frankly she couldn't think of what else to do without appearing ridiculous and childish—she felt a spurt of red-hot electricity zap through her body until every inch of her was galvanised into shrieking, heightened awareness of the dangerously sexy man standing in front of her.

'That would be nice,' she said a little breathlessly. As soon as she could she retrieved her scorching hand and resisted the urge to rub it against her trousers.

Alessio didn't miss a thing. She was a different person when she was concentrating on a computer. Looking at a screen, analysing what was in front of her, working out how to solve the problem he had presented, she oozed self-confidence. He idly wondered what her websites looked like.

But without a computer to absorb her attention she was prickly and defensive, a weird, intriguing mix of independent and vulnerable.

He smiled, turning her insides to liquid, and stood aside to allow her to pass by him out of the office.

'So we have a he or a she who goes to a certain Internet café, or more likely a variety of Internet cafés, for the sole reason of emailing me to, well, purpose as yet slightly unclear, but if I'm any reader of human motivation I'm smelling a lead-up to asking for money for information he or she may or may not know. There seem to be a lot of imponderables in this case.'

They had arrived at the kitchen without her being aware of having padded through the house at all, and she found a glass of fresh lemonade in her hands while he helped himself to a bottle of mineral water.

He motioned to the kitchen table and they sat facing one another on opposite sides.

'Generally,' Lesley said, sipping the lemonade, 'This should be a straightforward case of sourcing the computer in question, paying a visit to the Internet café—and usually these places have CCTV cameras. You would be able to find the culprit without too much bother.'

'But if he's clever enough to hop from café to café…'

'Then it'll take a bit longer but I'll get there. Of course, if you have no skeletons in the cupboard, Mr Baldini, then you could just walk away from this situation.'

'Is there such a thing as an adult without one or two skeletons in the cupboard?'

'Well, then.'

'Although,' Alessio continued thoughtfully, 'Skeletons imply something...wrong, in need of concealment. I can't think of any dark secrets I have under lock or key but there are certain things I would rather not have revealed.'

'Do you honestly care what the public thinks of you? Or maybe it's to do with your company? Sorry, but I don't really know how the big, bad world of business operates, but I'm just assuming that if something gets out that could affect your share prices then you mightn't be too happy.'

'I have a daughter.'

'You *have a daughter*?'

'Surely you got that from your search of me on the Internet?' Alessio said drily.

'I told you, I just skimmed through the stuff. There's an awful lot written up about you and I honestly just wanted to cut to the chase—any articles that could have suggested that I needed to be careful about getting involved. Like I said, I've fine-tuned my search engine when it comes to picking out relevant stuff or else I'd be swamped underneath useless speculation.' *A daughter?*

'Yes. I forgot—the "bodies under the motorway" scenario.' He raised his eyebrows and once again Lesley felt herself in danger of losing touch with common sense.

'I never imagined anything so dramatic, at least not really,' she returned truthfully, which had the effect of making that sexy smile on his face even broader. Flustered, she continued, 'But you were telling me that you have a daughter.'

'You still can't erase the incredulity from your voice,' he remarked, amused. 'Surely you've bumped into people who have had kids?'

'Yes! Of course! But…'

'But?'

Lesley stared at him. 'Why do I get the feeling that you're making fun of me?' she asked, ruffled and red-faced.

'My apologies.' But there was the echo of a smile still lingering in his voice, even though his expression was serious and contrite. 'But you blush so prettily.'

'That's the most ridiculous thing I've ever heard in my life!' And it was. Ridiculous. 'Pretty' was something she most definitely was *not*. Nor was she going to let this guy, this *sex God* of a man—who could have any woman he wanted, if you happened to like that kind of thing—get under her skin.

'Why is it ridiculous?' Alessio allowed himself to be temporarily side-tracked.

'I know you're probably one of these guys who slips into flattery mode with any woman you happen to find yourself confined with, but I'm afraid that I don't go into meltdown at empty compliments.' *What on earth was she going on about?* Why was she jumping into heated self-defence over nonsense like this?

When it came to business, Alessio rarely lost sight of the goal. Right now, not only had he lost sight of it, but he didn't mind. 'Do you go into meltdown at compliments you think are genuine?'

'I…I…'

'You're stammering,' he needlessly pointed out. 'I don't mean to make you feel uncomfortable.'

'I don't…err…feel uncomfortable.'

'Well, that's good.'

Lesley stared helplessly at him. He wasn't just sinfully sexy. The man was beautiful. He hadn't looked beautiful in those pictures, but then she had barely taken them in—a couple of grainy black-and-white shots of a load of businessmen had barely registered on her consciousness. Now, she wished she had paid attention so that she at least could have been prepared for the sort of effect he might have had on her.

Except, she admitted truthfully to herself, she would still have considered herself above and beyond being affected by any man, however good-looking he might happen to be. When it came to matters of the heart, she had always prided herself on her practicality. She knew her limitations and had accepted them. When and if the time came that she wanted a relationship, then she had always known that the man for her would not be the sort who was into looks but the sort who enjoyed intelligence, personality—a meeting of minds as much as anything else.

'You were telling me about your daughter...'

'My daughter.' Alessio sighed heavily and raked his fingers through his dark hair.

It was a gesture of hesitancy that seemed so at odds with his forceful personality that Lesley sat up and stared at him with narrowed eyes.

'Where is she?' Lesley looked past him, as though half-expecting this unexpected addition to his life suddenly to materialise out of nowhere. 'I thought you mentioned that you had no family. Where is your wife?'

'No *sprawling* family,' Alessio amended. 'And no wife. My wife died two years ago.'

'I'm so sorry.'

'There's no need for tears and sympathy.' He waved aside her interruption, although he was startled at how easily a softer nature shone through. 'When I say *wife,* it might be more accurate to say *ex-wife*. Bianca and I were divorced a long time ago.'

'How old is your daughter?'

'Sixteen. And, to save you the hassle of doing the maths, she was, shall we say, an unexpected arrival when I was eighteen.'

'You were a *father* at eighteen?'

'Bianca and I had been seeing each other in a fairly loose fashion for a matter of three months when she announced that her contraceptive pill had failed and I was going to be a father.' His lips thinned. The past was rarely raked up and when it was, as now, it still brought a sour taste to his mouth.

Unfortunately, he could see no way around a certain amount of confidential information exchanging hands because he had a gut feeling that, whatever his uninvited email correspondent wanted, it involved his daughter.

'And you weren't happy about that.' Lesley groped her way to understanding the darkening of his expression.

'A family was not something high on my agenda at the time,' Alessio imparted grimly. 'In fact, I would go so far as to say that it hadn't even crossed my radar. But, naturally, I did the honourable thing and married her. It was a match approved by both sides of the family until, that is, it became apparent that her family's wealth was an illusion. Her parents were up to their eyes in debt and I was a convenient match because of the financial rewards I brought with me.'

'She married you for your *money*?'

'It occurred to no one to do a background check.' He shrugged elegantly. 'You're looking at me as though I've suddenly landed from another planet.'

His slow smile knocked her sideways and she cleared her throat nervously. 'I'm not familiar with people marrying for no better reason than money,' she answered honestly.

Alessio raised his eyebrows. 'In that case, we really *do* come from different planets. My family is extremely wealthy, as am I. Believe me, I am extremely well versed in the tactics women will employ to gain entry to my bank balance.' He crossed his legs, relaxing. 'But you might say that, once bitten, twice shy.'

She made an exceptionally good listener. Was this why he had expanded on the skeleton brief he could have given her? Had gone into details that were irrelevant in the grand scheme of things? He hadn't been lying when he had told her that his unfortunate experience with his ex had left him jaded about women and the lengths they would go to in order to secure themselves a piece of the pie. He was rich and women liked money. It was therefore a given that he employed a healthy amount of caution in his dealings with the opposite sex.

But the woman sitting in front of him couldn't have been less interested in his earnings.

His little problem intrigued her far more than *he* did. It was a situation that Alessio had never encountered in his life before and there was something sexy and challenging about that.

'You mean you don't intend to marry again? I can understand that. And I guess you have your daughter. She must mean the world to you.'

'Naturally.' Alessio's voice cooled. 'Although I'll be the first to admit that things have not been easy between us. I had relatively little contact with Rachel when she was growing up, thanks to my ex-wife's talent for vindictiveness. She lived in Italy but travelled extensively, and usually when she knew that I had arranged a visit.

She was quite happy to whip our daughter out of school at a moment's notice if only to make sure that my trip to Italy to visit would be a waste of time.'

'How awful.'

'At any rate, when Bianca died Rachel naturally came to me, but at the age of fourteen she was virtually a stranger and a fairly hostile one. Frankly, a nightmare.'

'She would have been grieving for her mother.' Lesley could barely remember her own mother and yet *she* still grieved at the lack of one in her life. How much more traumatic to have lost one at the age of fourteen, a time in life when a maternal, guiding hand could not have been more needed.

'She was behind in her schoolwork thanks to my ex-wife's antics, and refused to speak English in the classroom, so the whole business of teaching her was practically impossible. In the end, boarding school seemed the only option and, thankfully, she appears to have settled in there with somewhat more success. At least, there have been no phone calls threatening expulsion.'

'Boarding school…'

Alessio frowned. 'You say that as though it ranks alongside "prison cell".'

'I can't imagine the horror of being separated from my family. My brothers could be little devils when I was growing up but we were a family. Dad, the boys and me.'

Alessio tilted his head and looked at her, considering, tempted to ask her if that was why she had opted for a male-dominated profession, and why she wore clothes better suited to a boy. But the conversation had already drifted too far from the matter at hand. When he glanced down at his watch, it was to find that more time had passed than he might have expected.

'My gut feeling tells me that these emails are in some way connected to my daughter,' Alessio admitted. 'Reason should dictate that they're to do with work but I can't imagine why anyone wouldn't approach me directly about anything to do with my business concerns.'

'No. And if you're as above board as you say you are...'

'You doubt my word?'

Lesley shrugged. 'I don't think that's really my business; the only reason I mention it is because it might be pertinent to finding out who is behind this. 'Course, I shall continue working at the problem, but if it's established that the threat is to do with your work then you might actually be able to pinpoint the culprit yourself.'

'How many people do you imagine work for me?' Alessio asked curiously, and Lesley shrugged and gave the matter some thought.

'No idea.' The company she worked for was small, although prominent in its field, employing only a handful of people on the creative side and slightly fewer on the admin side. 'A hundred or so?'

'You really skimmed through those articles you called up on your computer, didn't you?'

'Big business doesn't interest me,' she informed him airily. 'I may have a talent for numbers, and can do the maths without any trouble at all, but those numbers only matter when it comes to my work. I can work things out precisely but it's really the artistic side of my job that I love. In fact, I only did maths at university because Shane, one of my brothers, told me that it was a man's subject.'

'Thousands.'

Lesley looked at him blankly for a few seconds. 'What are you talking about?'

'Thousands. In various countries. I own several companies and I employ thousands, not hundreds. But that's by the by. This isn't to do with work. This is to do with my daughter. The only problem is that we don't have a great relationship and if I approach her with my suspicions, if I quiz her about her friends, about whether anyone's been acting strangely, asking too many questions…well, I don't anticipate a good outcome to any such conversation. So what would you have done if you hadn't done maths?'

Time had slipped past and they were no nearer to solving the problem, yet he was drawn to asking her yet more questions about herself.

Lesley—following his lead and envisaging the sort of awkward, maybe even downright incendiary conversation that might ensue in the face of Alessio's concerns, should he confront a hostile teenager with them—was taken aback by his abrupt change of topic.

'You said that you only did maths because your brother told you that you couldn't.'

'He never said that I *couldn't*.' She smiled, remembering their war of words. Shane was two years older than her and she always swore that his main purpose in life was to annoy her. He was now a barrister working in Dublin but he still teased her as though they were still kids in primary school. 'He said that it was a man's field, which immediately made me decide to do it.'

'Because, growing up as the only girl in a family of all males, it would have been taken as a given that, whatever your brothers could do, you could as well.'

'I'm wondering what this has to do with the reason I've come here.' She pulled out her mobile phone, checked the time on it and was surprised to discover how much of the day had flown by. 'I'm sorry I haven't been able to sort things out for you immediately. I'd understand perfectly if you want to take the matter to someone else, someone who can devote concentrated time to working on it. It shouldn't take too long, but longer than an hour or two.'

'Would you have done art?' He overrode her interjection as though he hadn't heard any of it and she flung him an exasperated look.

'I did, actually—courses in the town once a week. It was a good decision. It may have clinched me my job.'

'I have no interest in farming out this problem to someone else.'

'I can't give it my full-time attention.'

'Why not?'

'Because,' she said patiently, 'I have a nine-to-five job. And I live in London. And by the time I get back to my place—usually after seven, what with working overtime and then the travel—I'm exhausted. The last thing I need is to start trying to sort your problem out remotely.'

'Who said anything about doing it remotely? Take time off and come here.'

'I beg your pardon?'

'A week. You must be able to take some holiday time? Take it off and come here instead. Trying to sort this out remotely isn't the answer. You won't have sufficient time to do it consistently and also, while this may be to do with unearthing something about my own past, it may also have to do with something in my daughter's life. Something this person thinks poses a risk, should it be exposed. Have you considered that?'

'It had crossed my mind,' Lesley admitted.

'In which case, there could be a double-pronged attack on this problem if you moved in here.'

'What do you mean?'

'My daughter occupies several rooms in the house, by which I mean she has spread herself thin. She has a million books, items of clothing, at least one desktop computer, tablets… If this has to do with anything Rachel has got up to, then you could be on hand to go through her stuff.'

'You want me to *invade her privacy* by searching through her private things?'

'It's all for the greater good.' Their eyes locked and she was suddenly seduced by the temptation to take him up on his offer, to step right out of her comfort zone.

'What's the point of having misplaced scruples? Frankly, I don't see the problem.'

In that single sentence, she glimpsed the man whose natural assumption was that the world would fall in line with what he wanted. And then he smiled, as if he had read her mind, and guessed exactly what was going through it. 'Wouldn't your company allow you a week off? Holiday?'

'That's not the point.'

'Then what is? Possessive boyfriend, perhaps? Won't let you out of his sight for longer than five minutes?'

Lesley looked at him scornfully. 'I would never get involved with anyone who wouldn't let me out of his sight for longer than five minutes! I'm not one of those pathetic, clingy females who craves protection from a big, strong man.' She had a fleeting image of the man sitting opposite her, big, strong, powerful, protecting his woman, making her feel small, fragile and delicate. She had never thought of herself as delicate—too tall, too boyish, too independent. It was ridiculous to have that squirmy sensation in the pit of her stomach now and she thanked the Lord that he really couldn't read her mind.

'So, no boyfriend,' Alessio murmured, cocking his head to one side. 'Then explain to me why you're finding reasons not to do this. I don't want to source anyone else to work on this for me. You might not have been what I expected, but you're good and I trust you, and if my daughter's possessions are to be searched it's essential they be searched by a woman.'

'It wouldn't be ethical to go through someone else's stuff.'

'What if by doing that you spared her a far worse situation? Rachel, I feel, would not be equipped to deal with unpleasant revelations that could damage the foundations of her young life. Furthermore, I won't be looking over your shoulder. You'll be able to work to your own timetable. In fact, I shall be in London most of the time, only returning here some evenings.'

Lesley opened her mouth to formulate a half-hearted protest, because this was all so sudden and so out of the ordinary, but with a slash of his hand he cut her off before any words could leave her mouth.

'She also returns in a few days' time. This is a job that has a very definite deadline; piecemeal when you get a chance isn't going to cut it. You have reservations—I see that—but I need this to be sorted out and I think you're the one to do it. So, please.'

Lesley heard the dark uncertainty in his voice and gritted her teeth with frustration. In a lot of ways, what he said made sense. Even if this job were to take a day or two, she would not be able to give it anything like her full attention if she worked on it remotely for half an hour every evening. And, if she needed to see whether his daughter had logged on to other computer devices, then she would need to be at his house where the equipment was to hand. It wasn't something she relished doing—everyone deserved their privacy—but sometimes privacy had to be invaded as a means of protection.

But moving in, sharing the same space as him? He did something disturbing to her pulse rate, so how was she supposed to live under the same roof?

But the thought drew her with the force of the forbidden.

Watching, Alessio smelled his advantage and lowered his eyes. 'If you won't do this for me…and I realise it would be inconvenient for you…then do it for my daughter, Lesley. She's sixteen and vulnerable.'

CHAPTER THREE

'THIS IS IT...'

Alessio flung back the door to the suite of rooms and stood to one side, allowing Lesley to brush past him.

It was a mere matter of hours since he had pressed home his advantage and persuaded her to take up his offer to move into the house.

She had her misgivings, he could see that, but he wanted her there at hand and he was a man who was accustomed to getting what he wanted, whatever the cost.

As far as he was concerned, his proposition made sense. If she needed to try and hunt down clues from his daughter's possessions, then the only way she could do that would be here, in his house. There was no other way.

He hadn't anticipated this eventuality. He had thought that it would be a simple matter of following a trail of clues on his computer which would lead him straight to whoever was responsible for the emails.

Given that it was not going to be as straightforward as he first thought, it was a stroke of luck that the person working on the case was a woman. She would understand the workings of the female mind and would know where to locate whatever information she might find useful.

Added to that...

He looked at Lesley with lazy, brooding eyes as she stepped into the room.

There was something about the woman. She didn't pull her punches and, whilst a part of him was grimly disapproving of her forthright manner, another part of him was intrigued.

When was the last time he had been in the company of a woman who didn't say what she wanted him to hear?

When had he *ever* been in the company of any woman who didn't say what she wanted him to hear?

He was the product of a life of privilege. He had grown up accustomed to servants and chauffeurs and then, barely into adulthood, had found himself an expectant father. In a heartbeat, his world had changed. He'd no longer had the freedom to make youthful mistakes and to learn from them over time. Responsibility had landed on his doorstep without an invitation and then, on top of that, had come the grim realisation that he had been used for his money.

Not even out of his teens, he had discovered the bitter truth that his fortune would always be targeted. He would never be able to relax in the company of any woman without suspecting that she had her eye to the main chance. He would always have to be on his guard, always watchful, always making sure that no one got too close.

He was a generous lover, and had no problem splashing out on whatever woman happened to be sharing his bed, but he knew where to draw the line and was ruthless when it came to making sure that no woman got too close, certainly not close enough ever to harbour notions of longevity.

It was unusual to find himself in a situation such as

this. It was unusual to be in close personal confines with a woman where sex wasn't on the menu.

It was even more unusual to find himself in this situation with a woman who made no effort to try and please him in any way.

'I was expecting a bedroom.' Lesley turned to look at him. 'Posters on the walls, cuddly toys, that sort of thing.'

'Rachel occupies one wing of the house. There are actually three bedrooms, along with a sitting room, a study, two bathrooms and an exercise room.' He strolled towards her and looked around him, hands shoved in the pockets of his cream trousers. 'This is the first time I've stepped foot into this section of the house since my daughter returned from boarding school for the holidays. When I saw the state it was in, I immediately got in touch with Violet, who informed me that she, along with her assistants, were barred from entry.'

Disapproval was stamped all over his face and Lesley could understand why. The place looked as though a bomb had been detonated in it. The tiled, marble floor of the small hallway was barely visible under discarded clothes and books and, through the open doors, she could see the other rooms appeared to be in a similar state of chaos.

Magazines were strewn everywhere. Shoes, kicked off, had landed randomly and then had been left there. School books lay open on various surfaces.

Going through all of this would be a full-time job.

'Teenagers can be very private creatures,' Lesley said dubiously. 'They hate having their space invaded.' She picked her way into bedroom number one and then continued to explore the various rooms, all the time conscious of Alessio lounging indolently against the wall and watching her progress.

She had the uneasy feeling of having been manipulated. How had she managed to end up here? Now she felt *involved*. She was no longer doing a quick job to help her father's pal out. She was ensconced in the middle of a family saga and wasn't quite sure where to begin.

'I will get Violet to make sure that these rooms are tidied first thing in the morning,' Alessio said as she finally walked towards him. 'At least then you will have something of a clean slate to start on.'

'Probably not such a good idea.' Lesley looked up at him. He was one of the few men with whom she could do that and, as she had quickly discovered, her breathing quickened as their eyes met. 'Adolescents are fond of writing stuff down on bits of paper. If there is anything to be found, that's probably where I'll find it, and that's just the sort of thing a cleaner would stick in the bin.' She hesitated. 'Don't you communicate with your daughter *at all*? I mean, how could she get away with keeping her room—her *rooms*—as messy as this?'

Alessio took one final glance around him and then headed for the door. 'Rachel has spent most of the summer here while I have been in London, only popping back now and again. She's clearly intimidated the cleaners into not going anywhere near her rooms and they've obeyed.'

'You've just *popped back here now and again* to see how she's doing?'

Alessio stopped in his tracks and looked at her coolly. 'You're here to try and sort out a situation involving computers and emails. You're not here to pass judgement on my parenting skills.'

Lesley sighed with obvious exasperation. She had been hustled here with unholy speed. He had even come with her to her office, on the pretext of having a look at what her company did, and had so impressed her boss that Jake had had no trouble in giving her the week off.

And now, having found herself in a situation that somehow didn't seem to be of her own choosing, she wasn't about to be lectured to in that patronising tone of voice.

'I'm not passing opinions on your parenting skills,' she said with restraint. 'I'm trying to make sense of a picture. If I can see the whole picture, then I might have an idea of how and where to proceed.' She had not yet had time since arriving to get down to the business of working her way through the emails and trying to trace the culprit responsible for them.

That was a job for the following day. Right now, she would barely have time to have dinner, run a bath and then hit the sack. It had been a long day.

'I mean,' she said into an unresponsive silence, 'If and when I do find out who is responsible for those emails, we still won't know why he's sending them. He could clam up, refuse to say anything, and then you may still be left with a problem on your hands in connection with your daughter.'

They had reached the kitchen, which was a vast space dominated by a massive oak table big enough to seat ten. Everything in the house was larger than life, including all the furnishings.

'They may have nothing to do with Rachel. That's just another possibility.' He took a bottle of wine from the fridge and two wine glasses from one of the cupboards. There was a rich smell of food and Lesley looked around for Violet, who seemed to be an invisible but constant presence in the house.

'Where's Violet?' she asked, hovering.

'Gone for the evening. I try and not keep the hired help chained to the walls at night.' He proffered the glass of wine. 'And you can come inside, Lesley. You're not entering a lion's den.'

It felt like it, however. In ways she couldn't put her finger on, Alessio Baldini felt exciting and dangerous at the same time. Especially so at night, here, in his house with no one around.

'She's kindly prepared a casserole for us. Beef. It's in the oven. We can have it with bread, if that suits you.'

'Of course,' Lesley said faintly. 'Is that how it works when you're here? Meals are prepared for you so that all you have to do is switch the oven on?'

'One of the housekeepers tends to stick around when Rachel's here.' Alessio flushed and turned away.

In that fleeting window, she glimpsed the situation with far more clarity than if she had had it spelled out for her.

He was so awkward with his own daughter that he preferred to have a third party to dilute the atmosphere. Rachel probably felt the same way. Two people, father and daughter, were circling one another like strangers in a ring.

He had been pushed to the background during her formative years, had found his efforts at bonding repelled and dismantled by a vengeful wife, and now found himself with a teenager he didn't know. Nor was he, by nature, a people person—the sort of man who could joke his way back into a relationship.

Into that vacuum, any number of gremlins could have entered.

'So you're *never* on your own with your daughter? Okay. In that case you really wouldn't have a clue what was happening in her life, especially as she spends most of the year away from home. But you were saying that this may not have anything directly to do with Rachel. What did you mean by that?'

She watched him bring the food to the table and re-fill their glasses with more wine.

Alessio gave her a long, considered look from under his lashes.

'What I am about to tell you stays within the walls of this house, is that clear?'

Lesley paused with her glass halfway to her mouth and looked at him over the rim with astonishment.

'And you laugh at me for thinking that you might have links to the Mafia?'

Alessio stared at her and then shook his head and slowly grinned. 'Okay, maybe that sounded a little melodramatic.'

Lesley was knocked sideways by that smile. It was so full of charm, so lacking in the controlled cool she had seen in him before. It felt as though, the more time she spent in his company, the more intriguing and complex he became. He was not simply a mega-rich guy employing her to do a job for him, but a man with so many facets to his personality that it made her head spin.

Worse than that, she could feel herself being sucked in, and that scared her.

'I don't do melodrama,' Alessio was saying with the remnants of his smile. 'Do you?'

'Never.' Lesley licked her lips nervously. 'What are you going to tell me that has to stay here?'

His dark eyes lingered on her flushed face. 'It's un-likely that our guy would have got hold of this informa-tion but, just in case, it's information I would want to protect my daughter from knowing. I certainly would not want it in the public arena.' He swigged the remainder of his wine and did the honours by dishing food onto the plates which had already been put on the table, along with glasses and cutlery.

Mesmerised by the economic elegance of his movements, and lulled by the wine and the creeping darkness outside, Lesley cupped her chin in her hand and stared at him.

He wasn't looking at her. He was concentrating on not spilling any food. He had the expression of someone unaccustomed to doing anything of a culinary nature for themselves—focused yet awkward at the same time.

'You don't look comfortable with a serving spoon,' she remarked idly and Alessio glanced across to where she was sitting, staring at him. She wore a thin gold chain with a tiny pendant around her neck and she was playing with the pendant, rolling it between her fingers as she looked at him.

Suddenly and for no reason, his breathing thickened and heat surged through his body with unexpected force. His libido, that had not seen the light of day for the past couple of months, reared up with such urgency that he felt his sharp intake of breath.

She was not trying to be seductive but somehow he could feel her seducing him.

'I bet you don't do much cooking for yourself.'

'Come again?' Alessio did his best to get his thoughts back in order. An erection was jamming against the zipper of his trousers, rock-hard and painful, and it was a relief to sit down.

'I said, you don't look as though handling pots and pans comes as second nature to you.' She tucked into the casserole, which was mouth-wateringly fragrant. They should be discussing work but the wine had made her feel relaxed and mellow and had allowed her curiosity about him to come out of hiding and to take centre stage.

Sober, she would have chased that curiosity away, because she could feel its danger. But pleasantly tipsy, she wanted to know more about him.

'I don't do much cooking, no.'

'I guess you can always get someone else to do it for you. Top chefs or housekeepers, or maybe just your girlfriends.' She wondered what his girlfriends looked like. He might have had a rocky marriage that had ended in divorce, but he would have lots of girlfriends.

'I don't let women near my kitchen.' Alessio was amused at her disingenuous curiosity. He swirled his wine around in the glass and swallowed a mouthful.

With a bit of alcohol in her system, she looked more relaxed, softer, less defensive.

His erection was still throbbing and his eyes dropped to her mouth, then lower to where the loose neckline of her tee-shirt allowed a glimpse of her shoulder blades and the soft hint of a cleavage. She wasn't big breasted and the little she had was never on show.

'Why? Don't you ever go out with women who like to cook?'

'I've never asked whether they like to cook or not,' he said wryly, finishing his wine, pouring himself another glass and keeping his eyes safely away from her loose-limbed body. 'I've found that, the minute a woman starts eulogising about the joys of home-cooked food, it usually marks the end of the relationship.'

'What do you mean?' Lesley looked at him, surprised.

'It means that the last thing I need is someone trying to prove that they're a domestic goddess in my kitchen. I prefer that the women I date don't get too settled.'

'In case they get ideas of permanence?'

'Which brings me neatly back to what I wanted to say.' That disturbing moment of intense sexual attraction began to ebb away and he wondered how it had arisen in the first place.

She was nothing like the women he dated. Could it be that her intelligence, the strange role she occupied as receiver of information no other woman had ever had, the sheer difference of her body, had all those things conspired against him?

There was a certain intimacy to their conversation. Had that entered the mix and worked some kind of passing, peculiar magic?

More to the point, a little voice inside him asked, what did he intend to do about it?

'I have a certain amount of correspondence locked away that could be very damaging.'

'Correspondence?'

'Of the non-silicon-chip variety,' Alessio elaborated drily. 'Correspondence of the old-fashioned sort—namely, letters.'

'To do with business?' She felt a sudden stab of intense disappointment that she had actually believed him when he had told her that he was an honest guy in all his business dealings.

'No, not to do with business, so you can stop thinking that you've opened a can of worms and you need to clear off as fast as you can. I told you I'm perfectly straight when it comes to my financial dealings and I wasn't lying.'

Lesley released a long sigh of relief. Of course, it was because she would have been in a very awkward situation had he confessed to anything shady, especially considering she was alone with him in his house.

It definitely wasn't because she would have been disappointed in him as a man had he been party to anything crooked.

'Then what? And what is the relevance to the case?'

'This could hurt my daughter. It would certainly be annoying for me should it hit the press. If I fill you in, then you might be able to join some dots and discover if this is the subject of his emails.'

'You have far too much confidence in my abilities, Mr Baldini.' She smiled. 'I may be good at what I do but I'm not a miracle worker.'

'I think we've reached the point where you can call me Alessio. It occurred to me that there may have been stray references in the course of the emails that might point in a certain direction.'

'And you feel that I need to know the direction they may point in so that I can pick them up if they're there?'

'Something like that.'

'Wouldn't you have seen them for yourself?'

'I only began paying attention to those emails the day you were hired. Before that, I had kept them, but hadn't examined them in any depth and I haven't had the opportunity to do so since. It's a slim chance but we can cover all bases.'

'And what if I do find a link?'

'Then I shall know what options to take when it comes to dealing with the perpetrator.'

Lesley sighed and fluffed her short hair up with her fingers. 'Do you know, I have never been in this sort of situation before.'

'But you've had a couple of tricky occasions.'

'Not as complicated as this. The tricky ones have usually involved friends of friends imagining that I can unearth marital affairs by bugging computers, and then

I have to let them down. If I can even be bothered to see what they want in the first place.'

'And this?'

'This feels as though it's got layers.' And she wasn't sure that she wanted to peel them back to see what was lying underneath. It bothered her that he had such an effect on her that he had been able to entice her into taking time off work to help him in the first place.

And it bothered her even more that she couldn't seem to stop wanting to stare at him. Of course he was good-looking, but she was sensible when it came to guys, and this one was definitely off-limits. The gulf between them was so great that they could be living on different planets.

And yet her eyes still sought him out, and that was worrying.

'I had more than one reason for divorcing my wife,' he said heavily, after a while. He hesitated, at a loss as to where to go from there, because sharing confidences was not something he ever did. From the age of eighteen, he had learnt how to keep his opinions to himself—first through a sense of shame that he had been hoodwinked by a girl he had been seeing for a handful of months, a girl who had conned him into thinking she had been on the pill. Later, when his marriage had predictably collapsed, he had developed a forbidding ability to keep his emotions and his thoughts under tight rein. It was what he had always seen as protection against ever making another mistake when it came to the opposite sex.

But now...

Her intelligent eyes were fixed on his face. He reminded himself that this was a woman against whom he needed no protection because she had no ulterior agenda.

'Not only did Bianca lie her way into a marriage but she also managed to lie her way into making me believe that she was in love with me.'

'You were a kid,' Lesley pointed out, when he failed to elaborate on that remark. 'It happens.'

'And you know because…?'

'I don't,' she said abruptly. 'I wasn't one of those girls anyone lied to about being in love with. Carry on.'

Alessio tilted his head and looked at her enquiringly, tempted to take her up on that enigmatic statement, even though he knew he wouldn't get anywhere with it.

'We married and, very shortly after Rachel was born, my wife began fooling around. Discreetly at first, but that didn't last very long. We moved in certain circles and it became a bore to try and work out who she wanted to sleep with and when she would make a move.'

'How awful for you.'

Alessio opened his mouth to brush that show of sympathy to one side but instead stared at her for a few moments in silence. 'It wasn't great,' he admitted heavily.

'It can't have been. Not at any age, but particularly not when you were practically a child yourself and not equipped to deal with that kind of disillusionment.'

'No.' His voice was rough but he gave a little shrug, dismissing that episode in his life.

'I can understand why you would want to protect your daughter from knowing that her mother was… promiscuous.'

'There's rather more.' His voice was steady and matter-of-fact. 'When our marriage was at its lowest ebb, Bianca implied, during one of our rows, that I wasn't Rachel's father at all. Afterwards she retracted her words and said that she hadn't been thinking straight. God knows, she probably realised that Rachel was her lifeline to money, and the last thing she should do was to jeopardise that lifeline, but the words were out and as far as I was concerned couldn't be taken back.'

'No, I can understand that.' Whoever said that money could buy happiness? she thought, feeling her heart constrict for the young boy he must have been then—deceived, betrayed, cheated on; forced to become a man when he was still in his teens.

'One day when she was out shopping, I returned early from work and decided, on impulse, to go through her drawers. By this time, we were sleeping in separate rooms. I found a stash of letters, all from the same guy, someone she had known when she was sixteen. Met him on holiday somewhere in Majorca. Young love. Touching, don't you think? They kept in contact and she was seeing him when she was married to me. I gathered from reading between the lines that he was the son of a poor fisherman, someone her parents would certainly not have welcomed with open arms.'

'No.'

'The lifestyles of the rich and famous,' he mocked wryly. 'I bet you're glad you weren't one of the privileged crowd.'

'I never gave it much thought, but now that you mention it…' She smiled and he grudgingly returned the smile.

'I have no idea whether the affair ended when her behaviour became more out of control but it certainly made me wonder whether she was right about our daughter not being biologically mine. Not that it would have made a scrap of difference but…'

'You'd have to find out that sort of thing.'

'Tests proved conclusively that Rachel is my child but you can see why this information could be highly destructive if it came to light, especially considering the poor relationship I have with my daughter. It could be catastrophic. She would always doubt my love for her if she thought that I had taken a paternity test to prove she was mine in the first place. It would certainly destroy the happy memories she has of her mother and, much as Bianca appalled me, I wouldn't want to deprive Rachel of her memories.'

'But if this information was always private and historic, and only contained in letter form, then I don't see how anyone else could have got hold of it.' But there were always links to links to links; it just took one person to start delving and who knew what could come out in the wash? 'I'll see if I can spot any names or hints that this might be the basis of the threats.'

And at the same time, she would have her work cut out going through his daughter's things, a job which still didn't sit well with her, even though a part of her know that it was probably essential.

'I should be heading up to bed now,' she said, rising to her feet.

'It's not yet nine-thirty.'

'I'm an early-to-bed kind of person,' she said awkwardly, not knowing whether to leave the kitchen or remain where she was, then realising that she was behaving like an employee waiting for her boss to dismiss her. But her feet remained nailed to the spot.

'I have never talked so much about myself,' Alessio murmured, which got her attention, and she looked at him quizzically. 'It's not in my nature. I'm a very private man, hence what I've told you goes no further than this room.'

'Of course it won't,' Lesley assured him vigorously. 'Who would I tell?'

'If someone could consider blackmailing me over this information, then it might occur to you that you could do the same. You would certainly have unrivalled proof of whatever you wanted to glean about my private life in the palm of your hand.'

It was a perfectly logical argument and he was, if nothing else, an extremely logical man. But Alessio still felt an uncustomary twinge of discomfort at having spelled it out so clearly.

He noticed the patches of angry colour that flooded her cheeks and bit back the temptation to apologise for being more blunt than strictly necessary.

She worked with computers; she would know the value of logic and reason.

'You're telling me that you don't trust me.'

'I'm telling you that you keep all of this to yourself. No girly gossip in the toilets at work, or over a glass of wine with your friends, and certainly no pillow talk with whoever you end up sharing your bed with.'

'Thank you for spelling it out so clearly,' Lesley said coldly. 'But I know how to keep a confidence and I fully understand that it's important that none of this gets out. If you have a piece of paper, you can draft something up right here and I'll sign it!'

'Draft something up?' Under normal circumstances, he certainly would have had that in place before hiring her for the job, but for some reason it simply hadn't occurred to him.

Perhaps it had been the surprise of opening the front door to a girl instead of the man he had been expecting.

Perhaps there was something about her that had worked its way past his normal defences so that he had failed to go down the predicted route.

'I'm happy to sign whatever silence clause you want.

One word of what we've spoken about here, and you will have my full permission to fling me into jail and throw away the key.'

'I thought you said that you weren't melodramatic.'

'I'm insulted that you think I'd break the confidence you have in me to do my job and keep the details of it to myself.'

'You may be insulted, but are you surprised?' He rose to his feet, towering over her, and she fell back a couple of steps and held onto the back of the kitchen chair.

Alessio, on his way to make them some coffee, sensed the change in the atmosphere the way a big cat can sense the presence of prey in the shift of the wind. Their eyes met and something inside him, something that operated on an instinctual level, understood that, however scathing and derisive her tone of voice had been, she was tuned in to him in ways that matched his.

Tuned in to him in ways that were sexual.

The realisation struck him from out of nowhere and yet, as he held her gaze a few seconds longer than was necessary, he actually doubted himself because her expression was so tight, straightforward and openly annoyed.

'I am a man who is accustomed to taking precautions,' he murmured huskily.

'I get that.' Especially after everything he had told her. Of course he would want to make sure that he didn't leave himself open to exploitation of any kind. That was probably one of the rules by which he lived his life.

So he was right; why should she be surprised that he had taken her to task?

Except she had been lulled into a false sense of confidences shared, had warmed to the fact that he had opened up to her, and in the process had chosen to ignore the reality, which was that he had decided that he had no choice. He hadn't opened up to her because she was special. He had opened up to her because it was necessary to make her task a little easier.

'Do you?'

'Of course I do,' she said on a sigh. 'I'm just not used to people distrusting me. I'm one of the most reliable people I know when it comes to keeping a secret.'

'Really?' Mere inches separated them. He could feel the warmth radiating from her body out towards his and he wondered again whether his instincts had been right when they had told him that she was not as unaffected by him as she would have liked to pretend.

'Yes!' She relaxed with a laugh. 'When I was a teenager, I was the one person all the lads turned to when it came to confidences. They knew I would never breathe a word when they told me that they fancied someone, or asked me what I thought it would take to impress someone else...'

And all the while, Alessio thought to himself, you were taking lessons in self-defence.

Never one to do much prying into female motivations, he was surprised to find that he quite wanted to know more about her. 'You've won your argument,' he said with a slow smile.

'You mean, you won't be asking me to sign something?'

'No. So there will be no need for you to live in fear that you will be flung into prison and the key thrown away if the mood takes me.' His eyes dipped down to the barely visible swell of her small breasts under the baggy tee-shirt.

'I appreciate that,' Lesley told him sincerely. 'I don't know how easy I would have found it, working for someone who didn't trust me. So I shall start first thing in the morning.' She suddenly realised just how close their bodies were to one another and she shuffled a couple of discreet inches back. 'If it's all the same to you, you can point me in the direction of your computer and I'll spend the morning there, and the afternoon going through your daughter's rooms just in case I find anything of interest. And you needn't worry about asking your housekeeper to prepare any lunch for me. I usually just eat on the run. I can fill you in when you return from London or else I can call you if you decide to stay in London overnight.'

Alessio inclined his head in agreeable assent—except, maybe there would be no need for that.

Maybe he would stay here in the country—so much more restful than London and so much easier were he to be at hand.

CHAPTER FOUR

LESLEY WAS NOT finding life particularly restful. Having been under the impression that Alessio would be commuting to and from London, with a high possibility of remaining in London for at least part of the time, she'd been dismayed when, two days previously, he'd informed her that there had been a change of plan.

'I'll be staying here,' he had said the morning after she had arrived. 'Makes sense.'

Lesley had no idea how he had reached that conclusion. How did it make sense for him to be around: bothering her; getting under her skin; just *being* within her line of vision and therefore compelling her to look at him?

'You'll probably have a lot of questions and it'll be easier if I'm here to answer them.'

'I could always phone you,' she had said, staring at him with rising panic, because she'd been able to see just how the week was going to play out.

'And then,' he had continued, steamrollering over her interruption, 'I would feel guilty were I to leave you here on your own. The house is very big. My conscience wouldn't be able to live with the thought that you might find it quite unsettling being here with no one around.'

He had directed her to where she would be working

and she'd been appalled to find that she would be sharing office space with him.

'Of course, if you find it uncomfortable working in such close proximity to me, then naturally I can set up camp somewhere else. The house has enough rooms to accommodate one of them being turned into a makeshift work place.'

She had closed her mouth and said nothing, because what had there been to say? That, yes, she *would* find it uncomfortable working in such close proximity to him, because she was just too *aware* of him for her own good; because he made her nervous and tense; because her skin tingled the second he got too close?

She had moved from acknowledging that the man was sexy to accepting that she was attracted to him. She had no idea how that could be the case, given that he just wasn't the sort of person she had ever envisaged herself taking an interest in, but she had given up fighting it. There was just something too demanding about his physicality for her to ignore.

So she had spent her mornings in a state of rigid, hyper-sensitive awareness. She had been conscious of his every small move as he'd peered at his computer screen, reached across his desk to get something or swivelled his chair so that he could find a more comfortable position for his long legs.

She had not been able to block out the timbre of his deep voice whenever he was on the phone. She wouldn't have been able to recall any of the conversations he had had, but she could recall exactly what that voice did to her.

The range of unwanted physical sensations he evoked in her was frankly exhausting.

So she had contrived to have a simple routine of disappearing outside to communicate with her office on the pretext that she didn't want to disturb him.

Besides, she had added, making sure to forestall any objections, she never got the chance to leave London. She had never been to stay at a country estate in her life before. It would be marvellous if she could take advantage of the wonderful opportunity he had given her by working outdoors so that she could enjoy being in the countryside, especially given that the weather was so brilliant.

He had acquiesced although when he had looked at her she had been sure that she could detect a certain amount of amusement.

Now, in a break with this routine, Lesley had decided to start on Rachel's rooms.

She had gone over all of the emails with a fine toothcomb and had found no evidence that the mystery writer was aware of Bianca's past.

She looked around room number one and wondered where to begin.

As per specific instructions, Violet had left everything as it was and Lesley, by no means a neat freak, was not looking forward to going through the stacks of dispersed clothes, books, magazines and random bits of paper that littered the ground.

But she dug in, working her way steadily through the chaos, flinging clothes in the stainless-steel hamper she had dragged from the massive bathroom and marvelling that a child of sixteen could possess so much designer clothing.

This was what money bought: expensive clothes and jewellery. But no amount of expensive clothes and jewellery could fix a broken relationship and, over the past two days, she had seen for herself just how broken the relationship between father and daughter was.

He kept his emotions under tight control but every so often there were glimpses of the man underneath who was confused at his inability to communicate with his daughter and despairing of what the future held for them.

And yet, he wanted to protect her, and would do anything to that end.

She began rifling through the pockets of a pair of jeans, her mind playing with the memory of just how weirdly close the past couple of days had brought them.

Or, at least, *her*.

But then, she thought ruefully, she was handicapped by the fact that she found him attractive. She was therefore primed to analyse everything he said, to be super-attentive to every stray remark, to hang onto his every word with breathless intensity.

Thank God he didn't know what was going through her head.

It took her a couple of seconds before the piece of paper she extracted from the jeans pocket made sense and then a couple more seconds before the links she had begun to see in the emails began to tie up in front of her.

More carefully now, she began feeling her way through the mess, inspecting everything in her path. She went over the clothes she had carelessly chucked into the hamper just in case she had missed something.

Had she expected to find anything at all like this, searching through a few rooms? No; maybe when she got to the computer or the tablet, or whatever other computer gadgets might be lying around.

But scribbles on a bit of paper? No. She thought that teenagers were way beyond using pens and paper by way of communication.

What else might she find?

She had lost that initial feeling of intruding in someone else's space. Something about the messiness made
her search more acceptable.

No attempts had been made to hide anything and
nothing was under lock and key.

Did that make a difference? In a strange way it did,
as did the little things lying about that showed Rachel
for the child she still was, even if she had entered the
teenage battleground of rebellion and disobedience.

Her art book was wonderful. There were cute little
doodles in the margins of her exercise books. Her sta-
tionery was very cute, with lots of puppy motifs on the
pencil cases and folders. It was at odds with the rest of
what was to be found in the room.

An hour and a half into the search, Lesley opened
the first of the wardrobes and gasped at the racks of
clothes confronting her.

You didn't need to be a connoisseur of fine clothing
to know that these were the finest money could buy. She
ran her hands through the dresses, skirts and tops and
felt silk, cashmere and pure cotton. Some of them were
youthful and brightly coloured, others looked far too
grown-up for a sixteen-year-old child. Quite a few things
still had tags attached because they had yet to be used.

As she pushed the clothes at the front aside, she came
across some dresses at the back that were clearly too old
for a sixteen-year-old; they must have belonged to Rachel's mother. Lesley gently pulled a demure black dress
from the selection and admired the fine material and
elegant cut of the design. She knew that it was wrong
to try on someone else's clothes but she lost her head
for a moment and suddenly found herself slipping into
the gorgeous creation. As she turned to look at herself
in the mirror, she gasped.

Usually she was awkward, one of the lads, at her most comfortable when she was exchanging banter; yet the creature staring back at her wasn't that person at all. The creature staring back at her was a leggy, attractive young woman with a good figure, good legs and a long neck.

She spun away from the mirror suddenly as she heard the door open and saw Alessio look at her in shock.

'What are you doing here?' She felt naked as his eyes slowly raked over her, from the top of her head, along her body and then all the way back again.

Alessio couldn't stop looking at her. He had left the office to stretch his legs and had decided to check on how Lesley's search was coming along. He hadn't expected to find her in a stunning cocktail dress, her legs seeming to go on for ever.

'Well?' Lesley folded her arms defensively, although what she really wanted to do was somehow reach down and cover her exposed thighs. The skirt should have been a couple of inches above the knee but, because she was obviously taller than Rachel's mother had been, it was obscenely short on her.

'I've interrupted a catwalk session,' he murmured, walking slowly towards her. 'My apologies.'

'I was... I thought...'

'It suits you, just in case you're interested in what I think. The dress, I mean. You should reveal your legs more often.'

'If you would please just go, I'll get changed. I apologise for having tried on the dress. It was totally out of order, and if you want to give me my marching orders then I would completely understand.' She had never felt so mortified in her entire life. What must he be thinking? She had taken something that didn't belong to her and put it on, an especially unforgivable offence, considering she was under his roof in the capacity of a paid employee.

His 'catwalk' comment struck her as an offensive insult but there was no way she was going to call him out on that. She just wanted him to leave the room but he showed no signs of going.

'Why would I give you your marching orders?' She was bright red and as stiff as a plank of wood.

Any other woman would have been overjoyed to be the centre of his attention, as she now was, but instead she was staring straight ahead, unblinking, doing her utmost to shut him out of her line of vision.

He had never wanted a woman as much as he wanted this one right now. Mind and body fused. This wasn't just another of his glamorous, sex-kitten women. This thinking, questioning, irreverent creature was in a different league.

The attraction he had felt for her, which had been there from the second they had met, clarified into the absolute certainty that he wanted her in his bed. It was a thought he had flirted with, dwelled on; rejected because she'd challenged him on too many levels and he liked his women unchallenging.

But, hell…

'Please leave.'

'You don't have to take off the dress,' he said in a lazy drawl. 'I'd quite like to see you working in that outfit.'

'You're making fun of me and I don't like it.' She had managed to blank him out, so that she was just aware of him on the periphery of her vision, but she could still feel his power radiating outwards, wrapping around her like something thick, suffocating and tangible.

She felt like something small and helpless being circled by a beautiful, dangerous predator.

Except he would never hurt her. No; his capacity for destruction lay in his ability to make her hurt herself by believing what he was saying, by allowing her feelings for him get the better of her. She had never realised that lust could be so overwhelming. Nothing had prepared her for the crazy, inappropriate emotions that rode roughshod over her prized and treasured common sense.

'I'll pretend I didn't hear that,' Alessio said softly. Then he reached out and ran his hand along her arm, feeling its soft, silky smoothness. She was so slender. For a few seconds, Lesley didn't react, then the feel of his warm hand on her skin made her stumble backwards with a yelp.

His instincts had been right. How could he have doubted himself? The electricity between them flowed both ways. He stepped back and looked at her lazily. Her eyes were huge and she looked very young and very vulnerable. And she was still wobbling in the high stilettos; that was how uncomfortable she was in a pair of heels. He was struck with a pressing desire to see her dolled up to the nines and, with an even more contradictory one, to have her naked in his arms.

'I'll leave you to get back into your clothes,' he said with the gentleness of someone trying to calm a panicked, highly strung thoroughbred. 'And, to answer your question as to what I'm doing here, I thought I would just pop in and see if your search up here was being fruitful.'

Relieved to have the focus off her and onto work, Lesley allowed some of the tension to ooze out of her body.

'I *have* found one or two things you might be interested in,' she said with staccato jerkiness. 'And I'll come right down to the office.'

'Better still, meet me outside. I'll get Violet to bring us out some tea.' He smiled, encouraging her to relax further. It was all he could do not to let his eyes wander over her, drink her in. He lowered his eyes and reluctantly spun round, walking towards the door and knowing that she wouldn't move a muscle until he was well and truly out of the suite of rooms and heading down the staircase.

Once outside, he couldn't wait for her to join him. He was oblivious to his surroundings as he stared off into the distance, thinking of how she had looked in that outfit. She had incredible legs, an incredible body and it was all the more enhanced by the fact that she was so unaware of her charms.

Five brothers; no mother; karate lessons when the rest of her friends were practising the feminine skills that would serve them well in later life. Was that why she was so skittish around him? Was she skittish around *all* men, or was it just him? Was that why she chose to dress the way she did, why she projected such a capable image, why she deliberately seemed to spurn feminine clothes?

He found himself idly trying to work out what made her tick and he was enjoying the game when he saw her walking towards him with a sheaf of papers in her hand, all business as usual.

'Thank you.' Lesley sat down, taking the glass that was offered to her. She had been so hot and bothered after he had left that she had taken time out to wash her face in cold water and gather herself. 'First of all—and I'm almost one-hundred-per-cent sure about this—our emailing friend has no idea about your wife or the sort of person she was.'

Alessio leant closer, forearms resting on his thighs. 'And you've reached that conclusion because…?'

'Because I've been through each and every email very carefully, looking for clues. I've also found a couple of earlier emails which arrived in your junk box and for some reason weren't deleted. They weren't significant. Perhaps our friend was just having a bit of fun.'

'So you think this isn't about a blackmail plot to do with revelations about Bianca?'

'Yes, partly from reading through the emails and partly common sense. I think if they involved your ex-wife there would have been some sort of guarded reference made that would have warned you of what was to come. And, whilst he or she knew what they were doing and were careful to leave as few tracks behind them as they could, some of those emails are definitely more rushed than others.'

'Woman's intuition?' There was genuine curiosity in his voice and Lesley nodded slowly.

'I think so. What's really significant, though, is that the Internet cafés used were all in roughly the same area, within a radius of a dozen miles or so, and they are all in the general vicinity of where Rachel goes to school. Which leads me to think that she is at the centre of this in some way, shape or form because the person responsible probably knows her or knows of her.'

Alessio sat back and rubbed his eyes wearily. Lesley could see the strain visible beneath the cool, collected exterior when he next looked at her. He might have approached this problem with pragmatism and detachment, as a job to be done—but his daughter was involved and that showed on his face now, in the worry and the stress.

'Any idea of what could be going on? It could still

be that our friend, as you call him, has information on Bianca and wants me to pay him for not sharing that information with Rachel.'

'Does Rachel know anything about what her mother was like as…err…a young girl? I mean, when she was still married to you? I know your daughter would have been a toddler with no memories of that time, but you know how it is: overheard conversations between adults, bits and pieces of gossip from friends or family or whatever.'

Alessio leaned back in the chair and closed his eyes.

'As far as I am aware, Rachel is completely in the dark about Bianca, but who knows? We haven't talked about it. We've barely got past the stage of polite pleasantries.'

Lesley stared at his averted profile. Seeing them in repose, as now, she felt the full impact of his devastating good looks. His sensual mouth lost its stern contours; she could appreciate the length and thickness of his eyelashes, the strong angle of his jaw, the tousled blackness of his slightly too-long hair. His fingers were linked loosely on his stomach; she took in the dark hair on his forearms and then burned when she wondered where that dark hair was replicated.

She wondered whether she should tell him about those random scribbles she had found and decided against it. They formed part of the jigsaw puzzle but she would hang on until more of the pieces came together. It was only fair. He was a desperately concerned father, worried about a daughter he barely knew; to add yet more stress to his situation, when she wasn't even one-hundred per cent sure whether what she had found would prove significant in the end, seemed downright selfish.

The lingering embarrassment she had brought with her after the mini-skirt-wearing episode faded as the silence lengthened between them, a telling indication of his state of mind.

It would have cost him dearly to confide the personal details of his situation with his ex-wife. No matter that he had been practically a child at the time. No one enjoyed being used and Alessio, in particular, was a proud man today and would have been a proud boy all those years ago.

Her heart softened and she resisted the temptation to reach out and stroke the side of his cheek.

'I'm making you feel awkward,' Alessio murmured, breaking the silence, but not opening his eyes or turning in her direction.

Lesley buried the wickedly tantalising thought of touching his cheek. 'Of course not!'

'I don't suppose you banked on this sort of situation when you agreed to the job.'

'I don't suppose you banked on it either when you decided to hire me.'

'True,' he admitted with a ghost of a smile. 'So, where do you suggest we go from here? Quiz Rachel when she gets home day after tomorrow? Try and find out if she has any idea what's going on?' He listened as she ran through some options. He liked hearing her talk. He liked the soft but decisive tone of her voice. He liked the way she could talk to him like this, on his level, with no coy intonations and no irritating indications that she wanted the conversation to take any personal detours.

Mind you, she had so much information about him that personal detours were pretty much an irrelevance:

there really weren't that many nooks and crannies left to discover.

His mind swung back to when he had caught her wearing that dress and his body began to stir into life.

'Talk to me about something else,' he ordered huskily when there was a pause in the conversation. This was as close to relaxation he had come in a long time, despite the grim nature of what was going on. He had his eyes closed, the sun was on his face and his body felt lazy and nicely lethargic.

'What do you want me to talk about?' She could understand why he might not want to dwell ad infinitum on a painful subject, even one that needed to be discussed.

'You. I want you to talk about you.'

Even though he wasn't looking at her, Lesley still reddened. That voice of his; had he any idea how sexy it was? No, of course not.

'I'm a very boring person,' she half-laughed with embarrassment. 'Besides, you know all the basic stuff: my brothers; my dad bringing us all up on his own.'

'So let's skip the basics. Tell me what drove you to try on that dress.'

'I don't want to talk about that.' Lesley's skin prickled with acute discomfort. The mortification she had felt assailed her all over again and she clenched her fists on her lap. 'I've already apologised and I'd really rather we drop the subject and pretend it never happened. It was a mistake.'

'You're embarrassed.'

'Of course I am.'

'No need to be, and I'm not prying. I'm really just trying to grasp anything that might take my mind off what's happening right now with Rachel.'

Suddenly Lesley felt herself deflate. While she was on her high horse, defending her position and beating back his very natural curiosity, he was in the unenviable position of having had to open the door to his past and let her in.

Was it any wonder that he was desperate to take his mind off his situation? Talking relentlessly about something worrying only magnified the worry and anxiety.

'I—I don't know why I tried it,' Lesley offered haltingly. 'Actually, I do know why I tried it on. I was never one for dresses and frocks when I was a teenager. That was stuff meant for other girls but not for me.'

'Because you lacked a mother's guiding hand,' Alessio contributed astutely. 'And even more influential was the fact that you had five brothers.' He grinned and some of the worry that had been etched on his face lifted. 'I remember what I was like and what my friends were like when we were fourteen—not sensitive. I bet they gave you a hard time.'

Lesley laughed. 'And the rest of it. At any rate, I had one embarrassing encounter with a mini-skirt and I decided after that that I was probably better off not going down that road. Besides, at the age of fourteen I was already taller than all the other girls in my class. Downplaying my height didn't involve wearing dresses and short skirts.'

Alessio slowly opened his eyes and then inclined his head so that he was looking directly at her.

Her skin was like satin. As far as he knew, she had yet to make use of the swimming pool, but sitting outside for the past couple of afternoons in the blazing sun had lent a golden tint to her complexion. It suited her.

'But you're not fourteen any longer,' he said huskily.

Lesley was lost for words. Drowning in his eyes, her

throat suddenly went dry and her body turned to lead. She couldn't move a muscle. She could just watch him, watching her.

He would physically have to get out of his chair if he were to come any closer, and he made no move to do anything of the sort, but she was still overwhelmed by the feeling that he was going to kiss her. It was written in the dark depths of his eyes, a certain intent that made her quiver and tremble inside.

'No, I don't suppose I am,' she choked out.

'But you still don't wear short skirts...'

'Old habits die hard.' She gave up trying to look away. She didn't care what he thought—not at this moment in time, at any rate. 'I... There's no need to dress up for the sort of job that I do. Jeans and jumpers are what we all wear.'

'You don't do justice to your body.' He glanced at his watch. He had broken off working in part, as he had said, to check on Lesley and see whether she had managed to find anything in Rachel's quarters; but also in part because he was due in London for a meeting.

The time had run away. It was much later than he had imagined...something about the sun, the slight breeze, the company of the woman sitting next to him, the way she had frozen to the spot... He wondered whether any man had ever complimented her about the way she looked or whether she had spent a lifetime assuming that no one would, therefore making sure that she carved her own niche through her intelligence and ambition.

He wondered what she would do if he touched her, kissed her.

More than ever, he wanted to have her. In fact, he was tempted to abandon the meeting in London and spend the rest of this lazy afternoon playing the game of seduction.

Already she was standing up, all of a fluster, telling him that she was feeling a little hot and wanted to get back into the shade. With an inward, rueful sigh of resignation, he followed suit.

'You're doing a brilliant job, trying to unravel what the hell is going on with these emails,' he said, uncomfortably aware of his body demanding a certain type of attention that was probably going to make his drive down to London a bit uncomfortable.

Lesley put some much-needed physical distance between them.

What had happened just then? He seemed normal enough now. Had it been her imagination playing tricks on her, making her think that he was going to kiss her? Or was it her own forbidden attraction trying to find a way to become a reality?

It absolutely terrified her that she might encourage him to think that she was attracted to him. It was even more terrifying that she might be reading all sorts of nonsense into his throwaway remarks. The guy was the last word in eligible. He was charming, highly intelligent and sophisticated, and he probably had that sexy, ever so slightly flirty manner with every woman he spoke to. It was just the kind of person he was and misinterpreting anything he said in her favour would be something she did at her own peril.

'Thank you. You're paying me handsomely to do just that.'

Alessio frowned. He didn't like money being brought into the conversation. It lowered the tone.

'Well, carry on the good work,' he said with equal politeness. 'And you'll have the house all to yourself until tomorrow to do it. I have an important meeting in London and I'll be spending the night there in my apartment.' He scowled at her immediate look of relief. Hell, she was attracted to him, but she was determined to fight it, despite the clear signals he had sent that the feeling was reciprocated. Didn't she know that for a man like him, a man who could snap his fingers and have any woman he wanted, her reticence was a challenge?

And yet, was he the type to set off in pursuit of someone who was reluctant—even though she might be as hot for him as he was for her?

A night away might cool him down a bit.

He left her dithering in the hall, seeing him off, but with a look of impatience on her face for him to be gone.

She needed this. Her nerves were getting progressively more shot by the minute; she couldn't wait for him to leave. She went to see him off, half-expecting him suddenly to decide that he wasn't going anywhere after all, and sagged with relief when the front door slammed behind him and she heard the roar of his car diminishing as he cleared the courtyard and disappeared down the long drive.

She couldn't stay. Certainly, she wanted to be out by the time his daughter arrived. She just couldn't bear the tension of being around him: she couldn't bear the loss of self-control, the way her eyes wanted to seek him out, the constant roller-coaster ride of her emotions. She felt vulnerable and confused.

Well, she had found rather more searching through Rachel's room than she had told him. Not quite enough, but just a little bit more information and she would have sufficient to present to him and leave with the case closed.

She had seen the desk-top computer and was sure

that there would be a certain amount of helpful information there.

She had an afternoon, a night and hopefully part of the day tomorrow, and during that time she would make sure that everything was sorted, because she desperately needed to return to the safety of her comfort zone...

CHAPTER FIVE

LESLEY FLEXED HER fingers, which were stiff from working solidly on Rachel's desk-top for the past two and a half hours.

Alessio had given her the green light to look through anything and everything in his daughter's room and she knew that he was right to allow her to do so. If Rachel was under some sort of threat, whatever that threat was, then everything had to be done to neutralise the situation, even if it meant an invasion of her privacy.

However, Lesley had still felt guilty and nervous when she had sat down in front of the computer to begin opening files.

She had expected to find lots of personal teenage stuff. She had never been one of those girls who had sat around giggling and pouring her heart out to all her friends. She and her friends had mostly belonged to the sporting set, and the sporting set had only occasionally crossed over into the cheerleader set, which was where most of the giggling about boys and confiding had taken place.

However, the computer seemed largely to store school work. Lesley had assumed that the more personal information was probably carried on Rachel's tablet, or else her mobile phone, neither of which were in the house.

But she had found a couple of little strands that added to the building jigsaw puzzle.

Most of the really important information, however, had been gathered the old-fashioned way: pockets of jeans; scraps of paper; old exercise books; margins of text books; letters tossed carelessly in the drawer by the bed.

There had been no attempt to hide any of the stuff Lesley had gathered, and that made her feel much better.

Rachel might have given orders to a very pliant housekeeper not to go anywhere near her rooms, but had there been a little part of her that maybe wanted the information to be found? Was that why she had not destroyed notes that were definitely incriminating?

Lesley could only speculate.

By six that evening, she was exhausted. She ached all over, but she knew that she would be able to hand everything she had found over to Alessio and be on her way.

She felt a little panicky when she thought about getting into her little car and driving away from him for ever, then she told herself that it was just as well she was going to do that, because panicking at the prospect of not seeing him was a very dangerous place to be.

How had he managed to get under her skin so thoroughly and so fast?

When it came to men, she was a girl who had always taken things slowly. Friendships were built over a reasonable period of time. Generally speaking, during that protracted build-up any prospect of the friendship developing into something more serious was apt to fizzle out, which always reassured her that the relationship had not been destined.

But the speed with which Alessio had succeeded in filling her head was scary.

She found that even being alone in his house for a few hours was an unsettling business because she missed his presence!

In the space of only a couple of days, she had become accustomed to living life in the emotional fast lane; had become used to a heightened state of awareness, knowing that he was *around*. When she sat outside in the garden—working on her lap-top, enjoying the peace of the countryside, telling herself what a relief it was that she was not in the same room as him—she was still *conscious* of the fact that he was in the house. Somewhere.

With a little sigh of frustration, she decided that she would have a swim.

She hadn't been near the pool since she had arrived. She hadn't been able to deal with the prospect of him suggesting that he join her, even less with the prospect of him seeing just how angular, flat-chested and boyish her figure was.

He might have made the occasional flirty remark, but she had seen the sort of women he was attracted to. He had handed over his computer files to her and within them were photos of him with various busty, curvaceous, five-foot-two blonde bombshells. They all looked like clones of Marilyn Monroe.

But he wasn't here now, and it was still so hot and muggy, even at this hour of the evening.

When she looked at herself in the mirror, she was startled at how much it changed her appearance. However, she had seen herself in her navy-blue bikini sufficient times to be reassured that she was the same lanky Lesley she had always been.

Without bothering to glance at her reflection, she grabbed a towel from the bathroom and headed downstairs for the pool.

She should have felt wary venturing out with no one around, and just acres upon acres of fields and open land stretching away into the distance, but she didn't. In fact, she felt far more cautious in London, where she was constantly surrounded by people and where there was no such thing as complete darkness even in the dead of night in the middle of winter.

She dived cleanly into the water, gasping at the temperature, but then her body acclimatised as she began swimming.

She was a good swimmer. After being cooped up in front of a computer for several hours, it felt good to be exercising, and she swam without stopping, cutting through the water length after length after length.

She wasn't sure exactly how long she swam; maybe forty-five minutes. She could feel the beginning of that pleasant burn in her body that indicated that her muscles were being stretched to their limit.

At this point, she pulled herself up out of the pool, water sluicing down her body, her short, dark hair plastered down...and it was only then that she noticed Alessio standing to one side, half-concealed in the shadow of one of the trees fringing the side of the veranda.

It took a few seconds for her brain to register his presence there at all because she hadn't been expecting him.

And it took a few seconds more for her to realise that, not only was he standing there, but she wasn't even sure how long he had been standing there looking at her.

With an outraged yelp she walked quickly over to where she had dumped her towel on one of the chairs by the pool and, by the time she had secured it around her, he had walked lazily to where she was standing.

'I hope I didn't interrupt your workout,' he murmured without a hint of an apology in his voice.

'You're not supposed to be here!'

'There was a slight change of plan.'

'You should have warned me that you were going to be coming back!'

'I didn't think I needed to inform you that I would be returning to my own home.'

'How long have you been standing there?' She couldn't bring herself to meet those amused dark eyes. She was horribly conscious of what she must look like, with her wet hair like a cap on her head and her face completely bare of make-up—not that she ever wore much, but still.

'Long enough to realise that it's been a while since I used that pool. In fact, I can't remember the last time I stepped foot in it.' Water droplets were like tiny diamonds on her eyelashes and he wished she would look at him so that he could read the expression in her eyes. Was she genuinely annoyed that he had disturbed her, shown up unexpectedly? Or was she all of a dither because she had been caught off-guard, because he was seeing her for the first time without her armour of jeans, flats and faded tee-shirts? Clothes that neutralised her femininity.

He wondered what she would say if he told her just how delicious she looked, standing there dripping wet with only a towel that barely covered her.

He also wondered what she would say if he told her that he had been standing there for the better part of fifteen minutes, mesmerised as he'd watched her swimming, as at home in the water as a seal. He had been so wrapped up in the sight that he had completely forgotten why he had been obliged to drive back from London.

'Wait right here,' he urged suddenly. 'I'm going to join you. Give me ten minutes. It'll do me good to get rid of the London grime.'

'Join me?' Lesley was frankly horrified.

'You don't have a problem with that, do you?'

'No...err...'

'Good. I'll be back before you can get back in the water.'

Lesley was frozen to the spot as she watched him disappear back through the sprawling triple-fronted French doors that led into the conservatory.

Then, galvanised into action—because diving in while he watched was just out of the question—she hurried back into the water. What choice did she have? To have told him that she was fed up swimming and wanted to go inside, just as he was about to join her in the pool, would have been tantamount to confessing just how awkward he made her feel. The last thing she wanted was for him to know the effect he had on her. He might have some idea that she wasn't as impartial to his presence as she liked to pretend but her feelings were more confused than that and ran a lot deeper.

That was something she was desperate to keep to herself. She could just about cope if he thought that she fancied him; half the female population in the country between the ages of eighteen and eighty would have fancied the man, so it would be no big deal were he to include her in that category.

But it was more than that. Not only was she not the type to randomly fancy guys because of the way they looked, but her reactions to him pointed to something a lot more complex than a simple case of lust which could easily be cured by putting some distance between them.

She had just reached the shallow end of the pool

when Alessio emerged back out in the mellow evening sunshine.

Lesley thought that she might faint. Only now did she fully comprehend how much time she had spent daydreaming about him, about what he might look like under those expensive, casual designer clothes he was fond of wearing.

What would his body look like?

Now she knew: lean, bronzed and utterly beautiful. His shoulders were broad and muscled and his torso tapered to a narrow waist and hips.

He was at home with his body, that much was evident from the way he moved with an easy, casual grace.

Lesley sat on one of the steps at the shallow end of the pool, so that she was levered into a half-sitting position on her elbows while her long legs and most of her body remained under the surface of the water. She felt safer that way.

He dived into the water, as straight as an arrow, and swam steadily and powerfully towards her. It took every ounce of will power not to flinch back as he reared up out of the water and joined her on the step.

'Nice,' he said appreciatively, wiping his face with the palm of his hand, then leaning back just as she did.

'You haven't explained what you're doing here.' Lesley eyed the proximity of his body nervously.

'And I shall do that as soon as we're inside. For the moment, I just want to enjoy being out here. I don't get much by way of time out. I don't want to spoil it by launching into the unexpected little problem that's cropped up.' He glanced across to her. 'You're a good swimmer.'

'Thank you.'

'Been swimming a long time?'

'Since I was four.' She paused and then continued, because talking seemed a bit less stressful than remaining silent and concentrating all her energies on what he was doing to her. 'My father had always been a good swimmer. All my brothers were as well. After my mother died, he got it into his head that he would channel all his energy into getting me into competitive swimming. The boys were all a bit older and had their own hobbies, but he's fond of telling me that I was fertile ground for him to work on.' Lesley laughed and relaxed a little. 'So he made sure to take me down to the local swimming baths at least twice a week. I was out of arm bands and swimming by the time I was five.'

'But you didn't end up becoming a professional swimmer.'

'I didn't,' Lesley admitted. 'Although I entered lots of competitions right up until I went to secondary school, then once I was in secondary school I began to play lots of different types of sport and the swimming was put on the back burner.'

'What sport did you play?' Alessio thought of his last girlfriend, whose only stab at anything energetic had involved the ski slope. He had once made the mistake of trying to get her to play a game of squash with him and had been irritated when she had shrieked with horror at the thought of getting too sweaty. Her hair, apparently, would not have been able to cope. He wondered whether she would have submerged herself in the pool the way Lesley had or whether she would have spent her time lying on a sun lounger and only dipping her feet in when the heat became unbearable.

Any wonder he had broken up with her after a couple of months?

'Squash, tennis, hockey, and of course in between I had my self-defence classes.'

'Energetic.'

'Very.'

'And in between all of that vigorous exercise you still had time for studying.'

Hence no time at all for what every other teenage girl would have been doing. Lesley read behind that mild observation. 'How else would I have ever been able to have a career?' Lesley responded tartly. 'Playing sport is all well and good but it doesn't get you jobs at the end of the day.' She stood up. 'I've been out here for long enough. I should really get back inside, have a shower. Please don't let me keep you from enjoying the pool. It's a shame to have this and not make use of it, especially when you think that it's so rare for the weather to be as good as it has been recently.' She didn't give him time to answer. Instead, she headed for her towel and breathed a sigh of relief when she had wrapped it around her.

When she turned around, it was to find him standing so close to her that she gave a little stumble back, almost crashing into the sun lounger behind her.

'Steady.' Alessio reached out and gripped her arms, then left his hands on her arms. 'I should really talk to you about what's brought me back here. I've got quite a bit of work to catch up on and I'll probably work through the night.'

Lesley found that she couldn't focus on anything while he was still holding her.

'Of course,' she eventually managed to croak. 'I'll go and have a shower, and then shall I meet you in the office?' She could smell him—the clean, chlorinated scent of the swimming pool combined with the heady aroma of the sun drying him as he stood there, practically naked.

'Meet me in the kitchen instead.' Alessio released her abruptly. Just then every instinct inside him wanted to pull her towards him and kiss her, taste her, see whether she would be as delectable as his imagination told him she would be. The intensity of what had shot through him was disturbing.

'I...I didn't expect you to return; I told Violet that there was no need to prepare anything for me before she left. In fact, I let her go early. I do hope you don't mind but I'm accustomed to cooking for myself. I was only going to do myself a plate of pasta.'

'Sounds good to me.'

'Right, then,' Lesley said faintly. She pushed her fingers through her hair, spiking it up.

She left him watching her and dashed upstairs for a very quick shower.

She should have found his unexpected arrival intensely annoying. It had thrown her whole evening out of sync. But there was a dark excitement swirling around inside her and she found that she was looking forward to having dinner with him, stupidly thrilled that he was back at the house.

She told herself that it was simply because she would be able to fill him in on all sorts of discoveries she had made and, the faster she filled him in, the sooner she would be able to leave and the quicker her life would return to normal. Normality seemed like a lifetime away.

He wasn't in the kitchen when she got there half an hour later, with all her paperwork in a folder, so she poured herself a glass of wine and waited for him.

She couldn't think what might have brought him back to his country estate. Something to do with his daughter, she was sure, but what? Might he have discovered something independently? Something that would make it easier for her to tell him what she thought this whole situation was about?

He strolled in when she was halfway through her glass of wine and proceeded to pour himself a whisky and soda.

'I need this,' Alessio said heavily, sinking onto the chair at the head of the table and angling it so that he could stretch his legs out whilst still facing her. 'My mother-in-law called when I was in the middle of my meetings.'

'Is that unusual?'

'Extremely. We may well be on cordial terms but not so cordial that she telephones out of the blue. There's still that ugly residue of their manipulation, although I will concede that Bianca's mother was not the one behind it. And it has to be said that, for the duration of our divorce, it was only thanks to Claudia that I ever got to see Rachel at all. I can count the number of times that happened on the fingers of one hand, but then Claudia never was a match for her daughter.' He caught himself in the act of wanting to talk more about the destructive marriage that had made him the cynical man he was today. How had that happened?

'What did she want?' Lesley eventually asked.

'Rachel has been staying with her for the past four weeks. Pretty much as soon as her school ended, she decided that she wanted to go over there. She doesn't know a great deal of people around here and only a handful in London. The down side of a boarding school out in the country, I suppose.' He sighed heavily and tipped the remainder of his drink down before resting the empty glass on the table and staring at it in brooding silence.

'Yes,' Lesley contributed vaguely. 'It must be difficult.'

'At any rate, the upshot appears to be that my daughter is refusing to return to the UK.'

Lesley's mouth fell open and Alessio smiled crookedly at her. 'She's refusing to speak to me on the telephone. She's dug her heels in and has decided to set up camp with Claudia and, Claudia being Claudia, she lacks the strength to stand up to my daughter.'

'You must be a little put out.'

'That's the understatement of the hour.' He stood up and signalled to her that they should start preparing something to eat. He needed to move around. For a small window, he had been so preoccupied with her, with arriving back and surprising her in the swimming pool, that he had actually put the gravity of the situation to the back of his mind, but now it had returned in full force.

Strangely, he was thankful that Lesley was there.

As if knowing that he would return to the topic in his own time, Lesley began preparing their meal. She had earlier piled all the ingredients she would need on the counter and now she began chopping mushrooms, tomatoes, onions and garlic.

For once, his silence didn't send her into instant meltdown. Rather, she began chatting easily and pleasantly. She told him about her lack of cooking experience. She joked that her brothers were all better cooks than she was and that two of them had even offered to show her the basics. She could sense him begin to unwind, even though she wasn't looking at him at all and he wasn't saying anything, just listening to her rabbit on aimlessly about nothing in particular.

It was soothing, Alessio thought as he watched her

prepare the vegetables slowly and with the painstaking care of someone who wasn't comfortable in the arena of the kitchen.

Nor was he feeling trapped at the thought of a woman busying herself in his kitchen. He cleared as she cooked. It was a picture-perfect snapshot of just the sort of domesticity he avoided at all costs.

'So...' They were sitting at the kitchen table with bowls of pasta in front of them. She had maintained a steady flow of non-threatening conversation, and it had been surprisingly easy, considering she was always a bundle of nervous tension whenever she was in his presence. 'When you say that Rachel is digging her heels in and doesn't want to return to the UK, are you saying *for ever*, or just for the remainder of the summer holidays?'

'I'm saying that she's decided that she hates it over here and doesn't want to return at all.'

'And your mother-in-law can't talk her out of that?'

'Claudia has always been the pushover in the family. Between her bullying husband and Bianca, she was the one who got dragged into their plot and now, in this situation, well, it's probably a mixture of not wanting to hurt or offend her only grandchild and wanting to go down the path of least resistance.'

'So what are you going to do about that?'

'Well, there's simply no question of Rachel staying out there and going to school.' He pushed his empty plate to one side and sat back to look at her. 'I could have waited until tomorrow to come back here and tell you this but...'

'But...?' Lesley rested her chin in the palm of her hand and looked at him. The kitchen lights hadn't been switched on. It had still been bright when they had started preparing dinner, but the sun had suddenly faded, giving way to a violet twilight that cast shadows and angles across his face.

'I have a favour to ask of you.'

'What is it?' Lesley asked cautiously. She began standing to clear the table and he circled her wrist with his hand.

'Sit. Tidying can come later, or not at all. Violet will do it in the morning. I need to ask you something and I will need your undivided attention when I do so.'

She subsided back into the chair, heart beating madly.

'I want you to accompany me to Italy,' Alessio said heavily. 'It's a big ask, I know, but my fear is that, short of dragging Rachel to the plane and forcibly strapping her to the seat, she will simply refuse to listen to a word I have to say.'

'But I don't even know your daughter, Alessio!'

'If I cannot persuade my daughter to return to the UK, this will spell the end of any chance of a relationship I will ever have with her.' He rubbed his eyes wearily and then leaned back and stared blankly up at the ceiling.

Lesley's heart went out to him. Was that how it would be? Most likely. And yet...

'There's something you should see.' She stood up and went to the folder which she had brought down with her. This was the point at which she should now point out that she had gathered as much information as she could and it was up to him to do what needed to be done. In the end, it had been fiddly, but not impossible.

'You've found something?' Alessio was suddenly alert. He sat forward and pulled his chair towards her as she began smoothing out the various bits of paper she had found and the pages she had printed out over the past couple of days she had been at the house.

She had only given him a rough, skeleton idea of her findings before, not wanting to build any pictures that might be incorrect.

'I collated all of this and, well, okay, so I told you that I didn't think that this had anything to do with your wife…'

'Ex-wife.'

'Ex-wife. Well, I was right. I managed to trace our friend. He jumped around a bit, used a few different Internet cafés to cover his tracks, but the cafés, as I told you, were all in the vicinity of your daughter's school. It took a bit of time, but I eventually identified the one he used most frequently. Most importantly, though, in one of the very early emails—one of the emails you never identified as coming from him—he used his own computer. It was a little bit tougher than I thought but I got through to the identity of the person.'

Alessio was listening intently. 'You know who he is?'

'It would have been a bit more difficult to piece together conclusively if I hadn't discovered those very early emails when he'd obviously just been testing the ground. They were very innocuous, which is why he probably thought that they would have been deleted. I guess he didn't figure that they would still be uncovered and brought out of hiding.' She shoved the stack of printed emails across to Alessio and watched as he read them one by one. She had highlighted important bits, phrases, certain ways of saying things that pointed to the same writer behind them.

'You're brilliant.'

Lesley flushed with pleasure. 'I was only doing what you paid me to do.'

'So, build me the picture,' he said softly.

She did and, as she did so, she watched his expression darken and change.

'So now you pretty much have the complete story,' she finished. 'I gathered all this so that I could actually present it to you tomorrow when you returned. I was going to tell you that there's really nothing left for me to do now.'

'I still want you to come with me to Italy.'

'I can't,' Lesley said quickly, with a note of desperation in her voice.

'You've sorted all of this out, but there is still the problem of my daughter. Bringing her back over here with this information, it's going to be even more difficult.'

That was something Lesley had not taken into account when she had worked out her plan to present him with her findings and leave while common sense and her instinct for self-preservation were still intact.

'Yes, but it all remains the same. She's going to be—I can't imagine—certainly not warm and welcoming to the person who brought the whole thing to light.'

'But you have no personal axe to grind with her.' Would she come? It suddenly seemed very important that she was at his side. He was uneasily aware that there was an element of need there. How and why had that happened? He swept aside his discomfort.

'I also have my job, Alessio.' She was certain that she should be feeling horrified and indignant at his nerve in asking her to go way beyond the bounds of what she had been paid to do. Especially when she had made such a big effort to wrap everything up so that she could escape the suffocating, dangerous effect he had on her.

'You can leave that to me,' he murmured.

'Leave that to you? How do you work that one out?'

'I've just concluded a deal to buy a string of luxury boutique hotels in Italy. Failing business, mismanagement, feuding amongst the board members; that's what the trip to London was all about. I needed to be there to finalise the details with lawyers.'

'How exciting,' Lesley said politely.

'More so than you might imagine. It's the first time I shall be dabbling in the leisure industry and, naturally, I will want a comprehensive website designed.'

'You have your own people to do that.'

'They're remarkably busy at the moment. This will be a job that will definitely have to be outsourced. Not only could it be worth a great deal of money to the company lucky enough to get the job, but there's no telling how many other jobs will come in its wake.'

'Are you *coercing* me?'

'I prefer to call it *persuasion*.'

'I don't believe it.'

'I usually get what I want,' Alessio said with utter truth. 'And what I want is for you to come with me to Italy and, if this proves a helpful lever, then that's all to the good. I'm sure when I explain to your boss the size and scale of the job, and the fact that it would be extremely useful to have you over there so that you can soak up the atmosphere and get a handle on how best to pitch the project...' He gave an elegant shrug and a smile of utter devastation; both relayed the message that she was more or less trapped.

Naturally she could turn down his offer but her boss might be a little miffed should he get to hear that. They were a thriving company but, with the current economic climate, potential setbacks lurked round every corner.

Whatever work came their way was not to be sniffed

at, especially when the work in question could be highly lucrative and extensive.

'And if you're concerned about your pay,' he continued, 'Rest assured that you will be earning exactly the same rate as you were for the job you just so successfully completed.'

'I'm not concerned about the money!'

'Why don't you want to come? It'll be a holiday.'

'You don't need me there, not really.'

'You have no idea what I need or don't need,' Alessio murmured softly.

'You might change your mind when you see what else I have to show you.' But already she was trying to staunch the wave of anticipation at the thought of going abroad with him, having a few more days in his company, feeding her silly addiction.

She rescued papers from the bottom of the folder, pushed them across to him and watched carefully as he rifled through them.

But then, the moment felt too private, and she stood up and began getting them both a couple of cups of coffee.

What would he be thinking? she wondered as he looked at the little collection of articles about him which she had found in a scrap book in Rachel's room. Again, no attempt had been made to conceal them. Rachel had collected bits and pieces about her father over the years; there were photographs as well, which she must have taken from an album somewhere. Photos of him as a young man.

Eventually, when she could no longer pretend to be taking her time with the coffee, she handed a mug to him and sat back down.

'You found these...' Alessio cleared his throat but he couldn't look her in the eyes.

'I found them,' Lesley said gently. 'So, you see, your daughter isn't quite as indifferent to you as you might believe. Having the conversation you need to have with her might not be quite so difficult as you imagine.'

CHAPTER SIX

'THIS IS QUITE a surprise.' This was all Alessio could find
to say and he knew that it was inadequate. His daughter had been collecting a scrap book about him. That
reached deep down to a part of him he'd thought no longer existed. He stared down at the most recent cutting
of him printed off the Internet. He had had an article
written in the business section of the *Financial Times*
following the acquisition of a small, independent bank
in Spain. It was a poor picture but she had still printed
it off and shoved it inside the scrap book.

What was he to think?

He rested his forehead against his clenched fist and
drew in a long breath.

A wave of compassion washed over Lesley. Alessio
Baldini was tough, cool, controlled. If he hadn't already
told her, his entire manner was indicative of someone
who knew that they could get what he wanted simply
by snapping his fingers. It was a trait she couldn't abide
in anyone.

She hated rich men who acted as though they owned
the world and everything in it.

She hated men who felt that they could fling money
at any problem and, lo and behold, a solution would be
forthcoming.

And she hated anyone who didn't value the importance of family life. Family was what grounded you, made you put everything into perspective; stopped you from ever taking yourself too seriously or sacrificing too much in pursuit of your goals.

Alessio acted as he if he owned the world and he certainly acted as though money was the root of solving all problems. If he was a victim of circumstances when it came to an unfortunate family life, then he definitely did not behave as though now was the time when he could begin sorting it out.

So why was she now reaching out to place her hand on his arm? Why had she pulled her chair just that little bit nearer to his so that she could feel the heat radiating from his body?

Was it because the vulnerability she had always sensed in him whenever the subject of his daughter came up was now so glaringly obvious?

Rachel was his Achilles heel; in a flash of comprehension, Lesley saw that. In every other area, Alessio was in complete control of his surroundings, of his *life*, but when it came to his daughter he floundered.

The women he had dated in the past had been kept at a distance. Once bitten, twice shy, and after his experiences with Bianca he had made sure never to let any other woman get past the steel walls that surrounded him. They would never have glimpsed the man who was at a loss when it came to his daughter. She wondered how many of them even *knew* that he had a daughter.

But here she was. She had seen him at his most naked, emotionally.

That was a good thing, she thought, and a bad thing. It was good insofar as everyone needed a sounding board when it came to dark thoughts and emotions.

Those were burdens that could not be carried single-handed. He might have passed the years with his deepest thoughts locked away, but there was no way he would ever have been able to eradicate them, and letting them out could only be a good thing.

With this situation, he had been forced to reveal more about those thoughts to her than he ever had to anyone else. She was certain of that.

The down side was that, for a proud man, the necessity of having to confide thoughts normally hidden would eventually be seen as a sign of weakness.

The sympathetic, listening ear would only work for so long before it turned into a source of resentment.

But did that matter? Really? They wouldn't be around one another for much longer and right here, right now, in some weird, unspoken way, he needed her. She *felt* it, even though it was something he would never, ever articulate.

Those cuttings had moved him beyond words. He was trying hard to control his reaction in front of an audience; that was evident in the thickness of the silence.

'You'll have to return that scrap book to where you found it,' he said gruffly when the silence had been stretched to breaking point. 'Leave it with me overnight and I'll give it to you in the morning.'

Lesley nodded. Her hand was still on his arm and he hadn't shrugged it away. She allowed it to travel so that she was stroking upwards, feeling the strength of his muscles straining under the shirt and the definition of his shoulders and collarbone.

Alessio's eyes narrowed on her.

'Are you feeling sorry for me?' His voice was less cold than it should have been. 'Is that a pity caress?'

He had never confided in anyone. He certainly had

never been an object of pity to anyone, any woman, ever. The thought alone was laughable. Women had always hung onto his every word, longed for some small indication that they occupied a more special role in his life than he was willing to admit to them.

Naturally, they hadn't.

Lesley, though…

She was in a different category. The pity caress did not evoke the expected feelings of contempt, impatience and anger that he would have expected.

He caught her hand in his and held on to it.

'It's not a *pity caress*.' Lesley breathed. Her skin burned where he was touching it, a blaze that was stoked by the expression in his eyes: dark, thoughtful, insightful, amused. 'But I know it must be disconcerting, looking through Rachel's scrap book, seeing pictures of yourself there, articles cut out or printed off from the Internet.' He still wasn't saying anything. He was still just staring at her, his head slightly to one side, his expression brooding and intent.

Her voice petered out and she stared right back at him, eyes wide. She could barely breathe. The moment seemed as fragile as a droplet of water balancing on the tip of a leaf, ready to fall and splinter apart.

She didn't want the moment to end. It was wrong, she knew that, but still she wanted to touch his face and smooth away those very human, very uncertain feelings she knew he would be having; feelings he would be taking great care of to conceal.

'The scrap book was just lying there,' she babbled away as she continued to get lost in his eyes. 'On the bed. I would have felt awful if I had found it hidden under the mattress or at the bottom of a drawer somewhere, but it was just there, waiting to be found.'

'Not by me. Rachel knew that I would never go into her suite of rooms.'

Lesley shrugged. 'I wanted you to see that you're important to your daughter,' she murmured shakily, 'Even if you don't think you are because of the way she acts. Teenagers can be very awkward when it comes to showing their feelings.' He still wasn't saying anything. If he thought that she felt sorry for him, then how was it that he was staying put, not angrily stalking off? 'You remember being a teenager.' She tried a smile in an attempt to lighten the screaming tension between them.

'Vaguely. When I think back to my teenage years, I inevitably end up thinking back to being a daddy before I was out of them.'

'Of course,' Lesley murmured, her voice warm with understanding. At the age of fourteen, not even knowing it, he would have been a mere four years away from becoming a father. It was incredible.

'You're doing it again,' Alessio said under his breath.

'Doing what?'

'Smothering me with your sympathy. Don't worry. Maybe I like it.' His mouth curved into a wolfish smile but underneath that, he thought with passing confusion, her sympathy was actually very welcome.

He reached out and touched her face, then ran two fingers along her cheek, circling her mouth then along her slender neck, coming to rest at the base of her collarbone.

'Have you felt what I've been feeling for the past couple of days?' he asked.

Lesley wasn't sure she was physically capable of answering his question. Not with that hand on her collarbone and her brain reliving every inch of its caress as it had touched her cheek and moved sensuously over her mouth.

'Well?' Alessio prompted. He rested his other hand on her thigh and began massaging it, very gently but very thoroughly, just the one spot, but it was enough to make the breath catch in her throat.

'What do you mean? What are you talking about?' As if she didn't know. As if she wasn't constantly aware of the way he unsettled her. And was she conscious that the electricity flowed both ways? Maybe she was. Maybe that was why the situation had seemed so dangerous.

She had thought that she needed to get out because her attraction to him was getting too much, was threatening to become evident. Maybe a part of her had known that the real reason she needed to get out was because, on some level, she knew that he was attracted to her as well. That underneath the light-hearted flirting there was a very real undercurrent of mutual sexual chemistry.

And that was not good, not at all. She didn't do one-night stands, or two-day stands, or 'going nowhere so why not have a quick romp?' stands.

She did *relationships*. If there had been no guy in her life for literally years, then it was because she had never been the kind of girl who had sex just for the sake of it.

But with Alessio something told her that she could be that girl, and that scared her.

'You know exactly what I mean. You want me. I want you. I've wanted you for a while...'

'I should go up to bed.' Lesley breathed unevenly, nailed to the spot and not moving an inch despite her protestations. 'Leave you to your thoughts...'

'Maybe I'm not that keen on being alone with my thoughts,' Alessio said truthfully. 'Maybe my thoughts are a black hole into which I have no desire to fall.

Maybe I want your pity and your sympathy because they can save me from that fall.'

And what happens when you've been saved from that fall? What happens to me? You're in a weird place right now and, if I rescue you now, what happens when you leave that weird place and shut the door on it once again?

But those muddled thoughts barely had time to settle before they were blown away by the fiercely exciting thought of being with the man who was leaning towards her, staring at her with such intensity that she wanted to moan.

And, before she could retreat behind more weak protestations, he was cupping the back of her neck and drawing her towards him, very slowly, so slowly that she had time to appreciate the depth of his dark eyes; the fine lines that etched his features; the slow, sexy curve of his mouth; the length of his dark eyelashes.

Lesley fell into the kiss with a soft moan, part resignation, part despair; mostly intense, long-awaited excitement. She spread her hand behind his neck in a mirror gesture to how he was holding her and, as his tongue invaded the soft contours of her mouth, she returned the kiss and let that kiss do its work—spread moisture between her legs, pinch her nipples into tight, sensitive buds, raise the hairs on her arms.

'We shouldn't be doing this,' she muttered, breaking apart for a few seconds and immediately wanting to draw him back towards her again.

'Why not?'

'Because this isn't the right reason for going to bed with someone.'

'Don't know what you're talking about.' He leaned

to kiss her again but she stilled him with a hand on his chest and met his gaze with anxious eyes.

'I don't pity you, Alessio,' she said huskily. 'I'm sorry that you don't have the relationship with your daughter that you'd like, but I don't pity you. And when I showed you that scrap book it was because I felt the contents were something you needed to know about. What I feel is...understanding and compassion.'

'And what I feel is that we shouldn't get lost in words.'

'Because words are not your thing?' But she smiled and felt a rush of tenderness towards this strong, powerful man who was also capable of being so wonderfully *human*, hard though he might try to fight it.

'You know what they say about actions speaking louder...' He grinned at her. His body was on fire. She was right—words weren't his thing, at least not the words that made up long, involved conversations about feelings. He scooped her up and she gave a little cry of surprise, then wriggled and told him to put her down immediately; she might be slim but she was way too tall for him to start thinking he could play the caveman with her.

Alessio ignored her and carried her up the stairs to his bedroom.

'Every woman likes a caveman.' He gently kicked open his bedroom door and then deposited her on his king-sized bed.

Night had crept up without either of them realising it and, without the bedroom lights switched on, the darkness only allowed them to see one another in shadowy definition.

'I don't,' Lesley told him breathlessly as he stood in front of her and began unbuttoning his shirt.

She had already seen him barely clothed in the pool. She should know what to expect when it came to his body and yet, as he tossed his shirt carelessly on the ground, it was as if she was looking at him for the first time.

The impact he had on her was as new, as raw, as powerful.

But then, this was different, wasn't it? This wasn't a case of watching him covertly from the sidelines as he covered a few lengths in a swimming pool.

This was lying on his bed, in a darkened room, with the promise of possession flicking through her like a spreading fire.

Alessio didn't want to talk. He wanted to take her, fast and hard, until he heard her cry out with satisfaction. He wanted to pleasure her and feel her come with him inside her.

But how much sweeter to take his time, to taste every inch of her, to withstand the demands of his raging hormones and indulge in making love with her at a more leisurely pace.

'No?' he drawled, hand resting on the zipper of his trousers before he began taking those off as well, where they joined the shirt in a heap on the ground, leaving him in just his boxers. 'You think I'm a caveman because I carried you up the stairs?'

He slowly removed his boxers. He regretted not having turned some lights on because he would have liked to really appreciate the expression on her face as he watched her watching him. He strolled towards the side of the bed and stood there, then he touched himself lightly and heard her swift intake of breath.

'I just think you're a caveman in general,' Lesley feasted her eyes on his impressive erection. When he held it in his hand, she longed to do the same to herself, to touch herself down there. Her nerves were stretched to breaking point and she wished she was just a little more experienced, a little more knowing about what to do when it came to a man like him, a man who probably knew everything there was to know about the opposite sex.

She sat up, crossed her legs and reached out to touch him, replacing his hand with hers and gaining confidence as she felt him shudder with appreciation.

It was a strange turn-on to be fully clothed while he was completely naked.

'Is that right?'

As she took him into her mouth, Alessio grunted and flung his head back. He had died and gone to heaven. The wetness of her mouth on his hard erection, the way she licked, teased and tasted, his fingers curled into her short hair, made him breathe heavily, well aware that he had to come down from this peak or risk bringing this love-making session to an extremely premature conclusion, which was not something he intended to do.

With a sigh of pure regret, he eased her off him.

Then he joined her on the bed. 'Would I be a caveman if I stripped you? I wouldn't...' he slipped his fingers underneath the tee-shirt and began easing it over her head '...want to...' Then came the jeans, which she wriggled out of so that she remained in bra and pants, white, functional items of clothing that looked wonderfully wholesome on her. 'Offend your feminist sensibilities.'

For the life of her, Lesley couldn't find where she had misplaced those feminist sensibilities which he had mentioned. She reached behind to unhook her bra but he gently drew her hands away so that he could accomplish the task himself.

He half-closed his eyes and his nostrils flared with rampant appreciation of her small but perfectly formed breasts. Her nipples were big, brown, circular discs. She had propped herself up on both elbows and her breasts were small, pointed mounds offering themselves to him like sweet, delicate fruit.

In one easy movement, he straddled her, and she fell back against the pillow with a soft, excited moan.

She was wet for him. As he reached behind him to slip his hand under the panties, she groaned and covered her eyes with one hand.

'I want to see you, my darling.' Alessio lowered himself so that he was lightly on top of her. 'Move your hand.'

'I don't usually do this sort of thing,' Lesley mumbled. 'I'm not into one-night stands. I never have been. I don't see the point.'

'Shh.' He gazed down at her until she was burning all over. Then he gently began licking her breast, moving in a concentric circle until his tongue found her nipple. The sensitised tip had peaked into an erect nub, and as he took her whole nipple into his mouth so that he could suckle on it she quivered under him, moving with feverish urgency, arching back so that not a single atom of the pleasurable sensations zinging through her was lost.

She had to get rid of her panties, they were damp and uncomfortable, but with his big body over hers she couldn't reach them. Instead she clasped her hand to the back of his head and pressed him down harder on her breasts, giving little cries and whimpers as he carried on sucking and teasing, moving between her breasts and then, when she was going crazy from it, he trailed his tongue over her rib cage and down to the indentation of her belly button.

His breath on her body was warm and she was breathing fast, hardly believing that what was happening really was happening and yet desperate for it to continue, desperate to carry on shamelessly losing herself in the moment.

He felt her sharp intake of breath as he slipped her underwear down, and then she was holding her breath as he gently parted her legs and flicked his tongue over her core.

Lesley groaned. This was an intimacy she had not experienced before. She curled her fingers into his dark hair and tugged him but her body was responding with a shocking lack of inhibition as he continued to taste her, teasing her swollen bud until she lost the ability to think clearly.

Alessio felt her every response as if their bodies had tuned into the same wavelength. In a blinding, revelatory flash, he realised that everything else that had come before with women could not compete with what was happening right now, because this woman had just seen far more of him than anyone else ever had.

This had not been a simple game of pursuit and capture. She hadn't courted this situation, nor had he anticipated it. Certainly, there had come a point when he had looked at her and liked what he had seen; had wanted what he had seen; had even vaguely *planned* on having her because, when it came to him and women, wanting and having were always the same side of the coin.

But he knew that he hadn't banked on what was happening between them now. For the first time, he had the strangest feeling that this wasn't just about sex.

But the sex was great.

He swept aside all his unravelling thoughts and lost himself in her body, in her sweet little whimpers and her broken groans as she wriggled under him, until at last, when he could feel her wanting to reach her orgasm, he broke off to fumble in the bedside cabinet for a condom.

Lesley could hardly bear that brief pause. She was alive in a way she had never been before and that terrified her. Her relationships with the opposite sex had always been guarded and imbued with a certain amount of defensiveness that stemmed from her own private insecurities.

Having been raised in an all-male family, she had developed brilliant coping skills when it came to standing her ground with the opposite sex. Her brothers had toughened her up and taught her the value of healthy competition, the benefits of never being cowed by a guy, of knowing that she could hold her own.

But no one had been able to help her during those teenage years when the lines of distinction between boys and girls were drawn. She had watched from the sidelines and decided that lipstick and mascara were not for her, that sport was far more enjoyable. It wasn't about how you looked, it was about what was inside you and what was inside her—her intelligence, her sense of humour, her capacity for compassion—did not need to be camouflaged with make-up and sexy clothes.

The only guys she had ever been attracted to were the ones who'd seen her for the person she was, the ones whose heads hadn't swivelled round when a busty blonde in a short skirt had walked past.

So what, it flashed through her head, was she doing with Alessio Baldini?

She sighed and reached up to him as he settled back on her, nudging her legs apart, then she closed her eyes and was transported to another planet as he thrust into her, deep and hard, building a rhythm that drove everything out of her mind.

She flung her head back and succumbed to loud, responsive cries as he continued to fill her.

She came on a tidal wave of intense pleasure and felt her whole body shudder and arch up towards him in a wonderful fusing of bodies.

The moment seemed to last for ever and she was only brought back down to earth when he withdrew from her and cursed fluently under his breath.

'The condom has split.'

Lesley abruptly surfaced from the pleasant, dreamy cloud on which she had been happily drifting, and the uncomfortable thoughts which had been sidelined when he had begun touching her returned with double intensity.

What on earth had she done? How could she have allowed herself to end up in bed with this man? Had she lost her mind? This was a situation that was going nowhere and would never go anywhere. She was Lesley Fox, a practical, clever, not at all sexy woman who should have known better than to be sweet talked into sleeping with a man who wouldn't have looked twice at her under normal circumstances.

On every level, he was just the sort of man she usually wouldn't have gone near and, had he seen her passing on the street, she certainly would not have been the sort of woman he would have noticed. She would literally have been invisible to him because she just wasn't his type.

Fate had thrown them together and an attraction had built between them but she knew that she would be a complete fool not to recognise that that attraction was grounded in novelty.

'How the hell could that have happened?' Alessio said, his voice dark with barely contained anger. 'This is the last thing I need right now.'

Lesley got that. He had found himself tricked into marriage by a pregnancy he had not courted once upon a time and his entire adult life had been affected. Of course he would not want to repeat that situation.

Yet, she couldn't help but feel the sting of hurt at the simmering anger in his voice.

'It won't happen,' she said stiffly. She wriggled into a sitting position and watched as he vaulted upright and began searching around for his boxers, having disposed of the faulty condom.

'And you know that because?'

'It's the wrong time of month for that to happen.' She surreptitiously crossed her fingers and tried to calculate when she had last had her period. 'And, rest assured, the last thing I would want would be to end up pregnant, Alessio. As it stands, this was a very bad idea.'

In the process of locating a tee-shirt from a chest of drawers, he paused and strolled back to the bed. The condom had split and there was nothing he could do about that now. He could only hope that she was right, that they were safe.

But, that aside, how could she say that making love had been a very bad idea? He was oddly affronted.

'You know what. This. Us. Ending up in bed together. It shouldn't have happened.'

'Why not? We're attracted to one another. How could it have been a bad idea? I was under the impression that you had actually enjoyed the experience.' He looked down at her and felt his libido begin to rise once again.

'That's not the point.' She swung her legs over the side of the bed and stood up, conscious of her nudity, gritting her teeth against the temptation to drag the covers off the bed and shield herself from him.

'God, you're beautiful.'

Lesley flushed and looked away, stubbornly proud, and refusing to believe that he meant a word of that. Novelty was a beautiful thing but became boring very quickly.

'Well?' He caught her wrist and tilted her face so that she had no option but to look at him.

'Well what?' Lesley muttered, lowering her eyes.

'Well, let's go back to bed.'

'Didn't you hear a word I just said?'

'Every word.' He kissed her delicately on the corner of her mouth and then very gently on her lips.

In a heartbeat, and to her disgust, Lesley could feel her determination begin to melt away.

'You're not my type,' she mumbled, refusing to cave in, but his lips were so soft against her jaw that her disobedient body was responding in all sorts of stupidly predictable ways.

'Because I'm a caveman?'

'Yes!' Her hands crept up to his neck and she protested feebly as he lifted her off her feet and back towards the bed to which she had only minutes previously sworn not to return.

'So, what are you looking for in a man?' Alessio murmured.

This time, he drew the covers over them. It was very dark outside. Even with the curtains open, the night was black velvet with only a slither of moon penetrating the darkness and weakly illuminating the bedroom.

He could feel her reluctance, her mind fighting her body, and it felt imperative that her body win the battle because he wanted her, more than he had ever wanted any woman in his life before.

'Not someone like you, Alessio,' Lesley whispered, pressing her hands flat against his chest and feeling the steady beat of his heart.

'Why? Why not someone like me?'

'Because...' *Because safety was not with a man who looked like him, a man who could have anyone he wanted.* She knew her limits. She knew that she was just not the sort of girl who drew guys to her like a magnet. She never had been. She just didn't have the confidence; had never had the right preparation; had never had a mother's guiding hand to show her the way to all those little feminine wiles that went into the mix of attraction between the sexes.

But bigger than her fear of involvement with him was her fear of *not* getting involved, *not* taking the chance.

'You're just not the sort of person I ever imagined having any kind of relationship with, that's all.'

'We're not talking marriage here, Lesley, we're talking about enjoying each other.' He propped himself up on one elbow and traced his finger along her arm. 'I'm not looking for commitment any more than you probably are.'

And certainly not with someone like you; Lesley reluctantly filled in the remainder of that remark.

'And you still haven't told me the sort of man you would call "your type".' She was warm and yielding in his arms. She might make a lot of noises about this being a mistake, but she wanted him as much as he wanted her, and he knew that if he slipped his fingers into her he would feel the tell-tale proof of her arousal.

He could have her right here and right now, despite whatever she said about him not being her type. And who, in the end, cared whether he was her type or not? Hadn't he just told her that this wasn't about commitment and marriage? In other words, did it really matter if he wasn't her type?

But he was piqued at the remark. She was forthright and spoke her mind; he had become accustomed to that very quickly. But surely what she had said amounted to an unacceptable lack of tact! He thought that there was nothing wrong in asking her to explain exactly what she had meant.

His voice had dropped a few shades.

'You're offended, aren't you?' Lesley asked and Alessio was quick to deny any such thing.

Lesley could have kicked herself for asking him that question. Of course he wouldn't be offended! To be offended, he would actually have had to care about her and that was not the case here, as he had made patently clear.

'That's a relief!' she exclaimed lightly. 'My type? I guess thoughtful, caring, sensitive; someone who believes in the same things that I do, who has similar interests...maybe even someone working in the same field. You know—artistic, creative, not really bothered about the whole business of making money.'

Alessio bared his teeth in a smile. 'Sounds a lot of fun. Sure someone like that would be able to keep up with you? No, scrap that—too much talk. There are better things to do and, now that we've established that you can't resist me even though I'm the last kind of person you would want in your life, let's make love.'

'Alessio...'

He stifled any further protest with a long, lingering kiss that released in her a sigh of pure resignation. So this made no sense, so she was a complete idiot...

Where had the practical, level-headed girl with no illusions about herself gone? All she seemed capable of doing was giving in.

'And,' he murmured into her ear. 'In case you think that Italy is off the agenda because I'm not a touchy-feely art director for a design company, forget it. I still want you there by my side. Trust me, I will make it worth your while.'

CHAPTER SEVEN

EVERYTHING SEEMED TO happen at the speed of light after that. Of course, there was no inconvenient hanging around for affordable flights or having to surf the Internet for places to stay. None of the usual headaches dogged Alessio's spur-of-the-moment decision to take Lesley to Italy.

Two days after he had extended his invitation, they were boarding a plane to Italy.

It was going to be a surprise visit. Armed with information, they were going to get the full story from his daughter, lay all the cards on the table and then, when they were back in the UK, Alessio would sort the other half of the equation out. He would pay an informal visit to his emailing friend and he was sure that they would reach a happy conclusion where no money changed hands.

Lessons, he had assured her, would regrettably have to be learnt.

Lesley privately wondered what his approach to his daughter would be. Would similar lessons also 'regrettably have to be learnt'? How harsh would those lessons be? He barely had a relationship with Rachel and she privately wondered how he intended ever to build on it if he went in to 'sort things out' with the diplomacy of a bull in a china shop.

That was one of the reasons she had agreed to go to Italy with him.

Without saying it in so many words, she knew that he was looking to her for some sort of invisible moral back-up, even though he had stated quite clearly that he needed her there primarily to impart the technicalities of what she had discovered should the situation demand it.

'You haven't said anything for the past half an hour.' Alessio interrupted her train of thought as they were shown into the first class cabin of the plane. 'Why?'

Lesley bristled. 'I was just thinking how fast everything's moved,' she said as they were shown to seats as big as armchairs and invited to have a glass of champagne, which she refused.

She stole a glance at his sexy face, lazy and amused at the little show of rebellion.

'I came to do a job for you, thinking that I would be in and out of your house in a matter of a few hours and now here I am, days later, boarding a plane for Italy.'

'I know. Isn't life full of adventure and surprise?' He waved aside an awe-struck air hostess and settled into the seat next to her. 'I confess that I myself am surprised at the way things unfolded. Surprised but not displeased.'

'Because you've got what you wanted,' Lesley complained. She was so accustomed to her independence that she couldn't help feeling disgruntled at the way she had been railroaded into doing exactly what he had wanted her to do.

Even though, a little voice inside her pointed out, this rollercoaster ride was the most exciting thing she had ever done in her life—even though it was scary, even though it had yanked her out of her precious comfort zone, even though she knew that it would come to nothing and the fall back to Planet Earth would be painful.

'I didn't force your hand,' Alessio said comfortably.

'You went into the office and talked to my boss.'

'I just wanted to point out the world of opportunity lying at his feet if he could see his way to releasing you for one week to accompany me to Italy.'

'I dread to think what the office grapevine is going to make of this situation.'

'Do you care what anyone thinks?' He leant against the window so that he could direct one hundred per cent of his undivided attention on her.

'Of course I do!' Lesley blushed because she knew that, whilst she might give the impression of being strong, sassy and outspoken, she still had a basic need to be liked and accepted. She just wasn't always good at showing that side of herself. In fact, she was uncomfortably aware of the fact that, whilst Alessio might have shown her more of himself than he might have liked, she had likewise done the same.

He would not know it, but against all odds she had allowed herself to walk into unchartered territory, to have a completely new experience with a man knowing that he was not the right man for her.

'Relax and enjoy the ride,' he murmured.

'I'm not going to enjoy confronting your daughter with all the information we've managed to uncover. She's going to know that I went through her belongings.'

'If Rachel had wanted to keep her private life private, then she should have destroyed all the incriminating evidence. The fact is that she's still a child and she has no vote when it comes to us doing what was necessary to protect her.'

'She may not see it quite like that.'

'She will have to make a very big effort to, in that case.'

Lesley sighed and leaned back into the seat with her eyes shut. What Alessio did with his daughter was really none of her business. Yes, she'd been involved in bringing the situation to light, but its solutions and whatever repercussions followed would be a continuing saga she would leave behind. She would return to the blessed safety of what she knew and the family story of Alessio and his daughter would remain a mystery to her for ever.

So there was no need to feel any compunction about just switching off.

Yet she had to bite back the temptation to tell him what she thought, even though she knew that he would have every right to dismiss whatever advice she had to offer about the peculiarity of their relationship, if a 'relationship' was what it could be called. She was his lover, a woman who probably knew far too much about his life for his liking. She had been paid to investigate a personal problem, yet had no right to have any discussions about that problem, even though they were sleeping together.

In a normal relationship, she should have felt free to speak her mind, but this was not a normal relationship, was it? For either of them. She had sacrificed her feminist principles for sex and she still couldn't understand herself, nor could she understand how it was that she felt no regrets.

In fact, when he looked at her the way he was looking at her right now, all she felt was a dizzying need to have him take her.

If only he could see into her mind and unravel all her doubts and uncertainties. Thank goodness he couldn't. As far as he was concerned, she was a tough career woman with as little desire for a long-term relationship as him. They had both stepped out of the box, drawn to each other by a combination of proximity and the pull of novelty.

'You're thinking,' Alessio said drily. 'Why don't you spit it out and then we can get it out of the way?'

'Get what out of the way?'

'Whatever disagreements you have about the way I intend to handle this situation.'

'You hate it when I tell you what I think,' Lesley said with asperity. Alessio shrugged and continued looking at her in the way that made her toes curl and her mouth run dry.

'And I don't like it when I can see you thinking but you're saying nothing. "Between a rock and a hard place" comes to mind.' He was amazed at how easily he had adapted to her outspoken approach. His immediate instinct now was not to shove her back behind his boundary lines and remind her about overstepping the mark.

'I just don't think you should confront Rachel and demand to know what the hell is going on.' She shifted in the big seat and turned so that she was completely facing him.

The plane was beginning to taxi in preparation for taking off, and she fell silent for a short while as the usual canned talk was given about safety exits, but as soon as they were airborne she looked at him worriedly once again.

'It's hard to know how to get answers if you don't ask for them,' he pointed out.

'We know the situation.'

'And I want to know how it got to where it finally got. It's one thing knowing the outcome but I don't intend to let history repeat itself.'

'You might want to try a little sympathy.'

Alessio snorted.

'You said yourself that she's just a kid,' Lesley reminded him gently.

'You *could* always spare me the horror of making a mess of things by talking to Rachel yourself,' he said.

'She's not my daughter.'

'Then allow me to work this one out myself.' But he knew that she was right. There was no tactful way of asking the questions he would have to ask, and if his daughter disliked him now then she was about to dislike him a whole lot more when he was finished talking to her.

Of course, there were those photos, cuttings of him—some indication, as Lesley had said, that she wasn't completely indifferent to the fact that he was her father.

But would that be enough to take them past this little crisis? Unlikely. Especially when she discovered that the photos and cuttings had been salvaged in an undercover operation.

'Okay.'

Alessio had looked away, out through the window to the dense bank of cloud over which they were flying. Now, he turned to Lesley with a frown.

'Okay. I'll talk to Rachel if you like,' she said on a reluctant sigh.

'Why would you do that?'

Why would she? Because she couldn't bear to see him looking the way he was looking now, with the hopeless expression of someone staring defeat in the face.

And why did she care? she asked herself. But she shied away from trying to find an answer to that.

'Because I'm on the outside of this mess. If she directs all her teenage anger at me, then by the time she gets to you some of it may have diffused.'

'And the likelihood of that is…?' But he was touched at her generosity of spirit.

'Not good odds,' Lesley conceded. 'But worth a try, don't you think?' He was staring at her with an expression of intense curiosity and she continued quickly, before he could interrupt with the most obvious question: *why?* A question to which she had no answer. 'Besides, I'm good at mediating. I got a lot of practice at doing that when I was growing up. When there are six kids in a family, a dad worked off his feet, and five of those six are boys, there's always lots of opportunity to practise mediation skills.'

But just no opportunity to practise *being a girl*. And that was why she was the way she was now: hesitant in relationships; self-conscious about whether she had what it took to make any relationship last; willing not to get into the water at all rather than diving in and finding herself out of her depth and unable to cope.

Only since Alessio had appeared on the scene had she really seen the pattern in her behaviour, the way she kept guys, smiling, at arm's length.

He was so dramatically different from any man she had ever been remotely drawn to that it had been easy to pinpoint her own lack of self-confidence. She was a clever career woman with a bright life ahead of her and yet that sinfully beautiful face had reduced all those achievements to rubble.

She had looked at him and returned to her teenage years when she had simply not known how to approach a boy because she had had no idea what they were looking for.

For her, Alessio Baldini was not the obvious choice

when it came to picking a guy to sleep with, yet sleep with him she had, and she was glad that she had done so. She had broken through the glass barrier that had stood between her and the opposite sex. It was strange, but he had given her confidence she hadn't really even known she had needed.

'And mediation skills are so important when one is growing up,' Alessio murmured.

Basking in her new-found revelations, Lesley smiled. 'No, they're not,' she admitted with more candour than she'd ever done to anyone in her life before. 'In fact, I can't think of any skill a teenage girl has less use for than mediation skills,' she mused. 'But I had plenty of that.' She leaned back and half-closed her eyes. When she next spoke it was almost as though she was talking with no audience listening to what was being said.

'My mum died when I was so young, I barely remember her. I mean, Dad always told us about her, what she was like and such, and there were pictures of her everywhere. But the truth is, I don't have any memories of her—of doing anything with her, if you see what I mean.'

She glanced sideways at him and he nodded. He had always fancied himself as the sort of man who would be completely at sea when it came to listening to women pour their hearts out, hence it was a tendency that he had strenuously discouraged.

Now, though, he was drawn to what she was saying and by the faraway, pensive expression on her face.

'I never thought that I missed having a mother. I never knew what it was like to have one and my dad was always good enough for me. But I can see now that growing up in a male-only family might have given me confidence with the opposite sex but only when it

came to things like work and study. I was encouraged
to be as good as they were, and I think I succeeded, but
I wasn't taught, well…'

'How to wear make-up and shop for dresses?'

'Sounds crazy but I do think girls need to be taught
stuff like that.' She looked at him gravely. 'I can see
that it's easy to have bags of confidence in one area
and not much in another,' she said with a rueful shake
of her head. 'When it came to the whole game-playing,
sexual attraction thing, I don't think I've ever had loads
of confidence.'

'And now?'

'I feel I have, so I guess I should say thank you.'

'*Thank you?* What are you thanking me for?'

'For encouraging me to step out of the box,' Lesley
told him with that blend of frankness and disingenu-
ousness which he found so appealing.

Alessio was momentarily distracted from the headache awaiting him in Italy. He had no idea where she
was going with this but it had all the feel of a conversation heading down a road he would rather not explore.

'Always happy to oblige,' he said vaguely. 'I hope
you've packed light clothes. The heat in Italy is quite
different from the heat in England.'

'If I hadn't taken on this job, there's not a chance in
the world that I would ever have met you.'

'That's true enough.'

'Not only do we not move in the same circles, we
have no interests in common whatsoever.'

Alessio was vaguely indignant at what he thought
might be an insult in disguise. Was she comparing him
to the 'soul mate' guy she had yet to meet, the touchy-
feely one with the artistic side and a love of all things
natural?

'And if we *had* ever met, at a social do or something like that, I would never have had the confidence to approach you.'

'I'm not sure where you're going with this.'

'Here's what I'm saying, Alessio. I feel as though I've taken huge strides in gaining self-confidence in certain areas and it's thanks in some measure to you. I could say that I'm going to be a completely different person when I get back to the UK and start dating again.'

Alessio could not believe what he was hearing. He had no idea where this conversation had come from and he was enraged that she could sit there, his lover, and talk about going back on the dating scene!

'The dating scene.'

'Is this conversation becoming a little too deep for you?' Lesley asked with a grin. 'I know you don't do deep when it comes to women and conversations.'

'And how do you know that?'

'Well, you've already told me that you don't like encouraging them to get behind a stove and start cooking a meal for you, just in case they think, I don't know, they have somehow managed to get a foot through the door. So I'm guessing that meaningful conversations are probably on the banned list as well.'

They were. It was true. He had never enjoyed long, emotional conversations which, from experience, always ended up in the same place—invitations to meet the parents, questions about commitment and where the relationship was heading.

In fact, the second that type of conversation began rearing its head, he usually felt a pressing need to end the relationship. He had been coerced into one marriage and he had made a vow never to let himself be railroaded into another similar mistake, however tempting the woman in question might be.

He looked into her astute, brown eyes and scowled. 'I may not be looking for someone to walk down the aisle with, but that doesn't mean that I'm not prepared to have meaningful discussions with women. I'm also insulted,' he was driven to continue, 'That I've been used as some kind of trial run for the real thing.'

'What do you mean?' Lesley was feeling good. The vague unease that had been plaguing her ever since she had recognised how affected she was by Alessio had been boxed away with an explanation that made sense.

Sleeping with him had opened her eyes to fears and doubts she had been harbouring for years. She felt that she had buried a lack of self-confidence in her own sexuality under the guise of academic success and then, later on, success in her career. She had dressed in ways that didn't enhance her own femininity because she had always feared that she lacked what it took.

But then she had slept with him, slept with a man who was way out of her league, had been wanted and desired by him, and made to feel proud of the way she looked.

Was it any wonder that he had such a dramatic effect on her? It was a case of lust mixed up with a hundred other things.

But the bottom line was that he was no more than a learning curve for her. When she thought about it like that, it made perfect sense. It also released her from the disturbing suspicion that she was way too deep in a non-relationship that was going nowhere, a relationship that meant far more to her than it did to him.

Learning curves provided lessons and, once those lessons had been learnt, it was always easy to move on.

Learning curves didn't result in broken hearts.

She breathed in quickly and shakily. 'Well?' she flung at him, while her mind continued to chew over the notion that her involvement with him had been fast and hard. She had been catapulted into a world far removed from hers, thrown into the company of a man who was very, very different from the sort of men she was used to, and certainly worlds apart from the sort of man she would ever have expected herself to be attracted to.

But common sense had been no match for the power of his appeal and now here she was.

When she thought about never seeing him again, she felt faintly, sickeningly panicked.

What did that mean? Her thoughts became muddled when she tried to work her way through what suddenly seemed a dangerous, uncertain quagmire.

'I mean that you used me,' Alessio said bluntly. 'I don't like being used. And I don't appreciate you talking about jumping back into the dating scene, not when we're still lovers. I expect the women I sleep with to only have eyes for me.'

The unbridled arrogance of that statement, which was so fundamentally *Alessio,* brought a reluctant smile to her lips.

She had meant it when she had told him that under normal circumstances they would never have met. Their paths simply wouldn't have crossed. He didn't mix in the same circles as she did. And, even if by some freak chance they *had* met, they would have looked at one another and quickly looked away.

She would have seen a cold, wealthy, arrogant cardboard cut-out and he would have seen, well, a woman who was nothing like the sort of women he went out with and therefore she'd have been invisible. But the circumstances that had brought them together had uniquely provided them with a different insight into one another.

She had seen beneath the veneer to the three-dimensional man and he had seen through the sassy, liberal-minded, outspoken woman in charge of her life to the uncertain, insecure girl.

She was smart enough to realise, however, that that changed nothing. He was and always would be uninterested in any relationship that demanded longevity. He was shaped by his past and his main focus now was his daughter and trying to resolve the difficult situation that had arisen there. He might have slept with her because she was so different from what he was used to and because she was there, ready and willing but, whereas he had fundamentally reached deep and changed her, she hadn't done likewise with him.

'You're smiling.' Alessio was reluctant to abandon the conversation. When, he thought, was this dive back into the dating scene going to begin? Had she put time limits on what they had? Wasn't he usually the one to do that?

'I don't want to argue with you.' Lesley kept that smile pinned to her face. 'Who will you introduce me as when we get to Italy?'

'I haven't given it any thought. Where is all this hectic dating going to take place?'

'I beg your pardon?'

'You can't start conversations you don't intend to finish. So, where will you be going to meet Mr Right? I'm taking it you intend to start hunting when we return to England, or will you be looking around Italy for any suitable candidates?'

'Are you upset because I said what I said?'

'Why would I be upset?'

'I have no idea,' Lesley said as flippantly as she could. 'Because we both know that what we have isn't going to last.' She allowed just a fraction of a second in which he could have contradicted her, but of course he said nothing, and that hurt and reinforced for her the position she held in his life. 'And of course I'm not going to be looking around Italy for suitable candidates. I haven't forgotten why I'll be there in the first place.'

'Good,' Alessio said brusquely.

But the atmosphere between them had changed, and when he flipped open his lap-top and began working Lesley took the hint and excavated her own lap-top so that she too could begin working, even though she couldn't concentrate.

What she had said had put his nose out of joint, she decided. He wanted her to be his, to belong to him for however long he deemed it suitable, until the time came when he got bored of her and decided that it was time for her to go. For her to talk to him about dating other men would have been a blow to his masculine pride, hence his reaction. He wasn't upset, nor was he jealous of these imaginary men she would soon be seeking out. If they existed.

Her thoughts drifted and meandered until the plane began its descent. Then they were touching down at the airport in Liguria and everything vanished, except the reason why they were here in the first place.

Even the bright sunshine vanished as they stepped out and were ushered into a chauffeur-driven car to begin the journey to his house on the peninsula.

'I used to come here far more frequently in the past,'

he mused as he tried to work out the last time he had visited his coastal retreat.

'And then what happened?' It was her first time in Italy and she had to drag her eyes away from the lush green of the backdrop, the mountains that reared up to one side, the flora which was eye-wateringly exuberant.

'Life seemed to take over.' He shrugged. 'I woke up to the fact that Bianca had as little to do with this part of Italy as she possibly could and, of course, where she went, my daughter was dragged along. My interest died over a period of time and, anyway, work prohibited the sort of lengthy holidays that do this place justice.'

'Why didn't you just sell up?'

'I had no pressing reason to. Now I'm glad I hung onto the place. It may have been a bit uncomfortable had we been under the same roof as Rachel and Claudia, given the circumstances. I hadn't planned on saying anything to my mother-in-law about our arrival, but in all events I decided to spare her the shock of a surprise visit—although I've told her to say nothing to Rachel, for obvious reasons.'

'Those reasons being?'

'I can do without my teenage daughter scarpering.'

'You don't think she would, do you? Where would she go?'

'I should think she knows Italy a lot better than I do. She certainly would have friends in the area I know nothing about. I think it's fair to say that my knowledge of the people she hangs out with isn't exactly comprehensive.' But he smiled and then stared out of the window. 'I shudder to think of Claudia trying to keep control of my daughter on a permanent basis.'

The conversation lapsed. The sun was setting by the time they finally made it to his house, which they approached from the rear and which was perched on a hill top.

The front of the house overlooked a drop down to the sea and the broad wooden-floored veranda, with its deep rattan-framed sofas, was the perfect spot from which you could just sit and watch the changing face of the ocean.

Only when they had settled in, shown to their bedroom by a housekeeper—yet another employee keeping a vacant house going—did Alessio inform her that he intended visiting his mother-in-law later that evening.

'It won't be too late for her,' he said, prowling through the bedroom and then finally moving to the window to stare outside. He turned to look at her. In loose-fitting trousers and a small, silky vest, she looked spectacular. It unsettled him to think that, even with this pressing business to conclude, she had still managed to distract him to the point where all he could think of was her returning to London and joining the singles scene.

He wouldn't have said that his ego was so immense that it could be so easily bruised, but his teeth clamped together in grim rejection of the thought of any man touching her. Since when had he been the possessive type, let alone jealous?

'It will also allow Rachel to sleep on everything, give her time to put things into perspective and to come to terms with returning with us on the next flight over.'

'You make it sound as though we'll be leaving tomorrow.' Lesley hovered by the bed, sensing his mood and wondering whether it stemmed from parental concern at what was to come. She wanted to reach out and comfort him but knew, with unerring instinct, that that would be the last thing he wanted.

Yet hadn't he implied that they would be in the country for at least a week? She wondered why the rush was suddenly on to get out as quickly as possible. Did he really think that she had been using him? Had he decided that the sooner he was rid of her, the better, now that she had bucked the trend of all his other women and displayed a lack of suitable clinginess?

Pride stopped her from asking for any inconvenient explanations.

'Not that it matters when we leave,' she hastened to add. 'Would I have time to have a shower?'

'Of course. I have some work I need to get through anyway. I can use the time to do that and you can meet me downstairs in the sitting room. Unlike my country estate, you should be able to find your way around this villa without the use of a map.'

He smiled, and Lesley smiled back and muttered something suitable, but she was dismayed to feel a lump gathering at the back of her throat.

The sex between them was so hot that she would have expected him to have given her that wolfish grin of his, to have joined her in the shower, to have forgotten what they had come here for...just for a while.

Instead, he was vanishing through the door without a backward glance and she had to swallow back her bitter disappointment.

Once showered, and in a pair of faded jeans and a loose tee-shirt, she found him waiting for her in the sitting room, pacing while he jangled car keys in his pocket. The chauffeur had departed in the saloon car in which they had been ferried and she wondered how they were going to get to Claudia's villa, but there was a small four-wheel-drive jeep tucked away at the side of the house.

She had all the paperwork in a backpack which she

had slung over her shoulder. 'I hope I'm not under-dressed,' she said suddenly, looking up at him. 'I don't know how formal your mother-in-law is.'

'You're fine,' Alessio reassured her. A sudden image of her naked body flashed through his head with such sudden force that his heart seemed to skip a beat. He should have his mind one hundred per cent focused on the situation about to unravel, he told himself impatiently, instead of thinking about her and whatever life choices she decided to make. 'Your dress code isn't the issue here,' he said abruptly and Lesley nodded and turned away.

'I know that,' she returned coolly. 'I just wouldn't want to offend anyone.'

Alessio thought that that was rather shutting the door after the horse had bolted, considering she had had no trouble in offending *him*, but it was such a ridiculous thought that he swept it aside and offered a conciliatory smile.

'Don't think that I don't appreciate what you're doing,' he told her in a low voice. 'You didn't have to come here.'

'Even though you made sure I did by dangling that carrot of a fabulous new big job under my boss's nose?' She was still edgy at his dismissive attitude towards her but, when he looked at her like that, his dark eyes roving over her face, her body did its usual thing and leapt into heated response.

As if smelling that reaction, Alessio felt some of the tension leave his body and this time when he smiled it was with genuine, sexy warmth.

'I've always liked using all the tools in my box,' he murmured and Lesley shot him a fledgling grin.

His black mood had evaporated. She could sense it.

Perhaps now that they were about to leave some of his anxiety about what lay ahead was filtering away, replaced by a sense of the inevitable.

At any rate, she just wanted to enjoy this return to normality between them. For that little window when there had been tension between them, she had felt awful. She knew that she had to get a grip, had to put this little escapade into perspective.

She would give herself the remainder of what time was left in Italy and then, once they returned to the UK, whatever the outcome of what happened here, she would return to the life she had temporarily left behind. She had already laid the groundwork for a plausible excuse, one that would allow her to retreat with her dignity and pride intact.

It was time to leave this family saga behind her.

CHAPTER EIGHT

THE DRIVE TO Claudia's villa took under half an hour. He told her that he hadn't been back to Portofino for a year and a half, and then it had been a flying visit, but he still seemed to remember the narrow roads effortlessly.

They arrived at a house that was twice the size of Alessio's. 'Bianca always had a flair for the flamboyant,' he said drily as he killed the engine and they both stared at an imposing villa fronted by four Romanesque columns, the middle two standing on either side of a bank of shallow steps that led to the front door. 'When we were married and she discovered that money was no object, she made it her mission to spend. As I said, though, she ended up spending very little time here— too far from the action. A peaceful life by the sea was not her idea of fun.'

Lesley wondered what it must be like to nip out at lunchtime and buy a villa by the sea for no better reason than *you could*. 'Is your mother-in-law expecting me?'

'No,' Alessio admitted. 'As far as Claudia is concerned, I am here on a mission to take my wayward daughter in hand and bring her back with me to London. I thought it best to keep the unsavoury details of this little visit to myself.' He leaned across to flip open the passenger door. 'I didn't think,' he continued, 'That

Rachel would have appreciated her grandmother knowing the ins and outs of what has been going on. Right.
Let's get this over and done with.'

Lesley felt for him. Underneath the cool, composed
exterior she knew that he would be feeling a certain
dread at the conversation he would need to have with
his daughter. He would be the Big, Bad Wolf and, for
a sixteen-year-old, there would be no extenuating circumstances.

The ringing of the doorbell reverberated from the
bowels of the villa. Just when Lesley thought that no one
was in despite the abundance of lights on, she heard the
sound of footsteps, and then the door was opening and
there in front of them was a diminutive, timid looking
woman in her mid-sixties: dark hair, dark, anxious eyes
and a face that looked braced for an unpleasant surprise
until she registered who was at the door and the harried
expression broke into a beaming smile.

Lesley faded back, allowing for a rapid exchange of
Italian, and only when there was a lull in the conversation did Claudia register her presence.

Despite what Alessio had said, Lesley had expected
someone harder, tougher and colder. Her daughter, after
all, had not come out of Alessio's telling of the story as
an exemplary character, but now she could see why he
had dismissed Claudia's ability to cope with Rachel.

Their arrival had been unannounced; they certainly
had not been expected for supper. Alessio had been
vague, Claudia told her, gripping Lesley's arm as she
led them towards one of myriad rooms that comprised
the ground floor of the ornately decorated house.

'I was not even sure that he would be coming at all,'
she confided. 'Far less that he would be bringing a lady
friend with him...'

Caught uncomfortably on the outside of a conversation she couldn't understand, Lesley could only smile weakly as Alessio fired off something in Italian and then they were entering the dining room where, evidently, dinner had been interrupted.

Standing a little behind both Claudia and Alessio, Lesley nervously looked around the room, feeling like an intruder in this strange family unit.

For a house by the coast, it was oddly furnished with ornate, dark wooden furniture, heavy drapes and a patterned rug that obscured most of the marble floor. Dominating one of the walls was a huge portrait of a striking woman with voluptuous dark good looks, wild hair falling over one shoulder and a haughty expression. Lesley assumed that it was Bianca and she could see why a boy of eighteen would have been instantly drawn to her.

The tension in the room was palpable. Claudia had bustled forward, but her movements were jerky and her smile was forced, while Alessio remained where he was, eyes narrowed, looking at the girl who had remained seated and was returning his stare with open insolence.

Rachel looked older than sixteen but then Lesley knew by now that she was only a few weeks away from her seventeenth birthday.

The tableau seemed to remain static for ages, even though it could only have been a matter of seconds. Claudia had launched into Italian and Rachel was pointedly ignoring her, although her gaze had shifted from Alessio, and now she was staring at Lesley with the concentration of an explorer spotting a new sub-species for the first time.

'And who are *you*?' She tossed her hair back, a mane of long, dark hair similar to the woman's in the portrait, although the resemblance ended there. Rachel had her father's aristocratic good looks. This was the gangly teenager whose leather mini-skirt Lesley had stealthily tried on. She reminded Lesley of the cool kids who had ruled the school as teenagers, except now a much older and more mature Lesley could see her for what she really was: a confused kid with a lot of attitude and a need to be defensive. She was scared of being hurt.

'Claudia.' Alessio turned to the older woman. 'If you would excuse us, I need to have a quiet word with my daughter.'

Claudia looked relieved and scuttled off, shutting the door quietly behind her.

Immediately Rachel launched into Italian and Alessio held up one commanding hand.

'English!'

It was the voice of complete and utter authority and his daughter glared at him, sullenly defiant but not quite brave enough to defy him.

'I'm Lesley.' Lesley moved forward into the simmering silence, not bothering to extend a hand in greeting because she knew it wouldn't be taken, instead sitting at the dining room table where she saw that Rachel had been playing a game on her phone.

'I helped to create that.' She pointed to the game with genuine pleasure. 'Three years ago.' She dumped the backpack onto the ground. 'I was seconded out to help design a website for a starter computer company and I got involved with the gaming side of things. It made a nice change. If I had only known how big that game would have become, I would have insisted on putting my name to it and then I would be getting royalties.'

Rachel automatically switched off the phone and turned it upside down.

Alessio had strolled towards his daughter and adopted the chair next to her so that she was now sand-wiched between her father and Lesley.

'I know why you've come.' Rachel addressed her father in perfect, fluent English. 'And I'm not going back to England. I'm not going back to that stupid boarding school. I hate it there and I hate living with you. I'm staying here. Grandma Claudia said she's happy to have me.'

'I'm sure,' Alessio said in a measured voice, 'That you would love nothing more than to stay with your grandmother, running wild and doing whatever you want, but it is not going to happen.'

'You can't make me!'

Alessio sighed and raked his fingers through his hair. 'You're still a minor. I think you will find that I can.'

Looking between them, Lesley wondered if either realised just how alike they were: the proud jut of their chins, their stubbornness, even their mannerisms. Two halves of the same coin waiting to be aligned.

'I don't intend to have a protracted argument with you about this, Rachel. Returning to England is inevitable. We are both here because there is something else that needs to be discussed.'

He was the voice of stern authority and Lesley sighed as she reached down to the backpack and began extracting her folder, which she laid on the shiny table.

'What's that?' But her voice was hesitant under the defiance.

'A few weeks ago,' Alessio said impassively, 'I started getting emails. Lesley came to help me unravel them.'

Rachel was staring at the folder. Her face had paled and Lesley saw that she was gripping the arms of the chair. Impulsively she reached out and covered the thin, brown hand with hers and surprisingly it was allowed to remain there.

'It's thanks to me,' she said quietly, 'That all this stuff was uncovered. I'm afraid I looked through your bedroom. Your father, of course, would have rather I didn't, but it was the only way to compile the full picture.'

'You looked *through my things*?' Dark eyes were now focused accusingly on her, turned from Alessio. Lesley had become the target for Rachel's anger and confusion and Lesley breathed a little sigh of relief because, the less hostility directed at Alessio, the greater the chance of him eventually repairing his relationship with his daughter. It was worth it.

It was worth it because she loved him.

That realisation, springing out at her from nowhere, should have knocked her for six, but hadn't she already arrived that conclusion somewhere deep inside her? Hadn't she known that, underneath the arguments about lust and learning curves, stepping out of comfort zones and finding her sexuality, the simple truth of the matter was that she had been ambushed by the one thing she had never expected? It had struck her like a lightning bolt, penetrating straight through logic and common sense and obliterating her defences.

'You had no right,' Rachel was hissing.

Lesley let it wash over her and eventually the vitriol fizzled out and there was silence.

'So, tell me,' Alessio said in a voice that brooked no argument, 'About a certain Jack Perkins.'

Lesley left them after the initial setting out of the information. It was a sorry story of a lonely teenager, unhappy at boarding school, who had fallen in with the wrong crowd—or, rather, fallen in with the wrong boy. Piecing together the slips of paper and the stray emails, Lesley could only surmise that she had smoked a joint or two and then, vulnerable, knowing that she would be expelled from yet another school, she had become captive to a sixteen-year-old lad with a serious drug habit.

The finer details, she would leave for Alessio to discover. In the meantime, not quite knowing what to do with herself, she went outside and tried to get her thoughts in order.

Where did she go from here? She had always been in control of her life; she had always been proud of the fact that she knew where she was heading. She hadn't stopped for a minute to think that something as crazy as falling in love could ever derail her plans because she had always assumed that she would fall in love with someone who slotted into her life without causing too much of a ripple. She hadn't been lying when she had told Alessio that the kind of guy she imagined for herself would be someone very much like her.

How could she ever have guessed that the wrong person would come along and throw everything into chaos?

And what did she do now?

Still thinking, she felt rather than saw Alessio behind her and she turned around. Even in the darkness he had the bearing of a man carrying the weight of the world on his shoulders, and she instinctively walked towards him and wrapped her arms around his waist.

Alessio felt like he could hold onto her for ever. Wrong-footed by the intensity of that feeling, he pulled her closer and covered her mouth with his. His hand crept up underneath the tee-shirt and Lesley stepped back.

'Is sex the *only* thing you ever think about?' she

asked sharply, and she answered the question herself, providing the affirmative she knew was the death knell to any relationship they had.

He wanted sex, she wanted more—it was as simple as that. Never had the gulf between them seemed so vast. It went far beyond the differences in their backgrounds, their life experiences or their expectations. It was the very basic difference between someone who wanted love and someone who only wanted sex.

'How is Rachel?' She folded her arms, making sure to keep some space between them.

'Shaken.'

'Is that all you have to say? That she's *shaken*?'

'Are you deliberately trying to goad me into an argument?' Alessio looked at her narrowly. 'I'm frankly not in the mood to soothe whatever feathers I've accidentally ruffled.' He shook his head, annoyed with himself for venting his stress on her, but he had picked something up—something stirring under the surface—even though, for the life of him, he couldn't understand what could possibly be bugging her. She certainly hadn't spent the past hour trying and failing to get through to a wayward teenager who had sat in semi-mute silence absorbing everything that was being said to her but responding to nothing.

He was frustrated beyond endurance and he wondered if his own frustration was making him see nuances in her behaviour that weren't there.

'And I'm frankly amazed that you could talk to your daughter, have this awkward conversation, and yet have so little to report back on the subject.'

'I didn't realise that it was my duty to *report back* to you,' Alessio grated and Lesley reddened.

'Wrong choice of words.' She sighed. Here were the

cracks, she thought with a hollow sense of utter dejection. Things would go swimmingly well just so long as she could disentangle sex from love, but she was finding that she couldn't now. She spiked her fingers through her short hair and looked away from him, out towards the same black sea which his villa down the road overlooked.

She could see the way this would play out: making love would become a bittersweet experience; she would be the temporary mistress, making do, wondering when her time would be up. She suspected that that time would come very quickly once they returned to England. The refreshing, quirky novelty of bedding a woman with brains, who spoke her mind, who could navigate a computer faster than he could, would soon pall and he would begin itching to return to the unchallenging women who had been his staple diet.

Nor would he want a woman around who reminded him of the sore topic of his daughter and her misbehaviour, which had almost cost him a great deal of money.

'Would it be okay if I went to talk to her?' Lesley asked, and Alessio looked at her in surprise.

'What would you hope to achieve?'

'It might help talking to someone who isn't you.'

'Even though she sees you as the perpetrator of the "searching the bedroom" crime? I should have stepped in there and told her that that was a joint decision.'

'Why?' Lesley asked with genuine honesty. 'I guess you had enough on your plate to deal with and, besides, I will walk away from this and never see either of you again. If she pins the blame on me, then I can take it.'

Alessio's jaw hardened but he made no comment. 'She's still in the dining room,' he said. 'At least, that's where I left her. Claudia has disappeared to bed, and frankly I don't blame her. In the morning, I shall tell her that my daughter has agreed that the best thing is to return to England with me.'

'And school?'

'As yet to be decided, but it's safe to say that she won't be returning to her old stamping ground.'

'That's good.' She fidgeted, feeling his distance and knowing that, while she had been responsible for creating it, she still didn't like it. 'I won't be long,' she promised, and backed away.

Like a magnet, his presence seemed to want to pull her back towards him but she forced herself through to the dining room, little knowing what she would find.

She half-expected Rachel to have disappeared into another part of the house, but the teenager was still sitting in the same chair, staring vacantly through the window.

'I thought we might have a chat,' Lesley said, approaching her warily and pulling a chair out to sit right next to her.

'What for? Have you decided that you want to apologise for going through my belongings when *you had no right*?'

'No.'

Rachel looked at her sullenly. She switched on her mobile phone, switched it off again and rested it on the table.

'Your dad's been worried sick.'

'I'm surprised he could take the time off to be worried,' Rachel muttered, fiddling with the phone and then eventually folding her arms and looking at Lesley with unmitigated antagonism. 'This is all your fault.'

'Actually, it's got nothing to do with me. I'm only

here because of you and you're in this position because of what you did.'

'I don't have to sit here and listen to some stupid employee preach to me.' But she remained on the chair, glaring.

'And I don't have to sit here, but I want to, because I grew up without a mum and I know it can't be easy for you.'

'Oh puh…lease….' She dragged that one word out into a lengthy, disdainful, childish snort of contempt.

'Especially,' Lesley persevered, 'As Alessio—your father—isn't the easiest person in the world when it comes to touchy-feely conversations.'

'*Alessio*? Since when are you on first-name terms with my father?'

'He wants nothing more than to have a relationship with you, you know,' Lesley said quietly. She wondered if this was what love did, made you want to do your utmost to help the object of your affections, to make sure they were all right, even if you knew that they didn't return your love and would happily exit your life without much of a backward glance.

'And that's why he never bothered to get in touch when I was growing up? *Ever*?'

Lesley's heart constricted. 'Is that what you really believe?'

'It's what I was told by my mum.'

'I think you'll find that your father did his best to keep in touch, to visit… Well, you'll have to talk to him about that.'

'I'm not going to be talking to him again.'

'Why didn't you come clean with your dad, or even one of the teachers, when that boy started threatening you?' She had found a couple of crumpled notes and had quickly got the measure of a lad who had been happy to extort as much of Rachel's considerable pocket money as he could by holding it over her head that he had proof of the one joint she had smoked with him and was willing to lie to everyone that it had been more than that. When the pocket money had started running out, he must have decided to go directly to the goose that was laying the golden eggs: pay up or else he would go to the press and disclose that one of the biggest movers and shakers in the business world had a druggie teenage daughter. 'You must have been scared stiff,' she mused, half to herself.

'That's none of your business.'

Some of the aggression had left her voice. When Lesley looked at her, she saw the teenage girl who had been bullied and threatened by someone willing to take advantage of her one small error of judgement.

'Well, you dad's going to sort all of that out. He'll make the whole thing go away.' She heard the admiring warmth in her voice and cleared her throat. 'You should give him a chance.'

'And what's it to you?'

Lesley blushed.

'Oh, right.' She gave a knowing little laugh and sniffed. 'Well, I'm not about to give anyone a chance, and I don't care if he sorts that thing out or not. So. He dumped me and I had to traipse around with my mum and all her boyfriends.'

'You *knew* your mum…err…? Well, none of my business.' She stood up. 'You should give your dad a chance and at least listen to what he has to say. He tried very hard to keep in touch with you but, well, you should let him explain how that went—and you should go get some sleep.'

She exited the room, closing the door quietly behind her. Had she got through to Rachel? Who knew? It would take more than one conversation to break down some of those teenage walls, but several things had emerged.

Aside from the fact that everything was now on the table—and, whether she admitted it or not, that would have come as a huge relief to Rachel—it was clear that the girl had had no idea just how hard her father had tried to keep in touch with her, how hard he had fought to maintain contact.

And Alessio had no idea that his daughter was aware of Bianca's wild, promiscuous temperament.

Join those two things together, throw into the mix the fact that Rachel had kept a scrapbook of photos and cuttings, and Lesley suspected that an honest conversation between father and daughter would go some distance to opening the door to a proper relationship.

And if Rachel was no longer at a boarding school, but at a day school in London, they would both have the opportunity to start building a future and leaving the past behind.

She went outside to find Alessio still there and she quietly told him what she had learned during the conversation with his daughter.

'She thinks you abandoned her,' she reinforced bluntly. 'And she would have been devastated at the thought of that. It might explain why she's been such a rebel, but she's young. You're going to have to take the lead and lower your defences if you want to get through to her.'

Alessio listened, head tilted to one side, and when she had finished talking he nodded slowly and then told her in return what he intended to do to sort the small matter of a certain Jack Perkins. He had already contacted someone he trusted to supply him with information about the boy and he had enough at his disposal to pay a visit to his parents and make sure the matter was resolved quickly and efficiently, never again to rear its ugly head.

'When I'm through,' Alessio promised in a voice of steel, 'That boy will think twice before he goes near an Internet café again, never mind threatening anyone.'

Lesley believed him and she didn't doubt that Jack Perkins' life of crime was about to come crashing down around his head. It had transpired that his family was well-connected. Not only would they be horrified at what their son had done, and the drug problems he was experiencing, but his father would know that Alessio's power stretched far; if he were to be crossed again by a delinquent boy, then who knew what the repercussions would be?

The problem, Alessio assured her, would wait until he returned to the UK. It wasn't going anywhere and, whilst he could hand over the business of wrapping it up to a trusted advisor and friend, he would much rather do it himself.

'When I'm attacked,' he said softly, 'Then I prefer to retaliate using my own fists rather than relying on my bodyguards.'

Everything, Lesley thought, had been neatly wrapped up and she was certain that father and daughter would eventually find their way and become the family unit they deserved to be.

Which left her...the spectator whose purpose had been served and whose time had come to depart.

They drove in silence back to Alessio's villa. He planned on returning to his mother-in-law's the following morning and he would talk to his daughter once again.

He didn't say what that conversation would be, but Lesley knew that he had taken on board what she had said, and he would try and grope his way to some sort of mutual ground on which they could both converse.

Alessio knew that, generally speaking, the outcome to what could have been a disaster had been good.

Jack Perkins had revealed problems with his daughter that would now be addressed, and Lesley's mediation had been pretty damn fantastic. How could his daughter not have known that he had tried his hardest? He would set her straight on that. He could see that Rachel had been lost and therefore far too vulnerable in a school that had clearly allowed too much freedom. He might or might not take them to task on that.

'Thanks,' he suddenly said gruffly as they pulled up into the carport at the side of the villa. He killed the engine and looked at Lesley. 'You didn't just sort out who was behind this but you went the extra mile, and we both know, gentle bribe or no gentle bribe, you didn't have to do that.' Right now, all he wanted to do was get inside the villa, carry her upstairs to the bedroom and make love to her. Take all night making love to her. He had never felt as close to any woman.

No, Lesley thought with a tinge of bitterness, she really had had no need to go the extra mile, but she had, and it had had nothing to do with bribes, gentle or otherwise.

'We should talk,' she said after a while.

Alessio stilled. 'I thought we just had.'

Lesley hopped out of the car, slammed the door behind her and waited for him. Just then, in the car, it had felt way too intimate. Give it just a few more seconds sitting there, breathing him in, hearing that lazy, sexy drawl, and all her good intentions would have gone down the drain.

'Want to tell me what this is all about?' was the first thing he asked the second they were inside his villa. He threw the car keys on the hand-carved sideboard by the front door and led the way into the kitchen where he helped himself to a long glass of water from a bottle in the fridge. Then he sat down and watched as she took the seat furthest away from him.

'How long,' she finally asked, 'Do you plan on staying here?'

'Where is that question leading?' For the first time, he could feel quicksand underneath his feet and he didn't like it. He wished he had had something stronger to drink; a whisky would have gone down far better than a glass of water. He didn't like the way she had sat a million miles across the room from him; he didn't like the mood she had been in for the past few hours; he didn't like the way she couldn't quite seem to meet his eyes. 'Oh, for God's sake,' he muttered when she didn't say anything. 'At least until the end of the week. Rachel and I have a few things to sort out, not to mention a frank discussion of where she will go to school. There are a lot of fences to be mended and they won't be mended overnight; it'll take a few days before we can even work out where the holes are. But what has that got to do with anything?'

'I won't be staying on here with you.' She cleared her throat and took a deep breath. 'I do realise that I promised I would stay the week, but I think my job here is done, and it's time for me to return to London.'

'Your job here *is done*?' Alessio could not believe what he was hearing.

'Yes, and I just want to say that there's every chance that you and your daughter will find a happy solution to the difficulties you've been experiencing in your relationship.'

'Your job here...*is done*? So you're *heading back*?'

'I don't see the point of staying on.'

'And I don't believe I'm hearing this. What do you mean you don't *see the point of staying on*?' He point-blank refused to ask *what about us?* That was not a question that would ever pass his lips. He remembered what she had said about wanting to head back out there, get into the thick of the dating scene—now that she had used him to reintroduce her to the world of sex; now that she had overcome her insecurities, thanks to him.

Pride slammed in and he looked at her coldly.

'What we have, Alessio, isn't going anywhere. We both agreed on that, didn't we?' She could have kicked herself for the plaintive request she heard in her voice, the request begging him to contradict her. 'And I'm not interested in having a fling until we both run out of steam. Actually, probably until we get back to London. I'm not in the market for a holiday romance.'

'And what are you in the market for?' Alessio asked softly.

Lesley tilted her chin and returned his cool stare. Was she about to reveal that she was in the market for a long-term, for ever, happy-ever-after, committed relationship? Would she say that so that he could naturally assume that she was talking about *him*? Wanting that relationship *with him*? It would be the first conclusion he would reach. Women, he had told her, always seemed to want more than he was prepared to give. He would assume that she had simply joined the queue.

There was no way that she would allow her dignity to be trampled into the ground.

'Right now...' her voice was steady and controlled, giving nothing away '...all I want is to further my career. The company is still growing. There are loads of opportunities to grow with it, even perhaps to be transferred to another part of the country. I want to be there to take advantage of those opportunities.' She thought she sounded like someone trying to sell themselves at an interview, but she held her ground and her eyes remained clear and focused.

'And the career opportunities are going to disappear unless you hurry back to London as fast as you can?'

'I realise you'll probably pull that big job out from under our feet.' That thought only now struck her, as did the conclusion that she wasn't going to win employee of the week if her boss found out that she had been instrumental in losing a job that would bring hundreds of thousands of pounds to the company and extend their reach far wider than they had anticipated.

Alessio wondered whether her thirst for a rewarding career would make her change her mind about not staying on, about not continuing what they had. It revolted him to think that it might. He had never had to use leverage to get any woman into his bed and he wasn't about to start now.

Nor had he ever had to beg any woman to stay in his bed once she was there, and he certainly wasn't about to start *that* now.

'You misjudge me,' he said coldly. 'I offered that job to your boss and I am not a man who would renege on a promise, least of all over an affair that goes belly up. Your company has the job and everything that goes with it.'

Lesley lowered her eyes. He was a man of honour. She had known that. He just wasn't a man in love.

'I also think that when I decide to embark on another relationship.'

'You mean after you've launched yourself back into the singles scene.'

She shrugged, allowing him to think something she knew to be way off mark. She could think of nothing less likely than painting the town red and clubbing.

'I just feel that, if I decide to get involved with anyone, then it should be with the person who is right for me. So, I think we should call it a day for us.'

'Good luck with your search,' Alessio gritted. 'And, now that you've said your piece, I shall go and do some work downstairs. Feel free to use the bedroom where your suitcase has been put; I shall sleep in one of the other bedrooms and you can book your return flight first thing in the morning. Naturally, I will cover the cost.' He stood up and walked towards the door. 'I intend to go to Claudia's by nine tomorrow. If I don't see you before I go, have a safe flight. The money I owe you will be in your bank account by the time you land.' He nodded curtly and shut the kitchen door behind him.

This is all for the best, Lesley thought, staring at the closed door and trying to come to terms with the thought that she would probably never see him again.

It was time for her to move on...

CHAPTER NINE

LESLEY PAUSED IN front of the towering glass house and stared up and up and up. Somewhere in there, occupying three floors in what was the most expensive office block in central London, Alessio would be hard at work. At least, she hoped so. She hoped he wasn't out of the country. She didn't think she could screw up her courage and make this trip to see him a second time.

A month ago, she had walked out on him and she hadn't heard from him since. Not a word. He had duly deposited a wad of money into her account, as he had promised—far too much, considering she had bailed on their trip a day in.

How had his talk with his daughter turned out? Had they made amends, begun the protracted process of repairing their relationship? Where was she at school now?

Had he found someone else? Had he found her replacement?

For the past few weeks, those questions had churned round and round in her head, buzzing like angry hornets, growing fat on her misery until... Well, until something else had come along that was so big and so overwhelming that there was no room left in her head for those questions.

She took a deep breath and propelled her reluctant feet forward until she was standing in the foyer of the building, surrounded by a constant river of people coming and going, some in snappy suits, walking with an air of purpose; others, clearly tourists, staring around them, wondering where they should go to get to the viewing gallery or to one of the many restaurants.

In front of her a long glass-and-metal counter separated a bank of receptionists from the public. They each had a snazzy, small computer screen in front of them and they were all impeccably groomed.

She had worked out what she was going to say, having decided beforehand that it wasn't going to be easy gaining access to the great Alessio Baldini—that, in fact, he might very well refuse to see her at all. She had formulated a borderline sob story, filled with innuendo and just enough of a suggestion that, should she not be allowed up to whatever floor he occupied, he would be a very angry man.

It worked. Ten minutes after she had arrived, a lift was carrying her up to one of the top floors, from which she knew he would be able to overlook all of London. She had no idea how much the rent was on a place like this and her head spun thinking about it. She had been told that she would be met at the lift, and she was, but it was only as they were approaching his office that nerves really truly kicked in and she had to fight to keep her breathing steady and even and not to hyperventilate.

She was aware of his personal assistant asking concerned questions and she knew that she was answering those questions in a reassuring enough voice, but she felt sick to the stomach.

By the time they reached his office suite, she was close to fainting.

She didn't even know if she was doing the right thing. The decision to come here had been taken and then rejected and then taken again so many times that she had lost count.

The outer office, occupied by his personal assistant, was luxurious. In one corner, a massive semi-circular desk housed several phones and a computer terminal. Against one of the walls was a long, grey bench-like sofa that looked very uncomfortable. Against the other wall was a smooth, walnut built-in cupboard with no handles, just a bank of smooth wood.

It was an intimidating office, but not as intimidating as the massive door behind which Alessio would be waiting for her.

And waiting for her he most certainly was. He had been in the middle of a conference call when he had been buzzed by his secretary and informed that a certain Lesley Fox was downstairs in reception and should she be sent away or brought up?

Alessio had cut short his conference call without any preamble. His better self had told him to refuse her entry. Why on earth would he want to have anything further to do with a woman who had slept with him, had not denied having slept with him as part of her preparations for entering the world of hectic dating and then walked out of his life without a backward glance? Why would he engage in any further conversation with someone who had made it perfectly clear that he was not the sort of man she was looking for, even though they had slept together? Even though there had been no complaints there!

He had made sure that the money owed to her was deposited into her bank account, and had had no word from her confirming whether she had received it or not, despite the fact that he had paid her over and above the agreed amount, including paying her for time she had not worked for him at all.

The time he had wasted waiting for a phone call or text from her had infuriated him.

Not to mention the time he had wasted just *thinking* about her. She was hardly worth thinking about and yet, in the past few weeks, she had been on his mind like a background refrain he just couldn't get out of his head.

And so, when he had been called on his internal line to be told that she was there in the building, that she wanted to see him, there had been no contest in his head.

He had no idea what she could possibly want, and underwriting his curiosity was the altogether pleasant day dream that she had returned to beg for him back. Perhaps the wild and wonderful world of chatting up random men in bars and clubs had not quite lived up to expectation. Maybe having fun with the wrong guy was not quite the horror story she had first thought. Maybe she missed the sex; she had certainly seemed to enjoy every second of being touched by him.

Or, more prosaically, maybe her boss had sent her along on something to do with the job he had put their way. It made sense. She knew him. Indeed, they had landed that lucrative contract without even having to tender for it because of her. If anything needed to be discussed, her boss would naturally assume that she should be the one to do it and there would be no way that she could refuse. At least, not unless she started pouring out the details of her private life, which he knew she would never do.

He frowned, not caring for that scenario, which he immediately jettisoned so that he could focus as he waited for her on more pleasurable ones.

By the time his secretary, Claire, announced her arrival, through the internal line to which she exclusively had access, Alessio had come to the conclusion that he was only mildly curious as to the nature of her surprise visit—that he didn't care a whit what she had to say to him and that the only reason he was even allowing her entry into his office was because he was gentlemanly enough not to have her chucked out from the foyer in full view of everyone.

Still, he made her wait a while, before sitting back in his leather chair and informing Claire that his visitor could be ushered in—cool, calm and screamingly forbidding.

Lesley felt the breath catch jaggedly in her throat as she heard the door close quietly behind her. Of course, she hadn't forgotten what he looked like. How could she when his image had been imprinted in her brain with the red-hot force of a branding iron?

But nothing had prepared her for the cold depths of those dark eyes or the intimidating silence that greeted her arrival in his office.

She didn't know whether to keep standing or to confidently head for one of the leather chairs in front of his desk so that she could sit down. She certainly felt as though her legs didn't have much strength left in them.

Eventually, she only scuttled towards one of the chairs when he told her to sit, simultaneously glancing at his watch as though to remind her that, whilst she might have been offered a seat, she should make sure that she didn't get too comfortable because he didn't have a lot of time for her.

This was the guy she had fallen in love with. She knew she would have dented his pride when she had walked out on him, but still she had half-hoped that he might contact her in some way, if only to ask whether she had received the money he had deposited into her account.

Or else to fill her in on what had happened in his family drama. Surely that would have been the polite thing to do?

But not a word, and she knew that had she not arrived on his doorstep, so to speak, then she would never have seen him again. Right now, those brooding dark eyes were surveying her with all the enthusiasm of someone contemplating something the cat had inadvertently brought in.

'So,' Alessio finally drawled, tapping his rarely used fountain pen on the surface of his desk. 'To what do I owe this unexpected pleasure?' To his disgust, he couldn't help but think that she looked amazing.

He had made one half-hearted attempt to replace her with one of the women he had dated several months ago, a hot blonde with big breasts and a face that could turn heads from a mile away, but he had barely been able to stick it out for an evening in her company.

How could he when he had been too busy thinking of the woman slumped in the chair in front of him? Not in her trademark jeans this time but a neat pair of dark trousers and a snug little jacket that accentuated the long, lean lines of her body.

On cue, he felt himself begin to respond, which irritated the hell out of him.

'I'm sorry if I'm disturbing you,' Lesley managed. Now that she was here, she realised that she couldn't just drop her bombshell on him without any kind of warning.

'I'm a busy man.' He gesticulated widely and shot her a curving smile that contained no warmth. 'But never let it be said that I'm rude. An ex-lover deserves at least a few minutes of my time.'

Lesley bit her tongue and refrained from telling him that that remark in itself was the height of rudeness.

'I won't be long. How is Rachel?'

'You made this journey to talk about my daughter?'

Lesley shrugged. 'Well, I became quite involved in what was going on. I'm curious to know how things turned out in the end.'

Alessio was pretty sure that she hadn't travelled to central London and confronted him at his office just to ask one or two questions about Rachel, but he was willing to play along with the game until she revealed the true reason for showing up.

'My daughter has been…subdued since this whole business came out in the open. She returned to London without much fuss and she seems relieved that the boarding school option is now no longer on the cards. Naturally, I have had to lay down some ground rules for her—the most important of which is that I don't want to hear from anyone in the school that she's been acting up.' Except he had been far less harsh in delivering that message than it sounded.

Rachel might have been a complete idiot, led astray for reasons that were fairly understandable, but he had to accept his fair share of the blame as well. He had taken his eye off the ball.

Now, there was dialogue between them, and he had high hopes that in time that dialogue would turn into fluent conversation. Would that be asking too much?

He had certainly taken the unfortunate affair by the horns and sorted it all out, personally paying a visit to the boy's parents and outlining for them in words of

one syllable what would happen if he ever had another
email from the lad.

He had shied away from taking the full hard line,
however, confident that the boy's parents, who had
seemed decent but bewildered, would take matters in
hand. They both travelled extensively and only now had
it dawned on them that in their absence they had left
behind a lonely young man with a drug problem that
had fortunately been caught in the bud.

Rachel had not commented on the outcome, but he
had been shrewd enough to see the relief on her face.
She had found herself caught up in something far bigger
than she had anticipated and, in the end, he had come to
her rescue, although that was something he had taken
care not to ram home.

'That's good.' Lesley clasped her hands together.

'So is there anything else you want? Because if that's
all…' He looked at the slender column of her neck, her
down-bent head, the slump of her shoulders, and wanted
to ask her if she missed him.

Where the hell had *that* notion come from?

'Just one other thing.' She cleared her throat and
looked at him with visible discomfort.

And, all at once, Alessio knew where she was going
with this visit of hers. She wanted back in with him. She
had walked away with her head held high and a load of
nonsense about needing to find the right guy, wherever
the hell he might be. But, having begun her search, she
had obviously fast reached the conclusion that the right
guy wasn't going to be as easy to pin down as she had
thought and, in the absence of Mr Right, Mr Fantastic
Sex would do instead.

Over his dead body.

Although, it had to be said that the thought of her

begging for him was an appealing one. He turned that pleasant fantasy over in his head and very nearly smiled.

He was no longer looking at his watch. Instead, he pushed the chair away from the desk and relaxed back, his fingers lightly linked together on his flat, hard stomach.

Should he rescue her from the awkwardness of what she wanted to say? Or should he just wait in growing silence until her eventual discomfort propelled her into speech? Both options carried their own special appeal.

Eventually, with a rueful sigh that implied that far too much of his valuable time had already been wasted, he said, shaking his head, 'Sorry. It's a little too late for you.'

Lesley looked at him in sudden confusion. She knew that this was an awkward situation. She had appeared at his office and demanded to see him, and now here she was, body as stiff as a plank of wood, sitting in mute silence while she tried to work how best to say what she had come to say. No wonder he wanted to shuffle her out as fast as he could. He must be wondering what the hell she was doing, wasting his time.

'You're—you're busy,' she stammered, roused into speech as her brain sluggishly cranked back into gear just enough to understand that he wanted her out because he had more important things to do.

Once again, she wondered whether she had been replaced. Once again, she wondered whether he had reverted to type, back to the sexy blondes with the big breasts and the big hair.

'Have you been busy?' she blurted out impulsively, almost but not quite covering her mouth with her hand in an instinctive and futile attempt to retract her words.

Alessio got her drift immediately. No matter that the

question hadn't been completed. He could tell from the heightened colour in her cheeks and her startled, embarrassed eyes that she was asking him about his sex life, and he felt a groundswell of satisfaction.

'Busy? Explain.'

'Work. You know.' When she had thought about having this conversation, about seeing him again, she had underestimated the dramatic effect he would have on her senses. In her head, she had pictured herself cool, composed—a little nervous, understandably, but strong enough to say her piece and leave.

Instead, here she was, her thoughts all over the place and her body responding to him on that deep, subterranean level that was so disconcerting. The love which she had hoped might have found a more settled place— somewhere not to the forefront—pounded through her veins like a desperate virus, destroying everything in its path and making her stumble over her words.

Not to mention she'd hoped not to ask questions that should never have left her mouth, because she could tell from the knowing look in those deep, dark eyes that he knew perfectly well what she had wanted to know when she had asked him whether he had been 'busy'.

'Work's been...work. It's always busy. Outside of work...' Alessio thought of his non-date with a non-contender for a partner and felt his hackles rise that the woman staring at him with those big, almond-shaped brown eyes had driven him into seeking out someone for company simply to try and replace the images of her he had somehow ended up storing in his head. He shrugged, letting her assume that his private life was a delicate place to which she was not invited—hilarious, considering just how much she knew about him. 'What about you?' He smoothly changed the subject. 'Have you found your perfect soul-mate as yet?'

'What did you mean when you said that it was a little too late for me?' The remark had been playing at the back of her mind and she knew that she needed him to spell it out in words of one syllable.

'If you think that you can walk back into my life because you had a bit of trouble locating Mr Right, then it's not going to happen.'

Pride. But then, what the hell was wrong with pride? He certainly had no intention of telling her the truth, which was that he was finding it hard to rid his system of her, even though she should have been no more than a blurry memory by now.

He was a man who moved on when it came to women. Always had been—never mind when it came to moving on from a woman who had dumped him!

Just thinking about that made his teeth snap together in rage.

'I don't intend walking back into your life,' Lesley replied coolly. So, now she knew where she stood. Was she still happy that she had come here? Frankly, she could still turn around and walk right back through that door but, yes, she was happy she was here, whatever the outcome.

Alessio's eyes narrowed. He noticed what he had failed to notice before—the rigid way she was sitting, as though every nerve in her body was on red-hot alert; the way she was fiddling with her fingers; the determined tilt of her chin.

'Then why are you here?' His voice was brusque and dismissive. Having lingered on the pleasant scenario of her pleading to be a part of his life once again, he was irrationally annoyed that he had misread whatever signals she had been giving off.

'I'm here because I'm pregnant.'

There. She had said it. The enormous thing that had been absorbing every minute of every day of her life since she had done that home pregnancy test over three days ago was finally out in the open.

She had skipped a period. It hadn't even occurred to her that she could be pregnant; she had forgotten all about that torn condom. She had had far too much on her mind for that little detail to surface. It was only as she'd tallied the missed period with tender breasts that she remembered the very first time they had made love…and the outcome of that had been very clear to see in the bright blue line on that little plastic stick.

She hadn't bothered to buy more, to repeat the test. Why would she do that, when in her heart she knew that the result was accurate?

She had had a couple of days to get used to the idea, to move from feeling as though she was falling into a bottomless hole to gradually accepting that, whatever the landing, she would have to deal with it; that the hole wouldn't be bottomless.

She had had time to engage her brain in beginning trying to work out how her life would change, because there was no way that she would be getting rid of this baby. And, as her brain had engaged, her emotions had followed suit and a flutter of excitement and curiosity had begun to work their way into the equation.

She was going to be a mum. She hadn't banked on that happening, and she knew that it would bring a host of problems, but she couldn't snuff out that little flutter of excitement.

Boy or girl? What would it look like? A miniature

Alessio? Certainly, a permanent reminder of the only man she knew she would ever love.

And should she tell him? If she loved him, would she ruin his life by telling him that he was going to be a father—again? Another unplanned and unwanted pregnancy. Would he think that she was trapping him, just like Bianca had, into marriage for all the wrong reasons?

Wouldn't the kindest thing be to keep silent, to let him carry on with his life? It was hardly as though he had made any attempt at all to contact her after she had left Italy! She had been a bit of fun and he had been happy enough to watch her walk away. Wouldn't the best solution be to let him remember her as a bit of fun rather than detonate a bomb that would have far-reaching and permanent ramifications he would not want?

In the end, she just couldn't bring herself to deny him the opportunity of knowing that he was going to be a father. The baby was half his and he had his rights, whatever the outcome might be.

But it was still a bomb she'd detonated, and she could see that in the way his expression changed from total puzzlement to dawning comprehension and then to shock and horror.

'I'm sorry,' she said in a clear, high voice. 'I know this is probably the last thing you were expecting.'

Alessio was finding it almost impossible to join his thoughts up. Pregnant. She was pregnant. For once he couldn't find the right words to deal with what was going through his head, to express himself. In fact, he actually couldn't find any words at all.

'It was that first time,' Lesley continued into the lengthening silence. 'Do you remember?'

'The condom split.'

'It was a one in a thousand chance.'

'The condom split and now you're pregnant.' He leant forward and raked his fingers through his hair, keeping his head lowered.

'It was no one's fault,' Lesley said, chewing her lower lip and looking at his reaction, the way he couldn't even look at her. Right now he hated her; that was clear. He was listening to the sound of his life being derailed and, whether down to a burst condom or not, he was somehow blaming her.

'I wasn't going to come here...'

That brought his head up, snapping to attention, and he looked at her in utter disbelief. 'What, you were just going to disappear with my baby inside you and not tell me about it?'

'Can you blame me?' Lesley muttered defensively. 'I know the story about how you were trapped into a loveless marriage by your last wife; I know what the consequences of that were.'

'Those consequences being...?' When Bianca had smiled smugly and told him that he was going to be a father, he had been utterly devastated. Now, strangely, the thought that this woman might have spared him devastation second time round didn't sit right. In fact, he was furious that the thought might even have crossed her mind although, in some rational part of himself, he could fully understand why. He also knew the answer to his own stupid question, although he waited for her to speak while his thoughts continued to spin and spin, as though they were in a washing machine with the speed turned high.

'No commitment,' Lesley said without bothering to dress it up. 'No one ever allowed to get too close. No woman ever thinking that she could get her foot through the door, because you were always ready to bang that door firmly shut the minute you smelled any unwanted advances in that direction. And please don't look at me as though I'm talking rubbish, Alessio. We both know I'm not. So excuse me for thinking that it might have been an idea to spare you the nightmare of…of this…'

'So you would have just disappeared?' He held onto that tangible, unappealing thought and allowed his anger to build up. 'Walked away? And then what—in sixteen years' time I would have found out that I'd fathered a child when he or she came knocking on my door asking to meet me?'

'I hadn't thought that far into the future.' She shot him a mutinous look from under her lashes. 'I looked into a future a few months away and what I saw was a man who would resent finding himself trapped again.'

'You can't speculate on what my reactions might or might not have been.'

'Well, it doesn't matter. I'm here now. I've told you. And there's something else—I want you to know straight off that I'm not asking you for anything. You know the situation and that's my duty done.' She began standing up and found that she was trembling. Alessio stared at her with open-mouthed incredulity.

'Where do you think you're going?'

'I'm leaving.' She hesitated. This was the right time to leave. She had done what she had come to do. There was no way that she intended to put any pressure on him to do anything but carry on with his precious, loveless existence, free from the responsibility of a clinging woman and an unwanted baby.

Yet his presence continued to pull her towards him like a powerful magnet.

'You're kidding!' Alessio's voice cracked with the

harshness of a whip. 'You breeze in here, tell me that you're carrying my child, and then announce that you're on your way!'

'I told you, I don't want anything from you.'

'What you want is by the by.'

'I beg your pardon?'

'It's impossible having this sort of conversation here. We need to get out, go somewhere else. My place.'

Lesley stared at him in utter horror. Was he mad? The last thing she wanted was to be cooped up with him on his turf. It was bad enough that she was in his office. Besides, where else was the conversation going to go?

Financial contributions; of course. He was a wealthy man and in possession of a muddy conscience; he would salve it by flinging money at it.

'I realise you might want to help out on the money front,' she said stiltedly. 'But, believe it or not, that's not why I came here. I can manage perfectly well on my own. I can take maternity leave and anyway, with what I do, I should be able to work from home.'

'You don't seem to be hearing me.' He stood up and noticed how she fell back.

She might want him out of her life but it wasn't going to happen. Too bad if her joyful hunt for the right guy had crashed and burned; she was having his baby and he was going to be part of her life whether she liked it or not.

The thought was not as unwelcome as he might have expected. In fact, he was proud of how easily he was beginning to take the whole thing on board.

It made sense, of course. He was older and wiser. He had mellowed over time. Now that sick feeling of having an abyss yawn open at his feet was absent.

'If you want to discuss the financial side of things,

then we can do that at a later date. Right now, I'll give you time to digest everything.'

'I've digested it. Now, sit back down.' This was not where he wanted to be. An office couldn't contain him. He felt restless, in need of moving. He wanted the space of his apartment. But there was no way she would go there with him; he was astute enough to decipher that from her dismayed reaction to the suggestion. And he wasn't going to push it.

It crossed his mind that this might have come as a bolt from the blue for him, turning his life on its axis and sending it spiralling off in directions he could never have predicted, but it would likewise have been the same for her. Yet here she was, apparently in full control. But then, hadn't he always known that there was a thread of absolute bravery and determination running through her?

And when she said that she didn't want anything from him, he knew that she meant it. This situation could not have been more different from the one in which he had found himself all those years ago.

Not that that made any difference. He was still going to be a presence in her life now whether she liked it or not.

Lesley had reluctantly sat back down and was now looking at him with a sullen lack of enthusiasm. She had expected more of an explosion of rage, in the middle of which she could have sneaked off, leaving him to calm down. He seemed to be handling the whole thing a great deal more calmly than she had expected.

'This isn't just about me contributing to the mother and baby fund,' he said, in case she had got it into her head that it might be. 'You're having my baby and I intend to be involved in this every single step of the way.'

'What are you talking about?'

'Do you really take me for a man who walks away from responsibility?'

'I'm not your ex-wife!' Lesley said tightly, fists clenched on her lap. 'I haven't come here looking for anything and you certainly don't owe me or this baby anything!'

'I'm not going to be a part-time father,' Alessio gritted. 'I was a part-time father once, not of my own choosing, and it won't happen again.'

Not once had Lesley seen the situation from that angle. Not once had she considered that he would want actual, active involvement, yet it made perfect sense. 'What are you suggesting?' she asked, bewildered and on the back foot.

'What else is there to suggest but marriage?'

For a few frozen seconds, Lesley thought that she might have misheard him, but when she looked at him his face was set, composed and unyielding.

She released a hysterical laugh that fizzled out very quickly. 'I don't believe I'm hearing this. Are you mad? Get married?'

'Why so shocked?'

'Because...' *Because you don't love me. You probably don't even like me very much right now.* 'Because having a baby isn't the right reason for two people to get married,' she said in as controlled a voice as she could muster. 'You of all people should know that! Your marriage ended in tears because you went into it for all the wrong reasons.'

'Any marriage involving my ex-wife would have ended in tears.' Alessio was finding it hard to grapple with the notion that she had laughed at his suggestion of marriage. Was she *that* intent on finding Mr Right that she couldn't bear the thought of being hitched to him? It was downright offensive! 'You're not Bianca, and you need to look at the bigger picture.' Was that overly aggressive? He didn't think so but he saw the way she stiffened and he tempered what he was going to say with a milder, more conciliatory voice. 'By which I mean that this isn't about us as individuals but about a child that didn't ask to be brought into the world. To do the best for him or her is to provide a united family.'

'To do the best for him or her is to provide two loving parents who live separately instead of two resentful ones joined in a union where there's no love lost.' Just saying those words out loud made her feel ill because what she should really have said was that there was no worse union than one in which love was given but not returned. What she could have told him was that she could predict any future where they were married, and what she could see was him eventually loathing her for being the other half of a marriage he might have initiated but which had eventually become his prison cell.

There was a lot she could have told him but instead all she said was, 'There's no way I would ever marry you.'

CHAPTER TEN

THE PAIN STARTED just after midnight. Five months before her due date. Lesley awoke, at first disorientated, then terrified when, on inspection, she realised that she was bleeding.

What did that mean? She had read something about that in one of the many books Alessio had bought for her. Right now, however, her brain had ceased to function normally. All she could think of doing was getting on her mobile phone and calling him.

She had knocked him back, had told him repeatedly that she wasn't going to marry him, yet he had continued to defy her low expectations by stealthily becoming a rock she could lean on. He was with her most evenings, totally disregarding what she had said to him about pregnancy not being an illness. He had attended the antenatal appointments with her. He had cunningly incorporated Rachel into the picture, bringing his daughter along with him many of the times he'd visited her, talking as though the future held the prospect of them all being a family, even though Lesley had been careful to steer clear of agreeing to any such sweeping statements.

What was he hoping to achieve? She didn't know. He didn't love her and not once had he claimed to.

But, bit by bit, she knew that she was beginning to rely on him—and it was never so strongly proved as now, when the sound of his deep voice over the end of the phone had the immediate effect of calming her panicked nerves.

'I should have stayed the night,' was the first thing he told her, having made it over to her house in record time.

'It wasn't necessary.' Lesley leaned back and closed her eyes. The pain had diminished but she was still in a state of shock at thinking that something might be wrong. That she might lose the baby. Tears threatened close to the surface but she pushed them away, focusing on a good outcome, despite the fact that she knew she was still bleeding.

And then something else occurred to her, a wayward thought that needled its way into her brain and took root, refusing to budge. 'I shouldn't have called you,' she said more sharply than she had intended. 'I wouldn't have if I'd thought that you were going to fret and worry.' But she hadn't thought of doing anything *but* picking up that phone to him. To a man who had suddenly become indispensable despite the fact that she was not the love of his life; despite the fact that he wouldn't be in this car here with her now if she had never visited him in his office.

She had never foreseen the way he had managed to become so ingrained into the fabric of her daily life. He brought food for her. He stocked her up with pregnancy books. He insisted they eat in when he was around because it was less hassle than going out. He had taken care of that persistent leak in the bathroom which had suddenly decided to act up.

And not once had she sat back and thought of where all this was leading.

'Of course you should have called me,' Alessio said softly. 'Why wouldn't you? This baby is mine as well. I share all the responsibilities with you.'

And share them he had, backing away from trying to foist his marriage solution onto her, even though he had been baffled at her stubborn persistence that there was no way that she was going to marry him.

Why not? He just didn't get it. They were good together. They were having a baby. Hell, he had made sure not to lay a finger on her, but he still burned to have her in his bed, and the memory of the sex they had shared still made him lose concentration in meetings. And, yes, so maybe he had mentioned once or twice that he had learnt bitter lessons from being trapped into marriage by the wrong woman for the wrong reasons, but hadn't that made his proposal even more sincere—the fact that he was willing to sidestep those unfortunate lessons and re-tread the same ground?

Why couldn't she see that?

He had stopped thinking about the possibility that she was still saving herself for Mr Right. Just going down that road made him see red.

'I hate it when you talk about responsibilities,' she snapped, looking briefly at him and then just as quickly looking away. 'And you're driving way too fast. We're going to crash.'

'I'm sticking to the speed limit. Of course I'm going to talk about responsibilities. Why shouldn't I?' Would she rather he had turned his back on her and walked away? Was that the sort of modern guy she would have preferred him to be? He hung onto his patience with difficulty, recognising that the last thing she needed was to be stressed out.

'I just want you to know,' Lesley said fiercely, 'That if anything happens to this baby…'

'Nothing is going to happen to this baby.'

'You don't know that!'

Alessio could sense her desire to have an argument with him and he had no intention of allowing her to indulge that desire. A heated row was not appropriate but he shrewdly guessed that, if he mentioned that, it would generate an even bigger row.

What the hell was wrong? Of course she was worried. So was he, frankly. But he was here with her, driving her to the hospital, fully prepared to be right there by her side, so why the need to launch into an attack?

Frustration tore into him but, like his impatience, he kept it firmly in check.

Suddenly she felt that it was extremely important that she let him know this vital thing. 'And I just want you to know that, if something does, then your duties to me are finished. You can walk away with a clear conscience, knowing that you didn't dump me when I was pregnant with your child.'

Alessio sucked in his breath sharply. Ahead, he could see the big, impersonal hospital building. He had wanted her to have private medical care during the pregnancy and for the birth of the baby, but she had flatly refused, and he had reluctantly ceded ground. If, indeed, there was anything at all amiss, that small victory would be obliterated because he would damn well make sure that she got the best medical attention there was available.

'This is not the time for this sort of conversation.' He screeched to a halt in front of the Accident and Emergency entrance but, before he killed the engine, he looked at her intently, his eyes boring into her. 'Just try and relax, my darling. I know you're probably scared stiff but I'm here for you.' He brushed her cheek lightly and the tenderness of that touch brought a lump to her throat.

'You're here for the baby, not for me,' Lesley muttered under her breath. But then any further conversation was lost as they were hurried through, suddenly caught up in a very efficient process, channelled to the right place, speeding along the quiet hospital corridors with Lesley in a wheelchair and Alessio keeping pace next to her.

There seemed to be an awful lot of people around and she clasped his hand tightly, hardly even realising that she was doing that.

'If something happens to the baby…' he bent to whisper into her ear as they headed towards the ultrasound room '…then I'm still here for you.'

An exhausting hour later, during which Lesley had had no time to think about what those whispered words meant, she finally found herself in a private room decorated with a television on a bracket against the wall and a heavy door leading, she could see, to her own en-suite bathroom.

Part of her wondered whether those whispered words had actually been uttered or had they been a fiction of her fevered imagination?

She covertly watched as he drew the curtains together and then pulled a chair so that he was on eye-level with her as she lay on the bed.

'Thank you for bringing me here, Alessio,' she said with a weak smile that ended up in a yawn.

'You're tired. But everything's going to be all right with the baby. Didn't I say?'

Lesley smiled with her eyes half-closed. The relief

was overwhelming. They had pointed out the strongly beating heart on the scan and had reassured her that rest was all that was called for. She had been planning to work from home towards the beginning of the third trimester. That would now have to be brought forward.

'You said.'

'And—and I meant what I said when we were rushing you in.'

Lesley's eyes flew open and she felt as though her heart had skipped a beat. She had not intended to remind him of what he had said, just in case she had misheard, just in case he had said what he somehow thought she wanted to hear in the depths of her anxiety over her scare.

But now his eyes held hers and she just wanted to lose herself in possibilities.

'What did you say? I can't quite...um...remember.' She looked down at her hand which had somehow found its way between his much bigger hands.

'What I should say is that there was a moment back then when it flashed through my mind—what would I do if anything happened to *you*? It scared the living daylights out of me.'

'I know you feel very responsible...with me being pregnant.' She deliberately tried to kill the shoot of hope rising inside her and tenaciously refusing to go away.

'I'm not talking about the baby. I'm talking about you.' He felt as though he was looking over the side of a very sheer cliff, but he wanted to jump; he didn't care what sort of landing he might be heading for.

So far she hadn't tried to remind him that he wasn't her type and that they weren't suited for one another. That surely had to be a good sign?

'I don't know what I'd do if anything happened to

you because you're the love of my life. No, wait, don't say a thing. Just listen to what I have to say and then, if you want me to butt out of your life, I'll do as you say. We can go down the legal route and have the papers drawn up for custody rights, and an allowance to be made for you, and I'll stop pestering you with my attention.' He took a deep breath and his eyes shifted to her mouth, then to the unappealing hospital gown which she was still wearing, and then finally they settled on their linked fingers. It seemed safer.

'I'm listening.' *The love of his life*? She just wanted to repeat that phrase over and over in her head because she didn't think she could possibly get used to hearing it.

'When you first appeared at my front door, I knew you were different to every single woman I had ever met. I knew you were sharp, feisty, outspoken. I was drawn to you, and I guess the fact that you occupied a special place of intimate knowledge about certain aspects of my private life not usually open to public view fuelled my attraction. It was as though the whole package became irresistible. You were sexy as hell without knowing it. You had brains and you had insight into me.'

Lesley almost burst out laughing at the 'sexy as hell' bit but then she remembered the way he had looked at her when they had made love, the things he had said. *She* might have had insecurities about how she looked, but she didn't doubt that his attraction had been genuine and spontaneous. Hadn't he been the one to put those insecurities to bed, after all?

'It just felt so damned right between us,' he admitted, stealing a surreptitious look at her face, and encouraged that she didn't seem to be blocking him out. 'And the more we got to know one another the better it felt. I thought it was all about the sex, but it was much bigger than that, and I just didn't see it. Maybe after Bianca I simply assumed that women could only satisfy a certain part of me before they hit my metaphorical glass ceiling and disappeared from my life. I wasn't looking for any kind of involvement and I certainly didn't bank on finding any. But involvement found me without my even realising it.'

He laughed under his breath and, when he felt the touch of her hand on his cheek, he held it in place so that he could flip it over and kiss the palm of her hand. He relaxed, but not too much.

'Thanks to you, my relationship with Rachel is the healthiest it's ever been. Thanks to you, I've discovered that there's far more to life than trying to be a father to a hostile teenager and burying myself in my work. I never stopped to question how it was that I wasn't gutted when you told me about the pregnancy. I knew I felt different this time round from when Bianca had presented me with a future of fatherhood. If I had taken the time to analyse things, I might have begun to see what had already happened. I might have seen that I had fallen hopelessly in love with you.'

All his cards were on the table and he felt good. Whatever the outcome. He carried on before she could interrupt with a pity statement about him not really being the one for her.

'And I may not cry at girlie movies or bake bread but you can take me on. I'm a good bet. I'm here for you; you know that. I'll always be here for you because I'm nothing without you. If you still don't want to marry me, or if you want to put me on probation, then I'm willing to go along because I feel I can prove to you that I can be the sort of man you want me to be.'

'Probation?' The concept was barely comprehensible.

'A period of time during which you can try me out for size.' He had never thought he would ever in a million years utter such words to any woman. But he just had and he didn't regret any of them.

'I know what the word means.' The thoughts were rushing round in her head, a mad jumble that filled every space. She wanted to fling her arms around him, kiss him on the mouth, pull him right into her, jump up and down, shout from the rooftops—all of those things at the same time.

Instead, she said in a barely audible voice, 'Why didn't you say sooner? I wish you had. I've been so miserable, because I love you so much and I thought that the last thing you needed was to be trapped into marriage to someone you never wanted to see out your days with.' She lay back and smiled with such pure joy that it took her breath away. Then she looked at him and carried on smiling, and smiling, and smiling. 'I knew I was falling for you but I knew you weren't into committed relationships.'

'I never was.'

'That should have stopped me but I just didn't see it coming. You really weren't the sort of guy I ever thought I could have fallen in love with, but who said love obeys rules? By the time I realised that I loved you, I was in so deep that the only way out for me was to run as fast as I could in the opposite direction. It was the hardest thing I ever did in my entire life but I thought that, if I stayed, my heart would be so broken that I would never recover.'

'My darling… My beautiful, unique, special darling.' He kissed her gently on the lips and had the wonderful feeling of being exactly where he was meant to be.

'Then I found out that I was pregnant, and after the

shock had worn off a bit, I felt sick at the thought of telling you—sick at the thought of knowing that you would be horrified, your worst nightmare turned into reality.'

'And here we are. So I'm asking you again, my dearest—will you marry me?'

They were married in Ireland a month before their baby was born, with all her family in attendance. Her father, her brothers and her brothers' partners all filled the small local church. And, when they retired to the hotel which they had booked into, the party was still carrying on, as he was told, in typical Irish style. And just as soon as the baby was born, he was informed, they would throw a proper bash—the alcohol wouldn't stop flowing for at least two days. Alessio had grinned and told them that he couldn't wait but that, before the baby discovered the wonders of an Irish bash, she or he would first have to discover the wonders of going on honeymoon, because they had both agreed that wherever they went their baby would come as well.

And their baby, Rose Alexandra, a little girl with his dark hair and big, dark eyes, was born without fuss, a healthy eight pounds four ounces. Rachel, who was over the moon at the prospect of having a sibling she could thoroughly spoil, could barely contain her excitement when she paid her first visit to the hospital and peered into the little tilted cot at the side of Lesley's bed.

The perfect family unit, was the thought that ran through Alessio's mind as he looked at the snapshot picture in front of him. His beautiful wife, radiant but tired after giving birth, smiling down at the baby in her arms while Rachel, the daughter he had once thought lost to him but now found, stood over them both, her dark hair falling in a curtain as she gently touched her sister's small, plump, pink cheek.

If he could have bottled this moment in time, he would have. Instead, still on cloud nine, he leaned into the little group and knew that this, finally, was what life should be all about.

* * * * *

SECRETS OF THE PLAYBOY'S BRIDE

LEANNE BANKS

To Megan Crane, who said 'Obviously you have to write this book.' when I told her about my idea. There are few things that are more valuable than the encouragement of friends.

Leanne Banks is a *New York Times* and *USA TODAY* bestselling author who is surprised every time she realises how many books she has written. Leanne loves chocolate, the beach and new adventures. To name a few, Leanne has ridden on an elephant, stood on an ostrich egg (no, it didn't break), gone parasailing and indoor skydiving. Leanne loves writing romance because she believes in the power and magic of love. She lives in Virginia with her family and four-and-a-half-pound Pomeranian named Bijou. Visit her website at www.leannebanks.com.

One

Leonardo Grant caught the woman in his arms, absorbing her feminine impact and taking in swinging blond hair and seductive curves just before he felt something cold and wet slide down his chest.

"Oops," the blond woman said with a contrite expression, glancing from her nearly empty glass to his shirt. "I'm so sorry," she said. "I'm not usually such a klutz. I just wasn't watching where I was going. Let me get a napkin for you."

Despite the spill, the woman *emanated* class. No surprise, given she was attending one of Philadelphia's most exclusive charity events. He wondered who her date was. A woman this beautiful wouldn't have arrived alone. "No problem," he said smoothly. "I can get my own napkin."

"But I feel terrible. And you probably feel worse in that soggy shirt," she said motioning toward a waiter.

Charmed by how flustered she was, Leo allowed her to fuss over him for a moment while he studied her from head to toe. Silky shoulder-length blond hair framed an oval face with wide green eyes, a pert nose and a mobile, sensual mouth. He glanced lower, taking in her lean but curvy body. She worked out, he observed, taking in the slight muscle in her biceps. Her strapless dress revealed the tops of her creamy breasts and a narrow waist. The slit in her full-length gown gave him a peek at shapely legs.

A furrow formed beneath her brow as she mopped at his chest. "Maybe we could find you another shirt," she said.

Leo bit back a chuckle. He could have a shirt delivered to him in five minutes, but she was so much more interesting. "I can stand it," he said. "But we should replace your drink."

"I don't know," she said, full of doubt. "Maybe dumping my margarita on your shirt is a sign for me to stop even though that was my first one for the evening," she said.

He shrugged. "If at first you don't succeed," he said and extended his hand. "Leo Grant."

"Calista," she said, sliding her smooth, well-manicured hand in his. "Calista French. You've been such a good sport. I truly am sorry."

Her last name tripped a trigger, and Leo searched his memory for details. There'd been so many names over the years, names of people his guardian had tricked and used. Once Leo had run away, he'd tried to forget them all. He pushed the thought aside. "No more apologies necessary. You rescued me from boredom."

She held his gaze for an extra few seconds. "You don't seem the type of man to allow boredom."

He felt a flicker of sensual awareness snap between them. "I don't," he said. "I wasn't planning on staying long tonight anyway."

"Lucky guy," she said in a low, conspiratorial voice. "I'm a member of the group who sponsored the event, so I can't duck out until at least half-time. The only thing that makes it bearable is I really believe in the cause we're supporting this year. Support for Abused Children. A close second to that cause in my opinion is the mentoring program for inner-city youth."

"Are you a mentor?" he asked, surprised that a classy bombshell like her would spend her spare time with needy youth.

"Of course," she said, then shot him a look of sexy challenge. "Aren't you?"

"I could be," he said. "Maybe you could tell me more about the program sometime over drinks or dinner." He pulled a card from his pocket and pressed it into her hand.

Biting her lip, she searched his face. "I can have the program director give you a call. She's more knowledgeable about specific needs than I am."

"Are your turning down my invitation for dinner?" he asked.

She cleared her throat, but didn't fidget. "I was taught that a woman never makes the first call. Especially if she's spilled a margarita on the man. I should go. It's been a pleasure."

He watched her walk away, appreciating the curve of her backside. So, she didn't want to make the first move. He had no problem stepping up. Even though she'd neglected to give him her phone number, he could have it within minutes. He'd make a request now, he thought, reaching for his BlackBerry. Calista French stimulated his curiosity. When it came to women, Leo always got what he wanted. Unfortunately, once they discovered the extent of his wealth, women tended to fall over themselves to please him. At that point, he quickly became bored, but Calista intrigued him. Aside from her obvious assets, he'd liked the sound of her laughter and the sparkle in her eye. He'd been working nonstop lately. He could use a distraction, and she didn't seem the type to be overly impressed by his money. She oozed good breeding—something he certainly lacked. In the back of his mind, Leo was always looking for the perfect woman to make him *clean*.

Calista's heart pounded as she walked away from one of the wealthiest men in the world. Drawing in a calming breath, she accepted the bottle of water the waiter offered on her way to the opposite end of the grand ballroom. She rarely drank alcohol because she always had to be on guard. Since her father had died, there'd always been too much at stake.

Time would tell her if her fishing expedition with Leonardo Grant was successful. He was the kind of man who liked a challenge, and she had spent the last two months planning how to become *his* challenge. He was better looking in person than in the rare photographs she'd seen in the newspaper. Tall with dark hair and black eyes, he had a dangerous air that seemed to whisper beneath the surface.

She knew he was a huge benefactor of charitable causes. Probably paying his own version of penance for what his father had done, she thought bitterly. Not many people knew Leo Grant was the son of the late, unlamented Clyde Hawkins. Leo might have had enough money to pay for most of his past to go away, but she had a photograph of Clyde Hawkins and the boy who'd ruined her father. The boy in the photo was Leo Grant and he didn't know it, but he was going to help her.

On Sunday afternoon, Calista pulled her eight-year-old, but well-maintained, BMW in front of her cousin Sharon's home in the suburbs just as she did every week. Two hours from Philadelphia, the home had mostly insulated her twin sisters from the scandal that had wreaked havoc on their lives years ago.

Calista smiled at the beautifully-tended shrubs and flowers. Even with a son of their own, Sharon and her husband, Walter, had tended her sisters in the same loving way they approached everything. She walked up the steps to the small cottage and knocked on the door. "Hello? Anyone home?"

She heard a screech followed by pounding feet. The door flew open and her sister Tina and Sharon's son, Justin, elbowed each other. "Beat ya," Tina said and gave Calista a hug.

"Uh-uh," Justin said. "I got here first."

Despite the fact that Tina was seventeen and Justin was nearly fifteen, the two engaged in friendly competition at every opportunity.

Her other sister Tami appeared behind them with more predictable teenage cool. "As if it matters who gets there first," Tami said, yawning as she nudged past them. "Cal, can you take me for a mani-pedi? My nails are a mess."

"I wanted to ride go-karts," Tina said.

"Second that one," Justin said. "I'd win again."

Tami rolled her eyes. "Tina always gets her way. I'll watch."

"Maybe we could do both," Calista said. "Go-karts first, then a mani or pedi."

"I can't sit still long enough for a manicure, but I'll take the pedicure," Tina said.

"And you can just let me off at the ice-cream parlor," Justin said. "It's on the way."

Sharon appeared in the doorway and smiled. "Cal, sweetie, I didn't know you were here."

Calista reached forward to embrace her cousin. "I barely had time to knock with these two," she said.

Sharon ruffled her son's hair. "I shouldn't be surprised. What's the sister outing for today?" she asked.

"Looks like go-karts and a manicure," Calista said.

"What a combination," Sharon said. "Can I chat with you before you go?"

"Sure," Calista said, stepping inside the house. "And Justin can join us."

"For a manicure?" Sharon said.

"Go-karts and ice cream," Justin said.

"Hmm. We'll see," Sharon said and led Calista to the back porch. "Would you like something to drink?"

Calista shook her head. "I'm fine. What's up?"

"It's Tami," Sharon said quietly. "I caught her smoking again and I don't like the crowd she's hanging around. She got in well past her curfew last night and I think I smelled alcohol on her breath."

Calista's stomach clenched. It had been her most fervent goal for her sisters to grow up in a safe, nurturing environment until it was time for them to go to college. Since Sharon was a stay-at-home mom, and her husband, Walter, made a modest income, Calista provided all the necessary financial support for her sisters since she'd finished college three years ago.

Now, with both her sisters graduating from high school, Calista was determined that they would attend the college of their choice, regardless of the expense. There was also the added complication of Tami's asthma. Even with insurance, the cost of her medications and treatments had prevented Calista from being able to save extra money for her sisters' future.

"I'll talk to her," Calista said. "I know stepping up to parent my sisters hasn't been easy."

"Walter and I love them. We just wish we could better afford them," Sharon said wryly. "But I knew when I married a carpenter I wasn't destined for a life of luxury."

"I think you got a good deal. You got a life of love. That's more than many of us will ever see," Calista said, knowing a life of love wasn't likely in her own future. She couldn't imagine trusting anyone enough to let down her guard. Look what had happened to her mother, Calista and her sisters when they'd counted on her father.

"Speaking of love life, I can't believe no men have been asking you out," Sharon said.

"I may have met someone special recently," she said, laying the groundwork for the rest of her plan. "Time will tell."

"Oh, surely you can cough up more than that," Sharon said. "Is he kind? Funny? Gorgeous?"

She smiled at her cousin's priorities. Wealth hadn't even made the list. "It's too soon. I don't want to jinx it."

Hours later, after go-karts, a pedicure for Tami and Tina and ice cream for all, Calista snagged her sister Tami before she disappeared into the house. "Hey, what's the rush?" she asked, grabbing her sister's hand. "Sit here on the porch with me before I have to go."

"Graham is supposed to call," Tami said, speaking of her latest boyfriend.

"You can talk to him after I leave," Calista said.

"If Sharon lets me," Tami muttered, tossing her multicolored bangs from her eyes. "Honestly, I'm going to be eighteen in August, but the way she treats me, I may as well be in preschool."

"Slight exaggeration," Calista said in a dry tone she couldn't conceal.

Tami slid a rebellious sideways glance at her.

"August will be here before you know it and you'll be off to college."

"Freedom at last," Tami said.

"I hate to remind you, but college means more studying than ever," Calista said, then waved her hand to dismiss the subject. "How are things going for you lately?" she asked.

Tami regarded her suspiciously. "Sharon told you, didn't she?"

"Told me what?"

Tami sighed and glanced away. "She caught me smoking. I begged her not to say anything to you."

"Why?" Calista asked, her heart twisting. "I thought you and I were closer than that."

"We are," Tami said, fiddling with her hair. "I just didn't want you to be mad at me."

"I'm not mad. I'm worried. You know you have asthma, so you shouldn't stress your lungs by smoking. I just want you to be safe and happy." Calista gathered her sister into her arms. "That's all I've ever wanted for you."

"It was just once," Tami said and closed her eyes. "I've been thinking about Mom lately. I wish she hadn't died."

"I do too," Calista said, pulling back slightly and looking into her sister's eyes. "But we've got each other. Don't you forget that. If you need anything, anytime, give me a call. Just promise me you'll be safe."

"Promise," she said. "Prom is two weeks away. Are you still going to take us shopping for dresses next Saturday?"

"Wouldn't miss it," Calista said.

During the drive back to Philadelphia, she worried about her sister. Tami and Tina possessed diametrically opposed personalities. Tina was easygoing in her personal life, but competitive and intense with sports and grades. She would be eligible for scholarships and aid, but more money would be needed. Tami was intense about her personal relationships and had to be pushed to focus on academics. Fortunately, both her sisters were naturally intelligent and had been accepted at the colleges of their choice. Now, all Calista had to do was come up with hundreds of thousands of dollars to make it happen for them.

Leo glanced at the background information on Calista French for the third time. She hadn't lied. She was a card-carrying member of the exclusive women's society who'd sponsored the charity benefit, had graduated with honors from a top Ivy League university, was currently employed as an analyst for an insurance company and was active in local charities. Her mother and father were dead; her two sisters lived a couple hours away.

Her background was unblemished with the exception of her father's financial failure and subsequent death. Apparently her father was a terrible money manager;

however, Leo vaguely remembered that Clyde had pulled something over on a man with the last name French.

Another skeleton, he thought, gritting his teeth. He glanced at the photograph of Calista and remembered her smile and breathless laughter. Damn it, she made him curious. It might not be wise to pursue a woman whose life had been negatively affected by his pseudoguardian, but Leo was more tired than ever of being bound by his past. He picked up the phone and dialed her cell number.

"Hello?" she asked and her voice felt as if it seeped inside him like honey.

"Hi. Leo Grant. You said you couldn't make the first call," he said. "So I'm making it."

He heard the soft intake of her breath. "What a surprise. How did you get my number?"

"I have ways. Do you mind?"

She paused, a half beat that put him on edge. "No, I don't."

He grinned at the odd thrill that raced through him. "Good. Dinner tonight at Antoine's at seven. I'll have my driver pick you up wherever you say."

"I'm sorry. I can't tonight."

Unaccustomed to being refused, he felt a twist of irritation. "Tomorrow night?"

"I would like that," she said. "But there's no need for you to send a car. I can drive myself."

Calista hung up the phone and mentally checked step two off her list. The following afternoon, a last-minute meeting at work nearly made her late, but she rushed to pull herself together. Thank goodness for all the charm school classes her mother had required her to take. At the time, they'd seemed dreadfully old-fashioned, but now she was thankful to know how to present a calm face even when she didn't feel that way.

She strode into Antoine's and asked the maître d' to direct her to Leo's table. The man nodded. "Your dinner partner is at the bar," he said.

Glancing up to find Leo staring at her, she felt a dip in her stomach. No doubt about it, the man was as gorgeous as sin, but it was the intense way he looked at her that affected her. There was a hard-won strength about him that appealed to her despite the fact that she hated his father for what he'd done to her family. She smiled as he walked toward her. "Hello again," she said.

"Are you hungry?" he asked as the maître d' led them to a table in the corner next to the window.

"I will be as soon as I catch my breath," she said.

"Busy day?" he asked.

She nodded. "And always a minicrisis at the end of the day. How about you?"

"I just negotiated a new deal with a company in China. That will keep us busy for a while. Would you like something to drink? Don't I owe you a margarita?" he suggested with just a hint of sensual mischief in his eyes.

She laughed. "Thank you. I'll stick with one glass of wine tonight. What kind of business are you in?" she asked, even though she already knew quite a bit about Leo. She'd made it her mission to know as much about him as possible—even the kind of women he favored. She'd been pleased to learn he tended toward well-bred, well-educated blondes. Nice that she didn't have to dye her hair, she thought.

"Shipping and transportation," he said.

"And international since you just mentioned China," she said.

He nodded. "It's a must with the global economy. What about you?"

"I'm an analyst for Collier Associates. It's not my first love, but I have a great boss."

"What's your first love?" he asked and she noticed his voice had a caressing quality to it. She could almost feel it on her skin.

"I love astronomy, but now that I've worked for a couple years, I've decided it's better to enjoy that as a hobby," she said.

"So you like to study the stars," he said. "Interesting. How long have you had your head in the upper atmosphere?"

She smiled at his teasing tone. "Close to forever. I asked for a telescope when I was a very young child. A lot of kids get them, then they're abandoned in the attic. You strike me as the kind of man with both feet on the ground. Do you remember what you did with your telescope?"

"I didn't ever have a telescope," he said, with a chuckle that didn't meet his eyes. "I didn't have a childhood."

She blinked at his statement. "What? Everyone has a childhood. Unless you were hatched or are an alien."

He shook his head. "As far as I'm concerned, life for me began at sixteen. But enough about my boring past. I'd like to know more about you."

He was more charming than she'd planned, but she supposed she should have expected that. After all, he'd essentially been a grifter, a con artist. Wasn't that the job requirement for con artists?

Just after the server delivered their drinks, a man approached the table. He looked vaguely familiar to Calista, but she couldn't name him. She wondered if he was one of Leo's acquaintances, except he kept looking at her.

"Calista French. All grown up. I remember you as a young teen," the man said.

Calista searched the man's face but still couldn't recall him. "I'm sorry. I'm drawing a blank."

The man laughed but his eyes were cold. "William Barrett. I was one of your father's business partners."

Calista felt her blood drain to her feet. William Barrett had sued her father's estate and then gone after her mother after her father had died. She mustered a blank expression. "You're correct. I was very young. I hope you're enjoying your dinner. It's a lovely restaurant, isn't it?"

"Yes, it is. How is your mother these days?" he asked.

She couldn't quite keep from digging her fingernails into her palms, but at least her hands were in her lap out of sight. "My mother passed away several years ago."

Barrett raised his eyebrows. "Oh, I'm sorry. Of course, I knew about your father, but—"

The maître d' approached Barrett. "Sir, I've been asked by the manager to inform you that your party will receive a complimentary appetizer. We just need to know your preference. Your server has a menu at your table."

Barrett gave a loud bark of a laugh. "Must be my lucky day. Hope to see you again, Calista."

Calista said nothing and reached for her glass of wine, barely resisting the urge to hiss at the man.

"You don't like him, do you?" Leo asked.

"Was I so obvious?"

"You turned pale," he said.

"He treated my family poorly during a difficult time," she said.

"Then I'll tell his server to pour red wine on him," he said.

His suggestion lightened her mood. "Oh, they wouldn't do that on purpose," she said, feeling a slight pinch at the memory of the margarita she'd poured on Leo.

He lifted an eyebrow. "My personal assistant usually runs interference when I'm eating in a public place, but I allowed this man to approach because he might have been a friend of yours. Next time we're in public, I'll stick to my routine."

Although Calista had been raised in a relatively wealthy home, she'd never heard of her father employing an assistant for such a task. She glanced around. "Is your assistant here tonight?"

He nodded behind her and waved his hand. A brawny middle-aged man approached them. "George, this is Miss French. We'd prefer no interruptions for the remainder of the meal."

"Miss French," George said in a gruff voice with a nod.

"George, it's nice to meet you," Calista said, extending her hand.

Looking slightly uncomfortable, he shook her hand. "Pleasure to meet you also, Miss," he said then turned to Leo. "Enjoy your dinner, sir."

George turned around with his hands folded behind his back, creating a barrier between their table and the rest of the room.

Calista let out a sigh of relief. Barrett wouldn't be approaching her again that evening. "Must ask. What does he say to people who try to approach the table?"

"Mr. Grant and his guest would like to enjoy their meal

without interruption. Thank you for your consideration," he recited.

"Has it ever not worked?" she asked. "What happens if they ignore him?"

"That's only happened three times. George says, *I insist*."

"And if that doesn't work?"

He hesitated, then smiled. "You want to know about the one time that a man wouldn't take no for an answer? George is a former boxer, but he was homeless when I met him. He's my trainer and sparring partner."

Surprised, she stared at him for a moment. "Is he your bodyguard?"

Leo laughed. "Hell, no. He's the best friend I've ever had. I just had to find a way to get him off the streets and the only way I could do it was to employ him. Shocked?"

"Yes." She paused a second. "In a good way."

He lifted his glass and clinked it against hers. "To no more interruptions."

A couple hours later, Leo escorted her downstairs and outside. He was tall and moved with athletic grace. He oozed confidence, strength and mystery even though she knew his secret. Sliding his fingers through hers, he looked down at her. "Come to my house for an after-dinner drink," he said, his eyes full of invitation.

Her stomach dipped, taking her by surprise. "I can't. I have my car," she said.

"One of my drivers can pick it up for you," he countered.

She was stunned at the heat that rushed through her. "I have to go to work tomorrow," she said and suddenly remembered she was supposed to be seducing him. "Rain check?"

He leaned toward her and pressed his mouth against hers. Her breath left her body.

"Yeah," he said. "I'll walk you to your car."

She vacillated, not wanting him to see her older vehicle. "Um."

"I insist," he said and slid his hand behind her back.

They passed a homeless man on the sidewalk with a can for donations. She watched in amazement as Leo stuffed a twenty dollar bill inside. "Take care," he murmured to the man.

"Thank you," the homeless man said. "Go in peace."

Leo glanced at her and must have read the surprise on her face. "In different circumstances, that could be me," he said.

Something in his tone jerked at her heart. He spoke as if he had insider experience. She slid another assessing glance at him. Who was this man? He was different than she'd expected.

They arrived at her car in the parking garage and a black Town Car pulled alongside them. "Don't worry. It's just George. He's also one of my drivers," he said. "Are you sure I can't persuade you to extend the evening?"

"You probably could," she said, surprised at the breathlessness in her voice. She had a plan here, a strategy. She shouldn't be this attracted to him. "But I'm hoping to appeal to your better nature and that you'll encourage me to get the rest I need for my busy workday tomorrow."

Leo gave a rough chuckle. "My better nature? I'm not sure that exists." He lowered his head and pressed his mouth against hers. His mouth was both firm and soft, exploring and seducing. "Come to my lake house this weekend," he muttered against her lips. "It will be your reward for being a good analyst."

Calista sighed. "I can't. I have a previous commitment on Saturday."

"Break it," he said.

"I really can't," she said. "I promised to take my younger sisters shopping for prom dresses on Saturday." She shot him a teasing smile. "Wanna join us? Your opportunity to get up close and personal with teen girl drama."

"Sounds tempting, but I'll pass," he said dryly. "Will you be done by Saturday evening?"

"Yes. Why?" she asked.

"Then we can leave for the lake on Saturday evening. We'll take my helicopter. Say yes," he said.

She looked into his deep brown eyes and felt a shudder of intuitive warning reverberate inside her. "Yes," she said and wondered if she was making a huge mistake.

"Good." He glanced down at her car and frowned. "You won't be driving this car home tonight."

"Why not?" she asked then noticed her tires had been slashed. Her stomach dipped. "Oh, no! Are all of them—"

Checking the tires on the other side of the car, he nodded. "All four." He glanced at the car next to hers. "Look," he said. "All the tires of the cars in this row have been slashed. Damn vandals," he muttered and waved for George to approach.

Calista mentally added up the cost of replacing the tires and stifled a groan. She had neither the time nor the money to spare for this.

"Yes, sir," George said to Leo.

"We're going to need to get Miss French's car towed to the garage so her tires can be replaced. Just use our garage."

"No, that's not necessary," she said.

"I insist," Leo said. "You can stay at my condo. It's just a few blocks from here."

Panic surged through her. "Oh, that's crazy. There's no reason I can't sleep at my own place tonight."

"Your vehicle won't be ready until the morning," he said, then shot her a half smile. "Don't worry. You won't be all alone with me. I have staff."

Two

Moments later, Leo dropped his Town Car with the valet, and they took an elevator to the penthouse of an exclusive condominium building. A woman greeted them at the door. "Good evening, Mr. Grant. Can I get something for you?"

"Would you like another glass of wine?" Leo asked as they entered. "Margarita?"

She shot him a sideways glance. "Just water please."

"Water for both of us, Brenda. Thank you," Leo said.

"This is very nice," she said, looking around at the posh furnishings.

"It works when I'm spending a lot of time in the city," he said with a shrug. "I have another place just outside of town where I rarely stay. This is convenient."

Brenda returned with chilled water. Calista gulped hers down.

"Are you upset about your tires?" he asked, studying her face.

"It's a little disturbing even though it wasn't personal," she said and realized a big part of the reason she wasn't more upset was because Leo had been there with her. She would have to be very careful around him. It would be all too easy to enjoy having a strong, decisive man on whom she could count and let her strategy slide from being her top priority. "I'm just thinking I need to get up early in the morning so I can go back to my apartment before work. I think I'm ready to turn in. Where is the guest room?"

"You have a choice of two beds. The guest bed, or mine," he said with an undertone of seduction.

She felt a quick rush of forbidden temptation but pushed the sensation aside. "I'm not sure I'd get much sleep in your bed," she admitted in a whisper. "And sleep is what I need."

He slid his finger over her jaw. "If you say so," he said, then lowered his head and kissed her.

The light scent of Calista's perfume lingered for a few seconds after she walked down the hallway to the guestroom. He inhaled deeply, wanting to catch the last bit of her. The taste of her was still on his lips, but he wanted more. He couldn't remember wanting a woman this much, this quickly. He wanted her in his bed tonight.

Calista was the flesh and blood equivalent of his dream woman. Classy, well-educated, polished, yet warm, she could make him clean. With her by his side, he could travel with ease in any social circle. She would also be an asset to his business.

Yes, she would suit his needs nicely, in bed and out. After he seduced her, and he would, maybe he could con himself into believing she could make him clean on the inside, too.

* * *

The helicopter hovered over eastern Pennsylvania, landing on a helipad next to the lake, and what looked like a compound. A man approached the helicopter and took the luggage. Leo jumped out and helped Calista onto the ground, moving swiftly toward a vehicle waiting on the drive.

Moments later, they pulled into the back driveway of a three-story luxury mansion that sat directly on the lake. "Good for a little break, don't you think?" he asked as he led her into the huge house.

"Or longer," she said, taking in the polished wood floors and beautiful furnishings. More evidence that the con man had done very well for himself. He guided her to the room facing the lake and she stared out at the beautiful blue water and could have almost happily died from the serene view of the sunset.

"This is so beautiful. How do you tear yourself away?" she asked. "The view is just—" She broke off without adequate words to describe it.

"I get restless if I'm in one place too long," he said. "Plus, business can be very demanding."

"Hmm," she said and met his gaze. "If you say so."

He chuckled. "I bet you don't stay still for long either," he said.

She didn't, for other reasons, though. "Maybe, but this could tempt me."

"Good," he said, gazing at her through hooded eyes. "Dinner will be waiting for us on the terrace. Steak and lobster." A woman approached them. "Denise will show you to your room while I make some calls."

Denise led her to a beautiful room furnished with a queen-size bed, furniture upholstered in a soft pastel palette and Monet prints. The result was so soothing Calista could have happily closed the door and lived there the rest of her existence if she didn't have other responsibilities. She sank into a chair next to the window. Drinking in the peaceful reflection the moon cast on the lake, she felt her tension fade away. For a few sweet seconds, she felt safe.

A knock sounded on her door and the feeling disappeared. She must not forget that she was here for a reason. Calista stood and answered the door. "Yes?" she said to Denise.

"Mr. Grant invites you to join him for dinner," the woman said.

"Thank you," Calista said and grabbed her sweater. Peace was an illusion. She needed to continue with her strategy. "I'm ready now."

Denise led her to a porch that featured an outdoor heater. It was a clear night and she felt surrounded by the stars. "It's beautiful," she murmured.

"Yes it is," Denise said. "Mr. Grant will be here momentarily."

Sitting down next to the heater, she listened to the lap of the water against the shore. It didn't get any better than this.

Leo appeared and she met his gaze. "This is heaven. I don't care what your work demands are. I still can't comprehend how you can leave this place."

"You like it?" he said with an approving smile.

"What's not to like? Beautiful scenery, comfortable living conditions." She sighed.

"I'm glad you like it," he said.

"And have you noticed the stars?" she asked, looking up at the sky.

"No, but I would expect you to," he said. "See anything interesting up there?"

"It's more than interesting," she whispered.

"I may have to get a telescope so you can show me how interesting it is," he said.

A staff member appeared with a tray of food and served both of them. "It looks delicious," she said.

"No more than you," he said.

She bit her lip and looked down at her food. "What made you decide to build a lake home here if you fight staying here?"

"Something about it was irresistible," he said. "I missed the water. I miss the ocean too," he said. "I'll address the ocean another time."

"How can you miss the water? Haven't you spent your whole life in Philly?"

He paused. "No. I have vague memories of visiting the sea. I can't explain it. I just do."

She frowned, taking a bite of lobster. "But you said you had no childhood."

"Exactly," he said in a crisp voice. "Like I said, I can't explain it. It's like it's from another life. One of the few irrational things about me." He took a bite of steak.

She sensed he didn't want to discuss it further. Despite her desire to ask more, she delayed giving in to her curiosity. She had another job to do. "Thank you for inviting me. After the prom drama of the day, this is a huge relief."

He smiled. "How did that go?"

"Mostly good," she said. "My sisters are total opposites. Tami can be a trial, but she was good today."

"How often do you see them?" he asked.

"Almost every week," she said. "The love of my life."

He slid his hand across the table and covered hers. "Is that why you're not married?" he asked.

"It's more complicated than that. I guess I haven't found the right man yet," she said.

"Describe the right man," he said. "Similar backgrounds? Shared passage on the Mayflower? Same schools?"

"No," she said, laughing at the Mayflower comment. "Good head, good heart and crazy for me."

"That list doesn't sound that difficult," he said.

"You'd be surprised," she said. "What about you? Describe your right woman."

"Someone classier than I am to conceal my rough edges," he said. "Beauty doesn't hurt. Complete honesty. I'm not sure marriage is necessary, though."

"Many men don't," she said in a dry tone, her stomach tightening at his reference to honesty. How could he expect that of someone when he'd been the consummate liar?

"You disagree?"

"I believe in family. Marriage is part of family."

He shrugged. "I don't know much about family."

She gave a shrug in return. "Maybe you should learn."

He paused as he lifted his beer. "Is that a challenge?"

"I'll let you decide that," she said with a light laugh.

After dinner, they took a walk along the long dock that led out to the lake. His cell phone beeped and he glanced at the caller ID. "Excuse me, I need to take this. Won't be a minute. I've had a few blips with the China deal." He put the phone to his ear. "Leo Grant," he said and listened.

Calista walked further down the dock, torn between her next step with Leo and the sound of his voice.

"So our shipping agent in Hong Kong tried to charge more after we'd already loaded the merchandise for transport? Fine. Pay the surcharge this once, then call our second choice. After delivery is confirmed, cut the first guy loose and tell him we will be reporting his behavior to everyone in the shipping and merchandising business."

The ruthless tone in his voice made her throat tighten.

"That's my final word," he said. He turned off his cell and looked toward her. "That's done. We shouldn't have any more interruptions this evening," he said and moved beside her, sliding his arm behind her back.

"Why do I get the feeling that a guillotine has just fallen on some very foolish guy in Hong Kong?" she asked.

Leo shrugged. "He should have stuck to the deal. If someone tries to cheat me, they're history."

She felt a chill and a sliver of bitterness at his hypocrisy. How many times had his own father cheated people? How many times had Leo been a part of his father's schemes?

"Have I frightened you?" he asked. "There's no need as long as you're honest with me," he said, drawing her against him as he leaned against the small building at the far end of the pier. "Now let me make you forget about that unpleasant phone call."

His warmth surrounded her as he slid his hands down her back to her bottom and slid one of his hard thighs between her legs. A stab of sensual shock raced through her. "Leo," she began.

He dipped his head to her throat, rubbing his lips over her skin. "I bet every inch of you tastes delicious," he muttered, sliding his tongue over a sensitive spot. "I knew you would from the first minute I met you. Give me your mouth," he said and coaxed her lips into meeting his. Skimming one of his hands upward, he touched the side of her breast.

He emanated pure masculine strength and sexuality

and gave her the unmistakable message that he wanted to possess her. The primitive drive seemed to throb just beneath his clothes. Despite every reason she had to detest him, she was drawn to him like no other man. Here, she sensed, was a man with a will to match her own. Without conscious thought, she responded to him, sliding her arms up behind his neck, arching against him.

He took her mouth and she took his, drawing his tongue into the recesses. Heat scored her from the inside out, and her body called to his. His touch was tender, edged with roughness that only turned her on more.

He gave a low, carnal growl. "Let's go back to the house. I want you in my bed."

His words threw her into a maelstrom of confusion. She drew back from him catching her breath, trying to catch her sanity. She wanted to be with him intimately. She wanted him. But she had a plan. This relationship wasn't for her pleasure. It was for something far more important.

She inhaled another deep breath, reaching down deep for her conviction. "I want—" She broke off when she looked into his dark needy gaze and her mouth went dry. She couldn't look into his eyes at this close range. His gaze reflected the ache she felt inside her. She bit her lip and closed her eyes. "I'm afraid you're not going to understand this."

"Understand what?" he asked.

She forced her eyes open, but turned her gaze to his right shoulder. His strong, broad shoulder. "I want to go to bed with you."

"Good, let's—"

"But I can't," she quickly added.

Silence, so clear she could hear the water lapping against the dock, followed.

"Why?" he asked.

Summoning her courage, she met his gaze. "It's going to sound terribly old-fashioned, but I want to keep that for the man I marry. I don't think I'm cut out to be intimate with a lot of men. I don't want to make the mistake of giving my heart, myself, to a man and then being crushed because he isn't the right one."

He shot her a considering look then wiped his hand over his face. "You're telling me that you're saving yourself for marriage? That's the oldest trick in the book."

"I told you that you wouldn't understand. I'll leave in the morning," she said and turned away from him to walk back to the house. She crossed her arms over her chest, feeling the impending crush of defeat. Holding off on sex had been a calculated risk, but Calista had suspected that it would be difficult to motivate Leo to marry her quickly unless she waited.

Three seconds later, she felt her hand caught by his. "Not so fast," he said.

She stopped in surprise, searching his face.

"The least you can do is give me a chance to change your mind. Or see if you can change mine," he said.

Her heart racing a mile a minute, she shook her head. "I don't want to deceive you. I heard you talking earlier. You hate to be tricked. Again, it's best if I leave in the morning."

He lifted her hand to his mouth. "I'm not disappointed, or feeling tricked. I'm just surprised. Your outlook is unusual."

"I know, but I've watched so many of my friends make poor choices and wish they could take everything back. It's about more than the physical intimacy. I just think I'm one of those women who jumps all the way into the pool of commitment. I totally understand if you're not looking for that. Most men aren't." She added that last statement to spur his competitive nature. Leo wouldn't want to be compared to another man.

"I'm not most men," he said. "I'll show you to your guest room and we'll see how it goes."

She opened her mouth to tell him she had judged him correctly, but he covered her mouth with his finger. "I insist," he said in the sexiest voice she'd ever heard.

After Leo led Calista to the guest bedroom, he prowled his balcony, still aroused from the way she'd tasted, smelled and felt in his arms. He couldn't remember a time when a woman had turned him away from her bed. Although she'd done it without malice, it didn't diminish his sexual frustration. In fact, her desire not to manipulate him aroused him even more.

Many women had tried to trick him into marriage. A few had even feigned signs of pregnancy, but Leo had been very careful. He had no interest in binding himself to just any woman. At least, he hadn't until now. But he saw the advantage of linking himself with Calista. She was pure. She represented a fresh start.

Glancing out at the still lake, he considered taking a dip in the frigid water to quiet the heat Calista had generated in him and the longings he'd buried long ago. Did he really want a family? Was such a thing possible for him? His upbringing had been one move after another. He'd never known when his guardian father would take out his rage on him. He'd spent so many years braced for something horrible to happen to him. And it had, several times until he'd run away.

Leo wondered what it would be like to be loved by a

woman like Calista. He sensed she was the kind of woman who would marry forever. Look at her commitment to her sisters. She possessed a strength that drew him like a light in the darkness.

Was he considering marrying her? The notion shocked him. He barely knew her. Yet, he knew she was different. She'd known what it was like to be raised in a loving family—with relationships and ties she still worked to keep strong. She possessed the core of something he'd been searching for, for years.

He raked his hand through his hair. It wasn't just sex. He suspected he could seduce her into his bed despite her lofty goal. The sexual animal in him roared at the urge to take her, to make her his. He could and he suspected they would bring each other amazing pleasure.

For some strange, insane reason, however, he hesitated seducing her for the pure purpose of his gratification. It wasn't out of consideration for her principles. No. Her reticence called to his competitive nature. He wanted her to be convinced that he was the man she wanted. The man she couldn't turn down. He wanted her to come to him.

The next morning after breakfast, Leo took Calista out on his boat.

"The water is beautiful," she told him when they stopped near another pier.

"Want to swim?" he asked.

"I don't know," she said, giving the lake a skeptical glance. "How cold is it?"

"Depends on whether you're cold-blooded or warm-blooded," he said and stripped off his shirt. "Let's go in."

He felt her gaze linger on his chest then she seemed to

force her gaze away from him. "If you're sure," she said. "If I freeze, you have to promise to pull me out. Okay?"

"Promise," he said and watched her remove her shirt to reveal a bikini top that encased her full, creamy breasts. He could easily imagine them bare and wondered about the color and size of her nipples.

She kicked off her shoes to reveal slender feet with vixen-red toenails. He liked that touch of wildness she kept hidden from the rest of the world. He'd like to take care of all her wild urges. She pushed down her jeans, wiggling as she stepped out of them.

He fixated on the inviting curves of her waist and hips, feeling himself respond to the sight of her feminine figure. He took action to cool his arousal immediately. Diving into the water, he felt the cold wetness sink into his skin. Rising to the surface, he caught sight of her looking down at him from the boat.

"How cold is it?"

"Not cold enough to make icebergs," he said.

"That's not very encouraging," she said.

"Are you afraid?" he asked.

She immediately pursed her lips and lifted her chin. "Absolutely not," she said and jumped off the side of the boat. Seconds later, she bobbed to the ladder, gasping. "Omigod, you lied. This water is frigid."

"Well, it's not as warm as my pool at the house," he said, swimming toward her. "But it could be worse."

"When?" she asked. "In January?"

He laughed.

A wake from a boat riding past caused a wave and she reached for him with fear in her eyes. Concern rushed through him. "You're okay," he said, pulling her body against his. "I wouldn't let you drown. Damn, I should have asked if you're a swimmer."

"Of course I am," she said, her wide green eyes meeting his. Another wave rolled toward them and she clung to him more tightly.

"Are you afraid?" he asked, enjoying the sensation of her lithe body against his.

"Not really," she said, but her tone wasn't at all convincing.

"Nice try. You can tell me the truth now," he said, lifting her chin to meet his gaze again.

She shook her head and sighed. "It's silly."

"I bet not," he said.

"One time when I was a teenager, a friend invited me to the lake. Her father took us out in his boat. I didn't know it, but he'd had too much to drink. It was a windy, choppy day. I fell overboard and hit my head against the side of the boat."

Leo swore. "Why didn't you tell me? I wouldn't have forced you into the water."

"You didn't force me. Besides, I don't like it that I still get that knot in my stomach when I think about lakes and boats. Being a wuss is such a bore."

He admired her for trying to rise above her fear. "You could never be a bore."

"Just trying to be a brave little toaster," she said with a smile.

Her vulnerability grabbed at him, making him feel incredibly protective. "We can go back."

"No," she protested. "It's so beautiful here. I just might not be able to stand the water temperature very long. Although you are helping," she said, her eyelashes sweeping downward, shielding her eyes from him.

Despite the chilly water, arousal shot through him again. "Good to know I'm useful in some way," he said, sliding his hands around her back. The sunlight glistened on her light blond hair and the water droplets on her fair skin. He fought a strong urge to lick those droplets.

Instead, he took her mouth in a kiss. Her lips reminded him of the finest brandy, potent and addicting. He drew her tongue into his mouth and she made a delicious sound of arousal. Leo wanted to hear that sound again and again. He felt her shiver, but he wasn't sure if it was from arousal or cold.

"Let's go back to the house," he said and pulled her toward the ladder to the boat. "But you should know that when we ride on the boat the breeze will make you even colder."

"We could fish," she said.

He blinked, surprised at her suggestion. "You know how?"

"Of course," she said. "Do you? If you don't, I can show you."

He laughed at the lightning-fast switch from uncertainty to confidence. "I can fish," he said. "A long time ago, I fished for my supper."

She met his gaze. "Was that before or after you were hatched at the age of sixteen?"

"Both," he said and turned her toward the ladder. "You go first and I'll bring up the rear." She climbed the rungs and he was given an up close view of her gorgeous derriere in her bikini bottom. He groaned, wondering if he would be able to stick to his plan to make her come to him.

* * *

Hours later, Leo watched her lean back in the Jacuzzi and sigh. "What a great day," she said, then cracked open one eyelid. "Too bad the fish I caught was so much bigger than yours."

He chuckled. "Lady's luck," he said. "I couldn't show you up. You're my guest."

She opened both her eyes and scowled. "That's pure bull. The next thing you'll be doing is telling me you're not competitive."

"Only every bone in my body," he said.

She smiled and her gaze dipped to his shoulders in feminine appreciation. She'd done that several times today, so he knew she wasn't immune to him. He was winning her inch by inch. The notion filled him with a rush he hadn't experienced in a long time.

"Like the hot tub?" he asked.

She nodded, closing her eyes again.

"It's even better when you're naked," he said.

She opened her eyes to sexy slits. "And how would you know that?"

"It's in the manufacturer's instructions," he said.

A gusty laugh from her rippled all the way down his body to his groin.

"I dare you to take off your swimsuit," he said.

"I'm not sure that's a good idea," she said with a sigh.

"Even if I promise to keep my hands off of you?" he asked.

"The problem," she said as she moved closer to him and he pulled her onto his lap, "is that I won't want your to keep you hands off of me."

Three

As the helicopter landed on top of the high-rise in Philadelphia, Leo took Calista's hand and helped her onto the ground. Within moments, George was driving them in a limo toward her apartment. She turned to Leo. "This has been an incredible twenty-four hours. Thank you for everything."

"I'm glad you enjoyed yourself," he said and lifted his finger to stroke her cheek. "It doesn't have to end."

His touch distracted her, making her heart beat erratically. "What do you mean?"

"I'd like you to move in with me," he said.

Calista blinked, surprised by his speed and decisiveness. "Wow," she said. "That's fast." She took a breath. "It's very tempting, but as I've told you, I really want to be married before I live with a man."

"Why is that so important to you?" he asked with more than a trace of irritation on his face.

"I told you that I believe in family. A husband, wife and children can provide the ultimate joy, security and comfort for each other. I want that for myself. I want to give it to someone else," she said, her gut twisting because although she believed what she was saying, she knew it wouldn't come true for her.

"Was your upbringing that idyllic?"

She looked away, feeling a stab of shame about her father's financial disaster and death that never seemed to go away. "Of course not," she said. "Maybe because it wasn't idyllic, I'm determined to have something different for myself. It may sound crazy to you, but I want the security of family and a strong man."

He paused a moment, his dark gaze full of conflicting feelings. "It doesn't sound crazy. I just don't have much experience in that area." He covered her hand with his. "I want to spend more time with you."

"I want the same," she said quietly.

"Then come and live with me in my apartment. I'll make sure you won't regret it," he said, lifting her hand to his lips.

Even though they hadn't known each other long, Calista was more than a little tempted. There was a strength about Leo that drew something from deep inside her. His magnetism almost made her forget her purpose with him. Almost. His charm, though, belied any chance for security. He was accustomed to getting what he wanted from women without making a commitment. She wondered if she would possibly be able to seduce him to the point of marriage. Doubt surged through her.

"I'm sorry. I can't. I just can't," she said and fought the

fear that rose in her throat. "I really do understand if you don't want to continue with me. I'm sure you're used to a different kind of arrangement with women." She glanced outside the window. "Maybe we shouldn't have gone out in the first place, but I just couldn't resist you."

The limo stopped in front of her apartment building. She turned to Leo. "Thank you again for a wonderful time."

He helped her out of the limo and walked her to the security entrance. "My pleasure," he said. "Good night, Calista."

Calista tried to read his inscrutable expression and felt a sinking sensation in the pit of her stomach. He'd decided she wasn't worth the wait or the effort. She watched him walk out of her lobby and most likely out of her life. Though her ego stung, she was far more worried about her sisters' futures.

Swearing under her breath, she took the elevator to her small apartment. What was she going to do now? Pacing the length of her den, she tried to summon a plan B. If she went to bed with Leo, she would have no hope of marrying him. Plus, even though she found him physically attractive, she wasn't sure when her real feelings and thoughts about what he'd done to her father would leak past her facade. What if she slipped and told him she felt he was responsible? If he knew the truth…

Calista squeezed her eyes shut, feeling hopeless and trapped. She hated being deceptive, but she'd made this decision and she wasn't going to castigate herself for it. Her sisters deserved a good education and a better start than they'd had. They'd suffered the brunt of her family's implosion because of their youth. She would never be able to erase the shattered expressions on her sisters' faces when first her father had died and then less than two years later, they'd lost Mom, too.

Her head throbbing with tension, Calista tried to calm herself. Maybe she'd misread Leo. Maybe he would call her again.

Two weeks later, after no word from Leo, Calista saw the writing on the wall. Leo wasn't going to call. He was done with her. Bummed, but still obligated to attend the Brother-Sister Charity Auction, she accepted an invitation from Robert Powell, a man who worked in her office building. Amusing and seemingly easygoing, he'd asked her out several times. She hoped Robert could distract her from her disappointment.

Wearing a Betsey Johnson Spring dress she'd bought on sale, she greeted Robert in her lobby. His appreciative look provided a balm to her still smarting ego. At the auction, Calista mingled and introduced Robert to her acquaintances.

He slid his arm around her waist. "Do you realize I've been asking you out for months? You're worth the wait," he said and dipped his gaze suggestively over her.

Not wanting to encourage the flicker of sensual interest she glimpsed in his gaze, she shook her head. "Oh, not really. I'm not worth the wait at all. I'm just the good friend type, you know. Boring, works too much. All that."

He gave a low chuckle. "I don't think so."

"Calista." A voice that had haunted her captured her attention. "How are you?"

She swung around to see Leo Grant, larger than life, staring down at her. She might have needed to pinch herself if not for the gorgeous brunette on his arm. She forced her lips into a smile, thinking he hadn't waited long to replace her. "Fine, thank you."

"And your friend," Leo said, his gaze assessing Robert. "We haven't met."

"Robert Powell, this is Leo Grant," she said, refusing to inquire about *his* escort. The men exchanged handshakes. "Oh, look, they're starting the auction. I'm helping behind the scenes. I'll see you afterward, Robert. Please excuse me," she said and turned away.

Upset, she balled her fists at her side and strode toward the side of the ballroom where the items for auction were displayed. Forcing any thought of Leo from her head, she focused on tagging the items with the winners' names. After about forty-five minutes, the volunteer coordinator sent her for a break and she got a glass of water from the bar.

On her way back, Leo stepped in front of her, his eyes dark with what looked like anger. "You didn't waste any time, did you?" he asked.

"I could say the same for you," she retorted.

"She's the daughter of a friend I owed a favor," he said. "Not that I should have to explain myself."

"How convenient that she's drop-dead gorgeous. It must be a total chore to escort her."

He tilted his head and narrowed his eyes. "I could almost believe you're jealous."

"You would be wrong," she told him and moved to step around him.

He stopped her, his hand closing around her wrist like a handcuff. "Let's take this discussion somewhere private," he said and led her away from the crowd. He opened the door to an empty room, pulled her inside and closed the door behind him.

"Who is this Robert? Is he important to you?" he demanded.

Nervous, yet strangely thrilled to see him, she lifted her chin. "What's it to you? You haven't called me for two weeks."

"I've been out of the country."

She gave an indignant shrug. "I'm sure your cell phone has reception from everywhere in the world and maybe a few planets, too."

"Okay," he said. "I didn't want to call you. I wanted to give myself some time away from you. I didn't want to do anything impulsive."

Her heart hammered in her chest.

"You still haven't answered my question about Robert. Do you have feelings for him?" he asked flatly.

"No," she said. "No more than I would a friend. He's asked me out for months and I've turned him down."

"Then why did you agree to go out with him tonight?"

She paused and looked away with a sigh. "I was moping," she confessed.

"Excuse me?" he said.

She glanced back at him, peeved. "You heard me. I said I was moping. Because you haven't called me," she added reluctantly.

His eyes glittered as he looked at her. "Okay, I've thought about it for the last two weeks and made a decision. We'll get married."

Calista dropped her jaw in shock. "Excuse me?"

"I said we'll get married. I'd prefer just a living arrangement because of the legalities, but we can take care of that with a prenup." He paused, studying her carefully. "Unless you're adverse to a prenup."

Her thoughts still spinning as she tried to take it all in, she shook her head. "No, but—"

"Were you planning on a large formal ceremony? I understand women spend their entire lives mentally planning their dream weddings," he said as if the thought of it seemed insane to him.

"I suppose some do. I'd always thought I would want something small," she said. Calista had left fairy-tale wedding land shortly after her father's death. Her primary focus had been on survival, not having a huge society wedding.

"Good," he said in approval. "Then it's settled. I can have one of my assistants get together with you to make the arrangements. She knows the dates I'm available."

She held up her hand. "Wait just a second. You're moving at warp speed and I'm still trying to catch up. What made you think to get married?"

"I tried to put you out of my mind during the last two weeks. I found I didn't want to," he said.

Given the fact that they hadn't known each other very long, she was surprised at how his words got under her skin. It was a far cry from hearts and flowers. "I don't know what to say."

"Yes," he said.

She bit her lip and couldn't swallow a chuckle. "You didn't ask."

"Will you marry me?" he asked without missing a beat, his dark gaze holding hers.

"This is crazy," she whispered. Her heart lurched. After all her planning, could she really do this?

"Is that your answer?" he asked.

"No," she said, her lungs squeezing so tight she couldn't breathe. It was the best solution for Tina and Tami. His father owed her family for what he had taken from them. It was necessary. "Yes, yes."

Leo sat on the deck of his lakefront home the night before his wedding and shared Scotch with George. Calista and her family would arrive tomorrow morning via his helicopter. All the arrangements had been made. The only thing Leo had to do was show up at the ceremony tomorrow at noon and make sure not to see Calista before then. She had insisted. Silly superstition, but he would play along for her ease. With each passing day, she had seemed to grow more nervous.

George lifted his shot glass in salute. "I never thought I would see the day when you would marry a woman only a month after meeting her. Good luck to ya."

Leo shot George a sideways glance and lifted his glass. "Thank you. You haven't said much about my bride-to-be."

"What's to say?" George asked. "She's beautiful." He shrugged and tossed back the scotch, setting his glass down for a refill. "There's just something about her."

"What?" Leo asked, his antennae on alert. George was an excellent judge of character.

George frowned and squinted his eyes. "I can't put my finger on it. She's not evil," he said. "But there's something going on beneath the surface. The woman's more complicated than she seems."

Leo twirled the thought around in his head. "Most intelligent women are complicated."

"True," George said, nodding his head. "How'd the prenup go?"

"I insisted she have her attorney look at it. He put in a clause about her getting ten million after six months," Leo said. "Mine cut it down to two million. Her attorney didn't like it, but she signed." He shrugged. "She's so family-focused that I'm sure this wasn't her idea. It had to have come from her attorney."

"You're sure she doesn't know your guardian helped bring down her father?" George asked.

"How could she?" Leo asked, the familiar taste of bitterness filling his mouth at the mention of Clyde Hawkins. "It was ten years ago, and I've wiped out my association with him. Besides, that was one scheme I didn't play. I may have been introduced as Clyde's genius, gifted son, but I didn't have to do anything but validate Clyde's super success."

"Why are you marrying her?" George asked bluntly.

Not many would have the nerve to question his decisions, but he trusted George more than he trusted anyone else. "Besides the fact that I want to have sex with her?"

George chuckled. "Yes."

"I want the expanding Japanese and Indian markets, and I'm finding that the leaders of the companies I'm negotiating with aren't comfortable with my single status. I'm competing with other companies for the business. It's time to get a wife. Calista fits the bill. She's well educated and beautiful. She'll be an asset."

"So this is a business decision?" George asked.

"Mostly," Leo said. "The timing is good—no long engagement period."

George clicked his shot glass against his again. "I wish you a happy home then, Leo. After all you've been through, you deserve something good. I hope Calista will be good for you."

* * *

Calista practiced yoga breathing as the helicopter descended to Leo's helipad at the lake. In a matter of hours, she would be married.

"Omigod, this is amazing," Tami said, lifting her cell phone toward the window and taking a picture. "I have to text my boyfriend a photo. Will there be a photographer at the ceremony?"

"Yes," Calista said, taking another deep breath.

"Are you okay?" Tina asked. "You look whiter than usual."

"It's the helicopter," Calista insisted and forced a smile. "Did you enjoy the ride?"

"It was *sweet*," Tina said.

"What about you, Justin?" she asked her nephew.

"Cool," he said, clearly trying to appear unimpressed but not quite succeeding. "I want one of these when I grow up."

Sharon laughed. "Keep your grades up and go to college and you may have a shot at it."

The helicopter landed and several members of Leo's staff stood to greet them. A man helped her sisters, cousin, her cousin's husband and son out of the helicopter. Calista found herself pausing before she accepted the assistance of a man to help her step onto the ground. Every passing second drew her closer to the time when she would become Leo Grant's wife. Her heart raced in fear at the thought, then she looked at her sisters. So young, yet their childhoods had been stolen from them. The least she could do was to give them some security now and a solid start for their adult lives.

"Miss French," the man said, having been schooled in her appearance. She wondered from where Leo or his assistant had pulled her photograph, then pushed the thought aside.

"Thank you very much," she said and smiled.

"My name is Henry. I'm in charge of Mr. Grant's lake home. I have a special suite for you to dress for the ceremony. Mr. Grant has ordered rooms and food for the rest of your family," he said, guiding her down the walk. "I'm told that the second you are sequestered in your suite, I am to call Mr. Grant. He is in a room facing away from the lake."

She smiled. So, he had stuck to the agreement not to see her before the wedding. She had to like him for that. Her stomach dipped again. She would need to exhibit far more than like in their wedding bed tonight. She was terrified her true feelings for Leo would show.

Following Henry toward the suite, she heard her sisters gasp in approval as they walked inside Leo's home. *"Sweet,"* Tami said. "More pics."

"I can't remember being in a house this beautiful," Tina said, looking around.

Calista felt a twist of regret that she hadn't been able to provide more for her young sisters after her parents' deaths.

Her cousin studied her and broke away from her husband to come to Calista's side. "You need someone to help you get ready," Sharon insisted.

"I'll be fine. Just a little repair work on my hair and face, pull up my dress and I'm done," Calista said, the strange sensation of panic and numbness filling her again.

Sharon frowned. "I'll hang around anyway. A bride shouldn't be alone on her wedding day."

Perhaps her cousin was right. Calista was feeling the

unmistakable surge of fight-or-flight syndrome, and at the moment flight seemed most possible.

"This way, ladies," Henry said, guiding them up a curved stairway. "Jamal will take the rest of you to your rooms. Refreshments will be waiting."

"Thank goodness, I'm starving," Justin muttered.

"See you soon, bridie," Tami said with a broad smile.

"See you soon," Calista replied with much less enthusiasm.

Sharon helped Calista get dressed and encouraged her to eat. Calista couldn't swallow a bite. Even though this was the best possible result from her plan, she couldn't believe it was happening so fast.

"You look dazed and pale, sweetheart. Are you okay?" Sharon asked, her face full of worry.

"Just wedding-day jitters," Calista said with a smile.

"Are you sure this is what you want?" Sharon asked. "You haven't known Leo very long at all."

Calista recited her rehearsed response, "When it's right, it's right."

"But still," Sharon said, frowning.

A knock sounded on the door. "Oh, could you please get that?" she asked, thankful for the interruption. The photographer appeared. "Ready for me to take a few shots?"

"Of course," she said, smoothing her dress with her hands. "Sharon, come stand here with me."

Sharon shook her head shyly. "Oh, no. It's your time to shine. You look beautiful."

"But I want my close family members with me," Calista said. "Please get my sisters and bring them here."

Calista posed for several pictures before her sisters and Sharon returned. Then she took several pictures with them. Tami took a few pics with her cell phone. Calista drank in the sight of her happy sisters and reminded herself repeatedly that they were the reason she was doing this. Their lives would be so much better because she was marrying Leo.

One of Leo's staff poked her head in the doorway. "It's time," she said with a smile. "Are you ready?"

"Yes," Tami and Tina chorused, giggling with excitement.

Sharon placed a kiss on Calista's cheek. "I'll see you on the dock. You can still change your mind," she said.

How I wish. Calista smiled instead. "I'm all decided. Thank you for coming today."

"Wouldn't miss it," Sharon said. "Be happy."

Happiness for herself was the last thing on Calista's mind as she and her sisters walked down the staircase. Just before they stepped outside, Tami turned to her and adjusted her veil. "You really do look beautiful. Leo is one lucky dude."

Calista laughed. "You're sweet. Both of you look gorgeous yourselves."

"Do we really get to go for a boat ride after the ceremony?" Tina asked.

"Sure do. We're changing clothes and eating on Leo's yacht," Calista said. "Now let's get this over—" She barely caught herself. "Let's get this wedding on its way."

On either side of her, her sisters escorted her down to the dock. As she rounded the corner, she saw the minister, George and Leo. Her heart felt as if it dipped to her feet at the sight of him. Dressed in a designer black suit with a crisp white shirt and crimson tie, she knew the second he saw her. She felt the weight and heat of his gaze from yards away.

"Ready?" Tami asked. "Why did you stop?"

Calista had been so distracted she hadn't even noticed she wasn't moving forward. Tami glanced in the direction of Calista's gaze and gave a sigh. "He's pretty hot, isn't he?"

"Tami," Tina whispered. "Show some dignity. This is a wedding."

"You were the one ready to go jump on a boat before we'd even gotten to the dock," Tami retorted.

"Girls, you're supposed to be escorting me. Please stop arguing," Calista said, gritting her teeth. She began to walk again.

She felt Leo's gaze take her in from head to toe and wondered if he approved of the full-length A-line ivory chiffon gown with fitted sweetheart bodice that suddenly felt as if it was suffocating her. Her hair was half up, half down in loose curls. Pearl drop earrings dangled from her ears. She felt like a sacrificial bride from the Regency period.

Mentally rolling her eyes at herself, she stiffened her spine. *Cut the martyr act.* She was a woman taking control of her and her sisters' destinies. She only had to last six months. Not a lifetime.

She finally stood opposite the minister and focused her attention on the kindly faced man for a moment while she wondered if she would burn in hell for what she was doing. She felt a stab of guilt and brushed it aside. She couldn't have done this to just anyone. She'd chosen Leo because of what his father had done to her family. In the scheme of things, it was fair. It wasn't as if he would miss the money.

Lord, what thoughts to have while she was getting married. "Who gives this bride?" the minister asked.

"We do," Tami and Tina said and giggled. Tami took Calista's hand and reached for Leo's, then put them together. "Be good to my sister," she whispered to Leo. "Or I'll make your life a living hell. Ask Aunt Sharon. I can do it."

Leo blinked and shot Calista a bemused look. Embarrassed, Calista shook her head and mouthed *teenagers*. Leo's mouth lifted in a half grin and he nodded, both his hands enclosing hers.

Within seconds, she was held captive by his gaze as he began to recite the vows. "I, Leonardo Grant, take you Calista French..."

The rest of the ceremony passed in a daze. She looked down at the diamond and platinum band Leo placed on her finger. Was this real? Was this happening?

"Calista," Leo whispered. "Ring."

Biting her lip, she took the platinum band from Tina and pushed it down his finger. His hands were so much larger than hers, warmer and stronger. In a different lifetime, she wondered if she could have trusted him, relied on him. She remembered what his father had done and dismissed the thought. Deep, underneath it all, Leo was a liar, and she'd just joined with him in the biggest lie of her life.

"I now pronounce you husband and wife. You may kiss your bride."

Leo lowered his head and took her mouth with a kiss of possession and the promise of passion. He'd done his part. Now she would have to do hers.

Less than an hour later, they changed clothes and took Leo's yacht for a ride around the lake. After a late lunch that she didn't consume because she was still too nervous to eat, her sisters and Justin went for a swim. Leo made friendly small talk with all of her family. He promised her sisters that he would take them skiing next time they visited.

All too soon, the sun faded and the air turned chilly. The yacht returned to the dock and Calista kissed her family goodbye before Leo's helicopter took them away. She watched them go, fighting a feeling of abandonment. She felt Leo slide his hand behind her back and around her waist and closed her eyes, girding herself for the night to come.

"Thank you for letting them come," she said. "It meant a lot to me."

"You're welcome," he said, his lips twitching. "As long as Tami doesn't come after me with any sharp objects."

She laughed despite the way her stomach twisted with nerves. "She's a big bluffer. Very dramatic and emotional. She's the one who has asthma. She gives Sharon and me hives with some of the things she does, but she's got a big heart."

"Like her sister," he said and began to lead her back to the house.

"Hmm," she said in a noncommittal voice.

"You haven't eaten anything all day," he said.

She glanced up at him again, taking in his hard jaw and the sheer maleness of his physique. "How do you know?"

"My staff told me you ate nothing before the wedding, and I noticed that you ate nothing on the boat. Except for one bite of the cake."

"It was a big day."

"Yes, so I want you to eat something now. What shall I ask my staff to bring you?"

"I hate to bother them."

"You're not bothering," he said impatiently. "They are paid to do this. They spend a lot of time bored, so they're actually glad to have something to do."

Skeptical, she shot him a sideways glance. "Who told you that? Someone who wanted a raise?"

He chuckled. "If you don't tell me what you want, then I'll order a five-course meal."

"A turkey sandwich," she said quickly.

"Done," he said and squeezed her shoulders. She was still surprised at how kind he'd been to her sisters. She hadn't expected him to be an ogre, just distantly polite. Instead, he'd been charming. With his arm around her, she could almost believe he felt protective of her. Almost.

Four

Leo drank a beer while he watched Calista take a few bites of her turkey sandwich. Her gaze skittered from his and she took tiny sips from her water. It took him a moment to read her, but then realization jolted him. She was *nervous*. He'd noticed her nerves at the wedding, but assumed they would pass after the vow-taking.

She was still on edge, he noticed, and felt a foreign twist of tenderness toward her. Virginal nerves, he concluded. In this day and age, who would have thought it? There was no need to worry, he thought as he took in the sight of her. He could have easily seduced her before now. Some odd sense of ethics he hadn't known he possessed had made him pause.

No need for that anymore, he realized as he watched her lick her lips after she took another drink of water. "The sandwich was a good idea, thanks," she said.

"I frequently have good ideas," he said, holding her gaze.

"I'm sure you do," she said.

"It's been a long day," he said. "We should go up-stairs."

Calista's heart jumped into her throat. She'd known this would happen. Leo was now her husband. He would pay for the security of her sisters' future and she would pay by being his wife, albeit temporarily. Part of her couldn't dismiss the fact that this man was connected to her father's financial failure and subsequent death. In a way it would be making love with the devil.

She took a deep breath. There was no need to be melodramatic now. Leo was just a man, not a god or a devil. Right? Why was she so apprehensive? It wasn't as if she...

Stiffening her spine, she told herself to buck up to her end of the deal. "Can I grab another water?" she asked with a smile.

"I have plenty in my room." He extended his hand and his gaze fell over her like the heat from a midafternoon scorching summer day. She took his hand and he led her upstairs, stopping at his bedroom door to open it. Before she realized it, he swooped her up into his arms and carried her inside.

"Oh," she said. "A surprise."

"It's a tradition. Since you're a new bride, I thought you might enjoy it," he said, his face close to hers.

All too aware of his strength, she spotted a bottle of champagne and a tray of strawberries next to the huge bed that seemed to dominate the wall facing the windows. Lit candles provided a seductive ambiance. She clung to his shoulders. "I didn't know you were much for traditions."

"I'm not," he said. "But I don't have to buck all of them."

He set her down on the bed. "Now we can have a private toast," he said and popped open the champagne. He spilled the light golden liquid into one flute then another.

Giving her one of the glasses, he lifted his own. "To us and all the traditions we'll make and break together." He clicked his glass against hers. "Starting tonight."

Her heart hammered at the expression on his face. He looked as if he could literally consume her. She'd known he was highly sexual from the first time she'd seen him in person, but now she wondered if she would be able to... Pushing the thought from her mind again, she nodded and took a long drink of champagne, then another. She suspected, however, that she would need to consume the entire bottle to bring her anxiousness under control.

Leo sat on the bed and lifted his hand to cup her cheek. "There's no need to be nervous."

"I'm not," she said. "Really."

His lips lifted in a half grin. "You just need something else to think about," he said and lowered his mouth to hers. His lips were sensually rich and expressive. He rubbed his mouth from side to side, slipping his tongue inside when she took a half breath.

"You taste delicious," he murmured against her mouth. "And I plan on tasting every inch of you."

The vibration of his mouth on hers did things to her. She felt warmer, her face felt hot and her skin seemed ultrasensitive, hyperaware of his potent masculinity. He continued to kiss her, his caresses growing more aggressive. A shocking excitement flooded her.

How had that happened, she wondered. She'd been dreading this. *She had*. She felt his hand threading through the back of her hair, tilting her head to give him better access to her mouth. He pulled her against him and she instinctively clung to his strong shoulder, her champagne glass tilting precariously.

Leo pulled it from her hand, took a sip and then swore. Fire flickered in his eyes. "You're amazing…" He inhaled deeply, his nostrils flaring. He lifted the glass to her lips and she took a sip.

Setting the glass on the bedside table, he turned back to her and without a second of preparation, he pulled her shirt over her head. Three seconds later, he slid his arms behind her and unfastened her bra. Her breasts sprang free and he filled his hands with them. The sight and sensation of his tanned skin against her pale breasts was so sensual she had to close her eyes.

There was something primitive and carnal between her and Leo. She'd glimpsed flickers of it before and dismissed it as overworked imagination or hypersensitivity. He pulled off his shirt and his skin, molding to his muscles, glistened in the candlelight.

His strength, inside and out, called to her. She had been forced to be strong so long. What a temptation to be able to lean on someone else. And she suspected he was strong enough. She gave into the lure and slid her hands over his shoulders and biceps. "Good Lord, how did you get such an amazing body? Do you work out all the time?"

His teeth flashed. "No, but I have George to keep me in shape. I'm glad you appreciate it, since he beats the crap out of me."

He slid his finger over her bicep. "You do some working out yourself," he murmured.

She shivered again and his gaze slid to her breasts.

"Gotta keep up my delusion of having control over my life," she said.

His hands covered her breasts and she forgot what else she was going to say. He slid one of his hands down to her jeans and unfastened the top button. The sound of her zipper sliding downward felt as if it were magnified between her breath and his. He pushed her jeans and lace panties down over her thighs. She felt naked in more ways than one.

Her discomfort must have showed. "Looks like you need another distraction," he said and lifted the glass of champagne from the nightstand. He splashed some of the cool bubbly over her, shocking her with the chilled wet liquid.

"What are you—"

She broke off when his warm lips licked the champagne from her chest. Then he moved lower to her breasts. She bit her lip as her nipples grew hard and sensations swam to all her erogenous zones. She tried very hard not to arch her back, but her body acted out of its own volition.

"Good," he muttered against her nipples.

She felt as if her body began to spin. It had been so very long. She shouldn't let herself go. She hadn't in such a long time.

His hand slid between her thighs and he found her wet and swollen. Making a growling sound of approval, she felt him move away for several breaths. She began to come back down, but then he pulled her against his naked body. The sensation was so delicious and seductive she began to spin again.

"Leo," she murmured, wrapping her arms and legs around him. She wanted to absorb his strength, his passion, his life.

He swore under his breath. "Oh, damn it. I want inside you," he said and rolled on top of her. Pushing her thighs apart, he thrust inside her.

She blinked at the sensation, the thick, hard penetration of him.

A strange look crossed his face, and she couldn't prevent herself from wriggling beneath him.

He moaned and thrust again. The pleasure inside her grew. He began to pump. She clung to him, climbing higher and higher. Close, oh, so close, she was ready to burst free.

He sank inside her one last time, spilling his release in a long ecstasy-filled groan.

She bit her lip, still brimming with arousal, on the edge of a cliff, wanting to soar off of it. Something inside stopped her. Yawning need screamed inside her as deep as a cavern.

Leo rolled off of her, breathing heavily. "You weren't a virgin," he said. "You tricked me." A moment later, he rolled off the bed, grabbed his pants and left the room.

Calista stared after him as she tried to pull her mind and body together. Sexual need still hammered through her, clouding her mind. She felt as if she had no control of her body or mind. He'd taken both.

You tricked me. His words echoed through her mind. She hadn't thought he would know whether she was a virgin or not. After all, how many times had he had sex with a virgin? Her heart hammered with sudden fear. What if he annulled their marriage? What if, after all this, she still couldn't take care of her sisters?

Leo sat in the upstairs den with a bottle of scotch and bucket of remorse. His bride, the so-called virgin, had tricked him. What a fool he'd been, not wanting to seduce her lily-white sexual innocence from her. He hadn't wanted to taint her with his carnal needs in hopes that her purity would somehow cleanse his dirty past.

He chuckled with no humor. For a man who'd spent his youth deceiving others, he'd just experienced the biggest heist himself. He tossed back another shot of scotch. What was he going to do with her now?

The sound of a board creaking broke his solitude. He glanced up and saw her, wearing a white silk robe that belied her innocence. Her lips swollen from his kisses, her cheeks white and her eyes full of fear, she met his gaze. A surge of desire rolled through him. Lord, he was a fool.

"I never said I was a virgin," she said softly.

"You just inferred, suggested and did everything but say it," he said.

"You're not going to understand this," she said, crossing her arms under her chest.

"I can agree with that," he said, leaning back in his chair. He gave a cynical laugh.

He saw a flash of anger and defiance shoot through her green eyes, but she seemed to make an effort to quell it. She sat down in the chair across from his. "The truth is I had a sexual relationship during my sophomore year in college. It was a mistake. I thought I was in love. I thought he was the one. But he wasn't."

"Because he didn't have enough money?" he asked bitterly.

She narrowed her eyes and took a breath. "No. Because he lied to me and told me he loved me when he was involved with two other girls. That's when I knew I couldn't give myself that way again unless there was going to be a long-term commitment." She took another breath. "Yes, I made a mistake. Maybe you've never made a mistake. But if you had, then you'll know how it feels to want to make a fresh start."

He brooded over that for several seconds. God knows, he'd made a lot of poor choices. Who was he to hold this against her?

She stood and folded her hands in front of her. "I understand if you want me to leave."

His gut dipped at the prospect. "I didn't say that." He still didn't like that she'd deceived him. Part of the reason he had married her was he believed she was incapable of deceit. He'd obviously been wrong. A bitter taste filled his mouth. He hadn't been pure. Why should he expect anything in his life to be pure?

He downed another shot of scotch. "You take my bed for tonight. We'll discuss this in the morning."

She met his gaze and turned away. "Yeah, like I'm going to be able to sleep," she whispered and walked out of the room.

Calista stared up at the ceiling of Leo's bedroom with the covers wrapped tightly over her chest. This had been a disaster. He was bound to throw her out in the morning. Could she really blame him? He'd held off having sex with her because he thought she was a virgin and she'd let him think it.

She could kiss her sisters' future goodbye. She'd obviously mismanaged her charade. Calista wondered what she would do next. Would Leo annul their marriage? She couldn't believe he would give her a penny now. How horrid of a person was she to be thinking about money at this point?

She didn't want to think deeper than money, though.

She didn't want to think about whether she'd disappointed him. Or *hurt* him? Heavens, that had to be a stretch. The man was the personification of deceit. How could she even reach him, let alone hurt him?

Calista closed her eyes and counted backward from a thousand then counted backward again. Sometime during that second thousand, she drifted off.

In her sleeping but dreamless state, she felt the warmth of another body. A strong arm curved around her and drew her closer.

Her heartbeat accelerated. She rose to the surface of her sleep, and a hand slid over her hair, stroking. The touch soothed her and she drifted down again. When had someone stroked her hair? How long had it been? So long she couldn't remember…. She snuggled against the body that held her and sighed.

Minutes or hours later, she rolled over, encountering a hard chest and strong shoulders. Instinctively, she curled herself around the man and nuzzled her face against his throat.

"Calista," he said.

"Yes," she whispered, taking in the scent of him. She dipped her lips over his skin and darted her tongue out to taste him.

He sucked in a sharp breath and swore.

Feeling herself rise toward consciousness, she tasted him again, savoring the salt of his skin.

He gave her a gentle shake and she opened her eyes, encountering his dark gaze.

"Do you know what the hell you're doing?" he demanded.

"Do you want me to stop?" she whispered, her heart beating in her head, arousal surging inside her.

"Hell, no," he said and drew her mouth to his.

He kissed her and caressed and slid his fingers to her secret places, taking her to a different place. She wanted him inside her, craved his fullness expanding her, but he waited, taking her higher and higher.

She felt the tension inside her grow tighter and tighter. She didn't know if she could stand it.

"Give it to me, Calista. Give it to me," he coaxed, his fingers working their magic on her.

"Leo," she said, and suddenly she felt herself flung upward out of the stratosphere. Her climax twisted through her in fits and starts. She clung to him and he finally thrust inside her.

She moaned, feeling herself clench around him.

He groaned in response and thrust.

She arched against him, wanting to milk his response from him, needing every drop of his passion. He gave it and more.

Leo awakened the next morning with his bride in his arms. He felt a combination of cynicism and possession. He felt as if he'd been fooled. On the other hand, he felt as if he had gained a prize. Although she seemed innocent, he knew better. She'd come apart in his arms. Yet, even she had seemed surprised by the depth of her pleasure. That had given him enormous satisfaction. Knowing that he had taken her to new heights filled him with gratification.

Her blond hair was tousled over her eyes, her cheeks pink, her dark eyelashes fans against her fair skin. He suspected she didn't trust easily, yet she'd trusted him in marriage and in bed. That had to count for something.

As if she felt him thinking, she fluttered her eyes open. Her green eyes stared into his. She inhaled deeply and buried her head against his chest. "Good morning," she said.

He couldn't resist a surge of pleasure at the sensation of her voluptuous body rubbing against his. "Good morning," he murmured and exulted in her breasts against his skin, her naked thighs sliding through his.

She pressed her ear against his chest. "I can hear your heart," she whispered. "I can feel it."

There had been so many times when he'd been sure he didn't have a heart. He closed his eyes for just a second to drink in her essence then he used his chin to nudge her chin upward.

Her eyes met his, wariness warring with something he couldn't read. "Don't lie to me again," he said. "Don't mislead me. Don't shade the truth. Don't cheat on me. Do you understand?"

She gave a slow, solemn nod. "Yes."

"I'm glad we understand each other," he said and took her mouth and pulled her against him, determined to take her again.

After a night spent in Leo's bed, Calista awakened alone, feeling sore in secret places. She'd suspected Leo would have a strong sexual appetite, but she hadn't expected him to be quite so ravenous. And she hadn't expected he would make her so hot that during those private, primal moments she almost forgot who he was. She had the sinking feeling that she had gotten in way over her head. Grasping for something to quell her panic, she mentally flipped a page on the calendar. Technically, now that one night had passed, she had less than six months to go until she had completed her mission.

She rose from the bed and took a shower, allowing the

warm water to soothe muscles unaccustomed to such a strenuous, intimate workout. Drying off, she wrapped her hair in a towel, pulled on a too-large terry cloth robe and walked back into the bedroom.

The scent of bacon and waffles drifted toward her. She glanced at the balcony and spotted Leo sitting in a chair with his legs propped up while he read a newspaper. He wore a pair of jeans and an unbuttoned shirt that revealed his muscular chest. Her heart skipped a beat. She knew exactly how that chest felt against her naked breasts.

As if he'd heard her thoughts, he glanced up and met her gaze. "Good morning. Breakfast is waiting. I don't know what you like, so I told the cook to fix a little bit of everything." He lifted the large silver cover off the tray to reveal a feast of breakfast food.

"Good grief, that would feed a small foreign country," she said, her mouth watering at the sight of the fresh strawberries, blueberries and pineapple, along with the rest of the meal.

"What do you like?" he asked.

"Everything," she said, sitting down beside him. "I usually grab a quick bite or drink a breakfast shake before I walk out the door, so this is a splurge."

His gaze hovered on her. "No need to worry. You burned some calories last night."

She felt her cheeks heat. "So I did," she murmured and took a bite of waffle.

"Good?" he asked.

She nodded. "Delicious. Thank you. Don't you want anything?"

He lifted his cup of coffee to his lips. "I've already eaten."

After breakfast, she got dressed and Leo took her out on

his smaller boat. It was a warm, sunny day and she enjoyed the sights and sounds of the lake. He put down anchor in a private cove and she served the picnic the cook had packed for them, although she was still stuffed from breakfast.

In different circumstances, she would have been in heaven—married to a man who could take care of her and her family. A gorgeous, intelligent man full of passion with a sense of humor. She knew, however, that she didn't love him and he didn't love her.

"I need to take a trip to Japan in two weeks," he said. "I want you to go with me."

She mentally flipped through her work schedule. "That's short notice, but I'll check the company calendar."

"I'll be wanting you to join me on most of my trips," he said. "You may need to think about quitting your job."

She blinked at his suggestion and shook her head. "I couldn't do that. I work for a fabulous company with excellent benefits. I would be a fool to give it up."

"It's silly for you to worry about benefits now that you're married to me. You'll be covered under my insurance and I can give you an allowance twice your salary," he said.

Her throat tightened because she knew their marriage wasn't forever. If she gave up her job, she would be throwing away her future security. "There's no need to rush, and my company may be flexible. I would feel like a slacker if I didn't work at all."

"That's a first," Leo said with a crack of amusement in his voice. "I haven't met a woman yet who wasn't ready to dump her job for a life of leisure."

"Maybe that's part of the reason you married me and not the others," she said, lifting her chin.

"I doubt it," he said and pulled her against him. "But I'll give you a little time to work things out with your employer.

Just remember your first allegiance is to your husband," he said and took her mouth with his. "Always."

Calista felt a shiver of forewarning. It had been hard enough for her to hatch the plan of meeting and marrying Leo. He was such a strong man, inside and out, she wondered what she would be like after six months with him.

Two weeks later, Leo and Calista flew to Japan. Calista was still worried that she'd put her job in danger by insisting on taking the trip. Leo found her concern both irritating and sweet. She still didn't seem to comprehend how wealthy he was and that his wife would never want for anything.

Her brow furrowed as she studied her work assignments on her laptop.

Leo stroked that furrow with his index finger, startling her with his touch. "What—"

"You should relax. This is a long flight," he said. "I'm the one who has to be ready with facts and figures. You just need to look beautiful and act charming."

"Not quite. My boss expects me to have this assignment completed within three days. I'm sure jet lag will hit me before I know it, so I need to get it done while I have the energy."

"I don't know why you're fighting it. You may as well go ahead and quit," he said, turning back to his own preparations.

"I don't want to quit. I like my job. It gives me a feeling of accomplishment," she said. "I just need to learn how to juggle everything. I'll get there."

"We'll see," he said, shooting her a skeptical glance. "In a few weeks, we're going to India."

"India?" she echoed. "How in the world can I get off for two major trips within such a short time?"

"Exactly. Quit and I'll triple your salary," he said with a grin.

Not amused, Calista frowned. "It's not that easy."

"What's so difficult? I can cover all your expenses and more."

She hesitated a long moment. "I have some responsibilities with my sisters."

"I thought your cousin covered their expenses."

"They do as much as they can, but Tami has asthma and college is roaring toward us like a freight train."

"So tell my accountant what you need and he'll write a check. Money should be the last thing you're worried about. Instead, I'd rather you be prepared to meet my business associate and his family. My assistant completed a report for you," he said and handed a folder to her.

She lifted her eyebrows. "A report? I've been schooled in proper etiquette for at least a dozen countries."

"I know you have. One of your many valuable qualities," he said. "What you need to know is that you're not only meeting Mr. Kihoto and his wife, you may also meet his mistress, Shonana," he said.

"Mistress?" she echoed. "Surely he wouldn't flaunt that relationship with business associates."

"It depends on whether we go out to a nightclub," Leo said.

Indignant, she flipped through the report. "How am I supposed to pretend to his poor wife that her husband isn't a cheating jerk? Look, they have children," she said, pointing to the report, clearly appalled. "She's probably trapped in this marriage with an ogre."

Amused by her reaction, he bit back a smile. "I'm sure

she knows and accepts it," Leo said. "It's not unusual for a wealthy man to have a mistress."

She pressed her lips together in disapproval. "What's your opinion of it?" she asked.

"What he does in his personal life isn't my business," Leo said. "I just want to get the contract."

Silence followed and he glanced at her, finding her gazing at him thoughtfully. "Yes?" he asked.

"What is your opinion of taking a mistress for yourself?" she asked.

He laughed. "I have a beautiful, passionate wife. Why would I need a mistress?" he asked. "You're not worried, are you?"

She lifted her chin. "Of course not," she said and returned her attention to her report.

He noticed she fanned through the pages very quickly and wondered if she was truly taking in all the information. She set down the report and returned her focus to her laptop.

"What is Mr. Kihoto's age?" he asked.

"Fifty-three," she said without looking up from her screen.

"His wife?"

"Forty-five," she said.

"How long has he been CEO?"

"Twelve years. They have two children. A son and daughter. The son is oldest. He works for his father's company. He's married with a mistress too," she said, narrowing her eyes in disapproval. "His daughter is studying to be a doctor. No husband. No wonder," she muttered.

"Why do you say no wonder?" he asked, curious.

"With a father and brother who rule the roost and run

around, she probably would run screaming from marriage," Calista said. "Take control of your own life instead of giving it to a man."

Surprised by her reaction, he studied her carefully. "Is that why you don't want to quit your job?"

She hesitated a half beat, looking cornered and caught before she regained her composure. "From a personal standpoint, I gain satisfaction and confidence from completing my assignments with my job. Bringing that confidence into my relationship with you is a good thing. Plus, it's not as if we have children—"

Leo's stomach twisted at the mention of children. "And we won't have them, at least not for a long time, if at all."

She nodded. "I agree." She gave the report a little shake and shot him a considering glance. "It occurs to me that I know more about Mr. Kihoto, in some ways, than I know about you."

"Hmm. Really?"

"Well, aside from what happened before you were hatched at sixteen," she said.

"Life inside the egg was pretty boring," he said.

"I'm sure. But I know Mr. Kihoto's favorite food, favorite drink, favorite movie, and I don't know yours."

"Favorite food, lasagna. I had it a long time ago and I keep trying to find a restaurant that replicates the taste, but I haven't," he said. "Scotch or beer to drink, depending on my mood. Favorite movie, a tie between *Transporter* and *The Shawshank Redemption*."

She tilted her head to one side thoughtfully. "What did you like about *Shawshank*?"

"They were trapped, imprisoned, some were innocent. Morgan Freeman and Tim Robbins had to find their way to freedom," he said, thinking back to the days before he took his freedom into his own hands. It had required careful planning. He'd had to stick to his plan even when he was sweating with terror.

"You ever felt trapped?" she asked.

She had no idea. "Well, life inside an egg is bound to get claustrophobic," he said with a wry grin, pushing aside his darker memories. He was determined to leave his past in the past.

She nodded. "I guess we all have, at some point," she said and looked away.

He watched her, seeing another glimpse of the struggle between desperation and confidence. "When did you feel trapped?"

She bit her lip. "Mostly teenage years. A few times since then."

After her father's debacle, he realized. He wondered how much she knew about it. "What made you feel that way?"

"Family things," she said. "My father died and then my mother. My world turned upside down."

"You don't talk about your parents much," he said.

"Just as you don't discuss your time in the egg," she said, pushing back, clearly closing the door in his face. He didn't know why that bothered him, but it did.

"And now?"

"Now I try to depend on myself for my security," she said.

"Ah," he said, feeling another dig in his gut. He didn't like it that she didn't feel she could count on him, but he also understood it. Even though they were married, they didn't know each other very well. "Your job makes you feel more secure. In that case, keep it. Just negotiate more time away from the office."

She let out a sigh of relief, but he could swear she didn't want him to see it. One second later, her face brightened with a smile. "Favorite board game?" she asked.

"I haven't played board games in years," he said.

"Think back," she said.

He shook his head and strained his memory. "I don't remember much about it. This game had aircraft carriers and submarines and there was a grid and you had to guess the location of your opponent's ships—"

"Battleship," she said with a triumphant smile. "Bet you loved it."

"And what about you?" he asked. "What was your favorite?"

"In my younger years, it was Candy Land and Hungry Hippos," she said.

An image shot through his mind of Calista as a little blond-haired girl playing games. "And now that you're in your ancient mid-twenties?"

"Wii," she said. "I bought it for my sisters and occasionally whip their butts at bowling. I could probably whip your butt, too."

"Is that a challenge?" he asked.

"I'm sure you're too busy dominating the shipping business to play games," she said in a silky smooth voice, but the dare was still in her eyes.

"I might make an exception," he said and sent a text message to his assistant to purchase a Wii. "So what are the stakes for the winner and loser in your Wii bowling?"

She shot him a blank look and shrugged. "Bragging rights?"

He scoffed. "There's got to be more at stake than that," he said. "What's the use of playing?"

She laughed and shook her head. "For fun."

Five

The first thing that struck Calista as Leo's plane landed in Tokyo was the density. There were so many tall buildings tightly packed together. "They're so close," she murmured, looking out the window. She'd been so focused on her work that she hadn't had much time to think about exploring Tokyo while she was here.

"What would you like to see while you're here?" Leo asked. "I'll be in meetings most of the day and we'll have dinner with Mr. Kihoto, but there's no reason you can't explore. My assistant has arranged for a tour guide and interpreter for your convenience."

"I haven't even thought about it. What should I not miss?"

"Depends on how adventurous you are," he said.

"I still need to work while I'm here, but I should be able to sightsee a little bit," she said.

"Do you *ever* take a vacation?" he asked.

"Do you?" she retorted.

"Good point," he said. "You'll probably want to go shopping for souvenirs. The tour guide can escort you there. I have a few things in mind for you."

"What?" she asked.

"Surprises," he said and grinned. "You trust me, don't you?"

Her stomach dipped. *Yes and no*, she thought, surprised in a way that she trusted him at all. As long as Leo didn't know the truth about her plans for their temporary marriage, she suspected he would take care of her. But if he found out too soon... She shuddered at the thought.

At their hotel suite, Leo allowed her extra sleep to recover from jet lag. The next morning, she awakened to find him gone and instructions for contacting her personal guide. She got up and spent extra time in the bathroom, fascinated by the TOTO toilet, which actually lifted its lid as she approached and closed it as she left, all the while playing Mendelssohn.

She forced herself to work, although she was distracted by the beautiful small garden view from the window. After e-mailing one of her assignments to her office, she called the guide, a charming woman named Nakato. She went on a whirlwind tour, taking in the narrow streets, sounds and smells of Tokyo with a few shopping stops along the way. Nakato took her to a six-floor toy shop and she picked up a silly gift for Leo.

She dressed for dinner, fighting a sudden attack of nerves. When Leo walked through the door, she felt a whisper of relief until she saw his brooding expression. "How have your meetings gone?"

"Could be better. I learned that my biggest competitor

has already been here for a visit and Mr. Kihoto was impressed with him and his wife. I think Mr. Kihoto is a little put off by how young I am. At least having a wife means I've overcome one of his objections," he muttered under his breath.

Calista went very still, taking in his last comment. "Pardon me?" she finally said. "Did I hear you correctly? Are you saying you need to have a wife to get a business deal with this man?"

Still clearly distracted, he shrugged. "It's part of his expectations. My marital status doesn't have a thing to do with my business abilities, but having a wife smoothes the way."

"Are you telling me that you married me so I could smooth the way for your business deals?" she asked, shocked and almost hurt despite her own approach to the marriage. She couldn't possibly be really hurt because she didn't have any real feelings for him.

"I had several reasons for marrying you. I've demonstrated that," he said and flicked his gaze over her from head to toe. "I'll wash up and we can leave in a few minutes."

Calista paced from one end of the living area to the other, fuming. The more she thought about Leo's motivation for marrying her, the more upset she became. She remembered how he hadn't called her for weeks. He hadn't really had any feelings for her. He'd just been frustrated because his prospective business partners were reluctant with him because of his youth…and lack of a wife. So, what she'd really been was convenient. She wanted him to feel as vulnerable as she did.

"The limo's waiting," Leo said as he strode into the living area. "Let's go."

He took her elbow when they exited the elevator and she wrested her arm away from him. Despite the fact that she intended to divorce Leo in six months, she could barely swallow her indignation.

He shot her a look of cool curiosity as they got into the vehicle. "What's your problem?"

"You could have married just anyone," she said. "So, why me?"

"I told you before. You captured my attention."

"Plus I didn't want a big wedding. That was in my favor, too, wasn't it?"

Leo wiped his hand over his face in frustration. "Listen, there's no reason for you to pretend you're pissed off because part of the reason I married you was for practical reasons. You need to remember that you were very firm on getting married." His mouth tightened. "Despite the fact that you were not a virgin when we said our I-dos."

"I never said I was a virgin."

He lifted his hand. "This is nonsense. You and I have an explosive passion for each other. More than most married couples I'd say. You're getting what you want out of this bargain, and I am, too. If you wanted an emotional, romantic man, you picked the wrong guy. I never represented myself that way." He met her gaze. "Now, I want this deal. I don't want to feel like I've wasted my time by making this trip. So, just try to act like an adoring wife and you can resume your pissing fit after it's over. If it makes you feel better, I'll give you a blank check and you can shop off your anger tomorrow."

She stared at him in shock. "Do you really think going on a shopping spree is going to make me feel better about this?"

"Works with most women, doesn't it?" he asked as the limo pulled to a stop.

She would love to teach him a thing or two. After she secured her sisters' education and health care. She knew it was hypocritical, but his attitude still galled her.

"You're a jerk, but don't worry. I'll fake it," she said to him and got out of the limo.

Leo escorted her into the restaurant where a host greeted them.

"You're making a big deal out of nothing," Leo said under his breath. "Smile, darling. Here come the Kihotos."

The middle-aged couple approached and Leo made the necessary introductions. Calista smiled and nodded to each of them. "I have a small gift for you," she said to Mrs. Kihoto.

Mrs. Kihoto smiled shyly, but shook her head. "Oh, no, I can't accept."

Calista knew it was custom for the Japanese to refuse gifts up to three times. "Please do. It's very small and you would be doing me a favor."

Mrs. Kihoto gave a slow nod. "You're very kind and beautiful."

"Thank you. You're very generous to join us for dinner," Calista said and felt Leo's gaze on her.

When they sat down, he whispered in her ear, "Very nice. You surprised me."

She smiled, whispering in return, "Is this when you say 'good wife' and pat me on my head?"

She heard him smother a chuckle under a cough.

Calista successfully made it through the meal without stabbing Leo with her chopsticks and not pointing them in a culturally offensive direction. She even remembered to say the traditional *"Gochisosama deshita"* at the end of the meal.

Leo, again, appeared impressed. So did Mr. and Mrs. Kihoto. Calista collected her beautifully wrapped gift for Mrs. Kihoto and the woman also presented her with one.

"Oh, look at how beautiful," Calista said, admiring the gift. "You shouldn't have. Your company was a huge gift."

Mrs. Kihoto insisted and Calista thanked the woman and her husband again, relieved when she climbed into the limo.

"Very well done," Leo said. "I must show my gratitude. Since you're not interested in shopping one of my credit cards up to the limit, what can I get you?"

Calista leaned her head against the back of the leather seat and closed her eyes, the fiery brunt of her anger at Leo fading a little. She shouldn't have been surprised that his motive for marrying her was mercenary. And how could she blame him when her motive was almost as bad as his. The only thing that made her motive more honorable was that she was doing it for someone else, her sisters. Others might see that as splitting hairs. "I'd like a cheeseburger." She glanced at him out of the corner of her eye. "And maybe one of those TOTO toilets with all the bells and whistles."

He chuckled and loosened his tie. "Liked that, did you?"

"I was like a little kid. I think I played with it for thirty minutes," she confessed.

"I was the same way my first time too," he said.

She looked at him and felt a slight softening warring with her resentment.

He moved closer to her and pressed his mouth against hers. "You're an excellent wife."

"You were just surprised that I got Mrs. Kihoto a gift," she said. "I told you I'd been taught etiquette for several different cultures from the classes I took."

"True. I knew you were good. Just not this good," he said, sliding his mouth over her neck.

She felt a rush of heat despite her best intentions. He made her feel incredibly safe and challenged and irritated. He made her want to root for him. Probably part of his conman background, she thought cynically. That didn't keep her heart from beating faster.

"I'm taking you someplace the night before we leave," he said.

"Really?" she said. "Where?"

"It's a surprise," he said.

"No hints?" she asked.

He slid his hands to her waist and higher to her breasts. "What are you doing?" she whispered.

"Seducing my wife," he said. "Is it working?"

She felt as if she were melting into the leather upholstery. "Damn you."

"Too late. I've already been damned. But maybe you can redeem me," he said and slid her zipper down the back of her dress.

After a few days of combining work in the hotel suite and sightseeing, Leo awakened her before dawn. She covered her eyes. "Too early."

"I know, but Mrs. Kihoto was so impressed with you that she wants to take you somewhere special this afternoon," Leo said.

She peeked out from her fingers. "What?" she asked

suspiciously, taking in the sight of the too-gorgeous man who had somehow managed to distract her from the fact that she was peeved with him, that he was manipulative and lacking in human emotion.

"She wants to take you to a temple and Tokyo's best *onsen*," he said.

The temple was fine, but her drowsy mind tried to summon what she remembered about an *onsen*. "Sounds okay," she said and frowned. "*Onsen*? I can't remember—"

"You'll love it," he said. "Everyone loves it."

She rose onto her elbows and frowned. "What is *it*?" she asked.

"It's like swimming in a hot spring," he said.

The realization slowly sank in. "The communal bath," she said. "I'm going to have to get naked with your client's wife!"

"It's not that bad. You'll enjoy it. It will help you relax for your surprise tonight," he said and gave her another quick kiss. "I'll call you later."

"Leo," she said as he walked toward the door, but he kept walking. "Leo," she called and tossed a pillow that missed him by a mile. Frustration roared through her. She'd just been conned big time.

Hours later, after she'd visited a peaceful temple and taken a naked dip in a pool with a bunch of strangers, albeit feminine strangers who'd been fascinated by her fair hair, she reluctantly allowed herself to be driven to a different hotel for the evening. She was surprised by the modest outward appearance of the building. "This is different."

"Yes, it is," he said and led her inside the boutique establishment. They were led to a beautiful suite with a huge tub and expanded bathroom, but no bed. "Where do we sleep?"

"On the floor," he said.

"Oh, goody," she said.

He chuckled. "Don't prejudge. Our dinner will be served in our room."

"Can I have a fork?" she asked.

He nodded. "Yes."

A lovely meal of fresh fish was served via room service. Padded floor mats were rolled out onto the floor. Champagne was served with the meal.

"The champagne keeps it from being traditional, but I thought you might like it. I figured if they brought margaritas you might spill another one on me," he said, taking a sip of the bubbly.

"It's very quiet here," she said as she finished her last delicious bite. "I like it better than I thought I would."

"We're not done." He stood and extended his hand. "Come with me."

"Where are you taking me?"

"You'll like it," he said.

"That's what you said about the communal bathing," she said, reluctantly rising.

"And did you?" he asked.

"It wasn't as bad as I thought it would be," she admitted.

He led her into the bathroom where the huge tub was filled with steaming water with rose petals floating on top. She glanced at him. "I already had a bath today."

"It wasn't with me," he said and stripped off his clothes.

She looked at him, unable to tear her gaze from his body. The light was bright enough for her to see every well-defined muscle. In the past, when they'd made love, the power of his physique had distracted her so much that she couldn't study him. But now she could. As he turned his back to her, she took in his wide shoulders, the V-shape of his waist to his hips, his tight buttocks and long strong legs. He turned a certain way in the light and she saw thin white lines of abuse on his back and lower.

She stared at the marks, but then he stepped into the tub and turned around to face her. "Well?" he asked.

Rising to her feet, she pulled off her clothes. "I've already bathed three times today. I guess one more time won't hurt." She walked to the large steaming tub with the rose petals fanning away from the wake he'd caused.

He took her hand to steady her and she stepped inside, blowing a quick puff of air from her mouth. "Hot," she said.

"You'll get used to it," he said and pulled her into his arms. His nakedness felt delicious against hers. He was so hard where she was so soft. Pulling her down to her knees, he supported her.

"Yikes," she whispered at the heat.

"A little further," he said, splashing water over her shoulders. "Come on. A few minutes and you'll wish it were warmer."

"I don't think so," she said, but she allowed him to pull her the rest of the way into the tub.

He kissed her, taking her soft gasp into his mouth. She closed her eyes and the combination of the hot water and his naked body surrounding her made her feel as if she'd entered another dimension. She lifted her hands to his shoulders, her breasts rubbing against his chest. He nudged her thighs apart, wrapping her legs around his back so that she sat on his lap.

"Good?" he asked, rubbing his forehead against hers.

"Yes," she said, deciding she could let down her guard for just tonight. She was far from her sisters, far from her job and in the arms of a strong, strong man. "Very good."

Leo fed his bride a breakfast of fish, which she appeared to enjoy. After they'd made love last night, she'd slept like the dead. She often seemed as if a part of her was on guard, but he'd sensed something different in her. The woman usually seemed to be wound tighter than a clock, and damn if it wasn't his pleasure to unwind her. He watched her take her last bite and sigh with pleasure, similar to the way she sighed when he made love to her. Similar, but not the same.

"That was wonderful," she said.

"Good," he said. "Did it make up for your communal bath yesterday?"

"I'll tell you the truth. The communal bath was actually very nice and Mrs. Kihoto made it seem like the most natural thing in the world. She chatted and was very friendly." She paused and shot him a curious look. "Have you taken a communal bath with Mr. Kihoto?"

He nodded. "Last time I was here. It wasn't a big deal. Men aren't as hung up about their bodies as women are."

"That sounded sexist," she said.

"There are differences between men and women. Most of them are good," he said.

"Oh, really?" she said, lifting her chin.

He touched her pert nose. "You look snooty when you do that. Did you learn that expression in your girlie classes?"

"Girlie classes," she echoed. "You mean my etiquette classes."

He shrugged. "There weren't any guys in your class, were there?"

"No," she conceded. "I thought the classes were a waste of time the first two times I took them."

He stared at her, choking on his coffee. "How many times did you take them?"

"Four," she said with an expression of disgust. "I flunked them the first two times and my mother wanted to make sure I learned everything, so she made me take them a third time. Then I took the advanced level. I didn't want to take them again, so I got those right the first time."

He took another sip of coffee and watched the sunlight gleaming on her tousled hair. "You fought being civilized," he said.

Her lips twitched. "I wouldn't have put it that way." She rested her chin in her hands and studied him thoughtfully. "I want to ask you about something."

"Then ask."

She took a deep breath and frowned. "You have marks on your back. Were you injured at some time?"

Leo immediately pulled back. "Car accident when I was little."

Her eyes wrinkled in concern. "I'm sorry."

"I don't remember anything about it or anything before then."

"Oh," she said, a stunned expression on her face.

He could see the sympathy coming and was determined to stop it. "That was all before the egg," he said.

She didn't smile in return. In fact, she frowned. "Do you know how old you were?"

"Around eight," he said. "It doesn't matter."

"How can you say that? Don't you think it had an impact upon you?" she asked.

There'd been years when he'd fantasized about the family he must have had before the accident. Before Lilah and Clyde had rescued him. He knew his family had died in the crash, but he hadn't known how many siblings, if any, he'd had. He didn't know what his mother and father were like, if they'd treated him well. Now that he was grown, he suspected he'd been treated better by his real parents. How could he not have been?

"I don't focus on the past," he said. "I focus on the future."

"You don't think you can learn important things from your past," she said.

"I've learned everything I need to learn from my past. I don't dwell on what happened when I was child because if I did, I'd go crazy." He paused a half beat, refusing to give into the secret need for information about so many unanswered questions about himself. It was a fruitless endeavor. "We're flying out tonight. I've arranged for your guide to take you souvenir shopping one more time while I wrap up my last meeting with Mr. Kihoto. In the meantime, don't forget the trip to India in a few weeks. Have you cleared it with your boss?"

"I thought I would finish this trip before I start asking about another," she said, irritation leaking into her expression. "Are you sure it's necessary for me—"

"Absolutely sure," he said, standing. He was much more comfortable with her irritation than the sympathy he'd glimpsed.

She followed him to his feet, her irritation turning to anger. "And what if I can't?"

"If you can't find a way, then I'll help you," he said.

"That sounds like a threat," she said.

"No. It's a promise of assistance. Don't argue about this anymore," he said and headed for the bathroom.

"If you think you've married a submissive little Stepford wife, you are very mistaken."

He paused, thinking about her words. He turned to face her. "I never received any indication that you were submissive. I just understood that you were a reasonable adult willing to make the adjustments necessary in our marriage."

"And what adjustments will you be making?" she asked, crossing her arms over her chest.

"Whatever adjustments I make, they won't include continuing petty debates like this." He entered the bath and closed the door behind him, but not before he heard her make a sound of utter frustration.

Leo avoided her after that. It was amazing how much space the man could create around himself even in his personal jet. After they landed and returned to his condo, they might as well have been separated by a small city. *Fine*, she thought. She didn't mind. Every hour that passed when she didn't have to deal with Mr. Demanding was one less hour on her six-month time clock. His remoteness didn't bother her for at least two days. She had plenty of work to do. She visited her sisters and cousin and delivered the souvenirs from Japan and avoided her cousin's questions about her marriage.

The more she thought about what Leo had told her about the accident he'd had as a child, the more curious she because. On her return drive from visiting her sisters, she dialed the number for her P.I.

"Rob here. How you doing, Mrs. Grant?"

Calista made a face. "I haven't technically changed my name."

"Like that matters," he said. "Congratulations on bagging the big one."

She ignored his sarcasm. Rob had once wanted to date her. They'd become friends instead and he'd given her a cost break when she'd asked him to investigate the man who'd caused her father to go over the edge. "I learned something recently that has made me curious."

"What's that?" he asked.

"Leo was apparently in a terrible accident when he was about eight years old. He remembers nothing before that. Nothing about the accident."

"I stopped my investigation once I found out he was involved in the grifting scheme with your father," he said.

"Well, there's something about his childhood that bothers me. He won't talk about it."

"Probably because plenty of people would like to skin his late father and him," Rob said.

"Maybe," she said and mused about his response to her. "I probably shouldn't ask you to do any more digging."

"On your beloved husband," Rob said sarcastically.

"Okay. I get it. You don't want to help me. Can you at least point me in the direction I need to look if I want to get more information about his childhood?"

Rob laughed hysterically.

Calista frowned. "You don't have to be nasty about it," she said. "It's not like I'm asking for state secrets."

"I'll do it," he said. "You owe me drinks," he added and hung up.

"I can't take you for—" She broke off when she realized he was no longer on the line. Sighing in frustration as she approached Leo's condo, she slipped her key into the parking lot entry and tried to rein in her feelings. Her call to Rob had been impulsive and she shouldn't have made it. If Leo wasn't interested in his childhood, she shouldn't be either. Rob probably wouldn't find anything anyway.

Six

Calista's BlackBerry went off as she took her lunch in her office. Join Mr. Grant at 6:30 p.m. tonight for Philadelphia Business Owners dinner. Dress: business casual. Car will pick you at 6:00 p.m. at the downtown condo. Thursday night, George Crandall Museum for awarding of the LG Enterprises Scholarship Funds and Friday night Grand Celebration of the Arts on the Delaware River. More details to come. S. Miles, assistant to Leo Grant.

Calista stared at the text message from her husband's *assistant*. She shook her head. This wasn't even an invitation. It was a list of required appearances. *From his freakin' assistant.*

Her temperature rose with each passing second. She could barely contain her anger. Who did he think he was? Obviously, Mr. Important Leo Grant. Another text popped up and she strongly considered erasing it before she read it, but gave in to her curiosity.

Please confirm. S. Miles, assistant to Leo Grant.

She had two words for Mr. Miles and Mr. Grant and they were not Merry Christmas. Calista was so furious it was all she could do not to start screaming. Instead, she counted to ten. Twenty times.

She took a deep breath. First step, ignore the order. Second step, block Leo's assistant's number. Step three, work late and plan a long visit to the gym afterward.

Leo left the dinner early, wondering why Calista hadn't shown. In the back of his Town Car, he dialed her number, but his call went straight to voice mail. Irritation twisted through him. He wouldn't even have attended it, but the chairman of the organization had begged him. Little had he known he would be presented with an award for bringing new jobs to Philadelphia. The attention made him self-conscious. He was always wary of having his picture taken, especially if it might be put in the media. Even though he looked far different now from what he did as a young teenager, he always got a chill wondering if someone might recognize him.

He dialed her number again, but again it went to voice mail. Concern cut through him. He wondered if she was okay. It wasn't like Calista to turn off her phone. He was torn between an odd combination of missing his wife and not wanting her to ask questions about his childhood ever again. The conversation they'd shared that morning in Japan had opened old wounds he'd sworn to never revisit. There had been a time when he'd gone so far as to hire a private investigator to find out his past, but there'd been nothing except dead ends. Leo wasn't sure who his real parents or real family were and he'd had to face the fact that he never would. He hadn't wanted to claim Clyde as his father and was thankful he wasn't Clyde's son by blood.

"You're quiet tonight, Leo," George said from the front seat. "What's on your mind?"

"Regular stuff. I had nonstop international phone calls and meetings today. Barely had time to breathe," Leo said.

"Haven't seen your wife lately," George ventured, digging.

"We've both been busy since we got back from Japan," Leo said. "I have my work. She has hers, although I don't see why she continues. God knows, she won't need the money."

"She's a little more independent than you expected, isn't she?" George asked, glancing in the mirror.

"Yes, she is," Leo answered, unable to keep the irritation from his tone.

"If you'd wanted a tamer kitten from the litter, you shouldn't have chosen one with claws," George said. "She doesn't strike me as the type to take orders unless she sees a good reason for them."

Leo frowned. "Maybe."

"Odd that she won't quit her job. She's either very independent…" George said and paused a long moment.

"Or what?"

"Or she isn't sure the marriage is going to last."

The statement jarred Leo. He'd thought the prenup would hold her. "What the—"

"Just a thought. I could be wrong," George said as he pulled in front of the condo.

"Good night, George. Pleasant dreams," he said in a dry tone and got out of the car.

"You too," George called cheerfully.

Leo took the elevator to the penthouse and stepped inside. He stopped, listening for any signs of Calista. His housekeeper, Brenda, approached him. "Welcome home, sir. May I get something for you? A drink? Something to eat?"

He shook his head. "No thank you. Have you seen my wife?"

"Yes, sir. She came in about twenty minutes ago and went straight to the exercise room."

"Thank you, Brenda," he said and decided to fix his own drink. He went to his study and poured himself a scotch. Ditching his tie, he sat down and checked the overnight stock markets for a few minutes. He glanced at the clock and decided to head for the exercise room.

Opening the door, he spotted her running on the treadmill. She was moving at a fast pace and perspiration glistened on her arms and back. It wasn't at all unattractive to him. The way she ran reminded him of a cheetah in the jungle. She would be difficult for even the smartest, strongest predator to catch.

Seconds passed and she slowed. Gradually, she slid into a cooldown walk. Leo leaned against the wall and waited until she stepped off the treadmill and pulled out her earphones. She turned and her gaze landed on his, her green eyes widening in surprise before a twinge of anger came and went so quickly he wondered if he imagined it.

"Looked like a good run," he said. "Was it?"

She nodded. "Good stress reliever," she said and picked up a small dumbbell.

"Stressful day?" he ventured, walking forward, wondering

why in hell he hadn't insisted she join him in his bed since they'd returned from Japan.

"Still catching up from my time away."

"Did you get a message from my assistant?"

She wrinkled her brow. "I'm not sure. I got some sort of spam, so I decided to turn off my phone until I could contact my carrier about it."

"Spam?" he echoed, confused.

"It must have been. Some random guy I'd never met gave me all these dates and times I was supposed to make appearances."

He studied her for a long moment, but her eyes were wide with innocence. He cleared his throat. "Was the message from Samuel Miles?"

She frowned and shrugged her shoulders. "I don't know," she said. "It was so ridiculous I just dismissed it as spam."

Leo felt another surge of something stronger than irritation. "What was so ridiculous about it?"

She chuckled. "Oh, really. Think about it. If my husband wanted me to attend an event with him, he wouldn't send a message from his assistant. For one thing, it's incredibly impersonal. Plus the message wasn't a request. It was an order. Now that's insulting. And I just can't believe my husband would do something so incredibly ridiculous."

He was peeved and inexplicably amused at the same time. Her eyes batted in exaggerated innocence and he felt his lips twitch. "Point taken."

She met his gaze and took a deep breath. "Just so you know, I blocked his number."

"Whose number?" Leo asked.

"The person who sent me the spam," she said and lifted her chin. "I'm not your employee. I'm your wife."

He nodded. "In that case, wife, I'll expect you to join your husband in his bed tonight."

Her gaze flickered and she opened her mouth, but he spoke before she had a chance.

"Isn't that what husbands and wives do?" he challenged.

The next morning, Calista awakened after a night where Leo had pushed her to unbelievable sexual heights. She felt stretched and sore and amazing. Calista realized she'd never had a clue what sexual satisfaction meant before Leo. She wondered if he knew that, too. She glanced at the clock and dragged herself from Leo's huge bed. He, of course, had left a long time ago.

Stepping into the shower, she let the water spray over her, washing away her soreness and worries. When Leo made love to her, he took more than her body. He captured a bit of her mind, maybe even her soul. If she had one.

Rubbing herself dry with the Egyptian cotton towels, she returned to the bedroom and saw an envelope with her name on it propped on the bed. She picked it up, opened it and read it.

Would you meet me for lunch today? I have a charity obligation on Thursday and your presence would make it much more bearable. As it would for my obligation on Friday night.

He gave her his BlackBerry number. His request was infinitely more personal. Her heart twisted.

She typed her response. "Yes, yes and yes."

Hours later, she sat down to lunch with him at one of Philadelphia's most exclusive gourmet restaurants. "Thank you for meeting me," he said.

"Thank you," she said and took a sip of water from the glass that had already been poured. She looked at him, the man who had owned and occupied her body last night. "How's it going?"

"Could be worse," he said. "We got the Japanese account. I'm sure it's because of you."

"Not sure about that. Mrs. Kihoto made it easy. All I had to do was get naked in front of a group of Japanese ladies."

"Funny. Despite Mr. Kihoto's extracurricular activities, he respects his wife's opinion."

"Or maybe he just realized what a great deal you were offering," she said.

He flicked his gaze over her. "Maybe. What would you like for lunch? Anything is yours."

"Fish," she said. "I need all the brain food I can get. Especially after last night."

His lips lifted. "You flatter me."

"Not really," she said. "I just need to keep my mental energy going."

"Okay, salmon it is," he said.

Mere moments later, the waiter arrived with their lunch. Calista dug in, enjoying her seafood and focusing on her own meal rather than Leo. She needed her strength, her acuity. Heaven help her, she hoped the food would supply it.

She sipped from her water glass, refusing wine. "That was delicious."

"Yes, it was," Leo said, clicking his water glass against hers. "Would you like to go to the lake house this weekend?" he asked.

"I have to visit my sisters," she said.

"Bring them with you," he offered.

"Have you met them? I love them, but my sisters can be a royal pain," she said.

"So can you," he said, his eyes hooded with sensuality.

"Okay," she said. "But I've warned you."

She joined him for the events, dressing quickly after work. The first night he met her at home and made love to her. The second time, he took her in the limo. She wondered if she would ever feel normal again.

"This is kinda crazy," she told him as he held her in his arms.

"It's crazy in a good way," he said, kissing her.

"Are you sure about that?" she asked.

"Yeah, I am," he said.

Calista took a deep breath and deliberately drowned herself in him.

She felt him fold her around him as he slid inside her. She held onto him wanting more, wanting everything….

"I'm rolling onto my back," he said. "You can take me any way you want."

And she did, but at the same time, she was completely taken.

That weekend her sisters joined Calista and Leo at his lake house. Calista feared he would run screaming from extended close contact, but he managed. She was impressed at the way he handled them on his yacht. Then again, what wasn't to like about riding on a yacht?

Leo took Tina on an inner tube ride.

"Can I try it?" Tami asked, who was usually too cool to participate in what she deemed childish.

"Of course," Leo said. "You're up next."

After a few more minutes for Tina, Tami jumped off the side of the boat and positioned herself in the inner tube.

As Tina climbed on board, Calista wrapped a towel around her sister and hugged her. "That rocked," she said and glanced at Leo. "Your husband is the best."

Leo felt a surprising rush of pleasure at the teen's compliment. The appreciation he saw in Calista's gaze gave him an even bigger boost. Watching her interact with her sisters tugged at a long forgotten place inside him. Their teasing camaraderie reminded him of nights he'd spent wishing for a different family. He'd thought he'd buried those longings years ago. He couldn't help admiring the way the three of them had retained their sense of family even after all their losses and living apart.

"It does look fun," Calista said.

"You wanna go?" he asked, watching as her hair whipped around in the wind.

"Oh, no, that's okay," she said.

"You should try it," Tina said. "It's way easier than skiing."

Calista shook her head. "No—"

"Oh, don't be a wuss, Cal," Tina said.

"More than one can ride at a time," he said, remembering Calista's traumatic experience.

"I'll go with you," Tina offered.

"For some reason, that doesn't make me feel more secure, *daredevil*," Calista said and bumped her hip against her sister.

"It would work," Leo said, because he could tell Calista wanted to go. "Tina could go with you and Tami could watch."

"Come on," Tina said.

"Okay," Calista said. "But you better make sure Tami isn't texting instead of watching."

Minutes later, Calista took the plunge with Tina. He watched her younger sister coach her on the location of the grips. He wondered how often the girls switched roles, becoming the teacher instead of the student. Despite Tina's bold personality, she was gentle with Calista.

Out of the corner of his eye, he spotted Tami lifting her cell phone. "No texting when you're the lookout," he said.

"Who's texting? I'm taking pictures," she said. "Are you ready?" she called to Tina and Calista.

"Yes," Tina said.

"No," Calista said. "Okay," she amended when Tina rolled her eyes. "Just go very slowly."

Leo eased forward, escalating slowly. Hearing yelling voices, he glanced at Tami. "Tina wants you to go faster," she said.

"What about Calista?" he asked, focusing on piloting the boat.

"She's okay," Tami said.

Leo revved up the speed and took a few easy turns. He heard a scream during the last one and immediately slowed, glancing over his shoulder. "Is Calista okay?"

Tami was busy snickering and taking pictures with her cell phone. "They both got thrown."

"What?" he asked, searching the water for them.

"It happened during that last turn," Tami said, still snickering.

Leo spotted Tina screaming with glee then saw Calista yelling at the top of her lungs. Although she was wearing a life jacket, he was certain she was frightened. Stripping off his shirt, he jumped in the water and swam to her. She seemed to be struggling for breath.

"Are you okay?" he asked, pulling her to him.

She gasped then laughed. "Yes, I'm just going to kill my little sister. She did some sort of spinning thing with the tube during that last turn."

"So you really are okay?"

She met his gaze and her laugh faded. "Were you really worried?"

"I remembered about the time you fell off the boat," he said, feeling foolish.

"And you thought I was panicking," she concluded in a wry voice. "Reasonable assumption, but no, this time Tina distracted me. Thanks for jumping in for me, though," she said and smiled. "Had enough of my sisters?"

"The three of you have an interesting relationship," he said, pulling her toward the boat. "Tami is busy laughing at you, while Tina is goading you into taking a spin."

"That's sisters for you. I'm guessing you didn't have any," she said.

He met her gaze and felt a strange twist in his gut. "None that I can remember."

She hesitated, looking at him and biting her lip. "That must be awful. Not being able to remember," she said.

He couldn't bear her sympathy or her empathy. It caused an ache inside him that no pain medication would salve. "Maybe it wasn't worth remembering," he said and before she could respond, he added, "Go ahead and climb on board. You need to dry off. Here comes Tina."

Leo piloted the boat back to the dock in silence, thrown back in time to all those nights when he wondered what kind of family he'd had, what his parents had been like, if he'd had siblings and if they'd died instantly in the car crash that had left him with no memory and a foster father who had abused him. He pulled into the dock, lost in thought.

"Thanks," Tami said and hugged him.

He saw Calista watching them over Tami's shoulder and hugged the teenager. "My pleasure. I want copies of those pictures," he said.

Tami pulled back and smiled at him. "Deal," she said.

"What pictures?" Calista demanded.

"Just a few of you and Tina in the water," Tami said innocently. "I thought I'd post them on Facebook tonight."

Calista cringed. "Don't tag me. I don't want my boss seeing those."

"Why? Because he'll be jealous you were having such a good time with two hot almost-college girls?" Tami said.

Calista groaned. "Just don't. And maybe I should send both of you to a convent instead of a university."

Hours later, after eating dinner and viewing a chick flick in Leo's screening room, Calista climbed the stairs to Leo's bedroom and washed her face and brushed her teeth in the adjoining bathroom. Then she crept into his bed, carefully sliding underneath the covers.

"Did you have fun?" he asked, startling her.

She froze for two seconds then took a breath. "Yes. My sisters had fun, too. Thank you so much for making this happen. I can't tell you how much this means to me."

"I'm glad you enjoyed it. It was fun seeing you with your sisters. It's impressive that the three of you put things back together."

Her pleasure in the day dimmed a little. Leo would be all too well acquainted with how her family had imploded, especially her father. "My father wasn't perfect, but he was affectionate and he made us laugh. He tried to teach me to play golf."

"Tried?" he said.

"Not my forte. He was one of the most encouraging people I've known. I would hit a ball all wrong and he would say things like 'You almost got it.' 'That's a good start.'" She shook her head, her heart squeezing tight with the memories. "For the most part, he was extremely optimistic. Maybe a little too optimistic at times, but I miss him. I miss his smile and his laugh and his bear hugs."

Silence followed and Leo covered her hand with his. "You're lucky to have those memories."

She glanced up at him. "You must have some memories of your parents."

His jaw tightened. "None I want to remember."

Calista studied him, wondering what was really going on inside him. He clearly had no fondness for his father. She prodded him with memories of her own father. "When my father died, I couldn't believe it. How could someone so vital and positive be gone in an instant?"

He met her gaze. "That must have been hard," he said.

She gave a humorless laugh. "Hard doesn't describe it. Nothing prepared me for hearing that my loving father could have died so quickly. It wasn't possible."

Leo remained silent and she felt the dark tension coiling between them.

"There was a man who tricked him into investing a lot of money. He lost it all," she said. "He went from being the most optimistic man in the world to hopeless."

A long silence followed. "People, even good people, can

get into bad situations," he said. "At some point, everyone wants a break. An easy way out."

She searched his face. "You sound as if you have some experience with this."

He narrowed his eyes for a sliver of a moment and shrugged. "Must have been all that time in the egg."

"What was your father like? After the accident?" she asked.

"As you said, I was hatched," he said and she felt him pull away from her emotionally.

"But you had a father, didn't you?" she asked.

"No," he said, removing his hand from hers. The gulf between them suddenly felt like miles instead of inches, or heartbeats. "I didn't. You should get some rest. Your sisters will try to wear you out tomorrow."

She sank into her pillow and watched him turn away from her. She'd tried to get her digs in about her father and she'd succeeded. She'd pushed him away. He wouldn't make love to her tonight. He wouldn't hold her. That was what she'd wanted. Right? So, why did she feel so lonely?

Seven

Calista's cell phone rang just as she was finishing her work for the day. She glanced at the caller ID and saw that it was her P.I. friend, Rob. "Hi. Did you find something already?"

"I need to ask you a few more questions. Meet me for drinks," he said.

"I'm not sure that's a good idea," she said.

"Why? Afraid your meal ticket hubby will complain?" he asked.

Calista didn't like his attitude. "You know about my situation with my sisters. I don't appreciate you mocking it."

"Okay, okay. I was just trying to keep things light. Meet me at The Mark in thirty minutes," he said.

"Thirty minutes," she complained, but he'd already hung up. Rob was an excellent investigator, but lacking in social skills. She closed down her computer and got her car from the underground garage then drove to The Mark, which was more of a joint than a restaurant or a bar. There was no valet service, so she squeezed into a parking spot behind the building and walked swiftly to the entrance.

Stepping inside, she glanced around and caught sight of him waving from the bar.

"Hey, Princess," he said, kissing her on the cheek. "Looks like married life agrees with you." He wiggled his eyebrows. "I'm surprised you haven't quit your job."

"Then you don't know me well at all," she said, perching on the stool opposite his.

"Not as well as I'd like to," he said as a bartender nodded toward them. "What do you want to drink?"

"Ice water," she said.

He made a face. "You're such a buzz killer. Loosen up, it's happy hour."

"I'm not going home with liquor on my breath," she said.

"Check," he said. "Don't want to piss off Mr. Mega-Bucks before you get his donation. What kind of prenup did you sign?"

She shook her head. "None of your business. You said you had some questions."

He nodded. "What kind of accident was your rich little grifter in? What year was it? How old was he?"

She shrugged as the bartender gave her a glass of water. "He was eight," she said, taking a long drink.

"But you don't know for certain," he said.

"No, I don't."

"Okay, well find out everything you can about the accident, how old he was, what kind of injuries he sustained..."

"He must have had a severe concussion. He said he can't remember anything before the accident. He doesn't even remember the accident itself," she said, thinking back to the discussion she'd had with Leo. "He has scars. His skin on his back is rough."

Rob gave a low whistle. "Sounds like you're getting to know him very well."

She sighed and met his gaze. "Do you have to turn everything into either an insult or a double entendre?"

"I do my best," he said. "Okay, okay," he said at her expression. "Just find out as much as you can about the accident and how old Mr. Money was when it happened."

"Okay," she said and took another sip of water. "I'll be in touch."

"You're going already?" he asked.

"Yes," she said firmly and slid off her stool. Just as she approached the door, two policemen burst inside with a dog.

"Don't anybody move. We're here for an inspection," one of the officers said.

"Excuse me," she said. "I was on my way out."

"Not now you aren't," the officer said.

Calista waited impatiently as the officers led the dog around to sniff at various people. They found marijuana on three men and unregistered guns on five. That knowledge unsettled her.

Suddenly someone yelled, "Fire!"

She joined the stampede for the door, nearly being trampled by the people behind her. She felt a rush of something cold and wet over her dress and winced. Rushing into the parking lot, she gulped in breaths of air as she ran through the graveled parking lot toward the back of the building. A bouncer blocked her from proceeding.

"But my car," she protested. "My car is back there."

"There's been a fire in the kitchen," he said. "We can't allow you any closer."

"How am I supposed to get home?"

He shrugged his huge, overdeveloped shoulders. "Get a ride or call a cab."

Calista groaned to herself. This had been a disaster. Even though she had George's cell number, she refused to call it. How could she explain where she was? She gave the host a big tip and asked him to get a cab for her. Ten minutes later, she sat in a smelly taxi heading for Leo's condo. She remembered he'd said something about working late tonight. She could only hope that she beat him home.

Thirty minutes later, she rode the elevator up to the penthouse and walked inside, feeling a rush of relief. *There's no place like home*, she thought, even though this really wasn't her home. At least she felt safe here. She headed for the refrigerator and filled a glass with water then turned toward the stairs.

Out of nowhere, George appeared. "You're home late, Mrs. Grant."

She covered her chest with her hand. "You frightened me," she said.

"Sorry, ma'am," he said and twitched his nostrils. "If I do say so, ma'am, you smell a bit like booze and cigarettes."

"I met a client at a bar. I neither smoked nor drank alcohol tonight." she said. "I was glad to get out of there."

"You need to be careful. A woman who looks like you. You need to be safe," he said.

"I am," she said.

"Good," he said, studying her again. "Philly has its dark places."

She nodded. "I know. Do you know when Leo will arrive home?"

"Oh, he's already home. Upstairs," he said.

Her stomach sank. "Thank you,' she said and climbed the stairs. She walked into his suite and found him dressed in casual clothes, working on his laptop. He glanced up. "Late workday?" he asked.

She made a face. "I had a drink with a client. Next time, I'll just be rude."

He lifted an eyebrow. "You could always quit…."

"Later. I have bills to pay," she muttered.

He frowned. "What bills?"

"College tuition, medical bills," she said, distracted.

He nodded, saying, "Why isn't my accountant handling that? I can cover that."

He said it the same way he could cover gas or a meal at a fast-food restaurant.

She shook her head. "They're not your sisters."

"My sisters-in-law," he said.

She felt herself weaken. Temptation slid through her. Wouldn't it be nice not to have to worry about money? Wouldn't it be nice to know her sisters were taken care of? That was her eventual goal, anyway. What would it hurt if he took over her expenses now?

"Quit your job and I'll cover tuition," he said.

Calista snapped out of her fantasy world. If Leo started covering her expenses now what if their marriage fell apart before six months? She would be unemployed and scrounging to take care of her sisters. "No, thank you," she said.

"Why?" he asked.

"Because while it may be fine with me to stop working right now, and I'm not saying it is," she added, "what happens when I change my mind and decide I want to work again?"

"That's fine," he said with a shrug of his powerful shoulders. "You'll just need to work around—"

"There's the problem," she interjected. "I may not be able to work around your travel schedule. Surprisingly enough, many companies prefer their employees not to take off at the whim of their husbands."

"Damn," he said, striding toward her. "And I was so hoping I could tempt you into a life of slothful, indulgence." He pulled her into his arms and frowned. "You smell like cigarette smoke and—" He broke off. "Is that cheap whiskey?"

"Probably," she said, trying not to feel nervous. "At the last minute, some clients insisted I meet them at a bar. I had water," she said. "There was a fire, so the whole place was evacuated. I couldn't even get my car because it was too close to the fire."

"Hmm," he said. "Why didn't you call George?"

"I didn't want to bother him," she said. "So I called a cab. I'll get my car tomorrow."

"What was the name of this place you went tonight?"

"The Mark?" she said.

His eyes widened and he swore. "Who in hell wanted you to go to that dump?"

"They'd heard it was authentic Philly. I suggested something classier, but—"

"Don't go there again," he said. "It's a wonder a gang

fight didn't break out. If you must go, then call George or me. Preferably me." He paused. "Promise."

She bit her lip. "Promise."

He raked his hand through his hair. "I really want you to think about quitting. I'll take care of all your expenses, your debts."

Tempting, but she knew she'd better wait. He could change his mind and she'd not only have her sisters' college expenses and Tami's medical bills, she'd also be out of a job. "I'm not ready to quit yet, but thanks for the offer," she said and he kissed her. The strength of his body and personality quickly slid past her defenses. Had there ever been a time when she could let go and rely on someone else? Count on someone else? In every possible way?

"You feel so good," she said, sliding her hands over his chest and up to his shoulders. She sank against him and sighed against his mouth.

She felt him slide his fingers through her hair and tilt her head to give him better access. He kissed her deeply as if he were making his mark on her, possessing her. "I don't want you going to dangerous places."

"I've lived in Philly for a while. I'm not a complete novice," she said as he slid his mouth over her throat.

"But you haven't been married to Leo Grant. That changes things," he said.

She pulled back slightly. "What do you mean?"

"I mean it's possible that someone would want to take advantage of you because you're my wife," he said bluntly. "I won't let that happen. I refuse to be taken advantage of."

She felt a chill run through her at his cold-as-ice tone. "I don't understand what you're saying."

"I'm saying I've never had a wife before. Never had

anyone at risk. I've had my security detail on call for you, but in the future, I'll make sure they're always close by."

She frowned. "Close by?"

"Don't worry. You won't notice them. They'll just be available anytime you need them."

Calista didn't like the idea of being watched every minute. "I can't believe I would draw that much attention. I don't need that kind of supervision."

"It's not supervision," he said. "It's security. You're my wife. It's my job to take care of you."

She stared into his eyes, feeling a passion as deep as her bones. It struck her in her heart. "I'm not used to someone watching over me."

"Get used to it," he said and lowered his mouth to hers. "You're mine now."

He made love to her, rendering her speechless and nearly mindless. In the back of her mind, though, she remembered that she needed to get answers from him. After the glow of climax, she curled against him, still breathless. "I don't know your birthday," she whispered.

He swore. "Why do you need to know?"

"So I can bake you a birthday cake," she said.

He chuckled. "November 3," he said.

"What year?" she asked.

"I'm thirty-two. Why are you asking me this now?" he asked, pulling her naked body against his hard naked one.

"Because I want to know more," she said. "How old were you when you were in the accident?"

He stilled. "Why do you ask?"

Her heart hammered at his still, emotionless tone. "Because that was a big event in your life. As your wife, it's important for me to know the good and the bad things in your past."

He took a deep breath. "I was eight years old. I don't remember anything before or during the accident," he said, breathing heavily in the darkness of the room. "I hate it that I can't remember."

Her heart twisted at his words. "Maybe it's best that you don't," she said. "Maybe it's too painful."

"I would rather have a painful memory than no memory," he said and rolled onto his side, facing away from her.

Deep pain emanated from him. She felt it in her heart, in her pores, and her stomach twisted at the power of it. Confusion twisted through her. How could she feel such empathy for a man who'd had a part in her family's destruction? How could she feel such a connection to him?

She fought it for several moments, but she couldn't stop her arm from folding over his chest and sliding closer against him, her breasts pressed against his back. She felt his heavy sigh. Did she have that much of an effect on him? Did she bring him a little peace? Calista marveled at the thought, at the possibility of such power. It couldn't be true, she thought. It couldn't.

The following morning, George met him outside the condo building. "Good morning. How is Mrs. Grant?" George asked.

"Fine, this morning," he said and climbed into the back seat of his Town Car.

"I can't imagine what clients would want to meet her at the place she went last night," George said, his disapproval evident as he drove down the one-way street.

"I have no reason to believe she wasn't meeting clients.

She said they'd heard The Mark was an authentic Philly landmark," Leo said.

"For gangs," George said.

"She didn't seem to enjoy her time at The Mark," Leo said.

George paused a long moment. "True," he finally conceded. "What are you going to do about it?"

"About what?" Leo asked.

"About her security," George said.

"I'm going to assign a guard to her, but I'm going to tell him to stay on the down low," he said. "I don't want her to feel infringed upon because of her marriage to me," he said.

George gave a rough chuckle. "She'll have to be the dumbest girl in the world not to know that her life would turn upside down because she'd married you."

"She may know that, but I also think she's fighting it," he said.

Silence followed. "Could be," he said. "What are you going to do about it?"

"This is a marriage," Leo said. "It takes time to trust. She will trust me," he said. "And soon."

"But will you trust her?" George asked. "*Can* you trust her?"

"You know I don't trust anyone completely," Leo said. "I've given her your cell number if she ever needs it."

"Okay," George said . "But what if I find out she's doing something you wouldn't like?" he asked.

"Like what?" Leo asked.

"I don't know. Seeing an old boyfriend? Or a new one?"

"She won't," he said, because although he might not have Calista's trust and complete adoration, he knew he had her passion.

* * *

Calista's cell phone began ringing on Monday morning.

"Congratulations," said a distantly familiar voice.

Calista didn't recognize the number. "Excuse me?"

"It's Jennifer," she said. "Your roommate from college. I know we haven't kept in touch as well as we should, but I thought you would call me if you got married."

Calista frowned in confusion. "How did you know I got married?"

"It's in the paper today—a little sidebar in the society section about how Philadelphia's most eligible bachelor has been taken off the market. Aren't you the lucky one? How did you pull this off?" Jennifer asked.

"We met at a charity event," she said, fumbling as she tried to remember how she'd described her relationship to her cousin and sisters. "It was just one of those things where we instantly clicked. I wonder why it just made the paper. We've been married for weeks."

"Did you make an announcement?"

"No," she said and realized that probably wasn't very bridelike. For that matter, she hadn't even told her coworkers. "I've been so busy…" She hesitated. "With Leo," she said with emphasis.

"Well, we must get together for lunch. I want to hear all about this. You were so studious in college. Never took time for dating when you and I roomed together. And now you're married to *Leo Grant*. When can we get together?" Jennifer demanded.

"I don't know," Calista said, reluctant to face Jen's questions. "I'll have to look at my calendar. My work schedule—"

"Work," Jen echoed. "You're not still working, are you?

If I were in your shoes, I would have dumped my job before the ink dried on my marriage license."

A beep interrupted her, signaling another incoming call. "Oops, I'm sorry. I have another call. I need to go."

"Call me back," Jen said.

"Hello?" Calista said, this time recognizing the caller as a member from her elite women's society club.

"You little sneak," Rachel said. "Why didn't you bring your husband to our event last week?"

Calista swallowed a sigh. "We've both been terribly busy," she said.

"But the two of you went to other events together," Rachel complained.

"Those were required of him," she said. "I'm sorry I can't talk now, Rachel. I really need to get back to work."

"Work?" Rachel said. "Why are you working?" She laughed. "Oh, Calista, we should talk. Better yet, why don't you and Leo come over for dinner? Would Friday work?"

Calista blinked. "I need to ask Leo first. He's in so much demand with his company. I try to encourage him to take breaks," she invented. "Thanks for calling though. I'm sure I'll see you soon. Bye now," she said and hung up and turned off her phone. Peace, she thought, breathing a sigh of relief. At the touch of a button.

She heard a knock on her door. Wary because of her previous calls, she rose to answer it. Three of her female coworkers stood there with their faces wreathed in smiles. "Congratulations! We're so excited for you," Susan said.

"I'm sure you've already given notice," Anna said. "Do you know who is going to get your office?"

Calista dropped her jaw. "No, I—"

Hal, her boss, a middle-aged man, approached from behind the three women. He shook his finger at her playfully. "No wonder you wanted all that extra time off. You told me you got married, but you didn't tell me your husband's name."

Calista smiled weakly. "We wanted to keep things quiet."

"Why?" Susan asked. "This is the most exciting news we've had around here in a long time."

Her boss's assistant waved as she approached the group. "There's a journalist from *Philadelphia Magazine* on the phone. She wants to do a feature of you and your new husband. Wouldn't it be great if they put you on the cover?"

Not really, Calista thought. "Would you mind getting her e-mail and asking if I can get back to her? I would obviously have to discuss this with my husband." Even after being married for a month, those words sounded foreign coming out of her mouth.

"When do we get to meet him?" Susan asked. "Do you ever have lunch with him?"

"Don't be silly," Anna said. "You know she's already resigned. Haven't you?"

"No," Calista said. "I haven't. I don't plan to quit."

"Why?" Anna asked.

That same question was thrown at her over and over. Between those questions and the incessant phone calls, Calista was exhausted by the end of the day and she hadn't gotten any work accomplished.

Hal glanced into her office. "Busy day?"

She smiled but knew it was more of a grimace. "Times two," she said. "Don't worry. I'm taking work home, so I won't fall behind."

"I've been wondering if it might be best if you take a leave of absence," he ventured.

"Why?" she asked, her stomach clenching in fear. "I know there was a lot of disruption today, but I'm sure it will blow over quickly."

He shook his head and chuckled. "I think you're underestimating the level of interest people have in your marriage. My assistant was fielding calls for you half the afternoon."

"I'm sorry. I didn't think people would care that much. I'm sure it will get better," she said. "Please don't let me go."

"I'm not firing you," Hal said. "I just think it would be in the company's best interest and yours for you to take some time to get your ducks in a row about all this. And who knows? After you're off for a little while, you may decide you like it."

Panic rose inside her. "I really want to keep this job."

"I hear you. That's what you want now, but it could change. At least, take tomorrow and think about a short leave." His lips twitched. "You're a newlywed. Enjoy the moment."

Calista fought the terrible urge to cry. Before now, she'd been able to keep her marriage under the radar. Now that the news had exploded, it seemed like that was all anyone wanted to talk about with her. It was hard enough to fake her commitment to Leo and herself. With everyone gushing congratulations, best wishes and curiosity, all she wanted to do was scream that the marriage was temporary, so it wasn't necessary to get all worked up over it.

* * *

Leo walked through the door of his penthouse after going a round with George in the boxing ring down the block. The former pro hadn't cut him any slack either. He would be wearing a nice bruise on his jaw tomorrow.

His housekeeper met him at the door. "Good evening, Mr. Grant. Welcome home. What can I get for you?"

"Bag of frozen peas, please," he said.

He watched her eyes glint with a combination of humor and sympathy. "George was feeling his oats?"

He nodded. "He won't be feeling them tomorrow, though," he said. "I got one of his ribs pretty good after he blasted my jaw. Is Calista around?"

"Yes, sir. She went to the fitness room a little over an hour ago," she said.

"I'll look in on her," he said, barely waiting a moment before Brenda returned with the bag of peas. Immediately applying it to his jaw, he walked to the fitness room and saw Calista pacing from one end of the room to the other with a frown on her face.

"Bad day?" he asked.

Her head shot up and she met his gaze, not smiling. "It could have been better. It started out with my car getting towed from the parking lot of The Mark even though they wouldn't let me get to it last night."

"Did you call George?"

"No. I picked it up myself after work, which brings me to another subject," she said.

Irritation trickled through him. "I told you to call George if you needed help."

"Trust me. Picking up my car was cake compared to the rest of my day. Did you happen to see the newspaper this morning?"

Realization shot through him. "Oh, the little piece in the *Inquirer*. My assistant told me about it. I don't usually read the social column."

"How many calls did you get about it?"

He shrugged. "I don't know. My assistant screens my calls, and he knows I like my privacy."

"I could have used that kind of assistant today," she muttered.

"Do you want one?" he asked.

"No," she wailed. "I just don't want all these people calling me. My boss even suggested I take a leave of absence."

"I don't suppose this is a good time to say Hoo-rah," he said.

She shot him a dark look. "It isn't. For the most part, our relationship has been between you and me. We went out in public those few times last week, but I had no idea people would be so interested."

He shrugged. "People are interested in anything that involves money."

"I'd like to say that I disagree, but I can't," she said.

"What are you going to do?" he asked.

"I don't know," she said. "It was really disruptive at work today."

"So leave," he said. "Let me take care of your bills. They can't be that bad."

He watched her stiffen in response.

"I'm accustomed to taking care of myself," she said.

"You can take care of yourself, but it's not necessary to take care of your bills. I have more than enough to do that. I wish you wouldn't slam your head into the wall about it," he said.

"Easy for you to say. I guess this means I can make the India trip with no problem," she said.

"I've put that off. The son of the man I'm dealing with is getting married. His father is distracted," Leo said.

"Oh," she said.

"Yeah, oh," he said, extending his hand. "What's it going to take for you to relax?"

She lifted her chin, and he was drawn to the pride she took in herself and her choices. "What's it going to take for *you* to relax?"

He gave a low, dirty chuckle. "Never gonna happen," he said and pulled her against him. "But I'll cover you. Relax."

For a second, she looked as if she believed him, but then her eyes flickered. "You need to remember that I try not to count on anyone."

"I'm different," he said and pressed his mouth against hers.

"I'm starting to think you are," she whispered.

Her body felt delicious against his. She would feel even more delicious when he was sinking inside her. "I'll take care of you."

"I don't expect you to," she protested.

"Let me," he said, pulling her off her feet and into his arms. "Let me." He carried her into the master bath and made love to her.

Eight

Calista awakened each day the next week feeling a surge of panic. She should be working. She shouldn't relax. She needed to be earning money because, after all, her marriage to Leo could end before the six-month mark if he found out the truth about her. If that happened, she would be out of a job and her sisters would be without the funds for their education.

Calista cleaned their suite, then searched for things to do. Leo's housekeeper, Brenda, repeatedly approached her. "What can I do for you?" she asked. "How can I help you? You seem troubled."

"I'm unaccustomed to not working," Calista told her. "I don't know what to do with myself."

Brenda laughed in sympathy. "You're the only woman I know who has trouble relaxing."

"I feel like I should be doing something," Calista said.

"You are," Brenda said. "You're Mr. Grant's wife."

Calista tamped down another surge of panic. "I guess," she whispered.

"You need to let me do my job so you can do yours," Brenda said.

When Leo arrived home that evening, Calista laced and unlaced her fingers. "How was your day?" she asked, but her mind refused to let her listen to his answer.

Leo snapped his fingers in front of her face. "Calista. Earth to Calista."

"Sorry," she said. "My lack of a job is driving me insane."

His lips twitched. "Then spend more time volunteering."

She took a sip of wine and thought for a long moment. "Hmm."

He lifted his eyebrows in enquiry.

"The dog shelter—" She broke off. "That's it. I'll spend more time at the dog shelter. Thank you for the suggestion."

He swallowed a chuckle. "Glad I could help."

Two days later, she brought home a dog of indeterminate breeding. He could have been part bulldog and retriever or part Lab and cocker. The good news was that he was neutered. The bad news was that he was a puppy and liked to dig. She named him Pooh.

"Pooh?" Leo echoed in dismay, staring at the ugliest dog he'd ever seen. "But he's a dog."

"I didn't know what else to call him, so I decided to name him after my favorite Winnie-the-Pooh animal," she said, rubbing the puppy.

"But Pooh is a bear," he said.

"It's actually a compliment. Pooh is an animal with a big heart and big courage," she said earnestly.

"That's still weird as hell," he said, feeling a strange tug toward the animal. An overwhelming sense of longing twisted through him. He'd never had a pet when he'd lived with Clyde and Lilah, but he had a strange feeling that he'd had pets before. It was odd as hell.

"Does he have his shots? Does he have a leash?"

She lifted the leash and smiled. "I would have sworn you wouldn't be the least bit concerned about a dog."

"I wonder if he can catch a Frisbee."

She snickered. "Agility trials, here we come."

He met her gaze. "I have to help him overcome his name."

That night, they taught Pooh to catch a tennis ball in his mouth. Or Pooh just knew how to catch a tennis ball in his mouth.

Calista laughed in exhilaration beside him. "He's so fun."

"Yeah," Leo said and tossed another ball into the air in the game room.

Pooh chased it, catching it in his mouth. The dog had feel-sorry-for-me brown eyes combined with a panting doggy smile and ears that swung from side to side.

"We need to take him to the lake," he said.

"Or a dog park," she said.

He wrinkled his nose. "We can go to my estate just out of town."

"It will be a hassle for you to drive into town," she said.

"Not with the helicopter," he said.

She looked at him and smiled, her eyes sexy and challenging. "That's an awful lot of trouble just for a dog."

He gave a heavy put-upon sigh. "Since you've already committed us, we have to do the right thing."

She clutched his collar and pulled him against her. "You're a sucker," she whispered.

"Only when I want to be," he warned her.

"I like that about you," she said and pressed her mouth against his.

A week later, Rob called her. "I have info."

"What kind of info?" she asked.

"Important info. You gotta buy me a drink for this," he said. "You gotta buy me a lot of drinks. Meet me at The Mark," he said.

"No way," she said. "The last time I was there, the police raided the place, there was a fire and my car was impounded. Pick somewhere else."

"Man, you've gotten snooty since you married a gajillionaire," he said.

"Be reasonable," she said.

"Okay, you want snooty. How about the top of the Liberty Hotel?" he asked.

She bit her lip. "You don't know the meaning of the word discreet, do you?"

"You didn't want The Mark. This one's on you. Meet me tonight at six," he said and hung up.

Calista stared at her cell phone and scowled. How could she explain her absence from dinner? How could she explain her need to be away at that particular time? She sighed, but was determined to get answers. She would tell Leo's assistant that she wouldn't meet him for dinner tonight because she was shopping.

She went to the bar and waited. Ordering water, she waited and waited. She dialed Rob's number, but there was no answer. She waited for another hour then left.

Calista drove home because she didn't want George to know where she'd been. She swept inside the house and Pooh raced toward her, jumping up on her. The dog was a salve to her guilt. She rubbed Pooh's face.

"How was your shopping?" Leo asked, strolling toward her.

"Good," she said. "Good. How was your day?" she asked deflecting his question.

"Busy, as usual. Where are your dresses?" he asked.

She panicked for a few seconds. "They need to be altered."

He gave a slow nod. "Okay."

"Yes." She rubbed behind Pooh's ears. "How much trouble has he caused?"

"No more than you," he said.

She made a face at him. "I turned down three more invitations to dinner and sent regrets for more charity events. I unblocked your assistant, and he sent me a text message today that since we're not giving interviews we should make an appearance at something. Do you have a preference?"

"Something where we can leave early," he said.

She laughed at his dry tone. "Okay, I think my women's society club is holding a summer soiree scavenger party soon. I initially sent regrets, but the organizer keeps calling."

"Scavenger party?" he asked.

"It's creative," she said defensively.

He paused a half beat. "Can't deny that. Call your friend and confirm."

"There's also a Saturday Expand-my-brain volunteer workshop for people of all ages in a few weeks. They want people with all kinds of skills," she said.

"I have no idea how I could help in that situation," he said.

She smiled. "You underestimate yourself."

That night, he made love to her with more passion than he had before. He consumed her from head to toe, making her sated, but still hungry. When he finally sank inside her, she quivered around him, milking him with her wet, feminine secrets until he shot to the top.

For all the times he'd taken her, he still didn't feel married to her. He felt an incredible connection to her, yet, at the same time still separate. Being with her conjured up feelings he didn't understand, feelings he wasn't sure he wanted. She panted the same way he did. Her breath mingled with his.

"That was pretty amazing," she said, sliding her hands down his arms and searching his face. "What—"

"You," he said, "inspire me."

Her mouth curved into a smile. "Who? Me?"

"Yeah," he said, sliding off of her and pulling her against him. "You."

Within minutes, he drifted off to sleep. Visions drifted through his mind. He saw a dog with a wagging tail, little boys with dark hair and dark eyes. A woman scolded him. A man laughed, his joy evident.

He and the other boys ran to the dinner table. He beat one of the older ones and sat down to a plate of lasagna. The aroma of beef and sausage made his stomach growl. He took a bite. It was the richest, most delicious pasta dish he'd ever tasted.

"Leo, slow down. You'll make yourself sick," the woman said.

The man laughed again. "Don't worry. The boy has an appetite. Hunger is a good thing."

Leo woke up in a cold sweat. He sat straight up, panting, trying to make sense of his dream. The images tumbled through him again. He felt a hand on his arm. Calista's.

"What is it?" she asked in a groggy voice. "What's wrong?"

"Nothing," he said. "A strange dream."

"Hmm," she said. "A nightmare?"

"No," he said. "Just a dream." But he wondered because it had seemed so real, so very real. He slowly laid back down and took several deep breaths. Forcing his eyes closed, he saw the images he'd glimpsed earlier. He wondered if they were real or if they were wishes. Or if they held clues to his life before Clyde and Lilah.

Family? A father and mother? Brothers? Was it possible?

On Saturday, Calista dressed in jeans and a blouse to attend the expand-my-brain volunteer workshop. She found Leo, who had risen hours earlier, in his home office. For just a second she watched him, allowing her mind to play with the idea that he was her husband. If there'd been no ugly past between them, she wondered what would have happened between them, what could have happened. Her stomach twisted and she shook off her thoughts. She couldn't undo the past. "Are you ready to expand some brains?"

He flashed her a doubtful look. "I'm not sure I'm the best man for this job."

"Of course you are," she said. "You're smart. You're successful. What's not to like?"

"You weren't completely clear about what we'll be doing," he said.

"It could be anything from reading a book with a young child to helping with math. It won't be brain surgery," she said, although Calista was certain Leo was intelligent enough that he could have been a brain surgeon if that was what he'd wanted.

"I may not be the best example for young children," he said in a stilted voice.

"Why?" she asked, even though she knew he'd tricked dozens of people and made money off of it. "It's not as if you're a crook," she said.

His eyes barely flickered. "No, but there's always my misspent youth."

"Hmm," she said, feeling her anger shoot out of nowhere. So that was how he described it. His misspent youth. She took a quick breath and counted to ten to keep from saying what she really thought. "Nobody's perfect. You have a lot to offer."

His mouth lifted in a half smile as his gaze fell over her possessively. "Are you speaking from experience?"

Her mind slammed back to visuals of their heated lovemaking and she bit her lip, bothered by the way her feelings for him seemed to jerk from one end of the spectrum to the other. "An observation," she said.

He turned off his laptop and stood. "Okay, but I can only stay for an hour or so."

Forty-five minutes later, Calista helped an elementary-age girl named Kelly with division while a crowd formed around Leo. She assisted Kelly until the little girl's attention waned and her mother collected her. Curious about what Leo was discussing, she joined his class.

"Whenever you're selling anything to someone, including yourself, you have to find out what the buyer wants. What does the buyer need? Your job is to give him what he needs."

"What if you don't have it?" a young man asked.

"Then you tell him where he can get what he wants, or prove that your product is the answer to his problems. The biggest part of sales is listening to the buyer and helping him see that you're part of his solution. How many times have you gone into a store and asked for help only to have a salesman take you to the most expensive model of whatever you're looking for instead of asking you questions about what you want and need?"

"But I just sell candy for my community group," a little boy said.

"Then you sell the experience of being a part of making the world better by buying one of your candy bars. Be what your buyer is looking for—a clean, well-mannered young man," Leo said. "Same thing when you're looking for a job. Do your research. Find out as much as you can about the company where you're applying. Be prepared. You can learn a lot on the Web. You may even find out something about the person who will interview you."

"What if I ain't got no Internet?" another young man asked.

Calista watched Leo, wondering if this question would stump him. He looked so magnetic, so self-assured. She wondered if anyone ever succeeded in making him feel self-conscious.

"The library has Internet," he said. "All for now. Good luck with your future sales."

She saw the crowd, both adults and children, push toward him. Everyone seemed to want to shake his hand. It was almost as if they hoped his magic would wipe off on them. She wondered if he'd learned his selling technique from his father. A bitter taste filled her mouth. He'd certainly sold her father down the river. Yet, even now she could tell that he wasn't all evil. He appeared as if he sincerely wanted success for each person with whom he spoke. Was appearance the operative word? Underneath it all, what was he really thinking?

He glanced up and searched the crowd, his gaze landing on her. She felt a frisson of excitement at being singled out by him. Yes, the rest of the world knew she was his wife. But she knew the truth. He didn't love her and she needed something from him. Nodding in her direction, he walked toward her.

"Let's go," he said and slid his hand to her back as he guided her to the Town Car.

"What is it?" she asked. "They loved you. They were hanging on your every word."

His body was tense, his mouth taut. "Maybe. They hear what they want to hear."

"What do you mean?" she asked as he opened the door to the car and followed her inside.

"Home," he said to George.

"Which one, sir?" George asked.

"Out of the city," Leo said.

She studied his face and instinctively lifted her hand to his clenched jaw. "Why are you so upset?"

He caught her hand just before she touched him. "I'm not upset. " He shrugged, his eyes dark and full of tempestuous emotion. "Seeing them reminded me... It brought back memories."

"Of what?" she asked.

He narrowed his eyes and shrugged again. "Nothing I want to remember."

She felt a strange twinge of compassion at odds with her wall of defense against him. "You gave them hope."

His mouth twisted cynically. "That's what I was selling."

"You don't believe there's any hope?"

"I believe in hard work, good timing and good luck," he said. "It's not easy being poor and wanting a better life."

"No, but what you told them is true. Selling a product, selling yourself, is a life skill. Don't you believe that? Or were you just telling them what they wanted to hear?"

"No," he said. "I gave that up."

She lifted her eyebrows at his revelation. "When?"

"Shortly after my time in the egg," he said.

"But you still used your sales techniques," she said.

"Yes. I found out what the buyer wanted, but I also found out that people believe what they want to believe. Some are harder to read than others." He lifted his finger to her lips. "Like you. What do you want to believe, Calista? What do you want to believe about me?"

Her heart pounded at the intent way he looked at her. She feared he could almost read her mind. She swallowed hard over the sensation of her emotions wrapping around her windpipe and squeezing. "I want to—" She broke off. "I believe that you're a powerful, charismatic man. I believe some part of you wants a family," she added impulsively.

He lifted his eyebrows. "Is that what you believe or what you want to believe?"

Her thoughts whipped through her mind. She wanted to believe that he was a bad person and that she should feel no guilt about marrying him for his money. She wanted to believe that she couldn't have feelings for him because he'd been part of her father's downfall. "I don't believe that humans are hatched. Humans are born and want and need to be loved."

His eyes bored into hers. "A word of caution. Don't overestimate my emotional needs. I've spent a lifetime learning to live without. I'm not going to start now."

His statement made her blood run cold. "Are you saying you have no real feelings for me?" she asked. "If that's true, then why did you marry me? Oh, wait, you wanted a wife to make your business deals go through more smoothly. So why me? Other than the fact that I was convenient."

"I told you that you fascinated me."

"And you thought I could be an asset," she said, digging into the dirty truth as much for herself as for him. She had to find a way to keep him from getting to her.

"Yes, but many women could be an asset."

"So all women are interchangeable?" she asked.

"I didn't say that. I told you that you fascinated me. I couldn't get enough of you," he said, pulling her against him. "I still can't."

Her breath squeezed tight from her lungs again. "You don't have an emotional attachment to me and you never plan to. What do you expect of me?"

"Everything," he said. "Your mind, your body. Everything."

She gasped. "That's ridiculous, and it's not fair."

"I never said anything about being fair."

That night, he made love to her, consuming every inch of her, wringing a response from her that surprised even her. When she awakened in the morning, Calista felt like a prostitute. What was she selling in order to secure her sisters' future?

Feeling suffocated by her feelings and her fake marriage, she took Pooh and drove to visit her sisters. With each mile she put between her and Leo, she breathed a little easier.

She brought a picnic lunch to share with her sisters and cousin's family on the back porch.

"Best picnic food I've ever had," Sharon said afterward when the girls and Justin adjourned to play a video game.

"Leo's chef prepared it. He's amazing," she said.

"But of course. The great Leo would have nothing less than amazing, including his wife," Sharon teased.

"I'm not amazing, but I get the job done," she said cryptically.

Sharon stared at her and blinked. "What do you mean by that?"

Calista waved her hand. "Oh, nothing. I was just joking."

"How are things going with the newlyweds?" her cousin asked.

"Good," Calista said. "Great. Being Mrs. Leo Grant means I have a full-time job of turning down social invitations, so I quit my job."

Silence followed. "You don't sound happy about it."

Calista laughed to cover her discomfort. "Of course, I'm happy. I can become a lady of leisure now. What could be better?"

"If you say so," her cousin said.

"I do," Calista said. "How is Tami doing?"

Her cousin lifted crossed fingers. "I'm hoping better. She's still hanging out with a crowd I don't like, but she's been getting home on time. I worry now, but she'll be leaving for college in the fall and I won't be able to do a thing."

"I'm so lucky you worry about her. I do, too. If anything changes and you need help, let me know. Now that I'm not working, I can be down here in no time."

"Thanks for the offer, but I *think* I have it under control." Sharon glanced around. "Where'd your puppy go?"

"Oh, no," Calista said, a spurt of anxiousness driving her to her feet. "Pooh likes to chew. We better find him."

Minutes later, they found him in the kitchen, his head in the trash can. "Pooh! Stop!" Calista said, pulling on the dog's collar. "I'm sorry."

Sharon giggled. "No big deal. At least he didn't make a mess."

"Good point," Calista said. "I should probably head back now." She gave Sharon a hug. "Let me say goodbye to the rest of the crew."

She embraced her sisters, and her cousin's husband and son. As soon as she got into her car, Sharon's words weighed heavily on her. Was it so obvious to others that she was unhappy?

Pooh panted beside her, making a whining sound.

"What's wrong?" she said, patting the dog. "Did you find something in that trash can that didn't agree with you? Serves you right for being a naughty dog."

Pooh continued to pant, standing then sitting, standing again and whining.

"Sit down and rest," she said. "We'll be home before you realize it."

At that moment, Pooh got sick. Distressed, Calista pulled off on the side of the road and cleaned up as best as she could. She put Pooh outside and waited while the dog got ill again. After several moments, she put the dog back into the car and drove to Leo's home.

She called her cousin. "I hate to bother you, but could

you tell me what was in your kitchen garbage can? Pooh is sick."

"Oh, no. I can't think of anything that should bother him. Let me see, there was an empty can of tomato sauce, an empty carton of orange juice. I threw out some old grapes—"

Calista's heart sank. "Grapes, that's it. They're toxic to dogs."

"Oh, I'm so sorry, Calista."

"I need to get him to a vet. I'll call you later," she said and pulled in front of the house.

She ran inside and Meg, the housekeeper, greeted her. "Mrs. Grant, welcome—"

"Excuse me, I need to find a vet," she said. "The one I regularly use is downtown. Pooh is sick. He needs immediate treatment."

Meg shot her a blank look. "I'm sorry. I don't know of a vet. I—"

"I'll check my phone," she said, panicked. "We need an emergency animal hospital. Damn this is slow." While she waited, Meg brought her the yellow pages. Calista grabbed the book and ran toward the door.

"Where shall I tell Mr. Grant you are going?"

"Emergency vet," she called over her shoulder and rushed to her car. Before she could open the door, however, she heard footsteps behind her. She glanced back and saw Leo. "I just talked to Meg. What's the problem?"

Calista felt a twinge of relief at the sight of him. "He's sick from eating grapes out of my cousin's garbage. They're toxic to dogs."

Leo shook his head. "I didn't know that. Let's get him to the emergency vet."

"But I don't know where," she said.

"I do. George gave me a tip just before I headed out the door. Give me your keys. I'll drive."

Calista petted the dog as she sped on her way. Pooh's breathing was shallow and his eyes were closed. Even though she hadn't had the dog very long, Pooh had brought her enormous comfort during the last two weeks. She was devastated at the thought of losing the animal.

Leo spun into the graveled parking lot of the vet hospital and Calista carried Pooh inside. "He's had grapes," she said to the receptionist.

Within twenty minutes, the vet was working on the dog. Calista wrung her hands as she was instructed to wait outside. Wrapping her arms around herself, she fought tears as she paced. She felt like such a terrible owner. She'd barely had the dog two weeks and look what had happened.

Leo put his arms around her and the gesture undid her. She burst into tears. "Oh, Leo. I didn't think much of him getting into the trash until he got sick on the way home. I feel so awful," she said. "And he's been such a good little dog. He didn't deserve to have me practically kill him."

"You didn't kill him," he said, stroking her hair. "And you don't know how it's going to turn out."

"I should have been watching."

"Stop blaming yourself. Maybe he'll be okay," he said.

Perhaps it was crazy for her to cling to him, but she had no desire to resist. Leo might not admit it, but he was attached to the dog, too. Pooh was something that had drawn them together. She could laugh and forget about all her complicated resentment and desire for him. He could relax and enjoy a pet. She suspected he hadn't had a pet for a long, long time, if ever.

Seconds later, an assistant appeared. "Dr. Keller has him stabilized if you would like to see Pooh."

The middle-aged balding man with the sympathetic face extended his hand to Leo and Calista. "You did a good job getting him here so quickly. I think he'll recover."

Relief coursed through her and she swallowed a sob. "Thank you," she said. "I feel so terrible."

The vet shook his heard. "These things happen. He's lucky you got him here so quickly. We'll keep him overnight."

"Will someone be here to watch over him?" Leo asked.

"Of course," the vet said.

Leo nodded. "Here's my cell number," he said, handing the doctor a card. "Call me for any reason." He led Calista from the building to the car and opened the passenger door for her.

"I'm sorry I was such a sap," she said, sinking into the seat. "I'm usually more pulled together."

"People get attached to animals," he said, pulling out of the parking lot. "Unfortunately when you get a pet, you set yourself up for loss."

Calista blinked at his assessment. "If that's the way you think, then why did you act like you liked Pooh too?"

"I wasn't acting," he said, irritated. "I'd have to be an ogre not to like that dog. He's affectionate and playful. I'm just stating a fact. When you get a pet, loss is likely to be part of the equation."

"You say that as if you've had some experience in the area," she said, searching his face.

He frowned and swore under his breath. "None that I can recall," he said.

Calista looked at him and felt a strange shifting inside

her. He was the strongest, most compelling man she'd ever met. For all that strength, though, she sensed a need in him, a need he would likely deny. A need she wanted to fulfill. Where had the urge come from? It would be incredibly dangerous for her to give into her feelings, but she was beginning to wonder if she could stop herself. She felt as if she were walking on a precipice, and keeping the balance was becoming more impossible with each step.

If she were smart, she would turn her head toward the window and continue to play keep-away with her emotions. At the moment, though, she couldn't imagine doing that. She reached across the seat and put her hand on his arm.

He glanced toward her.

"Thank you for going with me," she said. "I could have done it by myself, but having you there made it easier for me. I've had to do most everything on my own since my parents passed away. I'm not used to depending on anyone."

"You're married to me. You can depend on me now," he said.

In the back of her mind, Calista knew she shouldn't, but just for a little while, she decided to allow herself the luxury of pretending that she could.

Nine

"I hope you don't mind, but I really don't feel like a big dinner tonight," Calista said after Leo led her into the house. She liked the feeling of his arms around her too much.

"You've had a rough day. Take a shower. I have a few more calls to make then I'll come upstairs and join you in about an hour," he said. "I'll ask Meg to bring up some sandwiches for us." He dropped a kiss on her forehead. "Go on," he said and gave her a gentle nudge.

Calista took his advice and climbed the stairs to Leo's suite. Instead of taking a shower, though, she gave into the temptation to take a bath. She had an hour after all. While she drew the water in the large, luxurious tub, Meg appeared with a glass of chilled wine. Calista smiled and thanked the woman. A thoughtful gesture from Leo, she suspected. She stripped and stepped into the tub, sinking into the hot water.

Her mind racing between worry for Pooh and concern for her sisters, she turned on the bathroom sound system to Michael Buble. She told herself to stop thinking for just a few minutes. Pooh was in good hands and she was working on her sister's future.

Lifting the glass of wine to her lips, she took a sip and closed her eyes.

"Well this is a sight for sore eyes," Leo said.

Her eyes flashed open at the sound of his voice and she sat up then sank under the water, her wine splashing on her chest. A sound of exasperation bubbled from her throat. "Did you consider knocking?"

"Hell, no," he said, resting one hand on his hip while his other hand held his glass of wine as his gaze seemed to devour her. "It was so quiet in here I wondered if you'd fainted." Moving toward her, he set his wineglass on the side of the tub, and her heart skittered like a stone tossed across a river.

"I obviously haven't," she said, watching as he pulled his shirt over his head and unfastened his slacks. Seconds later, his boxers hit the floor. Had the water grown hotter?

"You don't mind if I join you, do you?" he said more than asked as he stepped into the bath.

"You didn't exactly give me a chance to refuse," she said, trying not to be fascinated by the width of his shoulders and muscular body. His physique was impressive in *every* way.

"No need to thank me yet," he said with a wicked grin as he pushed her into a sitting position and slid behind her.

"Leo," she said. "I thought the objective was for me to calm down."

"You will," he said, skimming his mouth over her bare shoulder.

"How can—"

He held his wineglass to her mouth with the silent instruction for her to take a sip. She did, but she didn't feel one bit more calm. "I don't see—"

He slid her slightly to the side and tilted her head upward. "Trust me," he said and lowered his mouth to hers.

Trust him? How could she possibly? He slid both their bodies deeper into the water. She barely noticed the sound of him placing the wineglass on the side of the tub. His kiss was so compelling. A half-breath later, she felt his hand on her skin, skimming down to her breasts. The combination of the warm water, his seductive touch and the sensation of her back against his body sent every thought but him from her mind. He taunted her nipples at the same time as he drew her tongue deeply into his mouth.

She tried to roll over to face him, but he pulled back, shaking his head. "Uh-uh, not now."

Calista frowned, but his hand traveled down, further down between her legs and he found where she was already swollen and sensitive. She gasped against his mouth and he kissed her again. She felt his strength beneath her, his obvious arousal against her, as he kissed her and played with her sending her into the stratosphere. His caresses made her breathless, mindless. Her climax racked through her from head to toe. "Oh, Leo," she whispered.

"Now, you can turn over," he said.

She rolled over and covered his lips with her fingers. "No, now I want you to stand up."

He frowned, his eyes glittering with desire. "Why?"

"Just do it," she whispered.

Sighing heavily, he stood, the water coursing down his strong thighs, his erection jutting proudly. Still weak from the way he affected her, she rose to her knees and skimmed her hands up his thighs to cup him.

He let out a sigh of utter sexual frustration.

Holding his gaze, Calista lifted her lips and took him intimately into her mouth.

He said things that sounded like a combination of curses and longing. He wrapped his fingers in her hair and shook his head, drawing her head away from him. "Enough," he muttered.

Heedless of their wet skin, he picked her up and carried her into the bedroom, laying her on the bed, immediately following her down. "Hold on," he said. "I have to have you."

He took her in one sure thrust. She gazed into his dark eyes and the power she saw there made her feel as if she should look away. She felt as if he were taking more than her body. He was taking her soul.

When Calista awakened the next morning, she felt exhausted. Leo had made love to her several times during the night. She peeked through her fingers and saw that he was gone. She felt a twinge of disappointment, but told herself not to be surprised. Leo was almost always gone in the morning. A terrible loneliness sank inside her.

Growling in frustration, she threw off the covers and rose from the bed. "This is ridiculous," she muttered. "Lying in bed like some pitiful, sappy, helpless woman in love. I'm not helpless and I'm not in love," she told herself and glanced into the bathroom mirror. She'd made a plan, and she was working the plan.

The woman in the reflection, however, told a different

story. Calista lifted her fingers to her swollen lips. Her skin was pale, her eyes bloodshot, her hair a tumbled telltale tangle. Worse yet, the expression in her eyes was full of sadness and longing.

Unable to bear the sight of her naked emotions, she closed her eyes and turned away, taking a deep breath. She turned on the jets to the shower, determined to wash her vulnerability down the drain.

"Calista," Leo said from the doorway.

She jumped at the sound of his voice, wishing she was dressed. Instead, she crossed her arms over her chest in a feeble attempt to cover herself. "I thought you'd left."

"Almost," he said and offered her a steaming cup of coffee. "I waited to talk to the vet. They want to keep Pooh one more night."

Concern rushed through her as she accepted the coffee. "Did something happen? Did his condition worsen?"

He shook his head. "No, I just told them I want them to make sure he's well. In that case, he said they'd keep him another night on IV support. We should be able to pick him up tomorrow."

"You're sure?" she asked, setting the coffee on a table inside the bathroom.

He shot her a half grin. "Yeah, I'm sure." His gaze fell over her body. "Now, you'd better hop into that shower before I decide I need to distract you like I did last night."

Calista didn't know if her body or her emotions could take it, so she quickly stepped under the spray. She didn't linger, reaching for a towel as soon as she got out of the shower. She lifted the cup of coffee for a quick life-giving sip and noticed it was laced with vanilla and hazelnut. Surprised, she felt her heart take a dip. Leo took his coffee black. He wouldn't come within an inch of her girlie cappuccinos. She wondered if Meg or Leo knew her tastes.

Bombarded with more social invitations since they'd attended the expand-my-brain program on Saturday, Calista sorted out the few possible events she thought might interest Leo. She also talked with her sisters and cousin, reassuring them about Pooh.

Her cousin came back on the line after Calista finished talking to her sisters. "I hate to have to tell you this," she said. "But I'm pretty sure Tami has been smoking again."

Calista's stomach clenched. "But that's terrible for her asthma."

"I know. I've told her the same thing. I'm not sure what to do next. You know that when Fall rolls around, she'll go away to school and neither you nor I will be able to say a thing to her."

Calista sighed. "I'm not liking this," she said. "Not at all. Do you think it would help if she talked to a doctor?"

"I don't know. She's a teenager. It's hard to tell her anything. I'm keeping close tabs on her, though. I've told her I want her to start bringing her friends here instead of going out."

"What does she say to that?"

"She doesn't like it, but I'm not giving her much choice," Sharon said.

"Thanks. I'll think about this. There's got to be a solution," Calista said.

"I just wanted you to know. We'll talk soon," Sharon said.

"Yes, we will. Goodbye."

Calista stewed over the news about her sister after she

disconnected from the phone. Tami should know better. She'd had plenty of frightening asthmatic episodes.

"Mrs. Grant," Meg said, interrupting her thoughts. "You have a visitor. Mr. Rob Miller."

Calista felt a dart of surprise followed by extreme discomfort. "Oh. Um. He's a business colleague. Last week, he told me he needed to ask me a few questions about my projects. Please show him onto the back porch. I'll be down in just a moment."

Why had Rob shown up here without any warning? Her heart pounded in her chest out of fear. How could she explain him to Leo? Her hands turned clammy and she felt terror chill her to the bone.

Taking a deep breath, she struggled for composure. She would calmly arrange to meet him some other time at some other place. Calista walked from her makeshift office upstairs down to the back porch and closed the door behind her.

Rob turned to greet her. "Nice place," he said.

She bit her lip, but kept her voice low. "What are you doing here? Why didn't you call first?"

"Your cell phone changed. I called your work number and they said you were on extended leave. Hey, if you don't want the information—"

"No, no," she said, her stomach twisting. "What have you learned about Leo?"

"It's not just about Leo," he said. "It's about your father."

"What do you mean?" she asked.

"I hate to be the one to tell you, but I think you should know. I also knew you shouldn't see this in a report."

Her heart hammered against her chest in apprehension. "What? What is it?"

He moved closer to her and took her hand, lowering his voice. "Your father didn't die of a heart attack. He committed suicide."

Leo decided to leave the office early. Despite their trip to Japan, he realized he and Calista hadn't had a real honeymoon. Although he couldn't leave his business at the moment, he thought it would be a nice surprise to let her choose the place. Having a wife wasn't such a bad deal after all. Remembering how she'd melted in his arms the night before, he felt a new urgency to be with her again.

Meg greeted him as he walked into the house. "Welcome home, Mr. Grant."

"Thank you, Meg. Do you know where Calista is?"

His housekeeper paused. "She has a visitor. She's talking with him on the back porch."

Him? Leo frowned. He didn't like the sound of that. He walked through the house toward the back porch, stopping suddenly when he spotted Calista in another man's arms. His stomach gave a vicious, sickening twist. The man caressed her back as she clung to him.

Who the hell was this? What was he doing with her? What was she doing with him? This was his house, damn it.

Taking a sharp breath, he strode to the porch and threw open the door. "Anyone want to tell me what's going on?"

Calista pushed herself from his arms, clearly startled, a guilty expression crossing her face. "Leo?"

"Yes, it's me. Your husband. Introduce me to your—" He paused. "Guest," he said in distaste.

She licked her lips nervously. "This is Rob. He was just leaving."

"It didn't look that way," Leo said, staring the other man down.

The man lifted his hands. "Excuse me. I'll talk to you later," he said to Calista.

She cringed as the man left.

"You want to explain what I just saw?" Leo asked, clenching his jaw.

She walked toward him. "It's not how it seemed."

"Then how was it?"

"It's hard to explain," she said.

"I'll bet. How long have you been involved with him?"

"It's not like that," she said. "I swear."

"Then why were you in each other's arms?"

She closed her eyes for a second then took a deep breath. "He's a private investigator. He just told me that my father didn't die of a heart attack. He committed suicide. I never knew," she said in a broken voice.

"If he's a P.I., then why the hell was he holding you in his arms?"

"I've known him for a while. He's a friend."

"Just a friend?" Leo asked, full of doubt.

"Yes," she insisted. "You have to believe me."

"No. I don't," he said, suspicion trickling through him like acid.

Fear and dread darkened her gaze. "Leo, you have to believe I would never sacrifice our marriage for a stupid affair."

"Why not?" he asked, challenging her. How foolish he'd been, he thought. He'd actually been on the verge of trusting her.

She bit her lip. "I wouldn't. I couldn't." She closed her eyes. "My marriage to you is too important."

"Because I can give you money," he said, goading her.

She opened her eyes and stared at him in shock. She took a deep breath. "Not for me, but for my sisters," she finally said. "Yes, I need the money for their education and for Tami's health problems."

"Is that why you married me?" he demanded. "To take care of your sisters?"

Her eyes turned cold. "What room do you have to judge? I know you and your father pulled a grifting scheme over on my father. I thought his shame had killed him. It turns out he took his life because of what you and your father did."

Her words hit him like a block of ice. He stared at her in disbelief. "You knew about my father and me?" He shook his head. "Why didn't you just threaten to blackmail me?"

She gave him a blank stare. "Blackmail didn't occur to me. I wanted my sisters to get a good education and I couldn't pay for it. I've been too busy paying off other family debts," she said bitterly.

He laughed, but the sound was hollow to his own ears. "You used me."

She lifted her chin and met his gaze. "The same way you used me so you could get the Japanese account."

"Sweet little Calista," he said in disbelief. "I never would have thought it."

Pain shadowed her eyes. "I never would have done it if I didn't believe it was necessary."

He shook his head. "How long did you plan to keep going with this charade?" he asked.

"Long enough to secure my sisters' future."

"Six months," he said, remembering the prenup.

She crossed her arms over her chest. "So now you see why I wouldn't possibly risk an affair."

"Your sisters," he said.

She nodded. "That and the fact that I'm not the kind of woman to go to bed with one man while I'm married to another."

He gave another humorless chuckle. "I'll never know that for certain. Will I?"

Another shot of pain flashed through her beautiful green eyes. He could almost believe she felt some sense of remorse. Almost. He could pay her and send her away. He could send her away and give her nothing. He knew, however, that he'd had a part in bringing down her father. The bitter reality backed up in his throat. At this second, he detested the very sight of her. But it was as much because she held a mirror to him of his past sins.

"Take my room tonight. I'm going into town."

She blinked in surprise as if she'd expected him to send her away. He wanted to. He wished he could, but something inside stopped him. "You can pick up Pooh in the morning." He turned and walked away.

"Leo," she called after him.

He paused. "What?"

"I—" She broke off. "I didn't expect things to turn out this way."

He walked out the door.

He'd fallen for the biggest con of his lifetime. He'd been so willing to believe her, so determined to protect her. He'd thought she could make him clean, and she had to the outside world. With Calista as his wife, it was easier for people to forget the fact that his past was murky at best. Her presence had greased the wheels for some of his business deals, too.

Leo had a choice to make. He could either cut Calista loose or hold on. He could make her pay for using him. He could make her life miserable, but he wondered if he would be making himself miserable at the same time.

This wasn't a decision to be made in the heat of anger. He needed time and distance.

Calista didn't know what to do. She sure hadn't expected to blurt out her reasons for marrying him. She wasn't sure if she should leave or stay. The thought of her sisters and unexpected feelings for Leo made her stay. He was more than she'd thought he would be. She did everything she could to fall asleep. Exercise, take a bath, drink warm milk.

She went to bed, turned out the lights and her eyelids would not close. Sighing, she turned to her side and forced her eyes closed. Immediately, images of Leo raced through her mind. Leo laughing, Leo concerned about Pooh, Leo making love to her.

A tiny wail squeezed through her throat. What was she supposed to do?

Leo was a successful man, a hard man. Surely, he wasn't capable of being hurt. Surely she couldn't hurt him.

Inhaling deeply, she couldn't tear her thoughts away from him. She felt a connection to him that went deeper than the volatile lovemaking they'd shared. A part of her hated that she'd destroyed the possibility of sharing a future with him. She'd never intended that, she reminded herself. Never.

She closed her eyes again and mentally rocked herself to sleep.

The next morning, Calista picked Pooh up from the veterinary hospital. The dog was groggy, but wagged his tail in welcome. Despite her distraction with Leo, Calista's heart lifted.

"Hello, you naughty, sweetie pie. You scared the daylights out of me. You better not do it again," she scolded the dog.

Pooh just gave a doggy smile and licked her. Calista presented her card for the bill, but the receptionist told her it had already been paid. Leo, she realized. She still didn't understand why he hadn't just thrown her out. After all, he had all the cards since she'd told him the real reason she'd married him.

Her stomach twisted with a strange combination of guilt and loss as she drove to Leo's country home. She spent the day administering medication and TLC to Pooh and wondering what Leo would decide about their marriage. By nightfall, she felt more alone than ever. She took solace in Pooh's presence then went to bed for another mostly sleepless night.

With no word from Leo, she was stuck in limbo. Did he want to end their marriage? She couldn't imagine him wanting to stay with her. In that case, she needed to start searching the job market. Late the following afternoon, Calista's cell phone rang. The caller ID indicated it was her cousin. "Hi Sharon."

"Calista, I have bad news."

"What is it?" Calista asked, turning away from her laptop.

"Tami's been in an accident," she said, her voice quivering.

"Oh, no," Calista said, her heart jumping into her throat. "Is she okay? Is she in the hospital?"

"We're at the hospital right now. She has a few scrapes

and bruises." Sharon paused and lowered her voice. "She was driving drunk."

Calista closed her eyes and shook her head. Guilt rushed through her. Sharon had warned her that Tami had been having trouble, but Calista had buried her head in the sand, hoping that her sister had made a turnaround. "Oh my God."

"I thought she was doing better, but I was obviously wrong. If we could only get her away from that crowd she's been hanging around. And I hate to bring this up, but the ticket and visit to the hospital aren't going to be free."

"No. Of course not. I'll come right away."

"Call me when you get close," Sharon said.

"Will do," she said and turned off her laptop. She grabbed a change of clothes and was torn about telling Leo. Would he even care?

She didn't have time to agonize over it. She typed a text message that would go directly to his BlackBerry then headed downstairs to seek out Meg. "I've had a family emergency, so I need to leave. I'll probably be gone overnight."

Meg's forehead wrinkled in concern. "I'm so sorry."

"Thank you. Could you please watch Pooh while I'm gone?"

"Of course," she said. "I like having the little troublemaker around."

Calista got into her car and pulled out of the driveway. Two minutes later, her phone rang. She picked up. "Hello?"

"It's Leo," he said.

Her heart hammered in her chest at the sound of his voice. "Hi," she said.

"I got your message. What happened? Is Tami hurt?"

A knot formed in her throat. "Not very much physically hurt, but she's done some damage. She was driving my cousin's car and ran into a traffic sign. Unfortunately she was also drunk."

Leo swore.

"Yes," she said in agreement. "Sharon had said she was hanging around a bad crowd, and she'd thought the problem was solved by giving Tami an earlier curfew. I guess now we know that didn't work." She squeezed the steering wheel. "I'm worried about her."

Silence followed. "Maybe you should bring her to the house," he said.

Surprised, Calista blinked. "Uh," she said and cleared her throat. "I wasn't sure *I* should expect to stay at your house."

"I never told you to leave," he said.

"No, but you left," she said. "And I can't blame you after I told you—"

"We'll talk about that later. For now, you need to concentrate on Tami. If you bring her here to stay for a while, she'll have a chance to leave her mistakes in the past and refocus."

"Why would you offer your house to my sister?"

"There may have been a time when I shirked responsibility, but not now," he said in a rock-hard tone.

"You're sure?" she asked, fighting a combination of shock and relief.

"I wouldn't have said it if I weren't. Keep me updated," he said.

"Okay," she said. "Leo, thank—"

"Don't," he cut in. "Drive safely."

* * *

The following evening after Calista helped Tami get settled into a bedroom, Leo sipped a glass of whiskey in his suite as he waited for her. His pride had been stung when he'd learned she'd tricked him for money. After he'd taken time to cool down, however, he could only blame Calista so much. So far, she'd been reluctant to spend a dime of his money. He'd noticed she still paid her own bills from her own checking account. Another woman would have gone hog wild, buying everything in sight.

He also felt somewhat responsible for Calista and her sisters' predicament. He felt more than a twinge of guilt despite the fact that Calista's father had been weak. Like many fools, he'd believed what he wanted to believe. A man like that, with a devoted wife and children, didn't understand what he had.

The bedroom door opened and Calista appeared. She met his gaze solemnly. "Hi."

"Hi,' he said and waved to the chair beside him. "Have a seat."

She walked to the chair and sank into it. A glass of white wine sat on the table waiting for her. She took a sip then set it down. She looked tired, he noted.

"How is Tami?" he asked.

"She's trying to be tough, but she took a stuffed animal to bed with her," she said.

His lips twitched in humor. "Has she said anything?"

"Not much, and that's unusual. She did say she was sorry," she said.

"That's a good start. Realizing you did something wrong is the beginning of being different," he said and took another sip of whiskey. "I should know."

She met his gaze again. "Is that how it happened for you?"

"My so-called adoptive father beat me. He also threatened to beat my adoptive mother. He was manipulative. He trained me to lie, play games and exploit."

She bit her lip. "But you're not like that anymore, are you?"

He shrugged. "Everyone can be manipulative," he said and shot her a pointed look.

She glanced downward. "I can't say I'm innocent in that regard."

"You had good reasons," he said. "I accept that. In a way, I did, too. I was trying to survive. I don't like to be lied to."

"Most of us don't," she said, looking up at him. "Why haven't you kicked me out?"

"Aside from the fact that I still want you," he said and damned if he totally understood why. "It's the right thing to do. Even though my father set up the scheme to trick your father, I benefited from it. You suffered. Your father believed what he wanted to believe instead of the truth."

"He was a good man," she said.

"He may have been a good man, but he was flawed."

"That's a cruel thing to say," she said, her voice choking up.

"It's true."

She glanced away and a faint smile lifted her lips. "He knew how to make us laugh."

"Keep that memory," he told her, wishing he had some of the same kinds of memories.

"What do we do now?" she asked.

"What do you want to do?" he countered.

She fiddled with the stem of her wineglass. "I thought

for sure you'd hate me once I told you I married you to get support for my sisters."

"Do you really think I'm surprised that a woman would marry me for my money?" he asked.

"It's not totally like that," she said, shooting him a look of chagrin.

"Then explain to me how it is," he said, leaning back in his chair.

"I was only going to marry you for six months," she said.

"Ah," he said. "That clause in the prenup."

"Yes, I know it's shameful, but I didn't know how else to provide for Tami and Tina."

"Why didn't you just snag another wealthy man?" he asked. "The first one to come along?"

"Because it didn't seem right," she said. "At least, this way, you were partly responsible for my sisters becoming orphans. I told myself it was a six-month assignment, but the trouble was…" She trailed off and glanced away.

"The trouble was what?" he prompted.

"The trouble was that I liked you," she said with a fierce frown. "And in bed—" She shook her head. "Then you were wonderful about Pooh." She looked perplexed. "And now you're being wonderful about Tami."

He chuckled at her confusion. "Does this mean you want me to go back to your version of Satan?"

She looked at him for a long moment and shook her head. "No," she said softly.

Her expression made his gut knot. He didn't understand it and he sure as hell didn't like it, but he wouldn't ignore it. "You haven't said what you want," he said.

She took a deep breath. "I don't know. I didn't expect you to be like you are. In another situation, I wish you and my father had never met. I wish you and I could have met with no ugly history between us."

"Then let's do that," he said.

She swung her head upward to gape at him. "How?"

"Fresh start. Allow me to introduce myself." He leaned across the table and extended his hand. "I'm Leonardo Grant, your husband."

She stared at his hand for a long moment and paused. She met his gaze. "Hello, Leonardo Grant. I'm Calista French Grant, your wife," she said and slid her hand inside his.

He felt a rocking sense of possession that soared through his blood. "I'm going to want more than six months."

Her eyelids dipped, shielding her expression from him. "Okay."

He stood and tugged her from her chair and pulled her against him. "Starting tonight."

Two mornings later, Leo did his work from his home office. Calista took Pooh in for a checkup and he'd agreed to hang around until she returned. He asked Meg to tell him if and when Tami awakened. Midmorning, his housekeeper tapped at his door.

"She's up, sir," Meg said.

"Thanks. I'll be in the kitchen in a moment." He put his laptop on standby and walked into the kitchen where Tami sat at the bar looking lost.

"Good morning," he said.

She glanced up at him. "Good morning," she returned in a polite but flat tone.

"What do you have planned for today?"

"What can I do? I have no cell phone, no friends," she said.

"You didn't have real friends before," he said.

She crossed her arms over her chest. "You sound like Calista."

"There are worse places, you know," he said, sitting on the stool next to her. "The ghetto, jail."

"Not that you would know," she said.

"Actually I know more than most people would want to know about the ghetto," he said then shrugged. "Did Calista mention that we have horses here?"

"Yes, but I've never ridden."

"Want to learn?" he asked. "Or are you afraid?"

"I'm not afraid," she said. "But who could teach me?"

"That can be arranged," he said. "If you're interested."

"Okay. I'm interested," she said. "Please," she added as if she'd just remembered her manners.

"You have no idea how lucky you are that Calista loves you as much as she does," he told her. "You would be foolish to take that for granted."

Tami's lower lip trembled. "I let her down."

"Yes, you did," he said. "But you still have the opportunity to make her and everyone else who cares about you proud. Including yourself. So why don't you stop pouting and get on with it?"

"How can I? I have no phone, no car," she said.

"Prove you can make good choices. Take an online course and ace it," he said.

"She won't let me near the computer," she said.

"ETR," he said.

Tami frowned. "ETR?" she echoed.

"Earn the right," he said.

"How do I do that?"

"Ask Calista what you can do to help," he said. "What are your favorite pancakes?"

"Blueberry," she said.

"Meg," he called. "Can you please get Miss French some blueberry pancakes?" He walked away to let Tami think about what he'd said. Something told him she would go horseback riding today.

Leo left for a business trip and checked in with Calista several times. He arrived back in town late on Thursday night and headed directly for the shower. After drying off, he went to bed, inhaling her sweet scent as he lifted the covers. In the darkness, he saw the outline of her body and heard her even breathing. He craved the feeling of her naked body against his.

She was asleep, damn it. He would be a caveman to wake her. Closing his eyes, he inhaled deeply. Her scent wafted through him, torturing him.

Suddenly he felt her move and her hand was on his chest. "How did you talk her into horseback riding?" she asked, her breath sliding over his neck.

"I planted the idea," he said.

"Hmm," she said and slid her lips against his jaw. "And the online course?"

"I may have mentioned it," he said.

"I missed you," she whispered.

His heart hammered against his rib cage. "Show me," he told her.

Ten

Calista was relieved that Tami settled into a routine so quickly. Leo had suggested that Tami spend a semester at a local junior college before going away to school. Although Tami was disappointed, she seemed to understand.

Calista's cell phone rang and she glanced at the caller ID, unfamiliar with the number. "Hello?"

"Hi, this is your rock star P.I.," Rob said.

Calista's stomach twisted. "Hi Rob. Thank you for all the information you've sent me. I think I've learned as much as I need to at the moment, so I'll just send you a check."

"Whoa," he said. "You're not blowing me off, are you? Because you should know I've got some amazing new info. It's hot."

"What is it?" she asked reluctantly.

He laughed. "I'm not going to hand it over that easily."

Calista frowned. "What do you mean?"

"I mean now you're in a position to pay me what I deserve, and for this info, I deserve a lot."

Her stomach sank. "I really don't think I need any more information, but what were you planning to charge?"

He named a figure that took her breath away.

"You're crazy," she said. "I don't have that kind of money."

"Give me a break. You're married to the wealthiest man in Philly," he said, his voice full of cynicism.

"That doesn't mean I write checks off his accounts," she said.

Rob paused. "Oh. I wondered if he might tighten the leash on your spending habits after he walked in on you and me."

"Leo doesn't have a leash on my spending, and there's nothing going on between you and me. There never has been."

"If that's true, then you better find a way to write the check for this info, because if you don't want it, I'm going to sell it to the highest bidder and your sugar daddy may not like the way it turns out."

"Are you blackmailing me?" she demanded.

"No, just trying to get my pay. You have my number. Call me if you're interested, but don't wait too long," he said and hung up.

Calista stared at the phone, feeling sick to her stomach. Too upset to sit, she rose to her feet and paced. What did Rob know? He'd said it was *hot*. Would the information ruin Leo? She felt a knot of distress form inside her. She was regretting asking for Rob's help in the first place. She'd thought Rob would at least keep everything he learned confidential. She'd thought he would be ethical.

Ethical. The word hit her in the face. Why should she expect anyone in this situation to be ethical when she couldn't claim the same? Sighing, she shook her head. She was going to have to do something about this. She didn't know how, but she had to do something.

That night after she watched a movie with Tami, Calista joined Leo for a glass of wine and mustered her nerve. "I haven't mentioned this, but there are some checks I need to write and now that I'm not working…"

"Oh," he said with a careless shrug. "I set up an account for you before we got married. I've made a deposit, but my accountant can also add funds. I would have given you the checkbook before, but you were so adamant about not spending my money. You have tuition payments for Tina, don't you?"

She nodded, wondering if he still felt that was a sore spot.

"No problem," he said. "Anything else on your mind?"

She looked away. "Maybe."

"What?"

"This is awkward."

"What?" he asked.

"Back when you partnered with your father on his schemes, did you do any of that after you turned eighteen?" she asked.

"No," he said, his jaw tightening. "I ran away. I like to think my youth should excuse me, but I understood what I was doing, and I hated myself for it."

"But you've turned yourself around. Look at what you've become," she said.

"What's that?" he asked. "How would you describe what I've become?"

"You've become a man," she said. "You take responsibility for your choices. You're vibrant and intelligent, and you may not think it, but you have heart."

He shot her a sympathetic look. "I wouldn't count on that last one too much."

Disappointed and frustrated, she frowned. "You do. Look at what you've done for Tami."

"Some would say that's just payback," he said.

"Then what about our marriage?" she asked. "You want to stick with it. That says something about you."

"We made a deal, a bargain." He slid his hand under her chin. "I care for you. I want you. I'll take care of you. But don't expect the fairy tale. I think you and I both know better than that. Remember it and you'll be happier."

His ability to detach himself made something inside her freeze with fear. Was he truly incapable of emotion? Of love? Why did it matter? she asked herself. He was taking care of the financial end of things. That was all she'd ever wanted. Right?

Calista stared at him, suddenly slapped with the knowledge that her feelings for Leo ran deeper than she'd ever anticipated. And it hurt that he clearly didn't return her feelings.

"Calista?" he said, lifting his eyebrows. "You agree with what I've said, don't you?"

She bit the inside of her lip. "I see your point."

"Hedging," he said.

She played the girl card. "Do you really want to get into

a messy emotional argument with a female late at night?" she challenged with a smile.

"God, no," he said with a look of pure horror.

"Then let's go to bed," she said and told herself she would think about what he'd said some other time.

The next morning, she gave Rob a call. "I'd like to meet with you," she said.

"You have a check?" he asked.

"Yes, but you'll have to sign an agreement that you won't give any of the information you've discovered about my father or Leo to anyone else," she said firmly.

"Those are high demands. I could get some nice cash if I sold this to a tabloid," he said.

"Or not," she said. "Leo keeps a low profile. He's not a Hollywood star or a jet-setter, therefore, you could be taking the risk of getting much less. Or nothing."

"Oooh," he said. "Somebody grew kahunas. Okay, meet me at Liberty Bar at seven."

"No," she said. "I've got the check. We'll meet at three o'clock."

"No can do at three o'clock," he said. "I've got another job. Make it five-thirty and I can swing it."

Calista hated the timing, but she needed to get this taken care of immediately. "Okay. Don't be late," she said and hung up.

Calista visited the bar where she was supposed to meet Rob and waited. Thirty minutes passed and he finally showed up. "Where have you been?" she demanded.

"I got hung up," he said. "Where's the check?"

"Where's the information?" she retorted.

"You're getting tough, girl," he said and pulled out a manila envelope. "Check first."

"Signature first," she said and presented a legal document and copies for him to sign.

Rob read it and whistled. "You covered all the bases. Name changes and everything."

"If you want the money, sign it," she said.

He signed three copies of the document. "I don't suppose you'll give me a recommendation to your wealthy friends," he said.

"I don't like it that you changed the charge midstream," she said.

"That was only done after I realized I didn't have a shot at you," he said.

Calista felt nervous with each passing second. She had the odd feeling that someone was watching her, but she didn't know who. "Here's the check," she said.

Rob passed the folder to her and she stood. He followed and kissed her cheek. She drew back and frowned.

"You can't blame me. I came this close to a Philly Princess," he said, lifting his thumb and forefinger, pressing them together.

"You flatter yourself," she said and walked away. She got into her car and drove to Leo's house, the folder sitting beside her, nearly burning a hole in the passenger seat. It was dark when she pulled into the garage, and she winced when she saw Leo's car already parked in its regular spot.

Praying he wouldn't have noticed, she grabbed the folder and walked inside. The house was silent. George stepped into the hallway. "Mrs. Grant, where have you been?"

She didn't like his suspicious tone, or was it her imagination? "Out," she said. "And you?"

He raised his eyebrows in surprise. "Mr. Grant is looking for you."

"Where is he?" she asked.

"In your suite."

"Thank you," she said.

Her stomach clenched in knots, she climbed the stairs to their bedroom suite. She opened the door and found Leo facing the window, his hands on his hips. "Where have you been?"

"Out," she said, walking toward him, hating the wall he seemed to have drawn around himself.

He turned and threw some photos on the table beside him. "I see you met with your friend again," he said.

She glanced closer at the photos, seeing the damning visual of Rob kissing her cheek. Humiliation suffused her. "It's not what it looks like."

"Oh, really?" he said in a cold voice. "Then how is it?"

"Are you willing to listen?"

"Why should I?" he asked in a dead voice. "You'll only lie."

Her anger jumped inside her. "Stop it," she said. "You owe me the chance to explain."

"I owe you nothing," he said.

"Fine, then you'll never know what I spent a hundred thousand dollars of your money on. At this point, I don't even know. I just know I made Rob sign an agreement not to share the information."

Leo paused and frowned. "What the hell are you talking about?"

"Rob said he had information about you, but it was big. He told me I had to pay. That's why I asked you about money."

Realization dawned on Leo's face, but he was still cautious. "What information?"

She opened the folder. "Let's find out."

* * *

Leo scanned the report with skepticism. One of his security men had followed Calista and taken photos of her with the P.I. They'd been e-mailed to him and he'd printed them off, ready to throw her out of the house.

Now, he wasn't so sure. Calista's P.I. said his real name was Leonardo Medici and he had three brothers. Both his parents were dead. His father had died in a train accident. He was supposed to have died in the same accident, but an explosion threw him away from the train. He frowned as he read the story. Was it true? Was he the boy who'd survived?

According to the report, a woman had discovered him and taken him home. That was when Clyde had become his so-called adoptive father. That was when the abuse had begun.

"Oh my God," Calista whispered. She looked at him. "You survived a train wreck. Not a car accident."

He shook his head. "We don't know that for sure."

She lifted the written report, which was followed by photos of his brothers. "Look at them. They look just like you," she said. "They're your brothers."

Too stunned to take it all in, he shook his head. "I put my own P.I. on this. Why wasn't he able to find it?"

"Maybe, despite Rob's obnoxiousness, he got lucky and dug in the right place. Leo, this is amazing. Momentuous. You have to call your brothers. They will be so happy you're alive."

"How do you know?" he asked and shook his head. "What am I going to tell them? I had a criminal past and have a fake marriage."

Calista turned pale. "Is that what you really think?" she asked, shaking her head. "I know you don't believe in all the romance, but do you really believe our marriage is fake? I thought we'd both decided we wanted a fresh start. I thought that meant we were building something real."

Leo stood. The news about his family was too overwhelming. He didn't trust it. He didn't trust Calista. He didn't want to count on her. He'd learned he couldn't count on anyone. "What's reality? What's perception? I don't remember these brothers. They're not real to me. Why should I get in touch with them?"

"Because they're your family," she insisted. "And based on this report, they want to find you. Can you imagine how much pain they've experienced thinking you're missing or dead? For all these years," she said.

Leo walked to the window and stared outside. This was what he'd dreamed of for years, but he couldn't go after it. He'd changed from whomever he'd been when they'd known him. And not necessarily for the best.

Calista gently touched his arm. "Leo, I know you had a terrible childhood after the accident, but you've come out of it an amazing person. You've become a man I could fall in love with," she confessed and his gut tightened. "A man I have fallen in love with."

Her admission struck him at his core, but he couldn't accept it. He couldn't believe it. "My money is making life easier for you and your sisters. Don't mistake your gratitude for love, Calista."

He heard her shocked intake of breath and she snatched her hand away from him as if she'd burned it. Remorse surged through him. He hadn't wanted to hurt her, but he couldn't open up to her, especially now. "Calista," he said, turning.

She backed away, shaking her head, tears in her eyes. "No."

"Calista," he said again, moving toward her.

"No, really. Don't say another word," she whispered and ran from the room.

She didn't return to his bed that night and he didn't go looking for her. Leo stared at the ceiling for most of the night. He couldn't believe the P.I.'s report. He had brothers. His mother and father had died. Medici was his real last name. He whispered it. "Medici." It rolled off his tongue with a strange familiarity.

What had happened to his brothers, he wondered. What kind of course had their lives taken? He'd stopped reading the report midway. Unable to tamp down his curiosity, he got up and began to read it. Damien Medici, 35 years old, married, successful CEO of his own business. Rafe Medici, 33 years old, married. One son, another child on the way.

Something inside him twisted at the thought of a nephew.

Leo swore under his breath. He didn't know these people. This wasn't real to him and it never would be. He shoved the report into a drawer and glanced at the clock. Four o'clock in the morning. Screw it. He would go into the office. He couldn't stand being in his own skin at the moment. Work would be his panacea. It always had been.

When Leo arrived home that night, Meg greeted him, but Pooh didn't.

"Welcome home, Mr. Grant. Would you like a cocktail?" she asked.

Leo glanced around, frowning. "Where's the dog?"

"Oh, Mrs. Grant took him with her," she said.

"Excuse me?" he said, his gut tightening.

Meg nodded. "Mrs. Grant left this morning. She said she didn't know when she'd be back." Meg paused. "Shall I tell the chef to prepare your meal?"

He shook his head. "Just a sandwich will do. I'll be in my office." Feeling a sense of dread, he walked to his office. He'd been hard on her last night. Too hard? He wondered if she'd decided not to stay. He punched out the number to her cell phone, but it went straight to voice mail. No message, no note. Where had she gone?

The sense of dread in his gut grew to a large knot. Calista was gone. Tami was gone. Pooh was gone. And Calista wasn't answering her phone. Leo did the math and suspected Calista had left him for good.

The thought made every cell inside him hurt. The sensation shocked him. He hadn't believed he was that vulnerable. But maybe he was.

He swore underneath his breath. Leo had always told himself not to count on people, including Calista. He'd clearly failed. From the first minute he'd seen her, he'd wanted her. Aside from her obvious physical assets, she'd had a charm about her that made him feel warm inside. Just by her presence, she'd made everywhere they were together feel like home.

She'd made him want to open up to things he'd closed himself to in the past. She'd made him want to be the man she needed. The man who would take care of her and her sisters financially. The good man she could count on in an emergency. He'd seduced her and married her, but he couldn't give her what she'd ended up wanting and needing from him. The one thing he hadn't thought he would ever experience. Love. The biggest grifter scheme of all. Even though she'd known about his past, known that he was a con man, she'd made him feel like a real man.

Leo climbed the stairs to his bedroom, dreading entering it again. Once inside, the subtle remnant of the scent of her perfume haunted him. The possibilities he'd felt with her haunted him. He tried to push thoughts of her from his mind, but it was impossible. Images seeped inside him like smoke under the door. He wondered if he would ever be the same again. Did he want to be?

Everywhere he looked, he saw her, heard her laughter, felt her silky skin and warmth. He couldn't stand the memories. He had to get out of here.

George drove him to a hotel in downtown Philadelphia. "Is there something wrong with the penthouse?" he asked.

Only that Calista had been there and he needed to go somewhere she hadn't. It was the only way he could escape his thoughts about her. "No," Leo said, but added nothing.

"Are you meeting someone?" George asked.

Leo frowned at his longtime sparring partner. "God, no. I just need a different environment."

George glanced in the rearview mirror. "When is Mrs. Grant supposed to be back?"

"I don't know. You'll have to ask her," Leo said, staring out the window into the night.

"It's not my place to interfere," George said.

"That's right," Leo said. "It's not."

"But you could go after her," George said. "If you want her."

Leo narrowed his eyes, feeling as if his insides were being torn apart. He knew. He sensed it deep inside him. He'd smashed her overtures repeatedly. "It's too late."

* * *

Two days later, Leo felt like death warmed over. He hadn't slept more than a couple hours each night. Taunted by need for Calista and unanswered questions about his past family, he'd found no rest or peace. Staying at the hotel hadn't helped one damn bit. Now he just imagined he could smell her and hear her voice.

He cloistered himself in his office. He must have looked frightening. Even his assistant appeared reluctant to approach him. He received an odd text. Mr. Grant, your housekeeper called. There is a problem at your home in the country that needs to be addressed immediately.

Leo picked up his phone and paged his assistant. "I'm busy. What kind of problem?" Leo asked.

"I'm not certain sir. I only know she sounded upset when she called, sir," his assistant said.

Leo heard an odd nervousness in his assistant's voice. "Call her back and get specific information."

"I've already done that, sir, but there was no answer."

Leo frowned. "What the hell," he muttered.

"I'm very sorry for the interruption, sir. Shall I page George?"

"Yes," Leo said tersely.

His mood, which had already been nasty, deteriorated with each passing mile. As George drove inside the gates to the large home, he spotted a stretch limousine parked in front of his house. "What's going on? Don't bother with the garage. I'm getting to the bottom of this."

Leo strode up the steps to the front door. The house was completely silent. For once, Meg didn't greet him. He walked four steps into the foyer and Calista appeared.

Leo felt as if he were viewing an apparition. God knew,

he'd seen her in his dreams and mind every other minute during the last few days. "What are you doing here?"

She met his gaze and took a deep breath. "I'm about to piss you off."

Confusion rushed through him. The apparition spoke. "What are you talking about?"

"You know the old saying, If Mohammed won't come to the mountain, then the mountain must come to Mohammed?"

"Yes," he said, starting to realize that she wasn't a figment of his imagination. "Where have you been? Why did you leave?"

"I had to. I had to do it. If I really loved you, there was no other choice."

He felt as if she'd just punched him. "You're making no sense. Are you here to stay or not?"

"You might be throwing me out in a few minutes," she muttered. "I took Tami and Pooh to my cousin's house then flew to Atlanta to visit one of your brothers. They're waiting to meet you in the living room."

His heart stopped and his jaw dropped. "All of them?"

She gave a shaky laugh. "Once they heard you were alive, nothing would have stopped them." Her eyes filled with emotion. "You may not think you need them, but you do. And for them, you're the missing link."

Leo found that difficult to believe, but he couldn't resist the love shining from Calista's gaze. She'd made this trip out of love for him even though he'd brushed her hopes aside. How had he gotten so lucky? How had he managed to find the one woman who would see beyond his detachment with the world and burrow her way into his heart? Looking at her, he felt the magic of possibility again. She made him feel as if he really was better than his past.

"Come here," he said, staring at her in wonder. "You are the biggest miracle of my life. Never leave me again."

Calista's eyes filled with tears. "Oh, Leo, don't say that if you don't mean it."

"I do. I never thought I could love a woman like I love you."

Her mouth dropped open in breathless surprise.

"Yes," he said. "I love you."

She let out a sob of relief and lifted her hand to touch his face. "I knew when I did this that you might never forgive me, but I had to take the chance. I realize this might be difficult, but if you want me with you, I'll stay."

"Forever," he said. "All I want is forever."

She closed her eyes then opened them again. "You've got me."

He pressed his mouth against hers, needing to seal their promises to each other. Then he pulled back. "Time for me to meet my family," he said and he walked with Calista into the living room.

Three men with hair and eyes that matched his looked at him and in the dark, shadowy edges of his mind, a visual flashed of all of them racing toward the dinner table. He could almost smell the scent of spices, meat, sausage, tomatoes and fresh pasta.

"I don't have any concrete memories," he said, feeling compelled to break the news right away.

"They already know that," Calista said and stepped away from him.

One stepped forward. Leo remembered him from the P.I. report. "We can fill you in," he said and offered his hand. "Rafe," he added.

"I know," Leo said. "I read the report. I think I've memorized it." He glanced up. "Damien and Michael." He hesitated, an unbelievable whirlpool of feelings welling inside him. "My past isn't pretty."

"We don't care," Damien said, extending his hand. "We're just glad you survived."

Leo felt strange emotion form a knot in his throat as Michael walked toward him. There was turbulence in his eyes. "You need to know. You were on that train instead of me. If I hadn't gotten into trouble, it would have been me on that train. I wished for it so many times."

It struck Leo that he wasn't the only one carrying around a load of guilt. It also struck him that fate had dealt a hand in his life, bad and good. "Fate's a tricky witch," he realized and glanced at his brothers and Calista. "I can't be sorry for what I've gone through if this is what I've gotten in the end."

Epilogue

On New Year's Eve, the Medici brothers, *all* the Medici brothers, gathered at Michael's house in Grand Cayman to ring in the new year together. Although they had kept in touch since their first meeting, this was the first time they'd been able to come together due to their busy schedules. Everyone was happy to escape the winter blahs and relax at the Caribbean island. Calista sat next to Leo, happily taking in the hustle and bustle of the celebration.

Rafe juggled playing with his son, Joel, and holding his new baby daughter, Angelica. His wife, Nicole, took Angelica from his arms. "Time for her nap. You can't hold her all the time."

"If she didn't look like a miniature version of you, it wouldn't be a problem," he growled, taking his wife's lips in a quick kiss.

"Rafe is going to end up with twelve kids. He's a natural father," Damien said with a knowing glance.

Nicole shot him a look of horror. "I think twelve is tipping the scales. He'll be happy to enjoy some nieces and nephews." She smiled at Damien's wife, Emma, who was six months pregnant. "Just make sure you get them started changing diapers early on."

Damien looked at Emma with a skeptical raised eyebrow. "Do you really think you can talk me into changing diapers?"

Emma lifted his hand to her baby bump. "You tell me."

Damien's hard gaze softened and anyone could see he would do anything for his wife, including changing diapers.

Michael, sitting next to Leo, lifted a beer. "Cheers to Damien and Rafe for taking on father duty. I'll let you take the lead." He patted his wife's leg. "Bella and I are in no rush at all. Right?"

Bella shot him a pained look. "There's something I've been meaning to tell you."

Michael looked at her in confusion. "What?" he asked.

Silence fell over the tiled porch.

Michael's lovely wife shot him a nervous look. "You know how we were afraid I'd gotten a stomach flu?"

Michael set down his beer. "Yes, are you okay? Is it something more serious?"

"Well, my condition lasts about nine months and you might need to bone up on changing diapers, too. I'm pregnant. Is that okay?"

Michael's color drained from his face. "You're pregnant. How did that happen?"

"The usual way, sweetie. You remember that time in the limo when we left the opera early...."

"Oh, yeah," he said, realization crossing his face. Still stunned, he stared at her. "We're gonna have a baby?"

She nodded. "Are you upset?"

He shook his head and pulled her into his arms. "How could I be? You and I made this together."

Damien chuckled. "To Michael, uncle and father-to-be," he said, lifting his beer.

Everyone lifted their drinks. "Hear, hear," they chorused.

Lifting her own glass of lemonade, Calista felt a twist in her stomach. She wondered when she should tell Leo.

"Looks like it's in the water," Leo muttered to her as the group began to chatter with excitement. "We'd better be careful."

Calista mustered her courage. "I think it may be a little late for that," she whispered.

Leo swung his head around to stare at her. "Excuse me?"

"I wasn't really sure until day before yesterday," she said.

"Why didn't you tell me?" he asked in a low voice.

"I couldn't figure out the best time."

"Are you sure?"

Calista was feeling more nervous with each passing moment. "I took three at-home pregnancy tests and was also tested at the doctor."

"Do you want this?" he asked, his gaze intent and so focused on her they may as well have been the only ones around for miles.

"I do," she confessed. "I can't think of anything better

than making a new life with the amazing man I love more than anything."

He took her hand and this time his hand trembled. "You keep making me happier than I've ever dreamed I could be."

Her heart expanded in her chest so much it hurt. "You keep doing the same to me." She leaned forward and pressed her lips against his. "Don't stop."

"Never," he promised.

"Hey, Leo, take a break from your lovefest with your wife," Rafe said. "Do you shoot pool?"

"Yeah, I do," he said. "But I think we may need another round of drinks. Calista and I are going to have a baby." He shot Michael a stunned look. "Looks like you and I may be on the same daddy schedule."

Michael gave a half smile and moved toward him, extending his hand. Leo rose and shook his brother's hand. "This is one trip we can finally take together."

"To Leo and Calista," Damien said.

"Hear, hear," the families chorused.

"And to Aunt Emilia for pictures and encouragement," Michael said.

Leo toasted the aunt he'd met through his brothers' letters and photographs then pulled Calista against him. "Thank you for giving me all this," he said. "But mostly for giving me you."

* * * * *